Mother Eternal Ann Everlastin's
Dead

Mother Eternal Ann Everlastin's Dead

Pat G'Orge-Walker

KENSINGTON PUBLISHING CORP.
http://www.kensingtonbooks.com

DAFINA BOOKS are published by

Kensington Publishing Corp.
850 Third Avenue
New York, NY 10022

All Kensington titles, imprints and distributed lines are available at special quantity discounts for bulk purchases for sales promotion, premi-
ums, fund-raising, educational or institutional use.

Special book excerpts or customized printings can also be created to fit
specific needs. For details, write or phone the office of the Kensington
Special Sales Manager: Kensington Publishing Corp., 850 Third Avenue,
New York, NY 10022. Attn. Special Sales Department. Phone: 1-800-221-
2647.

Dafina Books and the Dafina logo Reg. U.S. Pat. & TM Off.

ISBN 0-7582-0380-2

First Hardcover Printing: July 2004
First Trade Paperback Printing: July 2005
10 9 8 7 6 5 4 3 2 1

Printed in the United States of America

ACKNOWLEDGMENTS

To my wonderful and spirit-filled husband, Robert; the journey has been and will continue to be awesome. Thank you for your unwavering love and support. Thanks to my three beautiful daughters, Gizel, Ingrid, and Marisa, and my grandchildren. I thank my surviving brothers and sisters along with countless other family members—especially aunts Ovella, Mildred, Katie, and Uncle Elbert. Your love has been as solid as a rock.

To my wonderful and pretty-as-a-picture pastor the Reverend Stella Mercado and my Blanche Memorial Baptist Church of Jamaica, New York, family. Thank you for all your support and prayers. I'd also like to thank New York State Assemblyman Tom Alfano. Thank you for my Woman of Distinction 2003 award. I am truly honored.

I would like to thank the entire Kensington Publishing Company, and my editor, Karen Thomas, and Jessica McLean in particular. Thank you to one of the hardest working women in publicity Ms. Renee Byrd and the staff at Sheba Diva Publicity. I must also thank Tonya Howard and Tina R. McCray for their publicity contributions and support.

Thank you to my literary agent, Djana Pearson-Morris, and my attorney, Christopher R. Whent. God also saw fit to place in my path Mr. Gary Bire, CEO of Seed Card of London, England. You've been a blessing in more ways than I can mention. There's nothing like having a boss and friend who's both spiritually and financially wealthy.

It was not easy to write comedy while the country was at war. The burden I carried as I continuously prayed for the safe return of Shoshona Johnson and the other POWs was a paralyzing experience for me, and I can't begin to imagine how they managed to survive. Personal dilemmas plagued me, and yet, God kept and delivered.

I'd like to thank Carol and Brenda at C&B Book Distributors, Emma Rogers at Black Images, Cush City, Borders, Black Expressions, PageNet, Waldenbooks (particularly Green Acres Shopping Mall),

Karibu and all the bookstores that have supported me. Fred Passmore (*www.sheeplaughs.com*), the Holy Humor Christian Comedian Organization, Elder Byron Harden, Cassianne Conty, Brenda O., Coy LeSone, Keitha V., and Brotha' Smitty. www.Holyhumor.org. Thank you to my theatre buddies, Sandra Reaves-Philips, Shay Youngblood and Broadway's beautiful Ann Duresque. All the radio stations online and off that supported my comedy ministry; in particular, "On the Same Page" with Maxine Thompson, "A Touch of Satin" with Parry "Ebony" Brown, "Literally Yours" with Donna Hill and the gracious Denise Campbell of "Book Lovers Haven," Larry Robinson and "Keepin' the Faith," and Delores Thornton of "Around 2 It." I'd also like to thank Audrey Crawford from Elite Investigations; your support has been amazing.

Thank you to my wonderful and supportive friend Tracy Price-Thompson. Thanks to Tee Royal and Raw Sistaz, Imani Voices, and numerous other book clubs around the country. I also thank Karen Simmons of *Sharper Magazine,* Veda Brown and the many churches, especially the United Missionary Baptist Association and other organizations that have supported my comedy ministry. I thank the many authors and friends who've supported me. To Barbara Easter and my Whist Queens family, thanks for everything. Finally, to my little ten-year-old protégé Raven Brewington . . . keep on writing. You're a star on the rise.

According as he hath chosen us in him before the founda-
tion of the world, that we should be holy and without
blame before him in love:

Having predestinated us unto the adoption of children by
Jesus Christ to himself, according to the good pleasure of
his will.

To God, be the glory.

—Ephesians 1:4-5

1

No Hope Now—Mercy Neva

Sunday afternoons in the small, gossip-driven town of Pelzer, South Carolina, were always an event within the numerous church circles. Folks got all dressed up in everything from pleats to cleats and made it to service. It had nothing to do with their religion. They just couldn't waste precious time on proper attire. They didn't want to wait to see who got dissed, or who had backslid since the past Sunday. Instead of greeting one another with "Praise the Lord," it was usually, "Chile, did you hear about so and so?" It didn't matter whether a racing fire truck was on its way to a raging fire or an exhausted mother in back-breaking pain was about to give birth. The response would always be, "Hold on. Let me stop what I'm doing so I can hear everything you got to say."

What was about to occur happened at the beginning of the fall season, and this Sunday afternoon shouldn't have been any different from others. The weather was still warm yet comfortable with many of the assorted petunias, jasmines and rosebushes on the corner of Shameless Avenue boasting brilliant colors despite their time for blooming being way past due. They, like most things in Pelzer, held on to their bright hues just to be stubborn and to see what would happen next.

Above a street that crossed Shameless Avenue named Last Exit Avenue, several white, rhythm-challenged pigeons fluttered their wings to the pulsating musical beats carried through the air from the radio-pumped music of Kirk Franklin, Mary Mary, Al Green and the Isley Brothers as the birds gathered on the telephone wires above the No Hope Now—Mercy Neva Church. In this neighborhood, the white birds were called pigeons. If they'd been fluttering and cooing, on the other side of town where the rich folks lived, they'd have been called doves.

The church played its music loud with a heavy emphasis on ear-splitting bass levels in desperation to attract more young people to Sunday services. Their only organist, thirty-year-old Brother Juan Derr, was barely five feet tall, cocky, with freckles that made him resemble a speckled barnyard rooster or the Howdy Doody puppet. He had short legs and flat feet. His flat feet looked like a pair of CDs dangling from his ankle. Juan Derr even pecked at the keys, with his head bobbing and no thought to musical rhythm. He was just like a rooster pecking at wiggly worms. He just kept stabbing at the keys hoping that he'd hit the right ones.

But the church kept him anyway even though he only knew how to play two songs, which he musically butchered every Sunday. Those songs were, "Stretch Out" and "Kumbaya," which were apparently two of the pigeons' favorites since they cooed and pranced on the telephone wires like they had mad cow disease whenever he played them.

That day, the pigeons flapped their wings and cooed loudly as if they were mocking the human that entered the small storefront church building below.

The building was once an open-all-night bodega owned by the late Mr. Pepe DuYuNo De Way to San Jose, and it still had the twice-shot-up, bulletproof, Plexiglas protection panel, which was streaked with patches of gray duct tape, covering the front.

The No Hope Now—Mercy Neva Church was pastored by the Righteous (in his own mind) Reverend Bling Moe Bling. The small church had a congregation of about seventy-five members. They were mostly related to one another through marriage with the exception of about five or six. Those five or six were the praying pillars. They were the ones who tried to keep the church spiritually afloat with their buoys of morality. They kept their tongues coated with praises and their lives a living testimony to their belief in God. They also happened to be the ones who were out of town at a missionary conference, that day, in nearby Williamston, South Carolina. With the church's spiritual parachutes absent, there was certain to be a free-for-all and a free fall on the horizon.

When Reverend Bling Moe Bling first founded his church, it had chipped wood-paneled walls and a worn-out yellow linoleum floor. He was doing so bad, he had to beg for and then borrow a couple of members from a nearby mission to use until he got on his feet and could convince others to join. Now, three years later, he'd made some progress. The church's chipped wood-paneled walls had been replaced with new matching brown-paneled walls and floor. It stood just five blocks away from the Ain't Nobody Else Right But Us—All Others Goin' to Hell Church. The five-block distance and the fact that they were both located in Pelzer was the only thing that the two churches thought they had in common. They actually had a lot more. Just like in the biblical cities of Sodom and Gomorrah, there were not ten people combined from both churches living a righteous life.

This particular morning two short but burly, thirty-five-year-old twin deacons named Luke and Warm Waters arrived at the No Hope Now—Mercy Neva Church in matching yellow Volkswagens with custom-made sunroof tops. Originally, the cars didn't have sunroofs. The holes were made from the angry swings of axes wielded by the twin sisters they dated, named Shay Nay Nay and Alizé, who still had a lot of vicious "home girl" traits. Those ruthless sisters had caught those shifty deacons laying unsupervised hands on a couple of female members. It appeared to be done in a nonspiritual manner and besides that, it was done in the parking lot after church service. No amount of praying, crying or threats of exorcisms from Luke and Warm could've stopped those women from remodeling the deacons' cars.

Deacons Luke and Warm were also the single, wanna-be playboy stepsons of Reverend Bling Moe Bling and the sons of his wife, First Lady Beulah Bling.

They drove up to the church that Sunday morning, and Deacon Luke was the first one to step from his car. "Ah. It's just another day that the Lord hath made, and I'm glad I made it to the church still looking as fine as I wanna be." He chuckled at his own testimony and walked with a proud gait. He favored wearing a gray Fedora and when he wore it, he'd move his head, slowly from side to side. He thought it made him look like a killer-diller ladies' man. What it made him look like was one of those bobble-head toys that folks love to place in their back car window. He also wore his Fedora to cover his ever-widening bald spot, which from a distance, without the hat, looked like a muddy desert pool.

Deacon Luke was older than his twin brother, Deacon Warm, by almost five minutes. He would've been older by only two minutes but someone started gossiping in the delivery room. In order to listen, his mama, Sister Beulah, clamped her knees together tightly and blanked out an on-coming hard, stomach-crunching contraction; one that would've killed any other woman or at the very least made having any more babies out of the question. "Hold on," she said, grimacing. "What did you say?" She was so determined to hear any little bit of gossip, she even stopped her own anesthesia drip to hear, clearly, what was going on. Instead of pushing, she started screaming, "You have got to be kidding. Please repeat that again—" And then, she screamed for real. Wasn't no woman that pain tolerant. It could also be the reason why her boys had all sorts of issues from the incubator on.

Showing off, Deacon Warm parked his car that Sunday with just one stubby pinky turning the steering wheel. He exited his car and followed a few feet behind his brother, Luke. Unlike Luke's egotistical walk, Warm's gait and control were a bit unsteady when he wasn't driving. He looked like a drunk trying to play a game of hopscotch as he fought gravity to remain upright. Deacon Warm also liked to wear red baseball caps. He wore a red cap regardless of what the rest of his outfit looked like or the occasion. He always said, "When the roll is called up yonder, the Lord will know me by my red baseball cap."

"Not by your works?" Deacon Luke would always ask while laughing.

"Nope. He'll know me by my red cap!" Deacon Warm didn't like his twin teasing him about something that meant so much to him.

"Well you'd better hope that ole Saint Peter ain't on fashion police duty," Deacon Luke teased, " 'cause you won't get in."

Actually, if Heaven did a background check, neither stood a chance of entering.

Deacon Warm ignored his brother because he couldn't think fast enough to say something witty or insulting back at him. Sometimes his brain was slower than a crippled tree sloth who had one paw tied behind his back.

On some Sundays, the twin deacons also served as both security guards and ushers. This day they would act as church security. They approached the church and stood inside the doorway. They were fitted, snuggly, side by side. Every time they moved to let someone enter, they looked like swinging doors. Armed with wide metal, paddled-shaped sensor wands, they scanned each person before permitting them to enter the church. Sometimes, if they were bored, they'd challenge someone.

"You can't wear that see-through halter top inside this church," Deacon Luke snapped with mock indignation while ogling a very well-built young lady whom he'd never seen before at the church but had definitely seen at the after-hours Beddy Bye club on a few Saturday nights. That's when he did his bimonthly backsliding. He continued salivating. "Unlike some other places that you may service,"—he paused to let his insinuation sink in before he continued—"at this service, we have a dress code."

Evidently, she wasn't smart enough to know that he'd called her a whore because he remained alive.

"That's right," Deacon Warm chimed in. He winked at his brother as he set his sensor scanner to *sensitive*. "Today is a church anniversary. The Mothers Board Anniversary to be exact. Everyone is supposed to wear white." The fact that neither he nor his brother was wearing white never entered his mind, or he just didn't care about hypocrisy. He moved in and started to scan the young lady from top to bottom, starting at her mousse-layered deep-brown French rolled hair, which contrasted perfectly against her taupe-colored complexion. He tried to outstare her but could not, so he taunted her instead, "Next time you make sure that it's a *white* halter top."

They weren't doing anything slick. The young lady really liked the attention. "Well, I didn't know that." She smirked, pretending indignation as she looked Deacon Luke straight in the eye, trying to remember where she'd seen the short, box-shaped man before. "I guess I'll have to miss this Sunday service," she said as she slowly turned around, giving them a peek at what they'd be missing.

The deacons weren't expecting her to leave. "Hold up! No need to be hasty. We all God's children," Deacon Luke whispered as he watched his brother slowly proceed with his wanton scanning. "We gonna let you slide this time." He was about to ask for her name and phone number so they could further discuss the church's dress code but the sound of a honking horn playing a slow version of "We're in the Money" caught his attention.

The honking horn was coming from a 2003 Rolls Royce limousine that had just turned the corner. It came around the corner, onto Last Exit Avenue, popping a wheelie with hydraulics that made it go up and down. Its horn was now blasting a hip-hop version of the melody to "We're in the Money."

The limo was beyond the stretch type; it was closer to the size of a small yacht. A blinding glare caused by the black-on-black waxed finish sent several pedestrians reaching for sunglasses as it came to a screeching halt. It took up the entire space reserved for buses. There was no mistaking its ownership. The silver-trimmed, double-braided-edged license plate read DISBME. It belonged to the one and only black widow queen herself, Mother Eternal Ann Everlastin'.

Mother Eternal Ann Everlastin' was the very rich widow of three wealthy church deacons. She was childless, and the only living relative known to her was a drunken nephew named Buddy; it was short for his late mother's favorite beer, Budweiser. She drank it every day, on the hour like she had stock in the company. He, on the other hand, favored Jack Daniel's. He drank the liquor constantly and would caress the bottle like it was his only friend.

Deacon Myzer was Mother Eternal Ann Everlastin's first husband; a tall handsome man who kept a constant smile on his clean-shaven face. Deacon Myzer was a James Earl Jones look-alike who'd inherited his considerable wealth from his father, Senator Dan Myzer.

Deacon Myzer, while in his youth, had once climbed the snow-capped mountains of Kilimanjaro. A year after he'd married Eternal Ann, he died suddenly at the age of forty after they went on a week-long camping trip in the Rocky Mountains. She told the authorities that he had slipped on a slippery chocolate mint patty wrapper.

Her second husband, Deacon Phil T. Luker, whose body had been discovered in a bear's cave, half eaten and surrounded by several empty chocolate mint patty wrappers had also mysteriously disappeared after they went on a hiking trip for a week in the Rockies. It happened almost three years to the day after he'd purchased a ten million dollar insurance policy.

Her last husband, multimillionaire, Deacon Shood B. Everlastin', heir to the Everlastin' Battery conglomerate, had his suspicions and wouldn't go hiking in the Rockies; so instead, he died from food poisoning. No one knew that he had a ravenous appetite for chocolate mint patties until they found a pocketful of empty wrappers, especially since both he and Mother Eternal Ann Everlastin' were known diabetics.

Rumors swirled around her fortune and her three husbands' misfortunes for years. Some called her the Curse of the Rocky Mountains, but Mother's bottomless pit of wealthy donations to every foundation ranging from Save the Aardvarks to the Police Athletic League finally squelched the chatter and all the federal investigations. Although, she never knew that behind her back, people still hummed the melody to "Killing Him Softly With Her Song."

Mother Eternal Ann Everlastin' wasn't always a member of the No Hope Now—Mercy Neva Church. She was once a longtime member of the Ain't Nobody Else Right But Us—All Others Goin' to Hell Church, which was currently pastored by the Reverend Knott Enuff Money. She had left that church because she couldn't get along with the then seventy-year-old Mother Pray Onn, who at that time was the chairperson of the Mothers Board and always thought that nobody knew God like she knew Him.

However, the real reason why the two old, feisty women didn't get along was a stupid one that usually caused a lot of tension between most women, in and out of the church. It was because they were both interested in a very virile sixty-five-year-old. He was a lifetime resident of Pelzer named Brother Benn Dead. Back in his heyday, his virility was legendary. He was the reason why most men and women in Pelzer were reluctant to date each other. They could never be sure, without a blood test, if they were brother and sister.

Brother Benn Dead was a young man by the two women's standards. It never mattered to them that he always kept a miniature, battery-operated resuscitator-on-a-rope handy and hidden under his shirt.

Brother Benn Dead claimed he had a heart condition and the few blue pills that often fell from his pockets were nitroglycerin not Viagra.

That lie would've worked if he hadn't needed emergency treatment every other month for a suspiciously chronic stiff throat and elbow. It usually happened after one of his outings to the local bingo hall, which was heavily frequented by lonely and unsuspecting females.

Anyhow, Brother Benn Dead claimed a heart problem and not a mental one. He decided that he'd be safer dating Mother Pray Onn. Satisfaction was more of a guarantee with whatever monies he could sweet-talk from her monthly pension. He was less likely to see sixty-six if he ever went on a camping date with Mother Eternal Ann Everlastin'.

"I don't need him or this church." Mother Eternal Ann Everlastin' pouted. She felt slighted and unforgiving while watching Brother Benn Dead and Mother Pray Onn blissfully happy. She packed away her dirty and well-used, fold-away shovel and several unopened boxes of chocolate mint patties. She secreted her frayed mountain-hiking map, which had several old smudged x marks on it and another new one drawn in pencil.

Several weeks later, after being snubbed by Brother Benn Dead, she met Reverend Bling Moe Bling at an invitation only Mo' Money Comin' revival. They joined together in a karaoke hymn contest that lasted well into the wee hours after the shouting and testa-lying was finished. That night, they won a Billy Banks ten-dollar-off discount coupon for Tae-Bo lesson, after lip-syncing a gospel version of the tune "Love Train," a secular song made popular by a group called the O'Jays.

"You have an amazing voice," Reverend Bling Moe Bling teased her. He'd watched in disbelief at the several large donations she'd placed in the many collection baskets without blinking an eye. "You sound like an mocha angel from on high. I just know there's a place for you in the choir—and no doubt, you'd be the lead soloist."

He laid a polite hand gently on her shoulder and whispered as best he could in a hoarse voice, "You know, I always knew that after God called me on my cell phone and told me to go and preach that He'd make a way for me to do it." Raising his head as though he were giving thanks, he continued, "God has sent me a singing angel; He's sent you."

Of course, the Reverend Bling Moe Bling wasn't aware that practically everyone to whom he told that story thought his cell phone must've been set on vibrate because no one either believed or heard God call him. He continued cooing little niceties lacing them with the prearranged Bible verses and sweetly massaged her ego until she finally reached into her purse for her checkbook.

"Ooh. Come on now." Mother Eternal Ann Everlastin' blushed. She somehow managed to push to the back of her mind, the annoying fact that the karaoke hymn CD had skipped during the entire time they'd been singing.

It should've been a clear clue, and it would've been to anyone but her.

They saw each other again in the hotel lobby as they checked out after the revival ended. Giving the appropriate good-byes, they determined that it would probably be months before they saw each other again. They promised to keep in touch by telephone.

It was hardly a week later, after her five thousand-dollar donation check cleared, that she received a phone call from Reverend Bling Moe Bling. Mother Eternal Ann Everlastin' was overjoyed to hear his voice. "Oh my goodness. It's so good to hear from you. I was just thinking about our duet together."

The Reverend Bling Moe Bling never believed in fixing things that weren't broke. It worked before at the conference and would probably work again, so he added a little nasal but raspy baritone to his voice and sweetly cooed. He thought he was smooth as butter armed with his scriptural arsenal of several prearranged Bible verses again. This time he was going for broke as he tried to sweeten the romantic Songs of Solomon.

When the Reverend Bling Moe Bling finished laying it on thicker than his rap sheet, one would've thought Barry White had called Mother Eternal Ann Everlastin'.

The phone had hardly clicked in its cradle before she had moved her membership, along with her considerable wealth to the Reverend Bling Moe Bling's little storefront church of No Hope Now—Mercy Neva.

It never bothered her that her new church was only five blocks away from her former pastor, Reverend Knott Enuff Money and his congregation. She was on her way to get a new start and, definitely, if her money was any good and she was certain it was, a loftier position.

It was when she showed up at the first Sunday service of her new church, wearing her most expensive "I should be the First Lady of somebody's church" hat that she got a big surprise. That was the day when she discovered that there was a Mrs. (Bertha) Bling Moe Bling.

The shocked Mother Eternal Ann Everlastin' also found out that the First Lady Bertha Bling, in her earlier years, had spent some less-than-quality time at a Women's Attitude Adjustment Center. She'd done time at the state's request for shoplifting and battery. The store security guard had determined that she shouldn't leave with property that wasn't hers. She'd determined that she didn't agree with his determination and beat him with his own nightstick.

Mother Eternal Ann Everlastin' also found out that even after Sister Bertha Bling claimed to have given her life to Christ, it seemed that there was a little taste of residual thug tendencies left in the first lady's personality.

According to First Lady Bertha Bling, she had only been studying the Bible for a short while and hadn't been fully delivered. She was still studying in the first five books, trying to learn how to pronounce the names of the begets, and wasn't up to the part in the Bible about turning the other cheek. And, sometimes it seemed like she wasn't in a big hurry to get to that last part. Most of the folks just nodded a "yes ma'am" to Bertha and gave her space.

It didn't take the Reverend Bling Moe Bling long to realize that he'd gone a bit too far in trying to entice Mother Eternal Ann Everlastin' into his fold, so he made sure that Mother Eternal Ann Everlastin' was appointed and ordained head of the Mothers Board, in less than an hour after she and her money had stepped foot through the door.

At that time, she was the oldest female in the church and the only one on the Mothers Board.

The word spread like wildfire through the five-block distance that Mother Eternal Everlasin' was moving her membership and her money and without so much as a letter of resignation. That bad news was too much for the greedy Reverend Knott Enuff Money and the Bishop Was Nevercalled. To lose such a wealthy member was something akin to blasphemy in their small minds. They hadn't given a second thought to her absence thinking that she was just away on a short vacation.

They would've much rather have lost their religion, if they'd had any.

The next Sunday morning the two men rose early and without so much as brushing their teeth or dabbing on baking soda or deodorant to mask their body odor, they rushed over to the little church they swore they'd never step foot in. They rushed from their cars ready to verbally fight with Reverend Bling Moe Bling who stood laughing at the front door.

The Reverend Knott Enuff Money and the Bishop Was Nevercalled called the Reverend Bling Moe Bling all kinds of names. They even tried lifting their arms to invoke a bolt of lightning to strike him. It was a good thing they didn't have that type of power or the three of them would've stood there smoking like three burning bushes.

The reverend and the bishop fought to keep Mother Eternal Ann Everlastin' like two lions over the last lioness—or the last millionaire in Pelzer.

The sounds of mayhem caused by the Reverend Knott Enuff Money and the bishop finally got her to come outside. They hadn't been able to invoke lightning but it had started raining. For about ten minutes, they stood out in the drenching rain on the sidewalk and tried begging and even bribery to keep her from leaving their church, ignoring the fact that she had already moved on.

"Mother Everlastin,' please come back," the bishop and the reverend pleaded.

They looked pitiful, as if someone had stolen the last communion wafer and watered down the wine.

"Y'all just look ridiculous," Reverend Bling Moe Bling said indignantly. He could hardly keep from laughing aloud. To keep himself appearing more devout, he added, "I'll run inside and get you two an umbrella to share."

That last remark from Reverend Bling Moe Bling was too much. He might as well have called their mamas an umbrella.

The Bishop Was Nevercalled suddenly broke away from the reverend and started his own brazen plea as he pulled his collar up higher to ward off the rain. "We will name one of the front pews after you. It will be up front with no cigarette burns, oil stains or broken slats," he promised.

The Reverend Knott Enuff Money looked at him like he was a spot of mucus, but that didn't stop Bishop Was Nevercalled from continuing his embarrassing plea. "You know you-you can take that to the the bank."

He'd started stuttering so Mother Eternal Ann Everlastin' knew he was lying. She usually suspected that he was lying as soon as his mouth opened, but when the stuttering came, she knew for certain.

Reverend Knott Enuff Money not to be outdone joined in and wept, "We'll even put a gold-layered plaque on the side of the pew so the whole church will know we were bought." He was pleading hard, with desperation. He started sweating the Jheri out of his Jheri curl, which was already napping up from the rain.

Bishop Was Nevercalled pushed the reverend out of the way with a hard shove. He crossed his fingers behind his back to lessen the lie he was about to tell and added in his usual stuttering manner, "We'll even run-run an ad in the newspaper, the *Daily BLAB,* to announce yo' good deed."

They'd been out there so long that the service had ended inside the church. None of their lies or pleas worked. Her unblinking, piercing and mistrusting brown eyes looked right through them. They couldn't move her money or her membership back to the Ain't Nobody Else Right But Us—All Others Goin' to Hell Church with a Jaws of Life machine.

She sucked her teeth, switched her hips, each movement shooting arrows of death at them and walked on through the rain and into her car. She rolled her windows down and hollered, "I'll see you later, Reverend Bling Moe Bling." She waved at him and suddenly stopped, adding while she pointed to the Reverend Knott Enuff Money and the Bishop Was Nevercalled who were still on the sidewalk, "It would be so nice if the sanitation department picked up the trash on Sundays, wouldn't it?"

She didn't wait for Reverend Bling Moe Bling to comment or to see how deep her words cut her former pastor and bishop. She rolled up her car window and got ready to leave.

Finally, with nothing more to lose, hopelessness overtook their good judgment. They jumped up and ran into the street. They lay flat out in surrender in front of Mother's gold-colored Bentley. She had the car before the 2003 Rolls Royce limousine. She'd given up the Bentley because she wanted to appear to sacrifice for the Lord and didn't want to seem too extravagant when she flaunted her wealth.

The bishop, not quite sure of Mother's driving skills, tried to rise up. The side of the Bentley snagged the hip pocket of Bishop Was Nevercalled, causing about twenty dollars in change to scatter all over the street. "Wait, Mother Everlastin', my-my pants are caught in yo' door and my-my money spilled out." He wasn't so hurt or upset that he didn't try to unhook his pocket and scamper to retrieve his change; after all, it was still money.

Mother Everlastin' ignored the bishop and her Bentley leaped forward and sped on a few feet. The car swerved right and left before it caught Reverend Knott Enuff Money's nappy Jheri curl wig on its side-view mirror as he bent down to plead through the window.

If she'd driven five miles faster, the headlines would have read: SIDE-VIEW MIRROR DECAPITATES PREACHER. Both of the men were temporarily stunned but managed to jump up and out of the way. They were both bruised and dirty with ripped pants pockets, a shriveled-up Jheri curl wig and leftover change scattered about the street.

The two of them were beyond scandalous. When she finally stopped the car, they ran over and apologized to her for being in her way. They even offered to take up an offering to replace the side-view mirror and have one of the homeless beggars give her a free car-wash from a bucket with a soapy fresh squeegee.

"Well suh. I've seen it all. Just strike 'em dead, Lord!" Mother screamed as her car surged ahead into traffic.

Having a conscience was foreign to those two scallywags. Before Mother Eternal Ann Everlastin' came into a ton of money from her somewhat questionable estates, they couldn't have picked her out in a crowd of two congregation members.

From that day forward and in her disgust, she vowed never to return to their church, not even for a Friends and Family Day celebration. She swore that she'd be dead before she would. She also got rid of the Bentley and bought herself a classy Rolls Royce limousine. She did that rather than to have to replace the side-view mirror.

This Sunday, no sooner had the sunroof of Mother's limo closed, than green and white pigeon poop rained down onto the roof. It was another sign of chaotic events about to happen.

Mother Eternal Ann Everlastin's tinted limo window rolled down slowly. She peeked out and around before she placed her twenty-carat diamond-rimmed sunglasses atop her silver-blue wig and screamed at the twin deacons. "Y'all gonna stand there gawking 'til the Rapture comes or are you gonna take my bags inside the church?"

Mother Eternal Ann Everlastin' had money but not a lot of class. Her tasteless actions showed that in her case class was something a person attended. It wasn't always available because of wealth.

A strong, gravelly male voice suddenly spoke and said politely, "I'll take those bags for you, ma'am."

She didn't bother to look in the direction of the voice or the extended hand. Instead, she opened her own door, then she turned up her nose and flipped her head to the side as any self-respecting and self-appointed queen would. "I don't remember asking you to help me!" Mother Eternal Ann Everlastin' snapped. Instead of letting her mean words carry the weight of her indignation, she kicked it up a notch. She slapped away the hand of her chauffer, Tiny, as if she were chastising a small child, as he tried to help her and the bags from the limo.

What was his crime? He'd attempted to lift the two heavy white leather shopping bags from the limo, using all the power of his squatty three-hundred-pound frame, without being asked.

She wanted who she wanted, when she wanted them. This Sunday, she wanted the twin deacons.

"Sure thing, ma'am," Tiny said as he tightened his jaw. "Why don't I just go and deliver these envelopes you gave me." His face looked like a red colander as beads of sweat seeped through his pores. He could hardly contain his anger as he said nicely through clenched teeth, "I'll let you deliver the one that you wanted done personally."

She didn't know her own strength, and Tiny's fat hand was stinging like a ferocious bee had stung through the meat and down to the bone. *Who in the world you think you slapping, you old crow,* he thought. He also thought about how much he needed his job to feed a wife and two kids who weighed almost as much as he. But family obligations still didn't stop him from wanting to slap the dark brown age spots off her tawny-colored face. Her moods swung like a pendulum. She could be so sweet when she wanted to be, but she had to want to be.

Tiny gently placed the bulky bags back down on the curb and returned, sulking to the limo and into the driver's seat. He slapped the ill-fitting chauffeur's cap back upon his head and then thought about taking off. When questioned by the police he could claim that he accidentally dragged her under the wheels of the limo.

Tiny took both hands and pulled the brim of the hat down around his head as he slyly looked around. "Aw shoot!" he grumbled as he frowned and pushed the hat back up on his forehead.

There were too many witnesses, plus he had looked over his shoulder and felt a little guilty when he spied the picture of the cross that hung accusingly from the church's swinging metallic sign.

He wasn't overly religious. Tiny thought most preachers were just schemers who used the pulpit to defraud, the way politicians used the ballot box, but he did fear God.

Mother Eternal Ann Everlastin' actually didn't need help from anyone. She was quite self-sufficient. She was built round and sturdy with short, skinny legs and long, spiked hairs that covered the top of her thin lips like a stiletto mustache. Everything on her face looked like it'd been hand-placed like a Mrs. Potato Head. Sometimes, she looked like a brown beach ball with legs or an M&M. When she wore a silver-blue wig, she looked like an angry catfish.

Mother also had a thing for hats and carrot sticks. She wore some of the most outrageous, handmade hats in Pelzer. She had a collection of curiosities but particularly one that was bright pink and shaped like a flamingo. That monstrosity came complete with a bird's bill and hand-stitched feathers. It also boasted a pair of webbed feet, which lay to the side of the hat, looking like windshield wipers waiting to slide.

She had two of them made by a local blind milliner named Mizz Du Boo. Mother liked Mizz Du Boo's handiwork and eventually she hired her to make *all her hats*.

All of Mother Eternal Ann Everlastin's hats were either pink or blue. That was because Mizz Du Boo's cousin Casper Boo was the night manager of a cloth factory. Blue and pink was normally over-stocked, and he was able to remove a bale or two without anyone becoming suspicious.

Of course, Mizz Du Boo advertised herself as chic and exclusive, even though Mother Eternal Ann Everlastin' was her only client. That was her claim, and she was sticking to it.

This particular Sunday, Mother Eternal Ann Everlastin' wore her hideous blue flamingo hat. Before leaving for church, she'd taken her time deciding. After all, Mother's hats had graced the cover of many of the local newspapers and supermarket rags. She even boasted that one of her pictures was placed in the town's post office on the "un-wanted" bulletin board. No one else could make that claim. No one else wanted to.

A couple of the townspeople had once said that Mother was actu-ally bald and that was the reason she wore the ugly hats. Soon after those same couple of townspeople came into a sudden fortune and they retracted their claims, which only made folks more suspicious. However, no one but Mother Eternal Ann Everlastin' knew why she loved carrot sticks so much and she never said; she was wealthy and didn't have to explain anything to anyone.

Meanwhile, Deacon Luke, who carried his mama's snooping DNA, had overheard the embarrassing rebuke levied by Mother Eternal Everlastin' on her chauffeur, Tiny. "Now, that's cold-blooded to the tenth degree," he muttered as he observed from a safe distance. How-ever, he knew which side of the bread the rich butter was spread. He raced to the curb and grabbed the white leather, fur-lined bulky shopping bags in both of his hands. The aroma of fried fish, pig feet and something that was undistinguishable tugged like tentacles at the long hairs protruding from his nostrils.

The overwhelming odors caused his stomach to growl uncontrol-lably. He yearned for the goodies in the bags, but he also knew better than to mess with whatever was in there. He scurried from the curb and became winded. For the final few feet, he had to waddle like a windup toy as he carried the bags inside the church. His heart was about to leave his chest from exhaustion as he placed the bags by the front pew, where she always sat.

A few minutes later, Deacon Warm, with Mother Eternal Ann Ever-lastin' clinging seductively onto his unsteady arm, gently led Mother to her seat. They walked as if they were staggering down the red carpet on Oscar night facing the lights from the rabid paparazzi cameras. Mother was happy to make it to her pew seat in one piece. She dropped his arm like it was hot and sat down. She smoothed her dress, allowing nothing but brown skin and blue veins on her pipe cleaner–thin legs to show. She then made sure that the flamingo beak on her hat was straight. From a distance she looked like she was a bird's nest.

Deacon Warm backed away from Mother. He did it, not out of respect, but because he never really knew when one of her moods would swing toward the danger zone. Deacon Luke came over and stood next to him. "Is there anything more you'd like for us to do, Mother?" they asked in unison.

"No, you two can go and do whatever it was that you were doing. I'll be fine. I'll just visit with a few of the other members until the service starts." Without even straining she lifted the heavy bags and placed them on the adjoining seat, so no one could sit too close to her royal personage.

A few minutes later Deacons Luke and Warm returned to the outside and resumed their duties. They scanned and taunted a few more visitors. They also had fun insulting a few of the members who hadn't been around for a while by asking them loudly, "What hell have you been through that's got you running out to the church this morning?"

It took about another thirty minutes of catcalls, unnecessary frisking and complaining before the deacons finished harassing and prodding the congregation members and several of the visitors coming through the church doors.

The service started with the members standing in place and the singing of the obligatory "Holy, Holy, Holy" from page one of the red hymnal. The hymn was sung with notes that sounded like everything from dog howls to gun shots. The music was supplied by a well-worn cassette tape because Brother Juan Derr, of course, didn't know how to play that well-known hymn. After about the twelfth repetition of the first verse, the congregation sat down. It was a signal for Reverend Bling Moe Bling to approach the podium and lead the members to the throne of grace. Of course, on his way to the podium his wife, First Lady Sister Beulah Bling could be heard murmuring, "kiss, kiss." Everyone knew that it meant, "Keep it short, stupid." She didn't talk much unless it was about someone else's business, but she ruled her husband.

Upon hearing Sister Beulah Bling's warning to the pastor, many of the congregation members started whispering and laughing at Reverend Bling Moe Bling's dilemma.

It was bad enough that he always wanted to preach a lot longer than he had material, but he couldn't have preached for a long time if his life had depended upon it. The problem was that he couldn't stand up for any long lengths of time because of a small leg problem.

He actually had one leg that was shorter than the other by about five inches. It was made that way because of being hit by a speeding boxcar when he was about twenty-two years old.

The accident happened after he'd been out of work for about a year. After struggling for a long time, he finally found a job as an underpaid valet, working long hours for the famous black illusionists and magicians Siegfreed and LeRoy. They were also animal trainers who worked the local circuit entertaining folks with two old toothless pussycats and a nearsighted pit bull named, Muffin.

One day, for some crazy reason, the Reverend Bling Moe Bling bet Siegfreed that Siegfreed couldn't get one of the old, toothless pussycats named Molars to eat out of Siegfreed's hand without being bitten. Siegfreed pretended that he didn't want to take the bet. After about five minutes he grew tired of pretending and said, "Bling, are you really betting me that I can't get old, toothless Molars to eat out of my hand without Molars biting me?"

Now being twenty-two at the time shouldn't have been an excuse for Reverend Bling Moe Bling to make that stupid bet; but that's the excuse he later gave. "What's the matter, Mr. Siegfreed? Are you backing out of the bet? I'm betting my whole week's salary of thirty dollars." He smiled as he envisioned winning the bet and, at two-to-one odds, having an entire sixty dollars to spend.

Well, of course, the Reverend Bling Moe Bling not only lost the bet when Molars gummed the food from Siegfreed's hand but had the extra embarrassment of the old toothless cat purring and rubbing against Siegfreed's leg when he finished.

"You only won the bet because you owned that cat."

"Exactly!" Siegfreed snatched the thirty dollars from Reverend Bling Moe Bling's hand and added, "When you get paid next week, would you care to make another bet that the other toothless cat Mush Mouth will bite me too?" he teased.

Later on that day, hungry and broke, the Reverend Bling Moe Bling was hit by a scooter made from old box crates as he fled from the outraged owner of a corner newspaper stand. He had stolen five Mary Janes and two Squirrel Nut candy pieces.

That little foray into crime had him laid up for about four years, and with no income or insurance, one leg naturally shriveled. Somehow, he did manage to put a leg brace on layaway from the U Break It, We Fit It medical supply store. Even on layaway, all he could afford was a used support; one that had not been certified as safe or even practical.

By the time he finally paid for it, it no longer fitted his shriveled leg. Instead, it looked more like he had a kickstand holding up his shortened leg. It looked that way because it actually was a kickstand disguised by a silver, hard plastic coating. However, in order to use it he had to vigorously shake his leg so that the kickstand would fall in place. When he did that, people would laugh and sing a line from the old Hucklebuck dance song: ". . . push your partner out, then you hunch your back, have a little movement in your sacroiliac, wiggle like a snake, wobble like a duck . . . That's the way you do it when you do the hucklebuck." He ignored the taunts and was satisfied to have something to aid him. He affectionately nicknamed it "My Support."

During his time of healing and laying around, accepting help from those who felt like giving it, he finally figured out what he had done wrong. "I should've never leaned against that newspaper stand to unwrap that candy," he later told a friend. The fact that he shouldn't have stolen or made a stupid bet never entered his mind.

Looking over the sea of irritated stares from the congregation and hearing the strong warning from his wife, the Reverend Bling Moe Bling preached a very short sermon that morning. He didn't want to wear the people out, especially since they were going to have another service later that day to celebrate the Mothers Board anniversary.

Before he gathered himself together to bring the Word, the Reverend Bling Moe Bling signaled for one of the members to cue the collection music. He kept James Brown's "The Payback" on the cassette player. As the music started, he beckoned the Deacons Luke and Warm to take their places at the offering table.

The offering table was actually an old brown fold-out picnic table that was covered with a custom-made white cloth with the words, *Give Until It Hurts* embroidered upon it in bright red letters. Two large metal pails sat upon the table. The pails were also painted red and they matched the nailed-down red and silver cash register at the end of the collection table. It was a leftover piece of equipment from when the church was once a store. According to Reverend Bling Moe

Bling, it was too hard to remove it so it became a part of the pulpit, which was built onto the end of the collection table.

The fact that Mother Eternal Everlastin' had given a ton of money to the church and there wasn't any apparent improvements was explained as her giving the money to the future church (the infamous Building Fund). That was the reverend's story and he was glued to it.

From out of nowhere appeared two other ushers, dressed in white with tool belts around their waists. The tool belts held a credit card swiper, a coin changer, a pack of Tic Tacs, a can of Pam oil spray (for those who had ashy ankles) and a couple of large-sized Pull-Ups diapers for the Mothers Board. The ushers stiffly led the congregation, one by one, to the deacons who stood next to the offering table.

Reverend Bling Moe Bling, tired of all the coins, including some foreign ones making their way into the collection plate every Sunday, had the Deacons Luke and Warm use the pat them down routine on each paying member. It was pretty much the same routine they used when they acted as security before service. For whatever reasons, they never did the coin search at the same time.

The clanging of the coins hitting the metal buckets was done so blatantly that several weeks before, the Reverend Bling Moe Bling had ordered the deacons to scan each person as they arrived at the collection table and find out who was bringing all that change instead of paper money. Every time they raised a wand, it kept making a *rat-tat-tat* sound of a machine gun because every member bought with them a pocket or pocketbook full of noisy change and lint. It was like going to war to get them to part with their paper money. They acted as though the dead presidents on the bills were their deceased family members.

As usual the deacons would reprimand the guilty member and solicit a promise that they would do better the next time. The next time never came.

All during the scanning process Reverend Bling Moe Bling cooed and soothed the members with more Bible verses while he kept one eye on the collection plate. When the collection was finally over and the monies blessed, the ushers and Deacons Luke and Warm returned to their posts on both sides of the sanctuary to guard and, of course, be of service to any who needed them; if they felt like responding.

It had taken them an hour to collect two offerings. Now they could restart the service, which would only last another ten minutes.

The Reverend Bling Moe Bling gave the benediction and asked that everyone return for that afternoon's anniversary celebration service.

"Please come back. We will have a few special guests this afternoon. And, as usual, I didn't get a personal RSVP from Reverend Knott Enuff Money, pastor of the Ain't Nobody Else Right But Us—All Others Goin' to Hell Church. He never responds, but I'm more saved than he is, so I won't be holding it against him. I'll just pray for him. Anyway, we did receive word that several of his members will be here to represent their church."

Mother Eternal Ann Everlastin' and the others wondered who the representatives would be. They didn't have to wait long because a loud response came from the congregation as soon as they heard the names.

"I believe we're gonna have Sister Betty coming here to represent their Mothers Board."

"It's gonna be boring," Sister Faker, one of the members seated in the front seat in the first pew nearest to the pulpit, whispered while she toyed with a section of her hair weave that was beginning to unravel. Whispering a little louder, she added, "Everyone knows that all Sister Betty knows how to be is holy." She started squirming in her seat to signal her impatience with what was being said. She was waiting for the benediction and didn't care if she was interrupting the Reverend Bling Moe Bling.

The Reverend Bling Moe Bling leaned over the pulpit, gripping it on both sides. He used his good leg, moving it up and down, to adjust the kickstand for his bad leg. When he felt comfortable, he loosened his grip on the pulpit, and with his most insincere smile, he said, "Sister Faker, I'm sorry if I'm keeping you from something—perhaps a hair appointment or something." His tone carried a none-too-subtle warning. Her look of false contrition satisfied him. He continued, "And, also, I need to mention that my understanding is that Sister Ima Hellraiser will be coming to cover this event for the *Daily BLAB.*"

Practically the entire church lunged forward from the pews and hunched over one another. Sister Faker, completely forgetting the warning she'd received less than a minute before yelled, "Oh. It's on now. You know I'm coming back if Sister Hellraiser is coming." The smiles and laughs that broke forth with a lot of high fives from the other members showed their approval as well as lack of spirituality.

The Reverend Bling Moe Bling would never admit it except under the threat of torture, but he, too, was a fan of Sister Ima Hellraiser.

Not only was she good-looking but she could slip out of more messes than anyone he knew. He appreciated a woman who knew her way around the law. If those same women knew a few Bible verses that would be a nice plus.

He pretended to be annoyed with the interferences and continued to tell them what was on the menu for the in-between services meal. He told them that fried catfish-in-a-blanket, smothered pig feet fajitas basted in yellow Jamaican hot sauce, third-degree chili and other delights were available in the church's backyard—for a price. "This food gonna make you feel like you eating manna from Heaven."

"What is manna?" one of the visitors whispered to a young man sitting next to him.

"I don't exactly know. But, as long as they drop a smoked ham hock in it, I'll be eating it," the young man replied.

The food had been supplied by none other than Mother Eternal Everlastin'. Her cooking along with her wealth and lack of fashion sense were renown in Pelzer.

The invitation from the pastor, along with the evil eye from Deacons Luke and Warm, mixed with the smile etched in the wrinkles on Mother Eternal Everlastin's face and the chaos assured by Sister Hellraiser's impending appearance made it impossible for the members to forgo the invite.

Soon the benediction was over and everyone had recovered from laughing too hard at the Reverend Bling Moe Bling when he forgot to push up his Support (the leg kickstand) before moving from behind the pulpit. That little memory lapse made him look like he was doing the Pee Wee dance as he shook and twisted, trying to grasp the edge of the pulpit to keep from falling.

The congregation of No Hope Now—Mercy Neva poured out through the back door and onto the lot behind the church. They did what many church folks did when they got together after a service— they talked about the short sermon, the long collections and the fact that no one thought to bring the hot sauce for the manna. And, of course, who would be given the job of keeping Sister Betty along with all of her "praise God" and strings of "hallelujahs" out of the way so Sister Hellraiser could add a little spice to the annual Mothers Board anniversary program. Everyone knew that there was a long-standing feud between Mother Pray Onn, who was Sister Hellraiser's aunt and fellow congregation member, and Mother Eternal Ann Everlastin'. If the two women got within scratching distance it would make it an event worthy of Pay Per View.

2

Ain't No Party Like a Funeral Party

No one could drink Kool-Aid like church folks, and the No Hope Now—Mercy Neva's backyard was littered with old empty Kool-Aid wrappers and dotted with little brown patches of grass. The between service meal was tasty, even without the traditional Hell-Naw hot sauce available and was quite passive compared to the others that had been held in the church's backyard. Even the pigeons kept their swooping and cawing to a minimum as they swooped down for scrapes.

Of course, there were several near-fights over meaningless stuff, but most folks wanted to defer their own drama for another time. They wanted to save their enthusiasm and energy for the afternoon service and whatever chaos Sister Hellraiser surely had in mind for their "precious" Mother Eternal Everlastin' Mothers Board anniversary service.

It was around 3:30 P.M., and the No Hope Now—Mercy Never Church's Mothers Board fifth anniversary was about to begin soon. The tiny church was packed. Word had gotten out, and people flocked to the church like ants. The Deacons Luke and Warm had to set up a few unsafe folding chairs outside on the rain-soaked sidewalk. Of course, several of the entrepreneurial-minded visitors brought items such as flimsy umbrellas and bags of cotton candy to sell to the sidewalk gawkers.

Sister Betty and Sister Ma Cile had already arrived and were inside greeting Mother Eternal Everlastin' with alternating hugs and well wishes. The old women had not seen each other in quite a while but the love was still there.

Both Sister Betty and Ma Cile conceded with pretended indignation that the matching white-on-white suits and white oversized pillbox-styled hats they wore paled in comparison to the big blue flamingo bird that sat upon Mother Eternal Everlastin's head.

"Mother Eternal, you sho can wear a hat," Ma Cile teased. "I wouldn't have the nerve to try and wear sumpthin' like that." That was saying a lot coming from Ma Cile, especially since most folks were afraid of her and that false blue eye that wobbled around in her eye socket when she became rattled or upset. The fact that she didn't have the nerve to wear a blue-feathered flamingo ugly hat, but would wear one false blue eye with her good brown eye was perplexing to say the least.

Sister Betty didn't open her mouth. It was apparent to her that her best friend, Ma Cile, had been pinching some of her industrial-strength snuff before they'd come to church. She'd learned a long time ago that trouble just naturally followed her and Ma Cile, so she didn't need to invite it. She would just hold her peace and pray. She would pray real hard.

"I'm so glad to see you two." A little tear appeared in the corner of Mother Eternal Ann Everlastin' eyes. She was just overjoyed to see her dear old friends. "And, Ma Cile, how's them sweet little grand-babies of yours? I bet they've grown quite a bit since the last time I had to pop June Bug's hands when he picked one of them green candy Life Savers off of one of my gorgeous hats." She chuckled while she blew a loose hat feather from her face and pushed one of the flamingo feet back to the side of her hat. She put her chubby arms with hanging brown flesh that resembled the wings of a flying squirrel around each of them. "I certainly miss our times together. I wanted to come by so many times and pick y'all up in my limo, but I didn't wanna seem uppity."

Ma Cile wiggled out from under the arm flap of Mother Eternal Ann Everlastin's embrace. "Uppity," Ma Cile echoed. "That B6663/4 bus runs whenever it feels like it. Now po' Sister Betty, she don't weigh but a few pounds compared to me, so she can walk a few feet and it won't bother her none. But me"—she patted one of her mas-sive hips, which made a sound like someone beating a drum or slap-ping an old rug—"with all this extra weight I'm carrying around on my hips, I can't be doing too much walking without my knees just cavin' in. So you can have as much uppity as ya want to. As a matter of fact, I'd probably like uppity," Ma Cile rattled on. She wasn't quite sure what *uppity* meant, but if it came with four wheels and ran on gas, she was certain she could deal with it.

Mother Eternal Ann Everlastin' gave Ma Cile a surprised look and started to respond, but the don't try and understand it arch in Sister Betty's eyebrow stopped her.

Mother Eternal Ann Everlastin', Ma Cile and Sister Betty continued chatting and then went among the visitors and members, greeting and reminiscing while they waited for the anniversary service to begin.

About ten minutes later, there was a noise heard from outside the church like a hoard of buzzing bees on a bear's butt. The Deacons Luke and Warm rushed through the door like there was a demon behind them.

There was.

Sister Betty knew by the hives that suddenly broke out on her arm and the twitch in her arthritic knee that ole Satan had left hell's door cracked and that Sister Ima Hellraiser had escaped.

The she-demon in a blond curly wig was tall, model-thin and beautiful, with a complexion the color of fresh honey, sauntered through the door dressed in a purple halter-top dress. The dress was totally inappropriate for church or daylight, but that was her style. She never said a word, content to wave with her long lavender-painted fingernail, indicating that no one should be in her space as she passed by.

The crowd, of course, spread like the parting of the Red Sea and closed just as quick as she passed. A few of the last to close the gap almost knocked the Deacon Laid Handz down upon his yellow Old Navy bellbottom pants bottom. The Deacon Playa-Playa as he was all but unaffectionately called, stumbled in behind her. He'd come along to operate the camcorder and whatever else Sister Hellraiser commanded with her grunts and finger pointing.

Deacon Laid Handz also hoped that the female pickings at the No Hope Now—Mercy Neva Church would offer him new flirting opportunities, especially since he'd worn out the ones at his own church. And, of course, he needed to escape Sister Carrie Onn. She was the forty something, unmarried, bane of his existence who always blocked the other females from getting too close to "her man" as she dubbed him, by sabotaging their efforts with lies, delicious home cooking and a good down-home hair-pulling exhibition, if necessary. Little Richard would preach without a perm or ultra light complexioned makeup before she let anyone get her man.

Sister Hellraiser greeted Rev. Bling Moe Bling with a smug kiss on the cheek. "Ooh, Reverend Bling Moe Bling, you just get finer and finer every time I see you. If you wasn't married and had that funny leg, I'd stolen you for myself a long time ago," she teased—sort of.

The Reverend Bling Moe Bling never knew what to say around her, so he said nothing.

Sister Hellraiser didn't want to leave his wife, Sister Beulah Bling, out of the picture, so she gave her a nasty, "see if you can top that" glare. Sister Beulah Bling smiled with an uncontrollable twitch dancing from the corners of her thick red lips. She filed away the she-devil's malicious insult, along with a dozen other verbal attacks doled out by Sister Hellraiser.

At first, Sister Bertha Bling buried the nasty insults in the deep recesses of her mind, but then she decided to let them rise, vicious insult by insult, to the surface. She was so mad that when she spun around and looked at the huge red, velvet-backed picture of Jesus in the Garden of Gethsemane hanging over the pulpit, it looked like she did a pirouette and a petit tour. She prayed under her breath, "Lord, I know that you have truly changed me, but Lord, you need to touch her 'cause she just don't know." Her eyes widened and blazed as she continued, "You know me, Lord. Back in the day, I'd have given a couple of crack heads about five dollars in change to redesign her face. Lord, you know they have skills with a box cutter and a can of spray paint." She let the sneer slide from her face, replacing it with one of sincerity and humility. "Since I can't do that, Lord, 'cause I don't wanna do no time, can you please just cut her down? I'm still a praying woman, Lord, so I ain't asking that you kill her; just maim her or turn her into a pillar of salt, Lord." She stopped and bowed her head while wiping a tear and finished her prayer, "I'll be forever grateful. Amen."

Sister Hellraiser, as was her custom, did her dirt and immediately forgot about it. She left the Reverend Bling Moe Bling standing like a statue supported by a kickstand and First Lady Bertha Bling performing ballet turns and praying. She walked in among the members and signed a few autographs. When she had her fill of their bowing and scraping, she then yelled at Deacon Laid Handz in a nice-nasty manner to set up the equipment. She completely ignored Mother Eternal Ann Everlastin', Sister Betty and Ma Cile. She didn't do it out of spite. She did it because she hadn't quite figured out just what kind of spin she would put on her coverage and didn't want to appear to favor the women, not that she would. That would be her story, and she was printing it.

It was time to get things cooking, and the recipe would be for disaster. Everyone there should've read the writing on the wall. Although, they probably did read it, and being the skeptics they were, most likely called the writing on the wall a forgery.

Several moments later, after things had calmed down a little, someone pushed the play button on the cassette player and a Shep and the Limelights song "Our Anniversary" started to play. The Reverend Bling Moe Bling limped to the pulpit. He took one hand and grasped the edge of the pulpit and shook his pants leg, lowering his kickstand and adjusting it at the same time. For whatever reason, known only to him, he always thought he was doing his adjustments without anyone seeing him. That was impossible because the pulpit was made out of see-through plastic and the acoustics were so bad that every little whisper was heard. When he finished fidgeting around, trying to adjust his bad leg, he looked up, embarrassed, with all the remorse of someone with his hand caught in a cookie jar. But he was their pastor and he needed to show them that it was he who ran things. So the Reverend Bling Moe Bling let out a pretend cough and asked the congregation to come to order. "I am going to turn this part of the program over to our distinguished Mothers Board president, Mother Eternal Ann Everlastin'. Let us give her our undivided attention."

That's how he ran things.

He didn't wait for any replies or comments from Sister Beulah Bling, whom he was certain if he had looked her way would have had her own idea of how the program was to go on. Instead, he started limping back to his chair, turned around and stood in front of it. He lifted his hand toward Mother Eternal Ann Everlastin' and beckoned her to the pulpit. He could almost feel the poisoned arrows in his back being thrown by the First Lady Beulah Bling as he navigated his weight from side to side on the cushioned seat. He re-adjusted the kickstand that supported his bad leg and sat there grinning.

Both Sister Betty and Ma Cile sat straight up in their uncomfortable wooden pew and smiled. Their faces lit up and nodded at the same time, as they gave Mother Eternal Ann Everlastin' their unspoken words of support.

Mother showed her appreciation by blowing them a kiss after shoving something in her mouth that she'd just taken from her dress pocket. Whatever it was it made her eyes roll around in ecstasy and turned her tongue dark. She was anxious to get started so she hurried as best she could to the pulpit. She adjusted the microphone and then looked at a piece of paper she held in her hand, as she began to speak.

"Good afternoon to everyone who is assembled in the place under the sound of my po' weak voice." She chuckled to herself at the word *po'* coming from her wealthy mouth and quickly swallowed what she'd been chewing. "I'd like to first give thanks to the Lord who let us see another day that He hath made." She stopped talking and looked annoyed. Once again, for about the tenth time that afternoon, she puckered her lips and blew at one of the blue Flamingo feathers, which was tickling her top hairy lip. "Give me just a moment," she remarked, and adjusted the bird's feet to fall to the back of the hat.

Satisfied and feeling a bit more comfortable, Mother Eternal Ann Everlastin' continued, "I'd like to welcome you all again to our fifth annual Mothers Board anniversary program. We plan on having a good time this afternoon." She glared around the room as if daring any one of them to doubt that they would have a good time.

Everyone just sat there, their faces frozen with expressionless stares.

Mother Eternal Ann Everlastin' appreciated their silent surrenders. "We gonna have a selection from our A choir followed by an attempt to sing from our B choir. When they finish messing that up, we'll have a solo by our Sister Petunia . . ."

Mother's tongue must've been getting heavy because she sure couldn't hold it in its place as she blabbed on. But she finally did stop speaking long enough to get some new information from Sister Beulah Bling, who, come hell or high water, was finally going to have a chance to give some input.

Sister Beulah Bling handed Mother a note while turning as she sucked her teeth and stuck out her tongue at her husband.

As usual he didn't respond. He realized that she was like a mighty oak tree and knew that at one time, every oak was once a nut that held its ground. His wife could plant herself like no one else he knew.

Mother Eternal Ann Everlastin' ignored the silent battle that went on behind her on the pulpit and took that opportunity to reach into her bag and retrieve an envelope. She took a few steps back and handed the envelope to Reverend Bling Moe Bling, who took it, figuring it had some monetary value. He quickly shoved it into his pocket in case his wife should ask for it.

Mother Eternal Ann Everlastin' stepped back to the pulpit, adjusted her reading glasses and scanned the note from Sister Beulah

Bling. Crumbling the note like it was a secret message, she said, "Never mind. It appears that both our A and B choirs were not able to get their color scheme together and I, for one, ain't having no fifteen different shades of white on *my*—I mean *our*—anniversary day."

She turned around and saw that Sister Beulah Bling appeared to be in agreement, so Mother continued giving orders. "We ain't gonna have nothing but first-class service this afternoon, so let us continue with the program."

Again, she absentmindedly turned and pulled something wrapped in silver foil from her top dress pocket and started unwrapping it while she continued speaking. "Y'all know that we always love to hear from Sister Petunia, and for those of you visiting for the first time, I'll explain. Because Sister Petunia is old and deaf, she'll be accompanied by Sister Peaches. Sister Peaches will do the signing for her. I know Sister Peaches is just as old, but she ain't as deaf. And, it's not that we think that y'all deaf, too, but when Sister Peaches signs, it helps Sister Petunia to keep her rhythm. I guess that's a deaf thing. I ain't sure."

Mother sat down in an empty seat on the pulpit. She moved around in her seat until her royal highness's butt found comfort and then motioned for Sister Petunia to come forward.

Sister Petunia was as tall as most basketball players and lemon-colored almost to the point of looking jaundiced. Her profile looked like an old wrinkled jelly bean. She was said to be nearing her nineties, but she dressed in a billowing silver-colored muumuu that made her look like she was the center pole in an old wobbly teepee. And wobble she did as she slowly walked toward the pulpit. She stood there completely still in the center of the floor, weaving like a disco ball near the offering table as if she were waiting for a signal to begin singing—perhaps a smoke signal.

Sister Peaches whose almond-shaped face sported a five o'clock shadow no matter what time it was inched across the floor with a lot of effort and stood next to Sister Petunia. Sister Peaches, black enough to be mistaken for a cave entrance, appeared to be just as old although rumored to have about five more Alzheimer-free brain cells than Sister Petunia. That particular Sunday, some of the five cells must've surrendered to the disease. It was evidenced by her see-through white crinoline dress, which could be seen through because she definitely forgot to wear a slip and probably didn't have on underwear.

Sister Peaches just stood there with a faraway look transfixed on her wrinkled face as if waiting for the announcement of the last spaceship leaving earth. She looked just plain put out.

It didn't take but a minute before Mother Eternal Ann Everlastin' was forced to stop looking at Sister Petunia because the silver-colored disco ball–shaped dress was starting to make her feel dizzy. Instead, she got up from her seat and went back to the pulpit. She turned toward the organist, Brother Juan Derr, and smiled as she spoke. "I just wanna remind you that you don't have to worry about playing no music for her 'cause she can't hear you."

The organist nodded, and she continued speaking while she unwrapped another piece of silver foil and stuck the contents of it in her mouth. With manners unbefitting the crown she'd given herself, Mother Eternal Ann Everlastin' chewed loudly while she spoke but folks could still make out what she was trying to say. "The next few words you hear mumbled will be from our soloist Sister Petunia."

It didn't matter how Mother Eternal Ann Everlastin' introduced Sister Petunia because Sister Petunia had other plans.

Sister Petunia looked like she had tears in her eyes as she signed to Sister Peaches that she had to use the ladies' room and she'd sing when she returned. Sister Peaches left Sister Petunia's side and inched her way up into the pulpit. She whispered the emergency situation to Mother Eternal Everlastin' who didn't appear to be too happy about the interruption in the program's flow. There wasn't too much Mother could do about it because Sister Petunia needed to pay her personal water bill and was about to get a head start. She was also about to lift her dress up in front of everybody at the same time that she dashed off the floor toward the unisex bathroom.

If Mother Eternal Ann Everlastin' was anything, she was quick on her feet. She shoved another one of the silver foil packets she favored back into her dress pocket and spoke. "Well, I guess we all know that I, Mother Eternal Ann Everlastin', may always have a few words to share, but Mother Nature certainly has the final one." She giggled at her little pun. That gave permission to everyone else to do the same. "So that we don't lose anymore time, we will have a selection from our very own, Brother Juan Derr. He will come to us in his own way. Let us receive him with a hearty amen."

Brother Juan Derr, caught off guard, spun around on his organ seat like it was a spinning top and then suddenly stopped. He cracked his knuckles so loud they sounded like cars backfiring; even he jumped up, nearly toppling over the organ bench as he attempted to dive under it. He looked around in embarrassment and caught a nasty glance from another of the members, a Korean couple by the name of Brother Won Note and his wife, Sister Noe Note, who were waiting to sing in a nearby pew.

In addition to the Notes' nasty glares, there was also a severe one coming from Ma Cile. It wasn't because she was angry; it was because she had suddenly become ill. "Sister Betty, I don't know what is wrong with me. I'm not feelin' too well. I think I'm gonna leave and go home. My stomach and ever'thang is just gurgling." She started to hold her stomach, and that was all she could hold. Suddenly the surrounding air took on a rather pungent smell as if demons had escaped from under her dress.

Sister Betty looked around as others in the pew started pinching their noses. "I'd go with you but I have to stay and represent the Mothers Board." She could've gone but really didn't want anyone to think that the not-too-pleasant odor was coming from her. "Just make sure you raise one finger when you leave, and take a cab." She looked at Ma Cile as Ma Cile's face became etched with discomfort. "I'll call you later," she added softly.

"That's okay. I'm just gonna git in my bed, and I don't wanna hear from nobody and about nothin'." Ma Cile didn't have time to explain any further because her stomach was on a race of its own, and it felt like it was gonna break a record sending stuff down to the finish line.

Ma Cile raised one stubby finger to signal to one of the ushers to come to assist her, but they acted like they didn't see her. It wasn't that they didn't see her; they did. They also smelled something foul coming from that direction and didn't feel spiritually fit to deal with whatever the problem or evil spirit was about.

Normally Ma Cile would've made a mental note of the snub but not that time. Instead, she took it upon herself to get up, and as she moved past the sitting congregants, she whispered, "Sorry. It's just some gas." Each person fell back in their seats, their heads hitting the back of the pews with a loud thud like a row of dominoes, as if she had slain them with power. She finally made it to the end of the pew with folks sprawled and strewn over their seats and waddled up the aisle and out the door, leaving Sister Betty to sit out the rest of the service by herself, as well as to later explain what had happened.

Brother Won Note and his wife, Sister Noe Note, were both short in stature with moon-shaped faces—him with a Mohawk and her with a widow's peak that threatened to peak at the tip of her wide nose. They wore matching blue satin floor-length robes embroidered with black dragons and were loudly clearing their throats. They let their heads fall back, allowing their tongues to vibrate, so they could vocally maim one of the hymns from the red standard hymnal book. They always sang "We'll Understand It Better By and By." However, when they sang it as a duet it always came out, "Deel Bunderhand It Chedda By in By." Their English was so bad that sometimes they couldn't understand each other.

They were allowed to sing anytime they wanted because they always gave huge offerings to the church. No one cared that it was monies earned off the sweat, as well as the patronage, of those who spent one dollar to get twelve oily pieces of chicken at the only Korean Krunchy Fried Chicken drive-thru in Pelzer, which happened to be owned by the Notes. The pieces of chicken were the size of a small kitten or a Chihuahua, and could've been just that, according to Chef Porky LePierre, owner of the El Diablo Soul Food Shanty, the competition next door.

By the time Brother Juan Derr got his seat adjusted where his feet almost met the pedals and he was ready to play, Sister Petunia had returned to the center of the floor with the hem from the back of her dress tucked in her panty waistband. With her bathroom emergency taken care of, she started to mutter her song.

Sister Peaches rushed to her side and started signing with her fingers frantically crisscrossing, like she was throwing up a gang sign— *your dress is stuck in the waistline of your drawers.* Sister Petunia knew that line wasn't a part of the verse and just completely ignored Sister Peaches. It was her turn to show what she had, and she certainly did.

In the meantime, Brother Juan Derr had turned his back to show his displeasure of being denied a solo but turned back around when he saw Sister Petunia's embarrassing situation.

Sister Betty just sat with eyes wide and mouth opened. She was stunned right along with the rest of the folks.

"Is she ever gonna finish and put her dress down?" Mother Eternal Ann Everlastin' mumbled as she waited impatiently for Sister Peaches to finish signing the song performed by the deaf Sister Petunia.

Finally it was over. Mother Eternal Ann Everlastin' spoke with mock humbleness as she sugar-coated and searched for appropriate words. "That was just lovely. Whatever it was that you were singing may not have been clear to us, and I'm here to say that it certainly wasn't, but we know Heaven was rejoicing."

She was so good with the smooth words that she sometimes surprised herself. She adjusted the microphone again and for about the fifth time since the program started, she pulled something from another silver foil wrapper and slipped it into her mouth. There were probably those who wanted to know what she was chewing but didn't dare ask. Whatever it was, she was really enjoying the taste.

"I have one other announcement to make. On another note, some of you may know and then some of you may not have read the church bulletin with big, bold black letters across the first two pages. Today is my seventy-first birthday."

The organist, Brother Juan Derr, started pecking out "Happy Birthday to Ya" and he did it with all eighty-eight keys plus a few more that weren't on the organ. The congregation, led by Sister Petunia, who did her usual sign-singing, sang their well wishes.

Mother waited until the very last chorus and then gave her best pretend blush and said humbly, "Y'all are so sweet. I thank God that He's kept me this long, and I just know in my heart and soul that He's gonna let me live to see one hundred—"

"Yes, He will," Reverend Bling Moe Bling called out. "He's gonna let you see at least one hundred and one."

And then it happened, and it happened very fast. Suddenly, without warning, Mother grinned and started babbling about how she was starting to have a vision. She said, "I feel the sensation of cold air. I believe the Lord is showing me a snow-capped mountain and I-I—" her eyeballs started rolling toward the back of her head but she continued, "I-I feel sunrays caressing my hair and the wind blowing through it. I hear the beautiful birds chirping. I-I feel a sensation like I've never felt before. God is givin' me a vision—"

She suddenly grabbed for the cash register that was nailed between the pulpit and the collection table, leaned over and fell on top of it.

The glint from the mysterious silver foil wrapper could be seen falling to the floor from Mother Eternal Ann Everlastin's hand.

Reverend Bling Moe Bling finally jumped up from his high-backed white cushioned seat and limped toward Mother Eternal Ann Everlastin'.

"Mother! Mother, are you alright?" At the same time, he bent down and with one hand he picked up the silvery piece of paper, thinking it might've held some money Mother was trying to hide.

Instead it was the silver wrapper from a snack size York peppermint pattie. Mother had not had a vision from God. Mother had felt too much of the sensation from eating a York peppermint pattie.

"Quick. Someone call an ambulance!" one of the members yelled to a nearby usher who just stood as still as she had been all during the service. When the usher didn't move fast enough, one of the other members snatched a cell phone from his pocket and dialed 911.

Just that quick, Mother Eternal Ann Everlastin' who thought she was having a vision from God at the podium and who wanted to live to be at least a hundred years old, instead died from an overdose of the cool sensation of a York chocolate peppermint pattie. She must've realized at the very last minute what was happening to her because later it took the paramedics and a huge vibrating, battery-operated chisel to pry her hands from the pulpit's cash register where she had just placed her tithes.

In the meantime, Sister Hellraiser thought she had captured the whole thing on film. When she found out that Deacon Laid Handz had been distracted by the sight of Sister Petunia's underwear tucked in the hem of her dress, and he had stopped taping, she completely freaked out. He had missed everything that happened from that point on. Sister Hellraiser lit on him like a rabid buzzard on a bunny rabbit. She was yelling so loud with several words totally unbefitting the church or the local bar until she started choking.

It was also a good thing that the paramedics were there that day. Trustees Ballen Tine Ale and Lett Lous, who in addition to being paramedics were also members of the We-Be Wishin' and Hopin' Military Universal Church. They gave Sister Ima Hellraiser emergency treatment while they waited for the county coroner to arrive.

While the paramedics worked on Sister Ima Hellraiser, poor Deacon Laid Handz lay sprawled out several feet away under a bunch of blank VHS cassettes, a broken camcorder and a microphone bent as only someone with supernatural powers could bend it. He had a huge knot on one side of his forehead, and his eyes looked as busted and as bloodshot as Mr. Magoo's. The paramedics had ignored his cries for help while they worked on Sister Hellraiser, with a few unnecessary chest massages until a sign of recognition lit up Trustee Ballen Tine Ale's face.

There was something very familiar about the man who lay

screaming and bleeding, wrapped in media tape. Paramedic/Trustee Ballen Tine Ale rose up and tipped close to where Deacon Laid Handz lay and with a threatening tone in his voice and swinging his stethoscope, he hissed, "I knew it was you! As messed up as you look, you can just lie there and wait on the coroner 'cause I'm about to kill you."

It appeared that paramedic/Trustee Ballen Tine Ale was also the husband of one of the members of the Ain't Nobody Else Right But Us—All Others Goin' to Hell Church, Sister Jaye Ale. The husband and wife attended different churches for different reasons. He went to a church that dismissed early whenever a championship game was playing; she went to one where she never felt convicted.

When he wasn't on duty on Sundays, after his own service, he always picked her up. He recognized Deacon Laid Handz as someone who one Sunday tried to lay hands on his wife in an unspiritual-like manner in the church parking lot. The deacon had fled that afternoon and this was the first time Ballen Tine Ale had seen him since that day.

"Oh, shoot!" said the other paramedic Trustee Lett Lous as he angrily stopped the unnecessary chest massage on Sister Hellraiser. He leaped up, rushed over, grabbed his partner by the arm and swung him around. "Man, you got to be professional about this!" he exclaimed with concern. "Don't do it. Whatever it is you about to do, now,"—he looked around with determination and whispered—"there's too many witnesses."

However, the Trustee Ballen Tine Ale would not be denied. He, too, quickly looked around and saw that everyone was basically huddled in corners. Some looked shocked. Others were busy taking notes. "Just stand in front of me," he told his partner, Lett Lous.

Before his partner could cover the two feet that stood between him and Deacon Laid Handz, Ballen Tine Ale had hauled off and with his heavy metal stethoscope, he whacked the Deacon Laid Handz across the domed part of the deacon's head. That metal stethoscope came down so hard on the deacon's head that it looked like it had been shaved with a lawnmower. It took out patches of hair, and what was left looked like little dark cabbage buds.

Now Deacon Laid Handz also had matching knots on his forehead. The bulging knots started to rise like growing acorns, and from a distance, they also looked like little devil-training horns.

Rooted to her pew seat, Sister Betty felt it was all a dream. Just that quick her beloved friend of more years than she could remember was gone. Gripping the back of the pew in front of her for balance, she finally got up. With her oversized Bible now lying in the bend of one of her tiny arms and a steady stream of tears that washed down into the folds of her wrinkled neck, she seemed to levitate through the melee to the church exit. She spoke to no one. She couldn't.

As Sister Betty left the church to go home, her mind began to wrap itself as best it could around what'd happened. As she shifted the weight of her oversized Bible on her arm, she thought to herself, *A York peppermint pattie. How in the world do you die from the sensation of a York peppermint pattie?*

She stopped trying to figure it out and wiped a tear that fell as she leaned against a parking meter. Somehow, she was able to hail a taxi, and she rode the rest of the way in silence. With one small and wrinkled hand, she hugged her big oversized Bible to her chest and groped at her large cross with the other. Many conflicting thoughts zigzagged across her mind. Each thought flashed like streaks of lightning bolts as she also struggled with how and when she would tell Ma Cile about their good friend's sudden passing.

Sister Betty remembered with sadness what Mother Eternal Ann Everlastin' had meant to her and to Ma Cile as well, and just how unpredictable life could be. Sister Betty looked out of the cab window up at the vast sky that suddenly took on a gray pallor and prayed silently, "Lord, hold her in your arms, and take care of her, Lord. I miss her already, and, Lord, when you come for me, please don't take me in any embarrassing fashion." She'd repent about that last request later.

All Sister Betty wanted to do was to get home and get into her prayer closet, which was only two brown down-filled throw pillows, one atop the other, at the foot of her sofa.

The first thing she wanted to do when she finally arrived home would be to take her phone off the hook. Except for God, she didn't want to see or talk to anyone.

It wasn't her intention to abandon Ma Cile by not calling her right away, but Ma Cile did say that she wasn't feeling well and didn't want to be disturbed. She was taking a big chance by not calling Ma Cile first. It was just possible that Ma Cile might've started feeling better and changed her mind about not answering her phone. There was a chance that someone else would give her the bad news. If that happened then she was sure Ma Cile would be very upset and probably would be calling her throughout the evening; but Sister Betty had many questions for God and a lot she needed to get off her own chest.

Just knowing that Mother Eternal Ann Everlastin' was gone made her even more aware of her own immortality; just as a car needed a tune-up every so often to have its insides checked for problems and to stay in the best running condition, Sister Betty needed a spiritual tune-up too. Who better to do it than the Master Mechanic of body, soul, mind and spirit? God.

Back inside the No Hope Now—Mercy Neva Church, the Reverend Bling Moe Bling, the Deacons Luke and Warm along with First Lady Beulah Bling just sat as if glued to their seats, looking bewildered. They had answered all the questions from the medics and had waited until the coroner arrived to pronounce the dead body as "officially" dead and to answer more of the same questions.

None of them could comprehend what had happened. Most of the church folks had left as soon as the coroner had arrived so they could go and spread the word. With most people gone and the church service interrupted as well as abruptly ended, there was nothing more that could've topped what had just happened—except the Lord's Second Coming.

It was agreed that the Reverend Bling Moe Bling, after he got home, would call Tiny, Mother Eternal Everlastin's limo driver and inform him of what happened. They then turned off all the church lights, set the alarm, triple-locked the church doors and went their separate ways home.

There were a lot of sad and surprised faces after the service that day. However, they recovered from their shock and many wondered who was gonna get all her money and property.

Mother Eternal Ann Everlastin' was really dead. Who would've thought it?

3

Beauty's Only Skin Deep, Gossipin's to the Bone

If the world was stunned way back when it was discovered that light traveled faster than the speed of sound, imagine how flabbergasted the entire town of Pelzer was when within twenty minutes of her death, everyone knew that Mother Eternal Ann Everlastin' had died. And that her death was unofficially caused by, of all things, an overdose of sensation from a York peppermint pattie.

The fuel for the faster-than-the-sound-of-a-speeding-bullet report of the sad news was none other than that queen of all blabbermouths, the always-up-in-somebody's-business phenomenon herself, Sister Carrie Onn. The forty-plus single, high-maintenance nutmeg-complected woman of considerable beauty whose real mission in life was to get a man. No one ever paid attention to her frequent claim that Jesus was her only man, and she didn't need any other man. Yet with the concentration and patience of a boa constrictor, she was just as determined to make Deacon Laid Handz her husband.

With no experience except the nosy DNA and sleuthing genes inherited from her mother, the stern and no-nonsense Mother Pray Onn, she managed to finesse being a petty snoop and a treacherous old maid into an art form.

It all went down later that Sunday afternoon after the morning service at her church, the Ain't Nobody Right but Us—All Others Goin' to Hell. It was after she realized there'd be no afternoon church service and couldn't find the Deacon Laid Handz that she decided to make use of her free time. She went home, took a shower and made a decision to treat herself to an afternoon of whatever she could get into.

As usual, Sister Carrie Onn never left her house without her American Express card and a need for gossip, so she'd gotten all dolled up in a lavender floral off-the-shoulder short dress. The dress was designed to show off her tanned Barbie doll–shaped legs and with just a few dabs of her signature Always Alone perfume, she got into her pearl-green 2000 Toyota Avalon XLS and started her drive into downtown Pelzer.

While she was momentarily stuck in traffic, sandwiched between a fire truck and a Good Humor ice cream cart, boredom set in, and that was never a good thing because it made her mind the devil's workshop. She turned on her radio, only there was nothing playing but gospel music on each of the three Pelzer stations. She wasn't in a spiritual mood since she couldn't find her man du jour. She looked into the rearview mirror, and to her horror she found a premature gray hair peeking out from her long neck. It stood, dead center, looking like a sliver of steel. She almost yanked the steering wheel from its column.

For certain, it wasn't looking good for her.

Sister Carrie Onn maneuvered her car in and around the other cars, honking her horn like she was the police. "Move outta my way. It's an emergency," she screamed at the other cars while giving them the bird. It wasn't a Larry Bird or a Tweety Bird, but the nationally known finger bird. Whatever she had learned or felt that was spiritual in church that morning left when that strand of gray hair arrived on her neck.

Many of the other Sunday drivers no doubt wanted to set up a roadblock. They could teach her the finer art of driving with manners, using the end of a gun. However, they recognized the crazy woman as the human wrecking ball, Sister Carrie Onn. As she weaved in and out of traffic, her nutmeg complexion contrasted darkly against the white scarf that whipped dangerously around her neck. She looked like a human cinnamon bun glued to a steering wheel.

The other drivers decided to just slow down, move to the side and let her pass. It wasn't worth the effort to try and fight with her because then they'd have to also fight with her mama, Mother Pray Onn, and worse than that, her cousin Sister Ima Hellraiser would surely take it to another level and make it newsworthy.

Sister Carrie Onn continued driving while profiling and perpetrating in style. She reclined the tan leather car seat and drove, laid back, with her mind on some mischief and some mischief on her mind. She drove nonchalantly with only one hand on the steering wheel in her pearl-green 2000 Toyota Avalon XLS. Her other hand was used to turn the broken knob on the volume on her static-filled illegal police scanner.

Soon Sister Carrie Onn was about a block away from her beauty appointment she'd made earlier in the day. She was on a mission to Shaqueeda's Curl, Wrap and Day Care Center next door to Pookie and Dem's Bogus Laundromat and Numbers Emporium for an emergency makeover. That gray hair had to go!

Suddenly, over the hissing and crackling noise of the police scanner, she heard the news. The details were sketchy but she heard the words *Mother Eternal Ann Everlastin's dead.*

That's all she needed. It wasn't that she was happy that Mother Eternal Ann Everlastin' had died, but sketchy details were always the best for her. That gave her room to be creative when she repeated the tantalizing tidbits until it resembled something else entirely.

With the skill of a professional stunt car driver or an underpaid parking valet, she managed to park her car with just one try. It was a magnificent and impressive feat, especially since the space was only big enough for two, maybe three Volkswagens, and two Volkswagens were already parked there.

"Tell me I ain't good," she exclaimed as she marveled at her driving skills. She had barely parked the car and stepped onto the sidewalk before she had her finger on the cellular speed-dial button. Her fingers were a blur as she managed to conference in enough people at one time to get the word out about Mother's sudden demise to half of Pelzer. She knew that once she got inside Shaqueeda's, it would only take another minute or two before the rest of Pelzer found out.

The only other thing the city of Pelzer, South Carolina, would have to wait for was the film at eleven on television channel Y-LIE.

Of course, she wasn't aware that they wouldn't have had to wait to see the action if Deacon Laid Handz hadn't been distracted earlier by the hem of Sister Petunia's dress trapped in the waistline of her underwear.

Sister Carrie Onn could hear some disturbance coming from the inside of Pookie and Dem's Bogus Laundromat and Numbers Emporium. She heard the clinking sound of plate-glass shattering, someone screaming obscenities, and the words *somebody better have my money!* Normally, she would have snuck around one of the spiny bushes and peered in to see what was happening, but not today. Besides, she wasn't wearing her bullet-proof vest, and she needed to make haste to Shaqueeda's to tell everyone the big news. Today, she didn't care if she wasn't the first to get her hair done. Being the first to tell the big news was her goal.

Inside Shaqueeda's Curl, Wrap and Day Care Center, there were about ten women of all shapes, sizes, hair lengths and textures. There was also one young man, daintily dangling his wrist while getting his manicure. Gospel celebrity and First Lady Shirley Caesar's soulful singing of "You Can Make It" softly flowed, her timbre coating the room with as much spirituality as possible, from an old straw-front covered Philco radio.

The patrons sat around on nine side-by-side assorted chairs and stools, one almost on top of the other, gossiping and commenting on things they knew nothing about. They were waiting for the only beautician in the place, Shaqueeda Uneeda Hairdone to finish her magic.

Each one of the waiting patrons looked like cartoon characters as they sat wrapped, taped and rolled inside the calico, Navajo and Kente-patterned kitchen of Pelzer's house of beauty.

Ché Shaqueeda. That's what was written in a green felt-tip marker on a sign that swung from a wooden slat that hung on the porch, but everyone knew its real business name was Shaqueeda's Curl, Wrap and Day Care Center.

Shaqueeda was the single, thirty-year-old octoroon midget who always wore an orange, down-to-the-hip hair weave with white strips of hair strategically placed. Shaqueeda looked like one of those orange-and-vanilla ice cream Popsicles. She had hips that stuck out like a peach slice was attached to each side. Her place was always packed, no matter when it was because she, alone, had a secret recipe for creating a head of hair that looked unique no matter the occasion.

One of her regular patrons, a science teacher at the nearby high school had once determined a part of her secret. He discovered from a few strands of hair he'd examined in a petri dish that she used a tablespoon each of Dax hair grease, Dixie Peach hair grease and Royal Crown hair grease. She added a gram of Nadinola bleaching cream, and a bottle of any store-bought brand of peroxide. He was so sure about his findings that he was almost ready to publish a paper that those ingredients were a definite part of the secret formula.

He would've made a fool of himself. What wasn't discovered was that Shaqueeda also mixed it all together with a little Argo starch to stretch it and she rubbed it in from the hair tip to the scalp instead of the other way. The hair always looked teased when she did it. Only Shaqueeda knew how to stir all that stuff together and no two hairstyles were ever the same. She was also very careful when she performed her beauty magic by layering lines, one-inch thick of Sulfur 8 dandruff grease into the scalp before any application. It was sure to keep any possible third-degree burns at a minimum.

The final styling came after Shaqueeda had washed the hair with her homemade concoction, which had a slight fried possum or sautéed gamey odor. "What's that odor?" some would say as they became faint, and then suddenly hungry.

While praying and chanting she'd circle her client. Then with a bunch of hair rollers, heavily coated with hot blessed oil, she'd stop and let her eyes roll to the back of her head. With the heated rollers held skyward, she'd spin around three times while thanking God for giving her the gift of hair styling. Shaqueeda would pull the hair so tight around those rollers, an instant face-lift couldn't be avoided. Many held their head up with pride and gratitude when they left Shaqueeda's chair. They thought they looked so good that they'd forget all about the pain in their neck from holding up the ten-inch high, concretelike plastered cones of hair.

The cost for one of Shaqueeda's creation didn't come cheap either; at least not by Pelzer's beauty shop standards. Her prices had risen dramatically. There was a time in her closet-sized, cluttered kitchen when she'd wash and rinse hair in a large silver mixing bowl for $2.50. After increasing the kitchen space by about five feet, which only spread out the clutter, then adding a double aluminum sink and a thirteen-inch black-and-white television, she decided that she should charge more—at the very least $7.50.

A lot of her patrons didn't mind the hefty increase because Shaqueeda wasn't above bartering. For instance, a large can of her favorite but hard-to-come-by B&B Baked Beans with the secret sauce recipe attached was always good for a two-color rinse and a one-layer dandruff treatment.

Shaqueeda's patrons also marveled at the way she handled her own five kids who were each claimed by six different fathers. She didn't have the heart to tell one of the possible baby daddies, who was about seventy-five and sported a stomach that resembled a large brown inner tube, that if he was ever able to look over that inner tube and into his pants he'd have realized that babies weren't something he could've made. He couldn't make much of anything. Most of the time he couldn't even make it to the bathroom on time. And, if he'd let the doctors examine him with his pants off, he'd have gotten disability added to his social security without a second opinion needed. But he was good for a few laughs and pocket change.

Shaqueeda also had ten other kids she baby-sat while she worked as a premiere ghetto beautician. She knew how to handle her business and never once stepped on those children's toes as they followed her around like a flock of ducklings.

Shaqueeda even had her own benediction and never let anyone leave before she prayed over them holding a can of Black and Could Be Lovely Stiff Goop. She'd say, "Until you make another appointment and return with the money you still owe me, may the Lord watch over you and the hair created by me with my holy rollers."

The activity was high inside as Sister Carrie Onn came blasting through the swinging doors of Shaqueeda's Curl, Wrap and Day Care Center like she'd been blasted from a rocket or like Deacon Laid Handz had finally asked her for a date. She was just that excited. "Y'all ain't gonna believe what's happened," she called out as she came to a screeching halt on the worn black rubber welcome mat. She wanted to blurt out the news so bad, she started salivating. This was her moment in the sun, and she was gonna stand there basking in it even if she got sunburned.

"We already know," Shaqueeda answered as she nonchalantly twisted a strip of aluminum foil around a wisp of red hair protruding from the bowed head of an unseen figure in a smock. But she wasn't finished pulling out that can of the So What attitude spray. She had to go and open up a thunderous cloud burst and drench Sister Carrie Onn's 411 by adding, "You way too late. The funeral director, Mr. Bury Em Deep was the second one this afternoon to tell me that Mother Eternal Ann Everlastin' dropped dead in the pulpit this morning. He called here asking me if I'd do her hair and makeup."

She never stopped popping her chicken-flavored chewing gum or adding more strips of the aluminum foil–filled concoction to the head of hair she'd been working on, while she added, "And then he had the nerve to ask me if I'd donate my skills." She frowned and blew a huge bubble with her gum. "I told him that I wasn't donating nothing. With all the money Mother Eternal Ann Everlastin' had, I know she must've set aside a check or some cash to have her hair and makeup done whenever she died."

It became so quiet that a butterfly banging its antennae against a cotton ball would've been heard.

Sister Carrie Onn turned an amber color and then added a slight blue tinge. She never had a chance to compose herself before another voice laced with vocal acidity spoke out from under a smock.

"Aw, Shaqueeda, come on. Don't be so modest. I don't care if you let folks know. You can tell Sister Carrie Onn in particular. Tell her that it was *me* who told you first about Mother Eternal Ann Everlastin'. Remember I told you about her falling over in the pulpit and never standing back up again." The voice giggled. "Mind you, not from a vision from God, but from the sensation of a York peppermint pattie." The head of aluminum foil–wrapped hair rose slowly and royally out from under the towel while continuing its taunt. "After all, Sister Carrie Onn and I are cousins."

The voice had a tinge of a nasty familiarity to it as it continued to rise with each word dipped and delivered in a cold-hearted mixture of surly meanness and spite. It could've only poured out from the Queen of Mean herself, Sister Ima Hellraiser. "Too bad you didn't call here first, dear cousin. I could've saved you the trouble of rushing over here." She stopped and gave Sister Carrie Onn a quick once-over. "Although you are definitely in need of Shaqueeda's individual attention and miracle magic. 'Cause quite frankly, my dear, you look *toh* up!" To kick the insult up a notch, she added, "You need to let Shaqueeda wax that gray hair you got sticking out from your neck."

Ouch!

She watched Sister Carrie Onn, the cousin she disliked the most, with the same dislike and lack of compassion as that shark in the movie *Jaws* displayed while he ate the captain.

Sister Carrie Onn's jaw dropped so fast and hard that it almost covered up that stubborn strand of gray hair on her neck.

"That's right, honey," someone in the room blurted out. "Sister Hellraiser came running through that door about thirty minutes ago with that faded red dye job spread around her face like peacock's feathers. Girl, before her big butt could sign in and plop down in that dye job chair, she'd told us everything . . ."

The voice laughed loud and alone. No one else had the nerve to laugh out loud but there were guts busting inside all over the place.

Sister Hellraiser's eyes shot poison-tipped darts with the speed of a nuclear rocket at the only mouth in town that could possibly compete with hers and Sister Carrie Onn's gossipy tongues. The competitor was none other than Brother Tis Mythang, the choir director and organist for the Ain't Nobody Else Right But Us—All Others Goin' to Hell Church. He was the Mad Hatter engineer of the gossip train.

Brother Tis Mythang was a thirty-year-old, slender, single man with a penchant for daintiness who loved to sing and play any James Brown and Kirk Franklin music and fancied himself as a Dottie Peoples expert.

He called himself a "Christian baller," but he was a baller on a budget, so he only came to Shaqueeda's once a month. It was his good fortune and everyone else's who was in need of a little entertainment that today he was there for his monthly touchup. He was no novice at starting trouble, only finishing it. No matter how many times he'd lost his dignity in a verbal battle, he'd find just a little more dignity to lose again in a rematch.

"Did I say something wrong?" Brother Tis Mythang smirked as he bravely met Sister Hellraiser's death glare with one of his own. He raised his newly polished pinky fingernail in midair. "You need to stop guzzling that hater aid. Don't stare at me and hate me 'cause I'm beautiful, darlin'. Just take a picture. It'll last longer." He continued meeting her stare with both his eyes squinted and one eyebrow arched like the superstar wrestler, the Rock, as he gently blew over the nail to dry it au natural. He tossed back his head, which was filled with large-size rollers for his coif, and with his other hand, he straightened the cartooned bib around his neck. *If I wasn't about to get a pedicure, I might've taken it to another level*, he thought. Instead he took delight in seeing the humiliation spread like cheap cement over both Sister Carrie Onn and Sister Ima Hellraiser's entire bodies. He watched them twitch in silence as he thought about how many times they'd done the same to him while challenging his manhood. He jerked his neck, Egyptian-style, and hissed, "Ah, payback on a Sunday at Shaqueeda's. There just isn't anything like it." He then started humming a Dottie Peoples song, one of his all time favorites, "On Time God."

In the meantime, one of the other patrons, Sister Love Lee, a member of the Path to the Kingdom Evangelical Center for Humanitarian Efforts, walked over and offered Sister Carrie Onn a sympathetic hand to gently lead her and the last bit of her self-esteem to the only empty seat left. "Here, darling, you have a seat. You look like you're about to pass out."

The woman tried to look a little too sympathetic. "Don't pay none of these folks any mind. It's such a shame what happened to Mother Eternal Ann Everlastin' . . ." Sister Love Lee droned on as she gingerly pushed Sister Carrie Onn down into the chair.

Too bad the chair was one of Shaqueeda's kids' little red rockers, although it was fit and fitting because Sister Carrie Onn certainly felt small enough to sit in it with room to spare. Like a robot, she sat down with her knees hunched up to her chest and did what anyone would do when they sat in a rocker; she rocked.

With all the chatter and laughter going on around Sister Carrie Onn, it took another five minutes for her self-control to return, but she didn't stop rocking. She hadn't felt that small and betrayed since Brother Two Ton had played her like a game of Sorry. He had told every member with a pair of unclogged ears at the Ain't Nobody Else Right But Us—All Others Goin' to Hell Church's Singles Auction and Desperation Banquet, that she'd asked him about a date, and he'd turned her down. He even took out an ad in the *Daily BLAB*. It was only partially true. She'd been talking to him about dates in a passing conversation. She'd meant a date, as in the fruit, and he'd misconstrued it. Knowing her reputation, he felt she was probably setting him up to hurt his feelings, so he turned her down first to make himself look good. It took her months to get over the humiliation of having the pint-sized four-hundred-pound man toss her to the curb before she ever wanted to walk on his oversized sidewalk. She knew that this travesty inside the hallowed walls of Shaqueeda's Curl, Wrap and Day Care Center would take much longer to get over because Sister Hellraiser and Brother Tis Mythang would see that it did.

Shaqueeda was determined not to lose Sister Carrie Onn, who was one of her best customers. She always came in on time, paid for the full treatment of hairstyling, nail and toe polishing, along with several chin hairs privately removed using beeswax and leftover collard greens pot liquor.

Shaqueeda didn't like the type of drama that made her establishment seem ghetto, although it was located in one. And, of course, she didn't mind whenever one of the local thugs—they called themselves part-time salesmen—from Pookie and Dem's Homeboyz Shopping Center strolled in. They sold everything from car rims to a portable breathing pump. At least they brought quality merchandise with them—it was stolen, but it was quality. She pretended to brush Sister Hellraiser's dyed red baby hairs in a down sweep alongside her ears but instead she put a dab of Jam gook on the hair and it made Sister Hellraiser look like she was wearing sideburns. Shaqueeda then purposely dropped the hood of the hair dryer down with a hard bang, squashing the curlers onto the top of Sister Hellraiser's head.

"Ouch!" Sister Hellraiser yelled. "Watch what you're doing."

Shaqueeda ignored Sister Hellraiser, and over her protests, she reached over and set the hair dryer to broil tha heifer and sashayed over to the rocker.

Shaqueeda's lips twisted with silent laughter as she left the injured Sister Hellraiser broiling under the hair dryer. Her wide hips narrowly missed knocking over several mystery-filled jars of strange-colored contents and several giant heating combs off the shelf as she approached Sister Carrie Onn. "Listen, honey. I already know that you've alerted everyone in Pelzer except for these here folks about Mother Eternal Ann Everlastin's unexpected death. Now, ain't you proud of that?"

She stopped and looked at Sister Carrie Onn. It looked like the rocker was slowing down, so perhaps Sister Carrie Onn was listening to her after all. "You got the word around to almost all the important folks in Pelzer, and that's something that neither Sister Hellraiser nor Brother Tis Mythang can claim. Come on. Pick up your mouth off the floor and go climb in one of my chairs. Let me try and perfect *perfection*."

Shaqueeda coaxed and sucked up to Sister Carrie Onn better than the servant who made the naked emperor believe that he was indeed wearing clothes.

Shaqueeda, after much cajoling, finally got Sister Carrie Onn into one of the other chairs so she could begin her magic. "You feeling better?" Shaqueeda asked as Sister Carrie Onn sank shyly into the seat.

"I guess I'm okay," Sister Carrie Onn answered timidly. "But, you know, it's kind of hot in here."

"Oh my goodness. Chile, I forgot I set that hair dryer on broil," she said, nodding over at Sister Hellraiser who looked like she was basting and marinating in her own evil juices.

Sister Hellraiser was hopping around under the dryer like a lobster trying to escape from the pot. Shaqueeda had purposely tied the bib around Sister Hellraiser's neck to the stem of the dryer so she couldn't escape the heat.

Shaqueeda ignored the desperate cries for help from Sister Hellraiser as she went back to tending Sister Carrie Onn. "I guess I should open a door," she called out to one of her children, "Li'l Linus, come out here and open the front door for Mama."

Linus, a small stocky boy of about nine, wearing a faded, hand-me-down-from-his-sister pink vest and football knickers walked past the front door and entered the kitchen. He was carrying a torn quilt blanket in one hand and sucking on a jam-crusted thumb on the other. He looked back at the front door he'd just passed and asked,

"Mama, why I got to be the one to open that door? Ain't it Camry or Corolla's turn to do it?" he asked, moaning.

Shaqueeda slammed down the jar she had started to open and glared while she spoke. "Linus, go open the door like I told you to do. You make sure you ball up a wad of newspaper and stuff it in the door frame so the door stays open. Hurry up. These flies ain't been out all day."

The day went on, and the gossip surrounding Mother Eternal Ann Everlastin's passing wound down. Sister Hellraiser was the first to leave. She was literally smoking after sitting under the hair dryer, which was set on broil. She looked like a beige hairy prune. She was so mad, she couldn't speak, but it didn't stop her from giving Shaqueeda a check dated for that Monday when she knew the funds wouldn't be available until that Thursday. There was nothing she could do about her damaged hair and she wasn't about to go inside the church looking like a shaved porcupine.

She wanted to turn around and place a slap on everyone who gawked, pointed and laughed at her misfortune. But she could get back at them by doing something none of them could. She was bound and determined to do something of notoriety at Mother Eternal Ann Everlastin's funeral. She just didn't know what.

Brother Tis Mythang would've left about the same time as Sister Hellraiser, but he was determined to milk the last tiny bit of gossip. He got so animated and excited talking about stuff that he'd heard from someone who wasn't even there when it happened that he smudged a freshly painted fingernail. He wouldn't leave until it was fixed, plus he wanted to make sure that Sister Hellraiser was completely gone from the area before he left.

"I wonder who will speak on Mother Eternal Ann Everlastin's behalf since she only got that nephew, Buddy. Everybody knows that he stays drunk all the time," Sister Love Lee said to no one in particular. "I think I'll call Sister Betty when I get home. She and Ma Cile are about the only longtime friends who would probably say something nice about her without wanting to get paid," she added.

The other newly coiffed patrons filed out one by one. Each commented on how they would all meet up at the wake and the funeral if for no other reason than to see if Buddy would show up to his aunt's funeral sober.

Sister Carrie Onn was actually the last one to leave. She bent Shaqueeda's ear with her half-baked plans of revenge, which she was determined to do to Sister Hellraiser. According to her, Sister Hellraiser would need to ask Mother Eternal Ann Everlastin' to "move over." The grave would be the only place she could hide.

Shaqueeda just closed her eyes and pretended she was listening to Sister Carrie Onn carry on. She mentally counted the money she was going to make from reconstructing the magical creations that adorned the heads of Sister Hellraiser and Sister Carrie Onn. If the laws of the planet were in full operation, those two would be back for touch ups on a wig or two before the funeral.

In the meantime, she needed to clean up and feed her brood as well as get the other children ready for when their parents returned to pick them up after the evening church service. She also needed to plan the magic she would perform on Mother Eternal Ann Everlastin'. It would take a lot of ingenuity to make a woman who fancied flamingo feathered hats and blue hair to look gorgeous in her coffin.

4

The Whole Town's Talkin'

Without question, by eight o'clock that night, after the evening church services were over in most of the churches in Pelzer, there wasn't a Christian or secular tongue that hadn't wagged or lied about Mother Eternal Ann Everlastin' departing the earth, riding out without a clue on that fatal sensation of a York peppermint pattie.

And after the shock of scandal wore off, peace seemed to follow rather quickly as folks decided whether they would attend the funeral, or as some others whom she'd aggravated called it, the festivities. Even the weather couldn't decide what to do. It thundered like demons were fighting one another one moment and then the next, calm winds blew like kisses from an angel's lips.

Although peace reigned outside, and despite the erratic weather inside of Mother Eternal Ann Everlastin's former church, the Ain't Nobody Else Right But Us—All Others Goin' to Hell Church, there was a religious war—or something akin to it—about to start. And it was beginning to brew on the inside of the mind of the Reverend Knott Enuff Money. In his study, he just sat as still as a rock one moment and then twiddled one of his Jheri curls the next. His face betrayed no expression as his head hung down with his chin resting on his chest. But that was because he was deep in thought, and for the first time, in a long time, he was feeling an emotion that was all but foreign to him. He was feeling a little sadness welling up on his insides. Since sadness usually did not accompany his greed-fed need, the feeling was new to him, and he didn't know how to handle it.

Suddenly, there was a hard rap on his study door. The knocking became persistent, with each rap accompanying the rhythm of the outside sound of thunder and filled with as much force as a hurricane. The explosive sound from the other side of the door slightly stunned the reverend and almost brought him out of his trance. But, like an old Negro spiritual, he would not be moved from his comfortable, shiny red, real leather chair, even though a tornado that stood only about four feet off the ground had blown into the room. The tornado's legs were bow-shaped and looked like a pair of parenthesis aided by a metal cane, wearing black-and-white saddle prescription shoes. It was cocooned in a plaid shawl. It wore its silver tresses in a tight bun and it hissed like a snake as it blew with gale-wind strength through the door.

The tornado's name was Mother Pray Onn; she was Sister Carrie Onn's gossipy DNA donator. Her mama. If there was a mistress of hell's manor, she would be it. She was powerful yet very short. Most people giggled cowardly behind her back about how she was short enough to be a teller at a piggybank. She always carried a spray can of industrial-strength Mace in a small handbag along with a serrated-edged Bible. If provoked by the least little word or action she was not above using either as a weapon.

According to Mother Pray Onn, one day while in her kitchen putting out a small grease fire that broke out from deep-frying bologna in a skillet, she'd had a vision while coughing on the smoke. In the vision she was told that she was to be the "keeper" of the church rules, the "keeper" of the church's direct line to God, as well as the "keeper" of the Reverend Knott Enuff Money's last good nerve. She was definitely a *keeper*, and no one was going to tell her that she was probably oxygen deprived or overcome from smoke when she thought she had that vision.

"What in the world!" Mother Pray Onn could feel her bun tightening on her head. "Something ain't right . . . I can feel it!"

Before she could continue with her spiteful tirade she was interrupted by another loud clap of thunder rumbling outside. "I hear ya, Lord. I know you want me to see what's going on in this room of iniquity!" she responded.

She was feeling unusually surly as she inched her arthritic hips inside the reverend's personal space and laid her bag, Bible and cane on a nearby shelf. With a touch of envy, she craned her wrinkled neck and peered over the top of her wide, double-sided bifocals to survey his purple and cherry wood-paneled, spacious office. She thought, *If I wasn't so saved, I'd wait until he went on another retreat and paint this room yellow.* She felt it should have been hers anyway and it was going to be, if she could scare enough votes out of the next church board meeting. *Yes, yellow would be a lovely color for my office,* she thought. *After all I am the head of the mothers board. I am a child of the King. I am royalty . . .* and it was while she was praising herself that she took a misstep and banged her crooked pinky toe that was shaped like a lobster's claw, against a hardwood chair. She swore and mumbled under her breath, in pain. She immediately let her head drop in self-reproach when she remembered that she was still inside the church. Her head plopped down hard enough to break an ordinary sinner's neck. "Lord, I'm sorry." Her head rose slowly as she opened her eyes to look toward the white stucco ceiling. "You know my heart."

In her mind, she wasn't really cussing in the Lord's house if she apologized and didn't say the swear words out loud. She considered it "cussing lite," and that was because she was a long-time member of the Child of the King Club and didn't do any heavy-duty cussing on Sundays and certainly not on church property.

It took another couple of minutes before both Mother Pray Onn and her crustacean-shaped pinky toe reclaimed any semblance of feeling, and all during those couple of minutes, the Reverend Knott Enuff Money never even looked up at her. He just sat in his chair with his shoulders hunched and head down, with one hand resting limply on one arm of his chair while the other hand still twiddled with one of his moisture-free Jheri curls. He twiddled it so much it was about to become one long dreadlock, and that would've defeated the whole purpose of him having a Jheri curl.

"I know this man ain't still ignoring me!" she muttered. She looked around the room for something to toss but still didn't see anything that wasn't tithe-bought so she just clenched her tiny fist hard enough for numbness to almost set in. Suddenly screaming out loud a few choice words, but not cuss words, didn't seem like such a bad idea after all, but just then she had another thought: *Maybe he's had a stroke or something.* It wasn't that she really cared if he did. She just couldn't understand how all of a sudden he wasn't afraid of her and was acting like she wasn't in the same room.

Mother Pray Onn took a couple of steps toward the shelf where she'd laid her cane. She grabbed the cane and turned it upside down, taking hold of the tip and deliberately banged its curved end against the side of the reverend's desk. She just barely missed nipping the top of one of his protruding brown wing-tipped shoes. "Oh, my. I'm sorry. I guess I must be getting old . . . Didn't see your big foot—"

She squinted like a hungry hawk and waited to see if the reverend would respond with one of his usual, under-his-breath snide remarks. He still didn't so much as flinch.

Mother Pray Onn was about to go into one of her lethal tirades, especially since there were no witnesses in the study except her, the reverend and her God. She wasn't concerned about the reverend hearing anything from her God. He wouldn't recognize the voice of God anyway because she knew he'd never heard anything from God before. It was her opinion that few people in her church, except for herself, had heard from God. Before she could look around to see what she could accidentally throw at him that wasn't recently tithe-bought, the door to the study swung open again, and the doorknob banged into the paneled wall. The door banged hard enough to cause several unread books on spiritual warfare and Bibles to fall from the bookshelf. One of the books, *Paradise Lost,* flew from the shelf and snipped the corner of her other pinky toe, which was shaped like a crab's claw, and once again she let a stream of a few more choice words escape from her pouting lips. She wouldn't even pretend to ask God to forgive her because she meant what she spouted that time and didn't care who heard her. Feet that hurt could make someone give up his closest friends to the law in alphabetic order or start cussing inside the hallowed walls of the church if he wasn't spiritually grounded.

Running through the door, panting like a leopard who'd missed its kill, came the Bishop Was Nevercalled. He withheld all the niceties. "Oh—oh my!" He stuttered whenever he was nervous or excited or about to tell a lie. Therefore, he stuttered practically all the time.

He ignored the painful look on Mother Pray Onn's wrinkled face as well as ignored the fact that no one had even bothered to say a welcoming hello to him. "I guess by now, y'all done-done heard about Mother Eternal Ann Everlastin' leaving for glory with a wad of-a wad of York peppermint pattie wrappers as her ticket."

The bishop, resembling a skinny white version of the Wimpy character from the *Popeye* cartoon, sporting large horn-rimmed, nearsighted-prescription bifocals, and who could barely read at a fourth-grade level and always followed the Reverend Knott Enuff Money instead of leading him, ranted on. He marveled at what he thought was an elegant and poetic way of saying, Mother Eternal Ann Everlastin' was dead.

By the time the bishop was through with his egotistical ravings, Mother Pray Onn's other pinky toe had regained a semblance of its feeling, and she was ready to do battle. "Have you lost your little mind? Of course, we heard about it two minutes after it happened." She leaned on her cane and with a blank look continued, "You know my niece Sister Hellraiser was covering the Mothers Board anniversary at the No Mercy Now—No Hope Neva Church event this morning."

Mother Pray Onn would have continued bragging but a sucking-teeth noise coming from the direction of the reverend's desk caught her and the bishop's attention.

"Are you two ever gonna shut your mouths?" snarled the Reverend Knott Enuff Money. "I can't even think with all the nonsense you two going on about!" He was running out of patience but he wasn't running his finger through his dried Jheri curl. The few strands that he'd absentmindedly twisted had become one long and stringy dread-lock. "Now look what you two done made me do!" He kept trying to free his finger from the dreadlocked tresses' powerful grip.

Any other time his dilemma would've seemed funny. "You mean to tell me that you was deliberately ignoring me?" Mother Pray Onn asked. She felt like leaping over the desk but with two slightly injured pinky toes, it made that feat impossible. So Mother Pray Onn just filed away the snub in the "payback" recess of her mind. She could wait.

"Reverend, you-you look so sad. I guess it don't matter that Mother Eternal Ann Everlastin' left us dirty and embarrassed, laying in the street, er-er while she moved her membership and her millions to that little ole storefront wanna-be-a-church." He was beginning to calm down, and his stuttering had almost slowed down but then he was about to tell a lie and the stuttering started up again. "You-you sho got a lot of forgiveness in your heart. I didn't think you had it in you." The bishop let a nervous grin creep across his pale face. He was almost proud of the reverend—almost. Just not enough to tell the truth about it.

The Reverend Knott Enuff Money was orbiting his own planet of self-worth and completely ignored the bishop. Instead, he just gave up on freeing his finger from his Jheri curled dreadlock and snatched the lock completely out. "Ouch! Look what y'all done made me do now!" He felt like using some of the same words he'd pretended not to hear, which Mother Pray Onn used earlier but decided against it.

In the meantime, Mother Pray Onn had managed with the help of her cane to hobble over to an unoccupied, though not as plush cushioned chair and sit down. She used the tip of her cane to ease off one of her thick-heeled, orthopedic saddle shoes and let out a sigh of relief. "Oh. Thank you, Lord for healing my pinky toes." She suddenly remembered that she was angry at the reverend and started back in on him. "Well, now that we know that you ain't sick or nothing and that you ain't going to apologize for worrying me like that, especially since you know how sensitive I am—"

Her other pinky toe abruptly started thumping and jumping like the lead drummer of the band in a half-time football segment. She took it as a sign to stop lying and continued with her harassment of the reverend. "Apparently, you must have something very important or devious on your mind to make you lose your manners." He didn't respond, so she continued, this time speaking softly as the pain in her pinky toe started to ebb. "Why are you so deep in thought, Reverend? I can tell you got something brewing around up there. Care to share it with the rest of us who are just sitting around with bated breath waiting for you to give an anointed word!"

Mother Pray Onn wasted no time in letting Reverend Knott Enuff Money know how aggravating he was becoming. If she had to sit through the pain of hurt toes and being ignored, he'd better have a good reason.

Acting as if he couldn't hear the agitation in Mother Pray Onn's voice, Reverend Knott Enuff Money replied, "It is about Mother Eternal Ann Everlastin'. I am so sorry she passed away so suddenly—"

"You see there," the bishop chimed in, "he-he can be sensitive and caring. After all these years of following him, I just didn't think I would witness it during my lifetime—"

Mother Pray Onn's mouth became so twisted, her two lips looked like one was about to loop around the other. Spit flew from the corner of her mouth as she verbally sucker-punched the bishop. "Bishop, will you please just shut your mouth. When you gonna realize that after all these years you ain't suppose to be following; you are supposed to be leading, but I'll handle you later. Right now I got to set the reverend back on track." She lifted her cane and shook it in the direction of the reverend as her words lit and stuck on him like flies on dung. "You act like you don't remember who your real friends are. You do remember that it was the oh-ain't-I-just-rich-and-wonderful Mother Eternal Ann Everlastin' who tried to come between Brother Benn Dead and me, and she tried to take away the Mothers Board presidency position from me as well."

"But-but, she didn't get either one." The bishop tried to reassure her in a sweet, stuttering manner. "And, besides that, she's dead." It was his feeble effort to dissuade Mother Pray Onn from whittling him down any further. He might as well have been talking to the howling wind outside because Mother Pray Onn wasn't hearing or having any of it.

"Go read sumpthin'." That was all she could say because she didn't want to chance any more profanity; however, she wasn't finished with her latest dig. "Oh, that's right, you can't read above the sixth-grade level."

The bishop wrung his hands because he couldn't wring Mother Pray Onn's neck—at least without the reverend's approval. "Why? Why you wanna hurt me like that? I told y'all that in confidence."

"You two are giving me a headache!" the reverend interjected. "With Mother Eternal Ann Everlastin' now dead, we got us a real problem." He finally got up from his chair. He'd been sitting in it for so long, his pear-shaped butt had left a pear-shape indentation in the cushion. He walked over to a far wall that contained a secret sliding panel. As usual, whenever he went to that particular wall he'd signal for whoever was around to turn their heads. This time he forgot to do it and instead, he pushed the panel back, exposing his secret code as he did and revealed a one-way mirror. He then pointed and sadly said, "You two. Come here. I want you to see what I see out there."

The bishop got up first and extended a hand to Mother Pray Onn, who immediately slapped it away until she realized that standing on her feet made her pinky toes hurt again. She grabbed his hand back and together he walked and she limped over and peeked out through the one-way mirror. They gave each other a questioning look, and turned to the reverend and then said, "We don't see nothing but the choir stand and the baptismal pool. What's the big deal about that?" Mother Pray Onn remarked and then fussed, "Got me standing up and limping over here for something that I've been looking at for the past fifty years."

The Reverend Knott Enuff Money started swaying slightly on his feet, and with both hands clasped behind his back, he indicated by sticking out his chin again at the one-way mirror, "I had been thinking about upgrading the baptismal pool."

"And?" Again, the bishop and Mother Pray Onn craned their necks, first to look again through the one-way mirror and then quickly at the reverend, waiting for him to hurry up and get to the point.

After a few seconds, which seemed more like five minutes, the reverend continued. "I was gonna upgrade the baptismal pool to a Jacuzzi!" Out of the blue, tears started to form in his eyes as he walked away from the one-way mirror and across to the other side of the room to a little hot plate on the counter. With his back turned to them, he lifted the carafe and poured something into small purple china cups for the three of them. He walked over and handed each of them a cup and then returned for his own. He took a sip and wiped away a tear. "Go ahead and drink up. I'll be alright."

Surprised by the reverend's crazier-than-usual actions Mother Pray Onn and the bishop slowly sipped the hot liquid while never taking their eyes off the reverend. In between sips which began to spread a warm, relaxing feeling over their bodies, they waited for him to continue speaking.

The reverend fidgeted for a coaster and then set his cup down on it. He leaned back in the chair and said, barely above a whisper, "Mother Eternal Ann Everlastin' paid a visit at my home just yesterday. She told me that she had been thinking about the church and that she'd never forgotten her experiences here. She asked me if I had any plans for improvements . . ." He stopped speaking. He seemed to let his mind wander for a moment as he reached over and took another sip from his cup.

Bishop Was Nevercalled sprang forward in his chair with his cup spilling over and blurted, "And, is that when you hit her up for a loan?" He was getting so excited at the prospect of big money coming in to the church and possibly into his hands that he didn't even feel the little drops of hot tea dribbling down one of his several chins. He didn't even stutter nor did he remember that Mother Eternal Ann Everlastin' was at that very moment, deceased.

The reverend quickly slammed down his cup. The cup missed the coaster, spilling some of the liquid onto the top of the cherry-wood desk. "No, I didn't hit her up for a loan!" the Reverend Knott Enuff Money shouted with indignation. "What kind of man do you think I am?"

That statement was the proverbial straw. Mother Pray Onn and the bishop quickly held up the little cups from which they had been drinking, and cautiously smelled the contents. Satisfied that there was nothing in the cups but hot tea laced with a little raspberry-flavored Arbor Mist wine, they began to look suspiciously over at the Reverend Knott Enuff Money. He looked like he was about *this-close* to being admitted into the Happy, Happy, Oh-So-Happy Hills sanitarium.

Mother Pray Onn gave a conspiring look to the Bishop Was Nevercalled who was slowly rising from his seat. He cautiously walked over and grabbed the reverend by his shoulders, lifted him up slowly from his chair and steered him toward a corner of the study, all the time pretending to say something that was personal. "Come on, Reverend. You can tell me, was it a lot of money?" The bishop droned on for another moment or two as he continued his efforts to distract the reverend.

As the bishop pretended to talk, man-to-man, with the reverend, it gave Mother Pray Onn a chance to limp on over to the reverend's desk and sniff his cup. Reverend Knott Enuff Money's cup reeked of pure raspberry-flavored Arbor Mist wine with just a hint of green tea to keep it within the church's "in moderation" health guidelines. It was what he always drank so she wasn't sure what to make of his strange behavior. She gingerly made her way back to her seat and took another sip from her own cup and raised her pinky finger, a sign that all was okay.

The Reverend Knott Enuff Money shook himself from the bishop's grasp and rebuked him. "I don't know why you whispering, Bishop. Mother Pray Onn can hear anything that we have to discuss."

The bishop backed away cautiously. He was now certain that the reverend had lost his mind because they were always discussing things that Mother Pray Onn wasn't supposed to find out about. "Anything you say, Pastor."

The Reverend Knott Enuff Money acted as if he hadn't heard the bishop and continued, "Besides, the reason I was so distraught was because Mother Eternal Ann Everlastin' forgot to endorse the check."

Before anyone could say anything or move an inch, the loud ringing from the desk telephone silenced them. "Who in the world could that be?" asked the reverend as he set his cup down and reached for the receiver. "Reverend Knott Enuff Money speaking." The reverend's eyes grew wide as he listened. After a few minutes had passed, he finally spoke into the mouthpiece. "Of course, y'all can hold Mother Eternal Ann Everlastin's funeral right here." Another moment of silence passed as he listened and then added, "Well, you understand that we will need a donation to feed all the folks 'cause Mother left her membership here some time ago, and it ain't like she's been coming." He suddenly stopped and caught himself as he thought about the envelope with the unendorsed check that Mother

Eternal Ann Everlastin' had left with him the day before. "Look, forget about a donation. I'll be happy to open my doors to any and all who want to come to her home going service. I'm sure there will be members of this church as well as those from yours who will be willing to donate food and whatever is needed. Just let me know when the service is going to happen." A smile suddenly spread across the reverend's face as he bid the caller good-bye.

After the reverend placed the telephone receiver back in its holder, he got up and pranced around the desk. He was truly savoring whatever was on his mind.

"Well, you gonna share with us what is going on? I must be losing my hearing because I thought I heard you give permission for you-know-who's home going service to be held here." Mother Pray Onn could feel her blood pressure rising. She was becoming so angry, she couldn't even bear to say Mother Eternal Ann Everlastin's name out loud. She snapped and wagged her walking cane in the reverend's direction. "Tell me. Am I going deaf? Are you gonna let that old lady have the last word in death after leaving us with a check that wasn't even signed?"

The bishop decided to err on the side of caution. He just sat and continued to sip his tea while he sat on the fence of indecision. It was where he felt the most comfortable and safest.

"Put yo' menopause on hold—" He really didn't mean to say it aloud.

Too late.

He never got a chance to finish his sentence. Mother Pray Onn came out of her chair so fast, she'd forgotten that she hadn't used her walking stick and hit her still-hurting baby pinky toe again against the same desk. "Ow!" She hobbled back to her seat and gave the reverend a look that would've killed a lesser man.

"Calm down. You didn't let me finish. I was only teasing you because everything in here is so tense."

The bishop came off his seat of indecision long enough to add, "I guess that wine-laced tea and that telephone call must've brought you out of whatever had you down about that huge donation." He needed to get the reverend back on track about the money and off Mother Pray Onn's bad side.

"Well, yes. We will let Reverend Bling Moe Bling and his congregation use our church to hold the home going service since their little storefront church is so small. It's the Christian thing to do. And, yes, they gonna end up paying, believe that. All I need to do is find out who is Mother Eternal Ann Everlastin's lawyer. Once I find out who is handling the legal end of things, we can make that check good."

"I know who her lawyer used to be, and perhaps he still is," the bishop said. "He's Mr. Cheatem. She used him when she plucked the riches of her first two husbands. I don't remember who she used to fleece the third one. Anyway, he has an office downtown, on the west side, with the law firm of Wee, Cheatem and How. It's in the same building as Councilman Hippo Crit's law office."

"Get me their number first thing tomorrow. And, when you've done with that make sure to put me in touch with her limo driver, Mr. Tiny—"

Mother Pray Onn, the Reverend Knott Enuff Money and the Bishop Was Nevercalled did what they always did whenever they came together: They schemed and plotted and somewhere during their time together, they'd remember who and where they were and would have the nerve to ask God to bless whatever craziness they were conjuring. They also asked God to touch Mother Pray Onn's toes. They were starting to swell up like blistered peanuts.

And, of course, they had the benediction because they needed God to protect them until they could come together and scheme again.

5

Reflections . . . Sister Betty

After a long cab ride through alternating downpours and drizzles, Sister Betty arrived home to a place that was immaculate, almost sterile in nature. She was a creature of habit who liked her life and her home organized. After arriving home, she would always immediately go into her hall closet and place her shawl on a hanger and her hat in its own hatbox. After slipping into a pair of comfortable house shoes, she'd go into her living room to put her oversized Bible in its place, which was on the end table beside her rocker. Everything in its place and a place for everything. But not tonight.

It was as if her whole world was filled with smoke and mirrors. All tricks. Nothing seemed real to her. Everything in this house she'd lived in for well over fifty years suddenly seemed foreign; everything in it did, including her God.

It wasn't that she'd never experienced death before. She had. The mephitic scent of death, which only she seemed to have smelled, trailed her all during her young teenage life and well into adulthood. It invaded her spirit and soul after she gave birth to a stillborn baby boy, and then in the same week, lost her young husband to another woman in another town.

Sister Betty couldn't stop her unwelcomed thoughts as she wandered through her house and into her living room as though it were the first time she'd been in there. Her eyes flooded with invading salty tears as she surrendered and let her mind travel back and revisit the people, the places and the woes she seldom thought about.

She stood in the middle of the room with her head hung and her hands held up in quiet submission, giving the past permission to return.

And return it did. The memories brought back the smells, the lacks and the frivolity of her youth.

She and her husband, seventeen-year-old Vernon, were barely out of the eleventh grade when she found out she was pregnant. He'd quickly married her to keep the town of Statesville, North Carolina's morality police tongues from wagging and ridiculing, and also because unknown to her, her father had threatened to kill Vernon.

During those times, a young lady (if she was indeed a lady) would never let a boy go all the way. She had waited all during the tenth grade for the tall, handsome and very popular Vernon Stephens to finally notice her. He eventually got around to noticing her after he'd carelessly worn out the God-fearing reputations and virginities of several other young women in the school. She didn't care about what he'd done before. She ignored the warnings from her friends and challenged them, calling them jealous. No matter how bad others thought he was, she had enough love to change him.

She didn't change him, but he certainly did change her. He changed her from the soft-spoken, well-behaved and obedient sixteen-year-old only child of Luke and Texanna to the girl who would straight-up lie to her parents' face and then sneak out to be with the town's resident sperm donor, Vernon.

It happened only a few months later, after a few dates and a few tall glasses of Mr. Tee's homemade corn liquor—they called it White Lightning back then. She was never sure if she'd let Vernon go as far as he wanted to go or as far as she wanted him to because the corn liquor had stolen her sense of consciousness and caution. She only remembered waking up to the smell of hay inside a neighbor's barn and the foul odor of musk that drifted up the nostrils on her young face as it poured from Vernon's sweaty body.

In the back of her mind, she somehow remembered grunting sounds; she wasn't sure which one of them made the noises. She did remember that her yellow dress was pulled up around her waist. The prickly hay beneath her was crumbled and stained with her red virgin blood.

The knotted pain that pulsated from the pit of her stomach down to the tip of her womanhood almost drowned out the breathy words that filtered through her hung-over haze. "You were the best." That's what she remembered Vernon softly whispering. Not "I love you," but *"you were the best."* She never found out what she was the *"best"* at.

Sister Betty could feel her knees begin to buckle as she brought her arms down hard enough for the skin flaps under her arms to make a smacking sound. She tried to reach for the arm of a nearby chair. She was barely able to grab it, but she did. She was fighting hard not to think about her past because she only wanted to talk to God about the events of that particular day. She had questions that only He could answer. However, her past was relentless in its persistent attack upon her mind, and it brought with it the buried memories that rushed to gain control of her again.

From that moment on, her life had changed for the rest of the year and it wasn't for the better. Inside that barn when Vernon either stole or she bequeathed him her virginity, the fall from grace was one long plunge. They'd married but she ended up leaving Statesville several months later after giving birth to a stillborn baby boy and her husband to another naïve woman.

Her last contact with her parents was when she visited them and stole fourteen dollars. Armed with an address of a white woman she'd heard about who needed someone to cook and clean in Pelzer, South Carolina, she left Statesville to mourn her past and said hello to a new future.

It was a mind-numbing bus ride to Pelzer, South Carolina. The rumbling brown box-shaped bus swaying from side to side, passing by the trees that stood with their roots planted in soils of pride. The trees were sparse with near-death leaves showing off their changing colors of brown to yellow and red to brown, slowly falling to become one with the earth and then to restart their youthful life cycle again in the spring.

They were the scenes that in her stolen youth the year before always excited her. Now the changing of the seasons meant nothing because her life had changed permanently. There would be no recycling or another chance at youth for her. She no longer had anything in common with those trees.

It was also during that somber bus ride that she'd met her soon-to-be dearest and best friend, Ma Cile. She was just known as Lucile back then. It was years later, after she'd had children and grandchildren that everyone started calling her Ma Cile—probably because she always tried to take care of folks and was bossy, just like someone's mother.

Ma Cile was about a year or two older and was returning from burying her husband, Charlie, in the nearby town of Catawba, North Carolina. She was traveling with her two young daughters who looked to be no more than three and four years of age. They rode for several miles without saying a word to one another, and it was during that time, as they sat in the rear of the old bus, that their pained expressions told their common story. It was etched in their swollen, water-filled eyes and in their the-world-done-beat-me-down looks and clothes. They had finally acknowledged each other's pain during a rest stop with a shy glance and a smile. After sharing their stories of loss, they then had tried to console each other, as best as two grieving women could. When Ma Cile found out that her newfound friend would be looking for a place in Pelzer to stay as well as to work, she immediately invited her to stay with her and the children. That was Ma Cile, even way back then. Strangers were only friends she'd not met before.

She only lived with Ma Cile and her small children for a couple of months before she'd saved up enough to get a room for herself. It was a tiny room with a common kitchen shared by four other renters, and it was only a block away. The drab cubicle came already furnished, so that saved a lot of money.

The rooming house was also home to another teenaged young woman who was to become one of her dearest friends. The young lady was named Eternal Ann. She'd gathered through small conversations what had brought her to Pelzer.

Eternal Ann had said that she'd recently moved to Pelzer after losing both of her parents to the bigoted and cowardly acts of some racists in Alabama. She'd left after her hardworking father, a man who worked eighteen hours a day raising hogs and tobacco, refused to be cheated out of his fertile land. Because he objected to selling the land he owned, he was hung from a tree in their own front yard. He swung as the moon watched, and he was still hanging as the sun came on duty the next morning. All during that night of cruelty and degradation, her mother who took in laundry to scrape together extra money was raped and beaten to death while the men who took turns at her also took turns looking out of the house window at her father swinging like a pendulum from a weeping willow tree.

Eternal Ann had heard everything from the secret closet as she hid down in the root cellar. She'd heard her father beg for the men in the white hoods and sheets to spare her mother's life, and she'd heard her mother scream out in pain as she begged the men to hurry up and take her miserable life.

Eternal Ann lay cooped up and frightened in the tiny root cellar, not distinguishing day from night for two days as the stench from her mother's decaying body filtered down into the small space. It was only when a neighbor happened upon the land looking to buy a hog discovered what'd happened and then searched for her that she was able to safely call out for help. She barely escaped Birmingham, Alabama, with her life. The kindness of the local church members collected enough money to secret her safely out of town. She'd come to Pelzer with only the clothes on her back and a few dollars secreted in her run-down brown-and-white brogan shoes.

Sister Betty and Eternal Ann worked for Mrs. Maximums, a young wealthy white woman who for whatever reason took a liking to the well-behaved and clean young women. But Eternal Ann wouldn't totally trust the woman because of the white color of Mrs. Maximums's skin, and couldn't bring herself to accept any kindness from Mrs. Maximums. She never saw it as reverse racism. As far as Eternal Ann was concerned, she was there to work, and that was all.

Mrs. Maximum allowed them to take home any leftover food and often gave them clothes that she no longer wanted or could wear. At that time, Ma Cile, Mother Eternal Ann Everlastin' and she all were about the same size, and they loved sharing the hand-me-down clothes. They would always add the leftovers to whatever Ma Cile had cooked or brought home from her day job at the local elementary school cafeteria so everyone had enough to eat.

From that time on, the three of them were always a part of one another's lives. Even though each ultimately walked a different path, they never strayed from their friendship. For years, they even attended the same church—the Ain't Nobody Else Right But Us—All Others Goin' to Hell Church. Back then it was pastored by the late Reverend Wasn't Evencalled. She'd seen Ma Cile through her trials with her children and then her grandchildren and over recent years, with her health. She'd been there for Mother Eternal Ann Everlastin' through the deaths of her various wealthy husbands as well as when she had decided to move her church membership to the No Hope Now—Mercy Neva Church. Both Ma Cile and Mother Eternal Ann Everlastin' had accepted without questioning Sister Betty's sanity that God had indeed called her on the telephone back in 1984, and they marveled and loved the change that had taken place in her Christian walk.

*   *   *

Sister Betty could feel the numbness subside in her hands as she loosened her grip on the chair's arm. The rhythm of her heart slowed in its acceptance of things beginning to return to as normal as things could be. As fast as the memories had come, they had finally left.

Sister Betty took the sleeve of her crumbled dress and wiped her eyes. She didn't realize that she was perspiring so heavily until she tried to remove her dress and it, along with her underclothing clung, wrinkled and damp, to her body. She still felt mentally distant, a stranger in her own home, and she had to navigate her way into the bedroom to find a robe to wear.

Without meaning to do it, she found herself walking back into the living room. That time she fell to her knees beside her living room sofa and without her throw pillows for support, she swayed, bowed and sobbed. She could hardly breathe as she implored, "Lord, I just don't see how you could take her like that."

She'd never questioned God about His business since He'd called her and showed her so much mercy, but tonight, she had more questions than answers. Like Jacob wrestling with the angel, she was not getting up until God showed her His plan.

Tonight, it was God's turn to be tested.

6

Reflections from the Reverend Knott Enuff Money

The Reverend Knott Enuff Money eased his silver Town Car into the rear of his long concrete-paved, winding driveway. He lived in a guarded and gated community called Williamston Heights. His house was a plantation-style red-brick with dark green shutters and stood two stories high in the middle of two acres of prime land. It was a grand house that was much too big for just him, but was just right in keeping up with the other expensive homes in that posh part of the Pelzer suburbs.

The house offered a lavish, state-of-the-art kitchen in which he hardly ever cooked or ate. There was a circular-shaped living room with an enormous gold-colored brick fireplace that never held a fire.

Upstairs were four bedrooms decorated in old-country French. Each was very spacious with a private bathroom.

He was very particular about who came to his house and therefore, when guests came to town, if they were not on his A list, he insisted the church pay to house them in expensive hotels.

To the Reverend Knott Enuff Money there was nothing unusual or extravagant about his lifestyle because he didn't have to pay for it. He had a huge congregation who took care of a few of his needs and all of his wants.

Normally, he would park his expensive car in the garage but not that night. He had more pressing matters. Too much had happened that day. Yesterday, when he was making plans about how to get back in the good graces of Mother Eternal Ann Everlastin', he hadn't counted on her dying so soon and in such a strange manner. He needed to sort it out.

It was at times like these that the Reverend Knott Enuff Money was glad he lived alone. At the church, there was always some sort of drama going on. Everyone demanded much of his time, although not much of his advice on religious matters.

Most of the members didn't understand his need or the requirements of getting to a mega church status. He was determined to bring the Ain't Nobody Else Right But Us—All Others Goin' to Hell Church and himself to that level, even if every member had to go broke to do it.

After taking off his clothes, and placing his Jheri curl wig on a silk-covered wig stand, the Reverend Knott Enuff Money took a long and much-needed shower. He donned a plastic shower cap to protect his few remaining hairs. The shower door slid easily in its tracks as he entered and held on to the sides of his glass-enclosed shower stall. He welcomed the powerful and steady shots of warm water that peppered his body. And for the next twenty minutes or so, he withstood the watery assault hoping that every blast would bring some relief.

After toweling off, the reverend left the steam-engulfed bathroom feeling his strength return. He marveled at his reflection in a long teakwood mirror as he slipped on a pair of baby blue silk pajamas. The mirror was deliberately kept in the vertical position so as to make him look slimmer. The silk pajamas were a gift from the Pastor's Aid Auxiliary and came wrapped in expensive paper along with a five-figure appreciation check.

When he finished all of his before-I-lay-me-down final touches, he went downstairs into his kitchen. He made a pot of strong yet soothing peppermint tea and then walked barefoot through the long mahogany-wood floor hallway and into his living room.

With everything that he needed to think over he still wanted to watch the late news. There was no doubt in his mind that news of Mother Eternal Ann Everlastin's sudden death would be worthy of, at the very least, a thirty-second blurb.

If there were any news regarding Mother Eternal Ann Everlastin's death on the local news channel, the Reverend Knott Enuff Money never saw it. As soon as he drank the last drop of the soothing hot tea and placed his tired feet upon the cushioned ottoman seat, which was activated to massage by a remote control, he fell into a deep slumber.

He felt as if he had fallen through a black hole as sleep engulfed his body and pushed him farther into a spiral as the memories grabbed at him as he descended. In his subconscious, he felt as though his entire body was twitching but it wasn't—instead it was his mind that kept ducking and dodging the deliberate thoughts and unpleasant places that he'd taken thirty years or better to forget.

"Knott—Knott! I know you hear me. Come on in here and hear what that pastor of the River Bend Eagle-Eye Temple has done with his ministry. That church only been up and running for about two years, and it's on about three radio stations now."

He could see the back of his mother, Sister Am Money's scarf-covered head bobbing up and down as she screamed out an excited high-pitched summons for him to come quickly into the living room. "My Lord, listen to the amen and hallelujah coming at him from his congregation. It sounds like it must be a huge church. He must have at least two or three hundred members." She stopped and dropped her head ever so slightly as if she had suddenly decided to whisper a prayer. After a few seconds, she threw her hands up in submission as she continued in a softer tone, "Come here and sit by me, Knott." She'd never turned around, yet she knew he was in the same room. "If we paid more attention and learned from successful preachers like him, perhaps our church would be on the radio too."

She looked much older than her fifty-five years as she sat wrapped in a dark brown oversized bathrobe, moving her skinny body side to side like that second hand on the small grandfather clock that rested, abandoned, over in the corner. "Come turn up the radio. I can barely hear him." Enveloped in jealousy, she leaned forward to hear the muffled and crackling sermon spewing from her old Philco radio. "I'm gonna have to get real hard-line with some of the members. They gonna have to throw in some more money or I'm gonna make you stop preaching there. I won't have you wasting your time preaching to small-minded folks in a little church. You can do that same thing to small-minded folks in a big church. We have got to build a fancy church. God said His people should have the very best. How we gonna show folks how prosperous God is if we ain't showing prosperity?"

It was always the same in the small house he shared with his mother that sat on a small plot in a small town. The same old threat that she gave every Sunday night after the day's service. She held double duty as both his mother and the first lady of the Bound and Determined Glory Maintenance Center in the little town of Belton, South Carolina. She took over the church's leadership after his fa-

ther's untimely death at the hands of another congregation woman's husband who had been released from prison a day early.

Reverend Knott Enuff Money's body suddenly stiffened as he thought about his father's death being almost as freakish as Mother Eternal Everlastin' dying from an overdosed sensation of a York peppermint pattie. It took another moment before his body suddenly submitted again to the uncontrollable memories.

With his mother more concerned about her reputation and community status, she never considered the impact her husband's death might've had on her twenty-year-old son. Contrary to what the congregation members wanted, she had her husband cremated. In her mind, it was a fitting send-off to someone who thought he was so hot. She had her reputation to consider and didn't need a bunch of her husband's crying whores at a funeral.

His father, the Right Reverend Will Money had been in his mid-forties, a six-foot-two, muscular, full-blooded Cree Indian with long, straight midnight black hair that he wore in a ponytail with a ribbon wound about it. He could pass for a Johnny Mathis look-alike with his bronze, baby-smooth skin and face that seemed to defy time. Whether he was singing or preaching, his deep baritone voice dripped over folks like sweet honey and imprisoned the listener with bars made of tight melodies and correct timbre words. The Right Reverend Will Money was the complete opposite of his mother who was much shorter, five years his senior, and couldn't even hum.

His father never claimed that God had called him to preach. A church just seemed natural to have because he'd always been a natural-born leader. It was only when he met his wife, Am, that a church became a good idea to have. It was a good idea because she had nagged him into believing it. He knew that she was ambitious and so he used her ambition to fill his lack of it.

The Right Reverend Will Money smiled a lot and always seemed to be satisfied with whatever he felt that God—or man—had placed in his path. However, it always seemed that the "whatever" always came embodied in the warm flesh of a young and shapely naïve female. He was never concerned with how big or how prosperous the church became because he was determined to get his little piece of Heaven while he was yet on Earth.

From the way he carried on, his little piece of Heaven on Earth was about as close as he would ever get to a heavenly home in the sky.

The entire church knew that his father cheated on his mother and yet they continued to financially support him, praised him whenever his name was mentioned and gave over their children for baptisms because he never preached about the wages of sin. He preached whatever would please the congregation's palate and he was good to look upon. The women wanted him, and their husbands wanted to be him.

Knott Enuff's mother always looked the other way. For her to make a scene would mean that she knew what his father was doing behind her back and that would mean humiliation and defeat in her purpose, a purpose that she was determined to achieve at all costs. Her unrelenting pride, her only son and her mental health were the collateral she used to ensure that she became Belton, South Carolina's finest first lady and pastor's wife.

She was going to make sure that her husband and her church became a household name, even if she had to fix a three-course breakfast and serve it to her husband and his whorish women as they lay in her own bed.

She had also insisted that her son marry young. "Knott, you gotta marry a pretty young thing so that folks will see you're the settled kind of man. God meant for every preacher to have a wife so he wouldn't have to go elsewhere and the church people wouldn't talk about him whenever he spoke to one of the females in the church." She was in complete denial about her own marriage or the state of it.

"I've fixed it up so that next week you can take Sister Leeola's daughter, Missy, to the church social. She's only nineteen but she's very light-skinned and she's got plenty of good manners and money. You gonna need that money to improve on the church building."

Neither he nor Missy ever stood a chance. It turned out that Sister Leeola was just as ambitious as his own mother. Within a year, he and Missy had married. Within two years after that, he and Missy had divorced. It wasn't an easy decision but neither of them had anything in common nor did they have any ambitions for an opulent church. At least at that time, he didn't.

It was two months to the day of his divorce that his mother fell sick. Every day while she lay in a deep coma, he came to the hospital. He promised her that he would do whatever she wanted. He would even ask Missy to remarry him if it would make her feel bet-

ter. Knott Enuff knew he was on shaky ground with God but he even tried a little praying.

His mother died without ever waking, and from that point on he believed that both God and his mother had abandoned him. God should've come to him and his mother should've never left.

As he watched the dingy white sheet pulled over his mother's face in that equally dingy white-walled hospital room, he repented that he'd been so selfish as to deny her a rest from her pain. So from that day forward, even after he'd left the church his father built and arrived almost penniless in Pelzer, South Carolina, he vowed to make it up to his mother. If God was pleased with some of the things he did, then that was okay too. From Heaven or hell, wherever his mother lifted her eyes she would see that he was still trying to build the mega church that she always wanted.

The Reverend Knott Enuff Money's unsettling trip down memory lane was interrupted by the persistent ringing of his telephone. He didn't want to answer it. A throbbing headache was in the beginning stages. He held his head in both hands while his eyes watered from the tortured memory of his life with an overbearing and egotistical mother. Her insistence that he preach, even though he, like his father before him, had never felt a call to do so, always pained him. The persistent ringing of the phone seemed almost violent but he could not move. He wanted to sit and wallow in this mystery because he felt those deep-seated memories held the answers to the nagging foreboding that he suddenly felt.

By the time he finally pushed himself up from his chair, the answering machine had picked up the call. He fell back down in the chair with a thud and listened as a male's raspy voice spoke with urgency.

"Reverend Knott Enuff Money! Oh great! Now you ain't home. I was hoping that you *would* be home. I need to talk to you about my aunt's funeral. Somebody told me that they think the funeral is gonna be held at *your* church. This is Buddy." The voice was screaming and was obviously intoxicated. "I know you remember me because it was you who put me out of your church! You need to listen to me. You can't put me out this time. I'm her only living close relative, and I need to have a say in how she's gonna be put away. You need to be calling me as soon as you get in from wherever you scamming people." (Pause, and there was the sound of guzzling.) "Where are you this time of night anyway? All you preachers are just alike. Y'all ain't never where you suppose to be when somebody needs help . . ."

There was a long beeping sound coming from the answering machine indicating that the allotted time for the message had ended.

The Reverend Knott Enuff Money was relieved that he had not picked up the telephone. How could he ever forget Buddy? There had not been a word or unwelcome visit from Buddy in several years.

He had asked Buddy, who was only twenty-two at the time, to leave the Ain't Nobody Else Right But Us—All Others Goin' to Hell Church because Buddy was openly gay and had swished his narrow hips one time too many at one of the convocations. The reverend had his own "don't ask, don't tell" policy that Buddy's in-your-face actions made hard to enforce. When he told Buddy that he had to leave, several of the other church members countered with their own suspicions about Brother Tis Mythang being of the same persuasion and hanging out in the same closet.

He told them that suspicions were not enough. Brother Tis Mythang had never admitted to being gay. Some of his other eccentric manners could be laid at the feet of others as well and should he let everyone go who they suspected of being gay? That's what he'd told the church board, but the real reason had nothing to do with Buddy's sexual preference. It was that Buddy had done everything imaginable, including stopping a payment on his aunt's twenty-five-thousand-dollar check to drive a wedge between the Reverend Knott Enuff Money and his aunt, Mother Eternal Ann Everlastin's money. And, of course, no one could stir up a service musically like Brother Tis Mythang, so he wasn't going anywhere.

Mother Eternal Ann Everlastin' sure left him in a mess. He had her unendorsed check to deal with and now there was Buddy, no doubt still openly gay as well as a drunkard. It was troubled times like these that he wished he'd been blessed with his father's good looks, real hair and honey-coated singing and soothing voice; he could use those tools to get Buddy to forgive him and gain entry into what he knew was Mother Eternal Ann Everlastin's wealthy estate fund.

He hadn't inherited his father's good looks or savvy and hypnotic DNA but he certainly had an abundance of his mother's greed, ambition and lack of conscience to make up for it. That's what had gotten him to where he was today. It would take some imagination but somehow, he was going to get what Mother Eternal Ann Everlastin' had left for him.

He turned off the lights and went upstairs to his room. He looked again at the expensive French pieces that adorned the room and believed in his heart that his mother would've been proud of all that he'd accomplished. If he never kept his word to anyone, he'd kept his word to her. On her deathbed, he'd promised he would make all her dreams come true. He had almost succeeded. He now had the big house, the big name, the expensive car and a church with more than one thousand members.

If he'd had God in the plan there would be no telling how blessed he would've become or how well he could've blessed others.

7

Let the Dead Bury the Dead

It had been two days since Mother Eternal Ann Everlastin's strange and sudden death and Sister Betty was still quite shaken up. The same day Mother had died, Sister Betty had gone home and wrestled with God for answers for most of the night. She had prayed and huddled beside her sofa.

"Lord, a peppermint pattie?" she questioned and walked the floor while she ranted, "Lord, a peppermint pattie?" And, when she couldn't speak the words, she questioned her God with outstretched hands. Sandwiched between sobs that caused her chest to hurt were unrelenting pleas of forgiveness for being a mere mortal.

In her mind, Mother Eternal Ann Everlastin' deserved better. God knew the woman's life from its inception to its finish, and for her to be humiliated in death was more than Sister Betty could take or accept.

For almost five decades, God was Sister Betty's beginning and her end, but sometimes in between she wished He'd share a little more of his mysterious plans. She needed to know about the ones she hadn't prayed about.

As hard as the death had hit Sister Betty, it practically tore Ma Cile's small world apart. Ma Cile couldn't seem to get a grasp of what had happened to someone whom she loved so dearly—and in such an unholy way. Sister Betty remembered Ma Cile's reaction when she had to call her with the sad news.

"What Mother Eternal Ann Everlastin' are you talkin' about?" Ma Cile asked as she struggled to understand. *"There must be an-*

other one somewhere because I just seen our own Mother Eternal Ann Everlastin' at her church earlier today." There was suddenly silence; nothing but dead air but it crackled with life as Ma Cile nervously laughed then continued erecting a mental wall of protection from reality. "Listen, I got ta go and see about Lil' Bit and June Bug. I hear them chil'ren in the bedroom playing and it's almost midnight. Them chil'ren know they oughta be in bed by now."

Again, the silence was almost deafening, but she could tell that Ma Cile had begun to choke up.

Sister Betty's heart almost broke again as she heard her dear friend start to cry.

"I'll talk to ya tomorrow, Sister Betty. I cain't talk no mo' now." The conversation ended abruptly, much like Mother Eternal Ann Everlastin's death.

Sister Betty finally heard from Ma Cile later on during the evening of the next day. Ma Cile tried to act like everything was alright. As a matter of fact, she called herself trying to cheer up Sister Betty. "You alright now? You were pretty much messed up last night."

Ma Cile was acting like it was Sister Betty who had fallen apart during their previous conversation. "I'm gonna come over and sit wit' you a spell. I'm sending June Bug and Li'l Bit over to Sister Need Moe's house to play with her children." Ma Cile stopped speaking and let out a little snicker, "She got about twelve head of chil'ren and two more won't even matter. She might not even know that they there." She became serious as she continued. "I'll come over and help you cook. You know Mother Eternal Ann Everlastin' gonna be real upset with us if we don't make that tater salad just the way she like it; you know she don't want nuthin' but cut up red onions in it and not them yella ones that most folks likes to put in it. And, we cain't put none of that sweet mayonnaise in it. She would rise back up and tell us all off . . ."

Ma Cile kept on chattering and Sister Betty kept on listening to her mindless banter because that's what friends did—they listened to each other even when one or the other didn't make sense.

Grief could be a terrible thing, and it could cripple the strongest. The two women were not immune.

That day, Ma Cile never sent her grandchildren to Sister Need Moe's, and she never came over to Sister Betty's house until the very next day because she didn't want to be alone and she knew she was not fit company for Sister Betty. She hoped that Sister Betty would be alright, but at that moment, she needed to do some praying, and she only wanted God to hear what she had to say.

It was two days since they'd lay eyes on each other when Ma Cile finally appeared on Sister Betty's doorstep acting as if they'd just spoken.

"Come on in, Ma Cile." Sister Betty took her friend by the hand, and the two old women walked into the kitchen. "Make yourself some tea, if you have a mind to do that."

Ma Cile poured the boiling water over a tea bag without any emotion or conversation. She sweetened it with a little honey and looked around Sister Betty's kitchen. There were pots and pans on the stove and in the oven. The aroma of cooking food suddenly lit up the room. It was the first time Ma Cile had smelled anything since sitting down.

"When you finish your tea, you can help me a little bit. I'm almost finished and some of the other members are gonna stop by and drop off some more food." Sister Betty took away the cup and saucer while she watched Ma Cile rise from the table like a puppet on a string with life as its puppeteer.

The two women piddled around in the kitchen for about another hour. Neither of them spoke an unnecessary word yet each understood what the other was thinking.

Ma Cile raced from one side of the kitchen to the other. Every once in a while, she'd let out a sigh and let a tear fall slowly down her fat cheek.

Ma Cile suddenly had a strange look upon her face when she finally broke the silence. "Remind me again. Why we got to cook all this food?" She wiped the sweat from her wrinkled brown brow with a clean white cotton handkerchief. "We done cooked everything but manna from Heaven." She stopped and picked up a green plantain from off the counter. This time she expressed amusement with caution. "Do ya think this might pass for manna? I could drop a smoked neck bone in with it."

Sister Betty never said a word. She just smiled even though her heart was torn in two. She was mourning the passing of life from Mother Eternal Ann Everlastin' and the passing of what little sanity Ma Cile had left.

Tired from all the cooking, Ma Cile felt around inside her starched white apron pocket and found her little tin of snuff. Before Sister Betty could answer or stop her, she had pulled her bottom lip forward and put about three pinches under her tongue. The snuff buzz hit her immediately. And, of course, when it did, she forgot that she'd asked Sister Betty about the recipe for manna and instead went over to stir one of the boiling pots.

Sister Betty wiped her tiny tired hands on her multi-stained plastic apron. She turned and looked Ma Cile directly in one of Ma Cile's eyes—the good one. "It's for our long-time good friend Mother Eternal Ann Everlastin'—she's gone on home to be with God," Sister Betty answered with caution. She spoke slowly, correctly pronouncing each syllable because it was the third time Ma Cile had asked her the same question.

Sister Betty thought that perhaps a little more warmed gingko biloba tea was what Ma Cile really needed to help her get through this and a lot less of that Railroad brand snuff she loyally favored. "The service should be starting in about an hour, so we need to pack up this food and whatever else the other members bring and get it over to the church." Sister Betty reached for several tin pans. "They will serve the food immediately after the funeral."

"Oh yeah. You did tell me we was doing that." Ma Cile's voice held a hint of sadness again. With heaviness of heart and even more of body fat, she placed her wrinkled brown right hand on the back of a chair to support the weight that sometimes bothered her lower back.

With one quick swoop she grabbed a tissue from her apron pocket with her left hand. With another tear running down her cheek from her good brown eye and the false blue eye looking upward, Ma Cile continued. "I guess I just don't wanna believe she's gone. Mother Eternal Ann Everlastin' was about the same age as us, wasn't she?"

Ma Cile did not wait for Sister Betty to answer. She just continued talking as she managed to move her heavy girth from the back of the chair into its seat. "Since she was on the Mothers Board at her church, too, do we have to say anything at the funeral on behalf of our Mothers Board?" Ma Cile asked.

She kept on asking questions because she felt like time was slipping by and there was nothing she could do about it. She also felt grateful that it wasn't her who was lying down in a casket in Mr. Bury Em Deep's funeral parlor waiting to be brought to the church. "I just don't see why they had to have the funeral so fast. I would've liked to keep her on this side of the grave with us a little longer. Are you gonna say somethin' at the funeral?"

"I'm not sure if I will, but I guess if you want, you can say something significant and spiritual about her. Perhaps a fond memory of an experience the two of you shared or something like that would be appropriate."

"Somethin' memorable, huh," Ma Cile said as she stopped to think for a moment. A smile soon replaced the sad look upon her face as she stood and came toward Sister Betty. "Ya know what? I think I will say somethin'. I sorta remember a few things."

"How can you say you remember a few things when you can't remember one single thing that I've repeated to you over and over just this morning?" Sister Betty mumbled and chuckled to herself. It seemed that the sad tension in the air was letting up just a little, but it was a welcome relief. "I was just wondering what it was you could say," she said, as she tried to judge just how serious Ma Cile was.

She waited for Ma Cile to answer and when she didn't Sister Betty continued speaking. "You want to tell me first before we go?" She was a little leery. She'd witnessed many of Ma Cile's memorable testimonies. Ma Cile sometimes shared a little too much information, and depending on the effect her snuff buzz was having on her, some of Ma Cile's testimony contained more than just a little fiction.

"Well, let me see," Ma Cile answered as she raised a corner of her hairnet to get her a stubby finger up under her good wig. She absent-mindedly scratched along a row of one of the little cornrowed plaits beneath her wig that looked more like a row of stitches. She let out a little cackle as she replaced the corner of her hairnet over her short gray hair.

Ma Cile lay back against one of the counters and clasped her hands as she thought about their recently departed friend. "I remembers the time when Mother Eternal Ann Everlastin' installed one of those Clappers in her house. It was somethin' she said she bought from one of those Home Shopper television shows. She said it took her a while but she finally got that contraption to working and when she did get it right, she set it on sensitive befo' she went to bed. Now befo' she closed her eyes to set about chatting with the Lawd, she took out her expensive false teeth that she finally had made at the Molars Teeth Emporium downtown on Gums Avenue."

Sister Betty hadn't realized that she had sat down on one of her kitchen chairs until she inadvertently bumped her bad knee. "Ouch!" she hollered.

Ma Cile was really into telling her story so she didn't even hear Sister Betty yell, instead she just kept on talking. "Later on, after she had fallen asleep, it must've gotten a little chilly."

Ma Cile suddenly stopped speaking to make sure Sister Betty was paying attention. Since Sister Betty stood there with her mouth gaped wide open, Ma Cile thought she must have been hanging on her every word, so she continued. This time, with her snuff buzz in overdrive, Ma Cile grabbed her stomach and another tissue to wipe away a tear that was beginning to form.

The tear was from laughter, as she continued. "I'm telling ya, Sister Betty, every time Mother Eternal Ann Everlastin' felt a chill, them gums would go to flappin' and her lights would turn on and off, on and off because of that Clapper thing. Sister Lou Louse—"

"Sister who?" Sister Betty interrupted, hoping she could get Ma Cile's attention and she'd shut up, but Ma Cile's mouth was on automatic, and it just kept on going.

"Sister Lou Louse. Ya know the woman who be getting rid of bad spirits and such. Anyway, she lived in that old rundown house next door. When Sister Lou Louse saw them flashin' lights coming from Mother Eternal Ann Everlastin's house, she thought it was a demon. So Sister Lou had her son—ya know, the crazy one who just come home from that mental institution over there on Nutt Street—go in and break down Mother Everlastin's door. There was po' Mother Eternal Ann Everlastin' sittin' with her legs crossed on the side of the bed in a pair of faded men's cotton boxer drawers that had the name Calvin Klein written on them."

"Huh!" was all a shocked Sister Betty could say as she raised her hand to silently ask God for His help. Doing this caused a slab of greasy fatback she had absentmindedly picked up to fly off the fork and out of her hand onto the floor, landing a few inches away from Ma Cile's feet.

Unfazed by whatever it was that had landed at her feet, Ma Cile continued, this time with a serious look on her face. "I don't know when it was that she first put them bloomers on, 'cause I don't wanna say nothing about her personal business, but when Sister Lou's son knocked down her door, everyone knew that Mother ain't neva married or dated nobody named Calvin! I think she wasn't always upfront with us and we was her very best friends." Her face turned sad again at the thought that their friend might have kept some of her personal business personal.

Sister Betty was still standing on the same little tile piece in a state of shock. The slice of fatback laid fried side up a few inches away. Even the smell of it, rising from the floor, could not shock Sister Betty back.

However, had Ma Cile known it was the piece of fatback that she had cooked with care just so she could eat it with a piece of corn bread, there might have been two funerals in the same day.

Finally, Sister Betty recovered. "Like I said, just a little too much information!" she muttered again as she returned to the task at hand. Sister Betty looked at her kitchen clock. It was time to clean up. The multicolored stains on the white Formica countertops told the story of the care she took in fixing her delicious southern cuisine.

Sister Betty was finished with her task; however, snuff usually made Ma Cile hungry so she decided to fix a little something to put in her stomach to quench her hunger. She went to the refrigerator and grabbed some bologna wrapped in wax paper. She threw two or three pieces into a frying pan.

Soon the aroma from the pan-fried bologna permeated the air. She tapped one foot as she waited for the evidence of a bubble in the center. That bubble meant that the bolagna was ready to be turned over and the edges slightly browned meant it was done, just right. Ma Cile, inhibited by the loss of one eye, which had been replaced by a store-bought false blue one, and the effects of snuff, kept missing the big bubble that popped up in the center of the bologna pieces. Of course, by the time she got finished stabbing the bologna it looked more like round Belgian waffles or brown pieces of Swiss cheese. Her hunger won out. No matter what it looked like, Ma Cile was eating it.

With so much time wasted, Sister Betty and Ma Cile raced to finish placing the foods in everything from Tupperware to brown Crown Royal bags. They even managed to find a few old jelly jars with Looney Toon cartoon characters and mismatched lids. They filled the jelly jars with the seasoned brown gravy complete with pieces of red onion and celery sticks. After another hour of small talk, mostly with Sister Betty repeating things two or three times before Ma Cile could understand them, by the time they washed the last pot and put away the dishes, Ma Cile's snuff was a memory.

The buzz from the doorbell startled both Sister Betty and Ma Cile. Without realizing it Ma Cile had followed Sister Betty to the front door. Sister Pert Near and her daughter, Sister Dawn Near, were leaning against the screen door for support. They were laden with several shopping bags.

"Y'all come on in. I'm so glad to see the both of you." Sister Betty extended her hand to take one of the shopping bags and in the meantime Ma Cile was standing so close behind her that she almost stepped on her feet.

Sister Pert Near and her daughter, Sister Dawn Near, just stood in the doorway locked in a stare with Sister Betty. It took them a moment to realize that it was Ma Cile standing behind her and not a giant shadow. "We're sorry we're so late," Sister Pert Near said. They walked through the door and looked at Ma Cile as though either she'd lost her mind or they had lost theirs. They couldn't understand why she stood so close behind Sister Betty or why she hadn't bothered to greet them. "How are you doing, Ma Cile?" Sister Dawn Near asked as she eyed her up and down with suspicion.

Ma Cile never said a word. Instead she snatched one of the shopping bags from Sister Pert Near's hand and went back into the kitchen, leaving Sister Betty to chat with the women.

"Can I take your wraps?" Sister Betty asked as she led the women into her living room.

Both women took off their matching white shawls, which revealed matching mother and daughter white plastic aprons. They had accessorized their outfits with black hairnets that had little white butterflies woven throughout. The flipped curls of their matching pageboy wigs peeked through the holes in their hairnets. "We thought we might stay for a while and help you with whatever else you need done," Sister Pert Near said. Without waiting for Sister Betty to reply, they walked back to her kitchen, passing by Ma Cile who had just left out of there and stood solemnly looking out of a hallway window.

The two Near women waddled around Sister Betty's tiny kitchen. Sister Pert Near, in her late sixties, widowed, and herself only a few months younger than Sister Betty, had wide hips that took up most of the kitchen space. Sister Dawn Near, single and about thirty years old with a tiny hourglass figure and with arms stretched wide, carried a large double boiler pot to the stove. She barely took up the size of one of Sister Betty's black-and-white floor tiles.

The Near women buzzed around in Sister Betty's kitchen for only about five minutes because there was hardly anything left to do. "Sister Betty, it looks like you've got everything pretty much under control. We are so glad that you volunteered to take our food contributions with you to the funeral. You know we were always fond of Mother Eternal Ann Everlastin', and we are so sorry that we won't be able to attend her funeral today." They started to walk out of the kitchen past Ma Cile who still stood without speaking while looking out of the hallway window.

"I didn't know I'd volunteered," Sister Betty remarked. "And I certainly didn't know that you two weren't going to the funeral. Why aren't you going? I thought we could all ride together."

"Oh, we thought we had mentioned that to you when we called earlier," they answered in unison. "We are driving over to Williamston. There's going to be two funerals over there today with quite a few handsome and eligible men." They stopped and looked at each other and smiled. "We always say just like the Bible do . . . 'let the dead bury the dead.' We are going over to the funeral to pick up among the living." They stopped suddenly and changed their smiles into looks of concern. "No offense."

"None taken," Sister Betty replied as she gave the women their shawls and bid them farewell and good hunting.

"Ma Cile, they've gone now. You can come on back into the kitchen and we'll finish up what we was doing."

Sister Betty barely managed to move her thin frame out of Ma Cile's way as Ma Cile whizzed past, enabled by an obvious industrial-strength, sneaked dose of snuff. "What was that you said?" Ma Cile asked as she raced back to the tile square where Sister Betty still stood.

"I said we can finish packing up everything. It seems that Sister Pert Near and Sister Dawn Near have both decided to attend another funeral over in Williamston. I guess they want to chase some living flesh, which is what they always seem to be doing."

Ma Cile dismissed Sister Betty's observations and added one of her own. "I hope a lot of folks show up. It would be a shame if a lot of folks didn't. Mother Eternal might've made some folks angry because every time she got married, she married well, but she's been living in Pelzer for as long as you have. She deserves to have a big funeral."

"I'm sure she will. She certainly had enough money to pay for a big one. I hear that Shaqueeda is donating her hairdressing skills and she'll make sure that Mother's body looks as natural as a body could possibly look adorned in flamingo feathers."

"You think they're really gonna bury her with all them feathers she favors?"

"More than likely, they will. I ain't never seen her without a feather. She'd look naked without them."

The two exhausted old women finished discussing how they

thought the funeral service should be while they took off their aprons, carefully folding them before they put them away.

After about ten minutes of playing bathroom tag, one waiting for the other, they finished dressing. "You look very nice in your black dress and pillbox hat, Ma Cile."

"I think you look very nice in your black dress and pillbox hat, too, Sister Betty."

After complimenting each other, they then decided they would go into Sister Betty's living room to watch a little daytime television. Sister Betty sipped on iced tea and sucked the pulp out of the lemons while making a sour face. Ma Cile, with time on her hands, unceremoniously dipped into her Railroad brand snuff while promising Sister Betty that it would be her last dip for the day. By the time the television show was over, Sister Betty was well rested and Ma Cile was cradled in one of her snuff, feel-no-pain, euphoric moments.

Sister Betty didn't feel any less nervous with Ma Cile's vow to lay off the snuff for a while. Instead, she felt a tight knot in her stomach.

She had a right to be nervous. Reverend Bling Moe Bling was going to give the eulogy. Brother Tis Mythang along with Brother Juan Derr would play the music. That meant a crippled preacher with his leg resting on a kickstand who claimed that God had called him to preach on his cell phone. Rounding out the circus would be a Kirk Franklin wanna-be choir director who played "Thriller" at every altar call and thought nobody knew what he was doing, along with another organist who only knew how to finger-peck one tune. If haunting was possible, she knew Mother Eternal Everlastin' was coming back with a vengeance.

"Are we gonna be takin' all this food to the church in a taxi?" Ma Cile suddenly asked as she carried the last of the shopping bags into the living room from the kitchen.

"Oh, I forgot to tell you. Tiny, Mother Eternal's driver, was supposed to come and pick us up but he said he had to take care of some last-minute important business that he felt Mother Eternal would've wanted him to do. He said he would get someone to pick us up but he didn't say who."

"Well, whoever is comin' needs to hurry up and git here. I'm startin' to sweat!" She stopped and used a piece of paper towel to wipe her cheeks. "I don't know why I'm startin' to sweat so."

Snuff, Sister Betty thought. She started to say something to try and calm Ma Cile down but then she looked out her living room window and was surprised to see the Reverend and Most Righteous

All Aboutme pull up in her driveway. He was driving his spotless cream-colored Porsche.

Before the Porsche, the fifty-something preacher had owned a lemon-colored Ferrari. He'd only had it for about six months but once he found out Reverend Over Priced owned one, he traded his in. If he was going to drive a big expensive car then he had to be the only one with it in the city of Pelzer. He always thought he was a one-of-a-kind sort of fellow, and everything he owned had to be too. He also thought that no one, except himself, knew his shiny black toupee made with acrylic hair was not real. Even when people laughed in his face he still thought he was fooling them.

Sister Betty watched him pull his wide girth, camouflaged under the weight of a two-piece blue Armani suit complete with vest and pocket watch, from his car. He took a moment to examine his reflection in the side-view mirror. After carefully scanning his spit-shined shoes, he did the same to the rest of the block.

Even with all the décor of a well-kept middle-class neighborhood in front of him, the Reverend and Most Righteous All Aboutme wanted to make sure that there were no undesirables lurking around to touch his car. If in the process he could make a few onlookers a little bit envious of his obvious wealth, he wouldn't be disappointed. After wetting his fingers to slick back a few strands of salt-and-pepper hair that peeked out from under his toupee, which was by now starting to frizzle from the humidity, he strutted up the walkway and rang the doorbell.

"Ma Cile, pull yourself together. The Reverend and Most Righteous All Aboutme is here to drive us to the funeral in his fancy car. You might want to grab one of my shawls in case they have the air condition running at the church. I know you feel hot now but you don't wanna catch your death of cold." Sister Betty took one look at Ma Cile as she waddled with her wide shoulders past her and on into the bedroom. She then added with sweetness and caution, "Ma Cile, since you are only a little bit heavier than me, grab two shawls for yourself."

By the time Ma Cile had huffed and puffed her way back from the bedroom with the two shawls in hand, the Reverend and Most Righteous All Aboutme was standing in the living room checking himself out again in Sister Betty's wall mirror.

He dispensed with all the niceties and was rather abrupt when he asked, "Sister Betty, how close to being ready is you and Ma Cile? I want to be on time, yet fashionably late. Other people may just go to a funeral. When you ride with me, you arrive at a funeral."

He was another sad but permanent resident in the state called denial.

Sister Betty told the reverend that they needed his help in placing the food for after the funeral into his fancy car.

He explained to her that his own mama couldn't drink a glass of water to down her life-saving medicine in his fancy car. No one ate nor drank in his car. As a matter of fact, he didn't transport his own groceries in that car. Instead he took a cab.

After threatening the Reverend and Most Righteous All Aboutme with promises of telling the entire congregation that he once wore clothes discounted from off the rack at Wal-Mart, he agreed to let them put their savory and aromatic foods in the trunk of his Porsche. They rode the rest of the way in silence because he was now in a foul mood and mumbling under his breath. Whatever he said was probably best not repeated in the presence of good Christian folks.

In the meantime, Sister Betty was praying that the reverend would be in a better mood since he was still among the living.

Sister Betty prayed and Ma Cile's snuff effect was wearing off and her false blue eye was starting to do its own thing.

In less than fifteen minutes they finally arrived in the front of the Ain't Nobody Else Right But Us—All Others Goin' to Hell Church. Normally, the Reverend and Most Righteous All Aboutme would wait to make sure that those he deemed out of his class were looking with envy before getting out of his car. Not this time. Instead of helping the two old women from the car, the Reverend and Most Righteous All Aboutme hurried to open his trunk. In his haste, he forgot to use the automatic key alarm and instead jammed the key in the trunk lock. He almost broke the key off in the lock rushing to take out the spicy smelling foods. Unfortunately for him, one of the bags contained the Looney Toon cartoon jelly jars with the seasoned brown gravy. One of the lids had popped open during the trip to church. When the Reverend and Most Righteous All Aboutme grabbed the bag, the greasy gravy spilled out of the jelly jar and onto the left pants leg of his blue Armani suit.

The Reverend and Most Righteous All Aboutme felt the hot and greasy brown gravy burn his leg. He looked down and when he saw the ever-widening gravy stain on his suit pants leg, he dropped the bag. When he dropped the bag, he broke the remaining jelly jars with the rest of the gravy and let out a howl. He hopped up and down, clutched his heart with one hand and his pants leg with the other, pulling it up over his knee and started bawling in the middle of the sidewalk.

He cried uncontrollably. "Oh Lawdy! Why Lawd? Why? Oh Lawd! Why? Why?"

One of the young deacons, thinking the reverend was overcome with grief, rushed over to the Reverend and Most Righteous All Aboutme and tried to console him with a firm pat on the back. "It's gonna be alright! You know the Lord giveth and the Lord taketh away."

The more the deacon tried to calm the Reverend and Most Righteous All Aboutme down the more he cried, and the more he cried, the more the deacon wanted to cry too. Finally the deacon could hold it no longer and just let loose with a river of remorseful tears. "Oh Lord, please Lord, give us the strength to go on," the deacon said, crying.

The Reverend and Most Righteous All Aboutme shrugged the deacon's hands away and just went to sobbing even louder. "Why didn't you just kill me, Lawd? Why did you have to stain me?" There was no humility in the Reverend and Most Righteous All Aboutme. Not even when his suit was damaged.

With both of them crying so hard, the deacon misunderstood what the Reverend and Most Righteous All Aboutme had said and he tried to add his own testimony. "Yes, Lord. I tried to abstain, too, but you know how Mother Eternal Everlastin' could turn a man's head. After all, she'd had three husbands . . . I'm so sorry, Lord!"

Between the two of them, they made so much noise, crying and whimpering that they probably would have been too loud to join a Mardi Gras parade. They cried on each other's shoulders and staggered up the church steps.

On their way up the steps the Reverend and Most Righteous All Aboutme realized that if he went inside the church with stained pants that the funeral would definitely not be about him. He yanked the deacon's arm from around his shoulder and dashed back down the steps to hail a cab. He was going home to quickly change but he wasn't going to chance driving his car and accidentally get gravy stains on the upholstery. After all, his possessions were his gods.

Two old women from the Mothers Board, Mother Eye and Mother DeClaire, wearing matching white crocheted caps and capes, peeked out from behind a bush. After a long wait, they crept out from the shadows and just stood by shaking their heads side to side as the reverend dashed past them, almost knocking them down. Their heads bobbed so hard with pretended disgust until their little caps slid down, almost covering their eyes. Finally Mother Eye turned and said to Mother DeClaire, "You see, I knew it! I knew Mother Eternal Ann Everlastin' had a little extra something going on. You ever seen her house? You and I ain't never gonna be able to live like that, and did she appreciate being one of the most richest women in town? Uh-huh! Carrying on with one of the poorest deacons in the church. That deacon ain't got enough money to ante up in a Monopoly game. Now you know that ain't right."

"It's just scandalous," Mother DeClaire said. "Now I know why that deacon could never pay all his deacon dues on time. He was giving his money to her. I remember when he got his telephone cut off. He was so far behind the phone company even went to his job and cut his phone off there too! You right! It's just scandalous. I'm so glad I ain't saved like that!"

When the two old supposed-to-be-saved women from the Mothers Board got finished tearing the dear and recently departed Mother Eternal Ann Everlastin' and the young deacon apart, they held hands, said a hypocrite's prayer and started to climb the church steps. Because of the arthritis that affected their hips but not their tongues, they climbed one step at a time.

As they passed by Sister Betty and Ma Cile, they stopped. Mother Eye whispered, "We must be strong because you know Mother Eternal Everlastin' was not only a good friend to you and this community, but she was a strong and God-fearing woman."

The other hypocrite, Mother DeClaire added, "She's gonna be missed."

They pretended to dab at a tear and almost tripped on the top step as they entered the church doors.

Sister Betty stood there in total disbelief, ignoring the two backbiting women while looking on at the Reverend and Most Righteous All Aboutme still clinging to the deacon.

"Have mercy on them, Lord." She hugged her big family-sized Bible close to her chest as if she thought a demon would jump from the two men and two women onto her. "Come on, Ma Cile. We'll get some of those young people to come outside and bring the rest of those bags of food inside. They should have everything set up so we can do what we need to do quickly and join in the funeral service."

Ma Cile was stunned, too, by the nice-nasty remarks from Mothers

Eye and DeClaire. However, she had promised Sister Betty that she would not take another pinch of her Railroad brand snuff no matter how bad someone got on her nerves. Instead, she grabbed a clean handkerchief from the cuff of her sleeve and dabbed her good eye. Giving one last tug to straighten her wig, she was now ready for the funeral.

It was time to let the dead bury the dead.

8

Go On Home, Mother Eternal Ann Everlastin'

Most of the church inside was adorned in purple and black with touches of blue feathers dotting the walls. All of this was done to let everyone know that they were going to bury someone of notoriety.

Reverend Bling Moe Bling limped down the church aisle wearing a loud, fire-engine red jumpsuit. "Mother would've loved to have seen me in this outfit," he whispered to Sister Bertha Bling who clung to his arm as though someone would mistake her for the recently deceased. He never mentioned that it was also the same red jumpsuit he wore when he first made Mother Eternal Ann Everlastin's acquaintance.

"Ouch!" Sister Bertha Bling shot back at her husband. "You need to watch how you stepping instead of cheesin' all these folks like you gonna get an offering. You nearly put a run in my pantyhose with that kickstand of yours." Without waiting for him to reply, she turned suddenly toward one of the ushers who had extended a helping hand and smiled, showing all twenty of her taupe-colored teeth. "Thank you so much. My husband is just overcome and that's why he's walking like he's playing hopscotch."

She took off her brown mink stole, which she wore no matter how hot it was and handed it to the usher with a look that read "take care of this like it was your firstborn child." With a run in her pantyhose that looked like a widening crevice that had escaped her scrutiny, she switched her wide hips, made all the wider by her orange pleated dress, on up to the pulpit.

Bishop Was Nevercalled was the next to come through the sanctuary doors. Remembering that he had stepped foot inside the sanctuary, he suddenly stopped. He yanked off his purple fedora, revealing a glistening bald head that threatened blindness as it shimmered in competition with the shiny purple satin suit he wore. He looked like the setting sun across the desert sand. It was not a good sign. When he looked like that, his sermon was usually just as dry as a desert. One of the ushers came toward him and with one hand arched behind her back and a finger over her lips to warn the people to stop snickering, she led Bishop Was Nevercalled to the pulpit.

Bishop Was Nevercalled sat down in one of the high-back velvet chairs. He leaned forward and placed his fedora under his chair next to an unread Bible, which was still in its plastic wrapper. He decided to do the Christian thing by speaking to someone he really didn't like. "It's been a long time," Bishop Was Nevercalled leaned over and whispered to Reverend Bling Moe Bling as he nodded in the direction of Sister Bertha Bling.

"Yes, it has been quite a while," Reverend Bling Moe Bling mumbled.

"We ain't seen you since you was laid out spread eagle begging for Mother Eternal Everlastin' to come back," Sister Bertha Bling chided.

"Well, she's coming back now, ain't she?" the bishop barked as he pointed to a spot about ten feet away from where they sat, which Mother Eternal Ann Everlastin's coffin would soon occupy. This time, he was so mad, he didn't even stutter. "At least, she never ran the risk of dying in our pulpit under suspicious and unholy circumstances. Ain't nobody I know ever died from eating no York peppermint pattie. I wouldn't be surprised if you didn't put something in the pattie. You look like you'd do something unnatural with a pattie."

He was about to forget where he was, and for what purpose, as he leaned forward in his chair and started to stand to sling another nasty barb at Sister Bertha Bling.

Just as the bishop stood up to go face-to-face with Sister Bertha Bling, Reverend Bling Moe Bling unlatched his kickstand, which fell out and caused the bishop to fall forward.

The bishop was too embarrassed to move back to his chair so he just stayed where he fell, and with one hand on a knee, he pretended to pray. After a moment or two, he jumped up and hollered, "Thank ya, Lord."

Sister Bertha Bling, never one to leave well enough alone, chided him again. "Yes, thank Him, Bishop. You know you just need to thank Him! You've certainly proved that God can clean up a mess!"

The bishop was about to forget his pulpit manners and rail into both of them when he suddenly felt the eyes of the congregation upon him; particularly the few members who had attended from the No Hope Now—Mercy Neva Church. They looked like they still had a little bit of thug residue and were just itching for a fight—or just itching because they hadn't washed. Either way, he'd bide his time. He filed the insult away in his head and instead he leaned back in his chair with his head raised toward the ceiling. It didn't seem as if he was going to get much respect from anyone, and he wanted to exercise his authority as the bishop.

Unfortunately for him, the only exercise he ever got was from jumping to conclusions.

While the bishop sat in his high-back cushioned chair sulking like a spoiled kid, the Reverend Bling Moe Bling and the first lady, Sister Bertha Bling, whispered back and forth. They ooh and awed about the opulence of the Ain't Nobody Else Right But Us—All Others Goin' to Hell Church and what they would do if they were running things. Each of them was so busy sulking, plotting and envying that they never noticed the buzz that was coming from the people.

It was supposed to be a funeral but the buzzing and whispers made it sound more like someone had disturbed a beehive.

The huge gold clock that hung over the choirs stand read twelve o'clock. High noon. However, as was his custom, the Reverend Knott Enuff Money arrived fashionably late. He was never on time for any church service and didn't plan on even arriving at his own funeral on time, let alone Mother Eternal Ann Everlastin's. He also knew that the church etiquette book, *Perpetrate Good Manners* said that everyone of high authority who sat up in the pulpit was supposed to lead Mother's coffin and family into the church. However, the funeral director, Mr. Bury Em Deep had informed him that according to Mother's last wishes, she wanted to have the Reverend Knott Enuff Money, the Bishop Was Nevercalled and the Reverend Bling Moe Bling waiting for her as her coffin rolled to a stop at the foot of the pulpit.

She also specifically requested that neither Sister Hellraiser nor the first lady, Sister Bertha Bling not be within twenty feet of her coffin. She also had the foresight to make sure that the ushers did not let Sister Carrie Onn in the church.

One look at the waiting pulpit told the funeral director that it may have been what she wanted, but it had nothing to do with the way things were actually going to happen. Flowers could be brought into the church, but with permission or not, First Lady Bertha Bling was already planted—in the pulpit.

It took a few moments but finally two old male ushers named Brother Flipper and Brother Willy who had served on the usher board for more than twenty years had frantically put on their white gloves and sprinted up the aisle. They almost tripped over each other as they tried to run side by side with about two inches of space separating them in the narrow aisle. Brother Flipper was about fifty years old, wore a salt-and-pepper wooly Afro wig and was extremely skinny. He was shaped and colored like an overripe banana, and with the tail of his coat flapping behind him, he looked like someone had tried to peel him.

Brother Willy was about sixty years old. He had exactly five strands of hair, which he counted every day and wore swept over his huge dome-shaped head like a raggedy feather duster. His skin was two shades deeper than black, and he looked like a round plum. Together, they looked like a crowded bowl of jiggling fruit as they ran toward the Reverend Knott Enuff Money who stood in the doorway with the sunlight bathing him from head to toe.

The Reverend Knott Enuff Money was wearing a long black satin robe with a high, fanned-out neck, which made him look like Dracula on a budget. The neck of the robe was covered by a clear plastic outer lining with some type of sponge material. The lining was attached by strips of Velcro to absorb the oily Jheri curl activator juice. There were also triangle-shaped little pieces of glitter sewn onto it. He was so fresh and so clean, and he almost blinded everyone in the back pew.

"Praise the Lord, Pastor," Brother Flipper said, out of breath from the few feet of sprinting as he took the brown leather briefcase from the Reverend Knott Enuff Money's hand. "We're here if you need us."

Not one to be outdone, Brother Willy added his two cents. "God is good, Pastor. I'll be standing at the pulpit should you have a need for an *experienced* usher."

As they started the slow and reverent walk down the aisle, each of the ushers verbally pulled at the reverend's ear like he was the last piece of taffy, with promises of undying loyalty and an extra tithe donation.

Under normal circumstances, the Reverend Knott Enuff Money would've ordinarily admonished the old ushers. He knew each of them wanted to be made chairman of the usher board. He had to admire their politics. Even a funeral couldn't stop them from trying to get ahead.

However, their efforts were futile. They still hadn't figured out that if they were going to get that position, they would've gotten it twenty years ago. Their methods were scandalous. He had to admire them for that, and he also had to keep his sad face from sliding. He had almost blown his outward show of sadness with a hint of an awkward smile. Somehow, he'd managed one little microscopic tear that ran down in a straight line and made his face look like it had a seam in it.

But nothing got past most of the folks inside the Ain't Nobody Else Right But Us—All Others Goin' to Hell Church. There were always one or two who still believed that throwing salt over one's shoulder would either bring them good luck or someone to love.

"Have mercy! Take a look at our pastor," one member whispered to another. "If he don't look pitiful like he's lost his best friend."

The other man looked past the first one, adjusted his glasses, which had slid down to the bridge of his nose and nodded in agreement.

As the ushers led the Reverend Knott Enuff Money past the pew, the same two men gave him a wide, encouraging smile and greeted him with raised hands and thumbs up.

Before the reverend could get two feet past the pew, the other man readjusted his glasses again and added, "He's probably looking sad because he couldn't tap into Mother Eternal Ann Everlastin's bank account." He reached inside his suit pocket and pulled out a wad of cash. "I bet you ten bucks he starts to bawling before everyone else can get started."

"I'll see that ten bucks and raise you another five that it will be the bishop who starts the waterworks first," the other man whispered as he retrieved his wallet.

"Let me get in on some of that action," Mother Eye butted in. She swiftly grabbed a soggy twenty-dollar bill from within one of the wrinkled folds between her breasts. "As a matter of fact,"—she stopped and reached back into the folds, retrieved more money, then leaned over and whispered—"I'll raise it by another five because I believe that the Reverend Bling Moe Bling will kick things off." She snickered to herself at the mention of the word *kick* because it reminded her of his kickstand leg rest.

The three of them had hardly gotten their money out when, from out of nowhere, one of the ushers raced over with a collection plate and snatched the money so fast, they all thought they'd been dreaming. They just sat there with their hands raised like they needed permission to get up and go to the bathroom.

"Thank you so much. We don't usually take up an offering at a funeral, but since y'all seem so anxious, we'll make an exception." The usher turned around even faster and disappeared. She looked like the evil witch in the *Wizard of Oz* melting after Dorothy had spilled water upon her.

Mother Eye and the other two members wanted to scream. They felt like they'd been robbed. But after all, they were in church, and at a funeral, no less. They didn't want to do anything unseemly.

The Reverend Knott Enuff Money walked very slow like he had something sticky on the bottom of his shoes. He looked like a strutting horse leading a parade. By the time he finally reached the pulpit, he immediately felt the thick tension in the air. It was so thick, he felt like he could've parted it like the Red Sea. He adjusted the wide standup collar around his robe and greeted the bishop with a handshake. "Bishop, glad to see you." He could read the look on the bishop's face, and it wasn't a happy story.

The Reverend Knott Enuff Money took another quick look around. He didn't see his backup team of Mother Pray Onn, Deacon Laid Handz and definitely not Sister Ima Hellraiser. He motioned for Brother Flipper to come to the pulpit.

Brother Flipper sprinted over to the pulpit with a pad and pen to write down whatever the pastor requested. He was determined to stay on the pastor's good side, even if it cost him a little of his dignity every time. "Yes, Pastor. What can I do? I noticed you motion for me 'cause Brother Willy's over there messing around attending to somebody who's having an asthma attack. That man doesn't know the meaning of prioritizing and being loyal to you." He was grinning so hard that his false teeth were about to escape. He was still grinning when he pushed them back into place.

The Reverend Knott Enuff Money craned his neck so far that it almost became entangled in the Dracula-looking collar of his robe. He glared at the patronizing usher and through closed teeth muttered, "Where are Mother Pray Onn, Deacon Laid Handz and Sister Ima Hellraiser?"

Brother Flipper flipped a page in his pad and looked over the many rumors that he'd written down so he could give his report to the *Daily BLAB* and whispered, "Well. Let me see." He pretended to squint so he could act like he was important. "It seems that Sister Ima Hellraiser won't be attending because she's having a bad hair day. And I know that Deacon Laid Handz is still laid up in the hospital from that beat-down he got Sunday night." He was about to run out of breath, so he stopped for about a second before he continued, "You know he's been doing some unauthorized anointing out in the parking lot on a few of the sisters. I guess he laid hands on the wrong one and got laid out!"

Brother Flipper was on a roll. He even ignored some of the hisses for him to be quiet. "Deacon Laid Handz fussed so much about a little tiny bump that threatened to scar his face until one of them night nurses slapped him across his butt real hard with a bedpan. I heard he's got to wait until the swelling goes down on one of his butt cheeks so they can peel the pan off." He took the look of shock on the pastor's face to mean that his information was very vital and welcome.

Brother Flipper moved in closer to the pastor because the choir had started singing and he wanted to make sure he was heard. He looked over the notes on his pad and whispered again, "Oh, I forgot to mention. A couple of them big-time preachers called. A Reverend Frank Reid, from Bethel AME in Maryland and a Bishop T. D. Jakes from that Potter's House Church, out in Dallas, Texas. They were calling to find out about sending condolences to Mother Eternal Ann Everlastin'. I guess she's been sending them money. Anyhow, I told them that when you had a chance you'd call them back."

The Reverend Knott Enuff Money was so mad that the heat from his head made the Jheri curl juice start pouring down onto his cape. For years, he'd wanted to be in the company of mega-church pastors, those two in particular, and Brother Flipper had messed things up. He couldn't speak, he was so outdone.

The choir sang louder, the reverend got hotter and Brother Flipper kept on talking. "Now about Mother Pray Onn. I know she didn't have much love for Mother Eternal Ann Everlastin'." He stopped and looked past the reverend to make sure that the bishop wasn't trying to get all up in their business. The bishop, as usual, sat there clueless as Brother Flipper continued. "You know it was all about the two of them a long time ago wanting the same man—ole Brother Benn Dead."

"Get to the point!" the Reverend Knott Enuff Money snapped. He needed to get the funeral over so he could return Bishop Jakes and Reverend Reid's phone calls.

"Oh, well," Brother Flipper said. "Anyway, supposedly Mother Pray Onn spent the night in the emergency room because she had two swollen pinky toes and they were supposed to be infected."

Brother Flipper was in his element. He'd had two conversations in a row with the pastor, and the pastor seemed to hang on to his every word.

"How do you know all this?" the Reverend Knott Enuff Money pressed.

"Because she called your study right after those big-time preachers called, which was about ten minutes before you arrived. Of course, me being filled with the spirit of discernment, I just knew she was lying, and I didn't want to bother you on this solemn occasion." Brother Flipper started grinning again. He was well pleased with himself.

Both Reverend Knott Enuff Money and his Jheri curl juice started spitting. "You have the spirit of discernment? Then how come you didn't know that when well-known pastors called me you were suppose to let me know immediately." He smiled wickedly as he saw the smile start to slide from Brother Flipper's face. "Don't worry about what I'm gonna do to you because when Mother Pray Onn finds out that you didn't give me that message, your life will be pretty much over. She's gonna spread you out in the same spot they're gonna have Mother Eternal Ann Everlastin' laid out."

Brother Flipper's ear-to-ear grin kept sliding and then froze on his face and that's when his false teeth fell out onto the pad he was holding. He either didn't even notice or he didn't care. He gummed an apology. "Pastor, I'm sorry. You ain't gonna tell her, are you?"

The Reverend Knott Enuff Money leaned over and with Jheri curl juice and spit flying out of his mouth like darts, he whispered into the ear of the frightened Brother Flipper, who by then had the same ashen color as the body in front of the pulpit. "Yep! You can count on it."

Brother Flipper grabbed his teeth and slipped them into his pocket, shut the notepad and dashed for the door. On the way, he took off his white gloves and threw them on a pew. He tossed his pad into a nearby wastebasket and then he threw his usher's badge to Brother Willy and sobbed, "I gave that man more than twenty years!"

Brother Willy just stood there in shock. He knew that Brother Flipper had never married but it certainly hadn't crossed his mind that he favored men. He didn't bother to reply. Instead, he figured he was a definite shoo-in for the chairman of the ushers board position. They'd been friends for more than a quarter of a century, yet Brother Willy didn't even say good-bye.

In the meantime, the Reverend Knott Enuff Money sat with a confused look upon his face. "Bethel Church and the Potter's House." He kept repeating it over and over. "All these years I've been wanting to talk to a mega-church pastor and that fool messes up."

Upon hearing the word *fool* the bishop asked, "You talking to me?"

"Never mind, Bishop." The Reverend Knott Enuff Money didn't want to get into any word games. He could be on the same level as those other mega preachers if he could fulfill his vision of a new Jacuzzi baptismal pool being installed. He also pushed the welfare of both Mother Pray Onn and Deacon Laid Handz to the side. They could be dealt with later by a visit from either him or someone from the missionary board.

The Reverend Knott Enuff Money quickly reached past the bishop and said, with a conniving grin upon his face, "Reverend Bling Moe Bling, Sister Bling, welcome y'all to my humble church, and I'm so sorry it has to be for such a sad occasion." Somebody was gonna ante up some cash.

"Thank you for allowing Mother to be sent on home. I know she would be so happy that you permitted all of her many friends to celebrate her home going from this luxurious sanctuary." Reverend Bling Moe Bling then flashed his own conniving grin.

Reverend Bling Moe Bling would've continued his rehearsed speech but he felt a hard tug on his sleeve, which caused him to turn around.

"Here, take this." Sister Bertha Bling handed her husband a balled-up tissue from her purse.

He mumbled under his breath, "What is the tissue for? I ain't started my crying yet." He turned back to the Reverend Knott Enuff Money and gave him another cheesy grin.

Sister Bling grabbed his arm and spun him around in his chair. "It ain't for your crying. It's for that big brown spot on your nose!" She huffed and sucked her teeth as she grumbled under her breath, "You sure you don't wanna use another tissue to wipe the reverend's behind? It would be a lot more sanitary than you using your nose."

Sister Bertha Bling was on a roll, and the only thing that stopped her mouth from issuing a check that it couldn't cash was the "well shut my mouth" sight of the choir director from her church, Brother Juan Derr. He was dressed in a black tuxedo, silver socks and black penny loafers with a dime in the band of each shoe. He also wore a silver cummerbund and was about to sit down at Brother Tis Mythang's brand-new, just-got-out-of-layaway Roland 600 electric organ.

There was a loud, sympathetic gasp from the pulpit and the people. It was for the impending beat-down that would soon be laid on Brother Juan Derr.

Oblivious, Brother Tis Mythang had his back turned away from his organ and was so busy giving last-minute instructions to the A, B, C and senior choir that he had not seen Brother Juan Derr do the unimaginable.

Fortunately for Brother Juan Derr, one of the other ushers, Brother Snap, had the presence of mind to run and grab a first aid kit from behind a vacant wheelchair that sat in the corner. He tossed the first aid kit across one of the aisles into the waiting arms of Brother Willy who back in his day had been a quarterback. Brother Willy caught the first aid kit just in time to make it back to the organ to give impending medical attention to Brother Juan Derr who sat with his pecking finger hanging in a very strange manner.

"What the—" Brother Tis Mythang, after he'd seen Brother Juan Derr about to flip his coattail over the organ seat, spun around like a ballerina and proceeded to prance all the way over to where Brother Juan Derr stood, too scared to move. When Brother Tis Mythang finished with Brother Juan Derr, Brother Juan Derr had another split in his tail—coat.

Brother Tis Mythang, after leaving Brother Juan Derr sufficiently punished and told off, ran to borrow a little nail glue from one of the male sopranos. He'd broken a nail and that was the only thing that kept him from fully maiming Brother Juan Derr—that and the fact that, he was only about three months away from finishing his probation from another little incident.

The Reverend Knott Enuff Money suddenly realized that the pulpit had an empty seat. He shot forward and grabbed the bishop's arm and pointed at it. "What in the world is going on?" He stopped pointing at the empty chair and pushed a loose lock of wet Jheri curl from his face, which he pinned with a bobby pin that appeared out of nowhere. "Where's the Reverend and Most Righteous All Aboutme? What happened to him?"

"Oh. Uh. I meant to tell you about that. It seems that he and one of the deacons had been messing around on the sneak with Mother Eternal Everlastin'. And-and, when the two of them got together outside the church earlier, they both was overcome with emotion after finding out that she had played them both."

His stuttering had returned, which meant that not only was he too excited, but he didn't have a clue as to what he was talking about.

"What! You mean they didn't get paid?" The Reverend Knott Enuff Money's eyes bulged, showing more confusion than normal.

"Yes, er . . . I was shocked too." The bishop was glad that he finally got the reverend's attention away from the patronizing grip of the brown-nosing Reverend Bling Moe Bling. "I don't know what they used to do with Mother Eternal Ann Everlastin' but whatever it was it made the Reverend and Most Righteous All Aboutme *stain* himself." He leaned to the side in his chair, very much pleased with himself and his up-to-the-minute reporting.

The Reverend Knott Enuff Money snatched the bishop back into his seat and challenged him. "Who in the world told you something like that?"

The choir suddenly started singing "I Love to Tell the Story."

Ignoring the obvious connection between the choir's selection and what he was saying, he continued. "I overheard Mother Eye and Mother DeClaire discussing it by the blessing dispenser before the doors to the sanctuary opened," the bishop replied.

"Well then, it must be true if they said it." The Reverend Knott Enuff Money's limited attention span was again diverted when he put his hand into his robe pocket and realized he still had Mother's unsigned check. He suddenly dropped his head and started dabbing at his eyes.

"You see that!" Mother Eye punched the man seated next to her as she pointed. "I just knew that the reverend was gonna start the waterworks before anyone else. I guess I would've lost my money anyway."

Of course, there were a few people who always played follow the leader, so when they saw the Reverend Knott Enuff Money drop his head and dab at his eyes, they started crying too.

Time started to pass and the huge gold clock that hung over the choir stand read one o'clock. It was way past the time to roll Mother's custom-made twenty-two-karat, gold-layered coffin down to her appointed spot at the heard of the church. It would be displayed just below the pulpit between enough flowers to make the spot look like a meadow—all bought and paid for by Mother herself. It was part of the funeral arrangements she'd planned. She was determined to go out in style and was thumbing her nose at Mother Pray Onn who worked on her funeral list every other week and who thought her funeral would be the cat's meow.

With nothing much to do until the funeral got into full swing except read the obituary, which read and looked like a sales brochure, a few people started to practice their crying. There were so many shoulders heaving and sighs heard until it looked and sounded like the entire sanctuary was doing a club wave. Some of the ushers ran around passing out fans with either Martin Luther King Jr. on the front or the family with the little girl wearing Shirley Temple curls sitting in front of her mother and father.

All of this was going on and they hadn't even started playing the traditional "Amazing Grace." That would be the signal to Mr. Bury Em Deep that it was time to bring Mother Eternal Ann Everlastin's coffin inside the church, so they could send her on home and everyone else could go on home too.

9

Some Things Just Don't Make Sense

Just as Mother Eternal Ann Everlastin' had instructed in the details she'd written for her own home going service, Sister Betty, Ma Cile, Shaqueeda and Mr. Bury Em Deep all surrounded the coffin, which was carried by six unknown white men hired by the Last Stop funeral home.

Sister Betty held a floral arrangement of blue-colored annuals with blue flamingo feathers hanging over the sides.

Ma Cile carried a bag of York peppermint patties. She felt very uneasy and superstitious carrying the very thing that had killed her friend.

Shaqueeda, as instructed, carried a comb, brush and a small makeup case along with a small compact shaving kit. She was to make sure that not a feather or a hair, whether it was on Mother's top lip or wig, was out of place as the people paraded past the coffin.

Finally, Mr. Bury Em Deep, the funeral director, carried his head up high as he led the procession. He did that out of respect for Mother Eternal Ann Everlastin'. He'd been in the business for more than thirty years and no one had ever been sent off the way she was about to go. She'd paid enough for her funeral to bury at least five others in the church with class.

And, of course, only Mother would've left instructions for six strangers—white strangers—to carry her remains. When she was alive, she always hired her own kind. She said that the only way she would hire a white man to take her anywhere, particularly since it was the KKK who murdered both her parents and sent her running for her life, was if she was dead. She was now dead and they were now hired.

It seemed as if Mother Eternal Ann Everlastin's coffin would never make it to its place at the altar.

The entourage had to stop several times because it seemed that someone forgot to close the lock on the top part of the coffin and once those blue flamingo feathers of Mother Eternal Ann Everlastin's burial hat got loose, they took on a life of their own. They were popping out of every corner of the coffin. Every time Shaqueeda would get one back in place and try to close the lid, another feather would escape. "Mother Eternal Ann Everlastin', cut it out," Shaqueeda muttered to herself. She had no doubt that wherever Mother was, she was still trying to run things her way.

The poor pallbearers were about to commit anarchy because Mr. Bury Em Deep, when he hired the white men didn't bother to check whether or not they were all about the same height and could carry the weight. They ranged from giant-size to midget. They kept complaining that not everyone was carrying their own weight and threatened to make the midget carry the coffin by himself if he didn't pitch in a little more muscle.

In the meantime, Brother Tis Mythang sat with one hand holding up his chin and rolled his eyes in boredom. He turned to one of the choir members who sat nearby, ready to sing a solo, and complained. "This don't make no sense. Why do I need to be sitting here if I ain't gonna play all the songs? And, why does Sister Petunia with her deaf self have to get up here and waste everybody's time trying to sing a song in sign language? And, Lord please, somebody explain to me what in the world is Sister Peaches supposed to be doing? If she calls herself doing sign language for Sister Petunia then I'm the Queen of Sheba."

The choir member wasn't really paying him any attention until he thought he'd heard wrong. He'd been too busy trying to pretend that he would act surprised if asked to sing. "You meant to say king, right?"

"Of course I meant to say king. They got me so riled up with this mess until I don't know what I'm saying."

Brother Tis Mythang had said exactly what he meant and meant exactly what he'd said. He just hadn't meant to say it aloud.

Sister Petunia and Sister Peaches had finished their singing and signing by the time the coffin arrived in the front of the altar.

There was a place reserved in the front pew for Sister Betty, and one with extra cushioning for Ma Cile. Sister Betty was there to read the obituary when called, and Ma Cile was there to run interference in case Mother Pray Onn, Sister Hellraiser or Sister Carrie Onn tried to disrupt the service. So far she hadn't seen any of them show up.

Mother Eternal Ann Everlastin' always thought ahead. Just in case those three connivers outlived her, she didn't want them messing with her when she couldn't fight back.

Shaqueeda took her place at the head of the coffin in case Mother needed any emergency hair and makeup done. She was also there to keep those blue flamingo feathers from poking the folks' eyes out as they passed by.

There was much pomp and sucking up by Mr. Bury Em Deep who because he was running behind schedule, decided he'd be the one to read the scriptures from both the Old and New Testaments to hurry things along. From the Old Testament, he read Song of Solomon 1:2: "Let him kiss me with the kisses of his mouth—for thy love is better than wine." And from the New Testament, he read 1 Thessalonians 5:16: "Rejoice evermore." All fitting, in his mind, to send Mother off. Of course, she'd asked for "Jesus wept" but he decided to add his own personal touch on that end.

They were about to get full swing into the funeral service when the doors to the church blew open again.

In the doorway, dressed in a blue wide-brim baseball cap and black muscle shirt and baggy pants stood Mother Eternal's driver, Tiny. It took a moment for most to recognize him because it was the first time they'd seen him not wearing his chauffeur uniform. He didn't even bother to take off his hat as he happily slid through the door, dragging another man behind him. He unceremoniously pushed the unwilling man in front of him a few feet, and then hollered, "See ya! I got someplace else I'd rather be!" And then, before he turned to leave, he walked over and pushed the man so hard again that the man almost fell on his face.

Mother Eternal Ann Everlastin's only close relative had finally arrived.

The man stood still for a moment, bewildered, with his eyes bulging like two dark balloons in an effort to see what was going on. He gave up on trying to figure out what was happening and instead, he started to stagger with what looked like a switch in his walk, like he was stepping over cracks in the floor or looking for a crack. He stopped every few feet to examine a plain brown bag that he held in one hand, take a swig and exhale the smell from his closest friend, Jack Daniel's liquor, from his dry and pasty lips.

It was Mother's drunken, thirty-year-old nephew Buddy. Either he didn't remember the occasion was his aunt's funeral or he was just too drunk to care. Buddy was shirtless and had on a pair of blue jeans with suspenders to keep them on his rail-thin body. He also wore sneakers without laces and looked as if he hadn't shaved—ever.

It wasn't like he had fallen off the wagon. It was more like he'd dived off.

Buddy's questionable connection to Mother Eternal Ann Everlastin' was that he was supposed to be the nephew of one of her dead husbands; some said the first one and others claimed it was the second one. He was also that infamous out-of-the-closet member that the Reverend Knott Enuff Money had thrown out of the church.

Brother Tis Mythang almost fainted as he laid his chest across the organ, somewhere between lower and middle C and whispered, "Buddy. Is that my Buddy?" He looked up to see who might be watching him, then decided he really didn't care as he whispered a little louder. "Buddy. You two-timing—" He stopped short because he suddenly remembered that telling too much would put permanent distance between him and his other love, his organ—the Roland 600 organ.

Better to keep folks guessing than to verify.

Under normal circumstances Buddy's late arrival for the funeral would have caused a round of eye daggers thrown his way, but for this sad occasion and because it was for Mother Eternal Ann Everlastin', the entire congregation and the pulpit stood with mock respect when he staggered in.

Two men dressed identically in black who turned out to be the Deacons Luke and Warm Waters from No Hope Now—Mercy Neva Church reached Buddy after his third spill and swig. They each grabbed him by his kinky-hair armpits, supporting him as best they could.

Only a few people knew that when the Deacons Luke and Warm were not hassling folks at the church, they worked at the funeral home to make a little extra cash. They needed the extra money for the extra sin they seemed to always be committing. From the somber looks on their faces, they took their funeral jobs serious. So, with stiff steps and lips tight, they led the bereaved and stinking drunk nephew to his honored seat on the front pew. Someone had grabbed the cushion from the seat just in case Buddy didn't know a pew seat from a toilet seat.

Without meaning to do it, both Sister Betty and Ma Cile slid across their pews like they were doing a sitting Electric Slide. Or perhaps it was the Macarena the way they were rapidly switching their hands from their noses to their heads to avoid his odorous assault.

As Buddy stumbled, he sobered up only enough to finally realize the reason why he was in his old church home. That's when he tried to open his eyes to muster up a few tears, but could not because that fifth bottle of Jack Daniel's liquor that he'd drank told him that everything was just fine. Everything with him was so mellow that he just started sliding off the pew like sap down a maple tree in the win-ter.

Deacons Luke and Warm raced over, caught him before he fell and threw him down on the pew like they were splattering a water-melon. It was hard enough to somewhat sober him up.

They threw him so hard that Ma Cile felt the vibration come through her cushion, race through her ample hips and up her spine. By the time the feeling reached her shoulders it had lost none of its power and Ma Cile had a lot for it to travel through.

When the hard wooden pew seat kissed Buddy's behind with a thud and a sharp splinter, he finally managed to open one eye. With his one eye now opened, he peeped around and saw Reverend Knott Enuff Money approach the podium. That Jack Daniel's liquor lied to Buddy again. It told Buddy that the Reverend was about to take up an offering. He slumped down again in the pew and bowed his head, as if in prayer. He stayed that way so long until he fell asleep, which only took about two seconds.

One of the newly appointed ushers was on her feet and on alert to make sure services at the church went by protocol. She was Sister Mentol Kase, about five foot nine of pure ebony rock with eyes that showed just as much emotion as a rock.

The first time that she ushered, which was only one other time be-fore the funeral, she'd looked like a robot. Sister Mentol Kase was built and acted like a construction worker, which was a good thing because she'd need to be tough to handle that crowd. She kept a box of Depends for some of the women on the Mothers Board. She was tired of them always calling her to excuse themselves to go to the bathroom. Near her seat, she kept a stethoscope and a small bottle of ammonia for those who feigned fainting around offering time. She also wore one tall-heeled prescription black shoe and a regular shoe. When she stood at her post, she looked like a black Leaning Tower of Pisa. She never said what caused the deformity and she looked too crazy for anyone to press her about it.

Unfortunately for Mother Eternal Everlastin's nephew Buddy,

Sister Mentol Kase never had a chance to serve at a funeral before. There had been no time to attend the Subtlety and Compassion class sometimes given to new members. Sister Mentol Kase had only joined the church two Sundays before. By the next Sunday, after reading two books of the "begets," she was made an usher.

This particular usher, Sister Mentol Kase had never testified or revealed that she was just out of the local mental hospital only a month when she joined the church. She had a mean temper and did not know her own strength. She tried to sprint down the aisle, but one foot barely touched the carpet, and the other kept threatening to topple her over. It took some doing but she finally got to where Buddy sat and slapped him real hard on his shoulder to wake him.

He pretended he didn't know where he was and automatically slapped Usher Mentol Kase back.

She crouched and tried the old rope-a-dope move with her prescription shoe planted while she pimp-slapped him twice.

Brought back to consciousness by the usher's hard slap, Buddy, now totally under the control of his lying friend, Jack Daniel's liquor, jumped up and assumed a karate stance. He assumed it because when he looked at Sister Mentol Kase with her one leg looking longer than the other because of her prescription shoe, he thought she was about to do a Crouching Tiger, Flying Dragon move on him.

"If you don't know who you messing with you'd better ask somebody!" screamed Buddy, slurring his words, which caused a little spit to fly out of his mouth.

Sister Mentol Kase was determined to keep her position as an usher. She stood her ground and growled back, "Really. Now just whom do you think I should ask?" she teased. She geared up, dodging and weaving, ready to deliver another pimp slap.

Buddy, encouraged once more by that lying Jack Daniel's liquor, answered without giving his dilemma careful thought. "You-you can ask anybody around here. They'll tell you that folks don't mess with me." He tried to push out his chest and kick out one leg, but only his breath came out kicking. "I'm part Indian, you know!"

"So what!" answered Sister Mentol Kase as she tried to circle him, limping like a three-legged lion sizing up its kill. "Everybody I know in Pelzer, South Carolina, is part Indian. What makes your tribe so bad that I should be afraid of you?"

Once again, that lying Jack Daniel's liquor told Buddy to put a sneer on his face because he thought he was getting to her. So with renewed and false confidence, he threw a sucker punch at her. He staggered and yelled, "I'm part Slap-a-ho."

Buddy, now the sucker, missed.

Sister Mentol Kase didn't.

He never saw the punch coming, but he did hear her say, "So what! I'm part Knock-'em-out." And she did just that. She hit him so hard that both he and that lying Jack Daniel's saw the stars, the moon and the Pillsbury Doughboy searching for his croissants with a flashlight in broad daylight.

Sister Betty, who was sitting far enough away to avoid Buddy's foul odor but not too far to hear them argue, sat with a surprised look upon her face. She'd been in Pelzer for a long time and had heard of many Indian tribes, but never one called Slap-a-ho. She started to intervene but instead decided she'd just stay out of harm's way and pray.

Everyone at the funeral, including the drunken and now knocked-out nephew Buddy was convinced that Sister Mentol Kase was crazy and definitely needed to be enlisted to serve on the pastor's aid committee. On the pastor's aid committee they always needed someone to block anyone from approaching the pastor. Anyone who did not have an offering showing in his or her hands could not come close.

Armed with the information that there was a crazy usher in their midst, no one stepped up to help him. The demented look on Sister Mentol Kase's face told the congregation that there was plenty more where that came from. It reinforced their decision. They decided that one funeral was enough for one day. So in order to save his life, they left the nephew Buddy knocked out next to the pew where he would have sat, if he had not been so stupid. They proceeded with the funeral.

When as much testifying and testa-lying, as possible, due to all the chaos on Mother Eternal Everlastin's behalf was over, the choir director, Brother Tis Mythang rolled his eyes in Buddy's direction. He sashayed from in front of the choir back over to the organ and ran his well-manicured fingers skillfully over the keys. He played about five songs in a row before a nasty glare from Reverend Knott Enuff Money told him that they were on the clock and he was about out of time. Brother Tis Mythang returned the glare and sucked his teeth and then jerked his head in rebellion.

Reverend Knott Enuff Money ignored him and decided to get his two cents in before he went on to introduce Bishop Was Nevercalled. "Well now, I'm just as overcome with grief as a few of y'all, so I'm gonna need some help from the choir to say a little something about Mother. I'm just gonna say one word, and I need y'all to sing a hymn."

Brother Tis Mythang wasn't quite sure what the reverend was up to but he'd go along with it for a little while.

"Power!" the Reverend Knott Enuff Money said firmly.

The choir, led by Brother One Note sang "There's Power in the Blood."

The Reverend Knott Enuff Money threw his head back yelled, "Grace!"

Again, the choir started singing. That time they sang "Amazing Grace," which was a funeral must.

Finally, the Reverend Knott Enuff Money got so caught up in the moment that he hollered, "Sex!"

Everyone just turned and looked at him. The choir didn't know what to sing.

However, Ma Cile was also caught up in the moment and she stood and started singing "Precious Memories" by herself.

A few people laughed a little and that seemed to add a little levity to the moment. The Reverend Knott Enuff Money had to chuckle a little too. "Thank you, Ma Cile. I'm sure that Mother Eternal Ann Everlastin' would've probably gotten a kick out of your solo." He suddenly turned off his false smile and replaced it with a look of seriousness. "Right now, if all hearts and minds are clear, I'm gonna present to some and introduce to others, our very own Bishop Was Nevercalled. After him, there will be words from the very fine pastor of the No Hope Now—Mercy Neva Church, Reverend Bling Moe Bling." He could feel the heat coming from Sister Bertha Bling because of his obvious snub to her presence on the pulpit, but he didn't care, and he didn't like her.

No sooner had the reverend finished the introduction, Brother Tis Mythang started playing Scott Joplin's "The Entertainer."

Both the bishop and the Reverend Knott Enuff Money, embarrassed by Brother Tis Mythang's show of total lack of respect in front of the Reverend Bling Moe Bling and the first lady, stomped their feet and jumped around. When they did that, Brother Tis Mythang started playing "Stretch Out" at twice its normal speed. Of course, since they were already on their feet and did not want to be embarrassed, both the reverend and the bishop started doing a church shout. They pranced around like they were under the anointing while lifting their hands in praise. If their hallelujahs had been sincere, they could've gotten applause from all the angels and the Lord himself.

When Brother Tis Mythang thought he had punished them enough, particularly since they were panting and blowing out of breath, he stopped playing.

Reverend Knott Enuff Money was dripping sweat and Jheri curl juice, which dimmed the shimmer from his new robe. He was seething and made a mental note to dock the choir director's pay and whatever else he could think of to get back at him.

Bishop Was Nevercalled, although still out of breath and clasping his chest, managed to start his eulogy. His theme was "Don't Let Worry Kill You Off, Let the Church Help." He threw his head back to throw out his best preaching whoop and then screamed, "Mother Eternal Everlastin' was a *working* woman when she was at the Ain't Nobody Else Right But Us—All Others Goin' to Hell Church."

The Reverend Bling Moe Bling jumped up out his seat, released the kickstand that was supporting his bad leg, reached over and patted the bishop on the back. As he did it, he got excited and hollered, "Didn't she know how to work it!"

The bishop, still mad from the earlier slight made by the Reverend Bling Moe Bling and particularly his wife, shrugged the reverend's hands off his shoulder and that's when suddenly a white silk, frilly handkerchief magically appeared in his hand. He looked up toward the ceiling and tossed the handkerchief up in the air. He caught it as it came down and hollered, "Mother Eternal Everlastin' is finally going on home to be with the Lord."

Brother Tis Mythang, playful as ever, couldn't help it. He started playing the 5th Dimension's hit "Up, Up and Away."

The bishop, trying in vain to ignore him, used the handkerchief to wipe his bald head while he geared up to whoop some more. He clutched the sides of the podium, shaking his shoulders from side to side. He moaned, "Y'all can go ahead and moan awhile for Mother. She certainly moaned for a plenty of folks while she occupied this church's moaners bench over in the corner. She really knew how to moan before she moved her membership over to that little storefront church, which ended up being her demise." He looked back at Sister Bertha Bling to make sure she got his gist.

She got it, and she would make sure that he got it later. She extended her middle finger and pretended to examine the nail polish on it for emphasis.

The bishop certainly got her gist but he was on a roll and wouldn't be stopped by a finger with or without polish. "Yes, y'all heard me. Go ahead and moan for the woman who sat for years on that moaners' bench."

Brother Tis Mythang quickly lifted one hand to start the choir who responded to the obvious tension cloaking the pulpit with a rousing gospel version of James Brown's "Get Up Offa That Thang."

The bishop was not amused, and being a closet fan of the younger generation's television program *106 and Park,* he glared at Brother Tis Mythang, and forgetting where he was he told him he'd better "Back that thang up." Realizing that everyone in the first ten rows probably heard him, he added, "Because you know, praise God, sometimes it's good to go back and redo that thang."

Of course, he wasn't making any sense, but he seldom did. About an hour into the eulogy, the music started sounding more like a jammin' oldies music hour than a funeral service.

Intermingled with the eulogy came whispered remarks from the congregation. They said everything from "I wish he'd just shut up!" to "Lord, just kill me so I can be like Mother Eternal Everlastin' and not hear that man's voice."

The bishop finally surrendered to the negative vibes he felt being thrown his way and brought the funeral service to a close. "Well, I'm gonna close out this eulogy, but I have a question for y'all. Those of y'all sitting out there sucking on Life Savers, is your life saved? If you was to get one of them stuck in your throat, right now, would you be prepared to meet your God like Mother Eternal Ann Everlastin' when she was overcome from the sensation of that York peppermint patty and died? Where you gonna be when the Lord come for you?"

Brother Tis Mythang was getting sick and tired of the bishop so he interrupted him and replied, "At the rate you going we gonna be still sitting right here!"

The bishop was about to say something that would've surely kept him out of Heaven, so instead, he smiled like he had enjoyed the comical rebuke. Of course, he forgot that he had not stuck to the program. Sister Betty had not read the obituary nor had anyone, except a few of the members from No Hope Now—Mercy Neva Church gotten up to make any remarks about Mother Eternal Everlastin,' nor had anyone read the many sympathy cards or floral acknowledgments. He had totally rewritten the program.

The funeral director, Mr. Bury Em Deep stood and motioned for Shaqueeda to take her seat next to Sister Betty and Ma Cile. He wasn't too worried about Buddy because Buddy was still knocked out or at the very least, he was quiet. The fact that the usher, Sister Mentol Kase, was still keeping her eye on him probably had a lot to do with his silence.

Mr. Bury Em Deep then called for the deacons Luke and Warm to come and open the upper half of the gold-plated coffin while the congregation, with the exception of those on the front pew, rose. He raised his hand and then he beckoned the people to file by and take one last look at the colorful floral-laden coffin containing Mother Eternal Everlastin's remains. He also told them to try and avoid getting slapped in the face or on the body by the blue flamingo feathers that by now looked like a bird caught in a metal trap.

Just then a powerful yet raspy voice whispered in Sister Betty's ear, "How's they gonna end the funeral when I ain't said my piece?" whispered Ma Cile, clenching her teeth as people passed by her trying to avoid looking at her bad eye and the blue flamingo feathers. "I told them ushers I had somethin' I wanted to say before I went to use the bathroom. I thought they would've at least call on me after the bishop finished lyin' all through his eulogy."

Oh no! Sister Betty thought. She figured Ma Cile had completely forgotten about giving her inappropriate recollection and that perhaps her snuff buzzes had worn off. She didn't know what to do.

Fidgeting around in her seat did not help Sister Betty come any closer to a solution. If anything, it made one of the ushers, Brother Willy, rush to her side to bring her a fan and a single tissue.

Ma Cile took advantage of Brother Willy's arrival. After he also threw a fan and a tissue at her, Ma Cile tapped him on the shoulder as he attempted to leave. When Brother Willy turned to respond, instead of looking into Ma Cile's good brown eye, the one that he thought she was looking at him with, he looked directly into her false blue one. Of course, that particular eye, unable to see, was looking past him and was focused on another mourner.

Brother Willy abruptly took off to help the other mourner who looked at Brother Willy like he was trying to assault her as he threw her a fan and a tissue. The woman suddenly started screaming and everyone thought that she was just overcome with emotion and ignored her.

However, Ma Cile was not about to give up. She started to rise to go after him, and that's when Sister Betty got an idea. She caught Ma Cile's hand and gently pulled her back into her seat.

"Ma Cile, wait," Sister Betty gently pleaded. "You know there's gonna be a feast after the service, and folks want to hurry up so they can all go back into the dining room and eat all that delicious food that it took us so long to make this morning. As a matter of fact, isn't that Brother Lead Belly sitting on the last pew near the doorway to the dining room? I bet you he probably smells those pig feet fajitas you cooked."

Sister Betty would have continued with her whispered pleadings but the pig feet fajitas clinched it. Everyone knew those were one of Ma Cile's favorite foods. She would have stopped the bus leaving for Heaven to take a bite out of a pig foot fajita.

"You right, Sister Betty," Ma Cile replied. Suddenly she almost forgot about the funeral of one of her good friends and was about to pass out just thinking about devouring an extra large pig foot fajita. She could almost taste it drenched with jalapeño peppers and Uncle Buster's Combustible Hot Sauce, washed down by a tall glass of iced vinegar water to cut the fat. She knew she was a bit heavy and was trying to watch her weight. Her problem was that she couldn't wait to eat.

Ma Cile turned around and tossed a wicked look toward Brother Lead Belly. A look that said, *If you thinkin' about eating one of my pig feet, you'd better think again or there'll be another funeral this afternoon.*

Of course, Brother Lead Belly thought Ma Cile was looking past him because just like the usher, he, too, was looking at her false blue eye. He continued staring innocently into space, deep in thought, never realizing that if he ate a pig foot fajita, he could die.

It was time for Sister Betty, Shaqueeda and Ma Cile, to rise and take a final look at their dear friend, Mother Eternal Ann Everlastin'.

Sister Betty pushed the fanning flamingo feathers aside as she reached into the coffin and caressed a face that only a few days ago had the softness of life. It was now hard with a grayish pallor, and she could hardly believe that it was the same face she'd looked into so many times over the years. She felt a bit unsteady and held on to the white satin lining that billowed from the inside of the coffin. The realization started seeping into the very core of her being that it would be the last time that she would lay eyes upon Mother Eternal Ann Everlastin'.

Sister Betty leaned over and with tears that seemed to flood both inside of her and out, she whispered, "Mother, you've been one of the best things that has happened to me since I left Statesville. My beautiful friend, you save a seat for me, and don't you fret none about going out the way you did. I know you and the Lord probably gonna have a good laugh about it on the judgment day." Another tear fell. As if it were trying to soften the hardness of the face, the tear seemed to gently kiss it as it inched its way down one cheek. "I'm gonna miss you. I love you . . ." Sister Betty could not continue. It was too much. All she could do was to ball up the soggy tissue in her hand so hard until it threatened to pop a vein and hold on to the side of the coffin with the other.

Ma Cile couldn't take it. She gestured for one of the ushers to come over. In the meantime, she gently tried to persuade Sister Betty to move away from the coffin. "Come on, Sister Betty. You know Mother gonna be mad at you if you make a scene." Ma Cile tried to muster a smile but her heart was breaking too. She'd seen the look on her best friend's face when Sister Betty felt the hardness of Mother Eternal Ann Everlastin's flesh. A flesh that was, once so soft and so beautiful.

Ma Cile waited until Brother Willy had escorted Sister Betty back to the pew and then she stepped forward. She leaned over, parted a few of the flamingo feathers for a good look, but she did not touch the body. She had not touched another dead body since her husband, Charlie, had passed away many years ago. She could never bring herself to do it. Instead, she just looked down at Mother and all the blue flamingo feathers and the flamingo feet that had managed to peek out from the side of Mother's hat. The sight of the flamingo feet bought a wide smile to Ma Cile's face. "Lawd have mercy. Mother ya sho know how to leave out in style. I'm gonna miss you somethin' terrible. I know you probably gonna save a seat fo' Sister Betty." She stopped and hung her head. Tears started to pour and a few of the tears looked like they were coming from her false eye. Ma Cile's ample bosom started to heave as she took a breath after each word. "If I promise not to bring my snuff to Heaven, would ya mind saving a seat for me too?"

Ma Cile quickly patted the satin lining of the coffin as if it were hot and returned to her place beside Sister Betty. She grabbed Sister Betty's hand and the two of them didn't speak but each heart knew the ache of the other.

After Sister Betty and the other mourners finished passing by the coffin and paying their final respects, the ushers, led by Sister Mentol Kase, got together and headed toward the front pew where Mother

Eternal Everlastin's drunken and still unconscious nephew, Buddy, had somehow managed to fall over next to a potted plant. They agreed that he still looked as potted as the plant. The ushers clasped hands and threw him from one to the other as they passed him by the coffin until they finally dumped him right back in the same spot where they'd picked him up.

The funeral director, Brother Bury Em Deep, simply shook his head in amusement and took a business card from his jacket pocket. He placed it in Buddy's torn pants pocket and whispered, "I'll be seeing you real soon. If you let us serve you, there is a ten percent discount because you were family."

While everyone stood, Brother Tis Mythang led the choir in another song, and the church waited for the pallbearers to pick up the coffin.

The midget was holding the biggest floral arrangement, which he threatened to drop because several of those flamingo feathers were still peeking out of the closed coffin. Every step he took a feather tickled him under his chin. He tried to wiggle and squirmed to avoid them. Instead, the feathers assaulted him and so did the nasty glares from those who thought he was being very disrespectful. He sucked in, enduring the tickling from the feathers. He prayed he'd make it to the door and back into the safety of the suburbs.

Finally the pulpit came down to lead the way. Of course, no funeral would be complete if there wasn't more drama at the end.

Sister Bertha Bling was still mad because not only had she not been able to speak when the bishop so abruptly ended the funeral, she never had a chance to do her whoop. She'd been practicing for months, behind her husband's back, because she, too, wanted to preach. She thought Mother's funeral was the perfect occasion for a trial sermon performance. She also figured that if her husband, Reverend Bling Moe Bling, could do it after getting the call from God on his cell phone, she could most certainly do the same. However, since the hour was late, she was willing to let bygones be bygones until she overheard the Reverend Knott Enuff Money tell her husband that the Ain't Nobody Else Right But Us—All Others Goin' to Hell Church expected a donation for opening their doors for someone who was no longer a member of the church. He had in mind to get as much money from them as he could since all he had for his troubles was one unsigned check.

And then, it was all over but the whoop!

"You crazy!" Sister Bertha Bling turned around and kicked the latch off her husband's kickstand, which caused his bad leg to fall forward. Instead of helping her husband to put the bad leg back onto the kickstand so he wouldn't fall over onto the bishop, she grabbed the kickstand with both hands. There were only about two or three feet between her and the Reverend Knott Enuff Money but it might as well have been an inch. She jumped on him with that kickstand like she was stomping the first roach to appear when the kitchen light came on. "You ain't gonna insult my church or me and my husband no more."

The reverend ducked to the side of the pulpit. "You crazy too! If you think I ain't gonna get paid, then you a bigger fool than your husband!" The Reverend Knott Enuff Money whipped his Dracula-looking robe behind his back and snatched one of the flamingo feathers that peeked out from the rear of Mother Eternal Ann Everlastin's coffin. He took a fencing stance with one hand, and with the other, he held the tail of his robe behind him. And whether he meant to or not, he started swinging that flamingo feather at Sister Bertha Bling.

A flamingo feather versus a wooden kickstand. There was only one way it could've ended.

By the time Sister Bertha Bling got finished explaining the futility of fighting with a feather against a wooden stool, the reverend looked more like a patched-up Frankenstein than a suave Dracula. Everywhere that stool landed on him, it left a big red welt. His face looked like an old road map as the veins angrily puffed up from his forehead down to his chin.

The bishop had decided to take advantage of all the chaos and was spurned on by Brother Tis Mythang playing a Nelly hit, "Hot in Herre." He took his foot and knocked the bad foot from under Reverend Bling Moe Bling, which caused him to fall forward. Reverend Bling Moe Bling banged his head and fell out, unconscious, right next to Buddy who hadn't moved, with the exception of someone else moving him since Sister Mentol Kase had introduced him to her Knock-'em-out tribe.

In the meanwhile, Sister Bertha Bling had caught the beating of her husband out of the corner of her eye. She turned her attention from the Reverend Knott Enuff Money to the bishop. It wasn't that she was trying to protect her husband, it was because she had some unfinished business with the bishop. She was getting a little winded from fighting with the Reverend Knott Enuff Money, so she just snuck up behind the bishop then knocked him out with the remains of the kickstand.

Now three bodies lay there next to the potted plant, which was becoming more popular than the corner seat over in the deacons section where most of them sat and slept during the service.

When Bertha Bling looked around to finish her fight with the Reverend Knott Enuff Money, he was being escorted away by the usher, Brother Willy. She would've enjoyed her triumph a lot more if she hadn't spied two of Pelzer's finest. They were racing down the aisle toward the pulpit, and they weren't coming for the service. Each had a pair of handcuffs in one hand while the other hand was on the butt of their pistols, which poked out from their holsters.

Sister Bertha Bling turned to run but Sister Mentol Kase who stood between her and the potted plant blocked her. She sneaked a peek at the usher's blazing eyes. The usher stood lopsided with her prescription shoe protruding and ready to drop-kick her. The way Sister Mentol Kase wielded that flashlight signaled Sister Bertha Bling would be safer with the police.

Sister Bertha Bling saved the policemen time by racing toward them. She was waving one of her white tissues to signal surrender.

As the police led Sister Bertha Bling away, they were stopped by Sister Betty. "Officers, please, we're here for a funeral and we need someone from the deceased's church to say something at the burial. If you take the first lady, Sister Bertha Bling, then we'll have no one because the others are laying over there potted—"

"That's right!" Sister Bertha Bling exclaimed as she wiggled her hands inside the handcuffs. "I'm all they have."

Mr. Bury Em Deep rushed over to Sister Betty's side. He stepped between Sister Bertha Bling, Sister Betty and the policemen. "Oh, don't worry about who's gonna speak at the burial. Mother Eternal Ann Everlastin' left instructions for that too. I'll be doing the speaking."

"Why would it be you?" Sister Betty asked with suspicion.

"Yeah, why would she want you to speak for her? You don't know nothing about her." Sister Bertha Bling was beginning to see her freedom slip away so she calmed down enough to use a little diplomacy. "She paid for a beautiful funeral, and I'm sure she hadn't planned on only having the funeral director speak on her behalf at the burial with both her pastor and first lady in attendance."

"She paid a ton of money for a grand funeral, yet it's me speaking on her behalf at the burial because Mother Eternal Ann Everlastin' knew that the leaders of both churches would no doubt show out at her funeral. She left instructions for me to have the police on standby so there wouldn't be too much time taken up for nonsense at her funeral." He stood there with each hand holding on to a collar tip while he rose up and down on the heels of his shoes. He was very proud of his oration abilities.

"You mean, she took care of everything and we don't need any of these folks?" Sister Betty asked, pointing to both Sister Bertha and the potted tree club. A smile took the place of concern, and she told the police, "Well then, officers, take her away, and we'll see about getting some help for those three over there if they haven't come to when we come back from the They All Dyin' to Git Here Cemetery." She was led away.

With all the noise that was going on, the bishop and Buddy never awoke but the Reverend Bling Moe Bling had come to. With help from someone who was standing near the potted plant to get a better view of the happenings, he rose.

The Reverend Bling Moe Bling limped behind the police, using the end backrest of each pew. He could see that they had Sister Bertha in tow, along with his shattered wooden kickstand for evidence. He stayed a safe distance away so she wouldn't see him. He was determined to ride in one of the limos to the cemetery. If she saw him, then he'd have to ride in the same lead car as Mother Eternal Ann Everlastin'—flamingo feathers, feet and all. He had to give it to Sister Bertha. She sure was feisty. She was screaming loud enough to wake up Mother Eternal Ann Everlastin' from her eternal rest.

The funeral procession filed outside and after deciding who rode in what limo, they got into the many cars and prepared for the ride to the cemetery.

Sister Bertha Bling was in a car too—a police car. From the inside of it, she got a chance to watch all the long, sleek black limos line up to leave without her, and if she wasn't so sure that her husband was still knocked out inside the church, she could've sworn that she saw him riding in one of the limos. As soon as she could arrange bail, she'd be back, and they needed to be afraid—very afraid.

Mother Eternal Ann Everlastin' had planned everything down to the last little detail but just like the old saying goes, "while you're making plans, life happens."

And, life would've gone on just fine if it weren't for the fact that although Mother Eternal Ann Everlastin' had been laid to rest, she left many folks upset with her. They couldn't get to her since she died so abruptly, but it wouldn't stop them from trying to get to her apparent heir, the drunken nephew Buddy, and what better place to do so than at the after-funeral get-together party.

10

Ain't No Party Like an Afta-Life Party

As usual, Mother Eternal Ann Everlastin' even had her way in death at the cemetery. The service was short and to the point, and nothing was mentioned that didn't reflect a positive note on her life. It went on without the usual graveyard drama—no one fell into the grave and no one tried to throw anyone in it either. Of course, when the last mound of dirt was tossed on the grave and all the floral arrangements set up according to Mother's instructions, it looked like a gaggle of blue-feathered flamingos were nesting.

The Reverend Knott Enuff Money, the Bishop Was Nevercalled, along with Sister Betty and Ma Cile, rode back to the church in a black stretch limousine. Mother Eternal Ann Everlastin' made sure that she put in her funeral plans that Ma Cile and Sister Betty should ride in style at least once; however, as clever as she was, she forgot to put down in the plan that she didn't want either the Reverend Knott Enuff Money or the bishop to step foot in her car, so they hopped in one side, and when they weren't shoved out through the open sunroof or kicked out the other side, they lay back and rested.

The ride back to the church was quiet with the exception of a soft hum from the car's air conditioner. Both Ma Cile and Sister Betty, tired from the activities of the past few days and the funeral, napped head to head while holding hands.

The Reverend Knott Enuff Money spent the entire ride trying to get information about the rest of Mother Eternal Ann Everlastin's plans from Mr. Bury Em Deep. "I know that you know more than what you're saying. If she planned this funeral with you then I know she also told you about what would happen to her fortune when she passed."

Mr. Bury Em Deep ignored the urgent pleas from the reverend and, instead, told the driver to drive faster. He needed to drop everyone off at the church and get back to the Last Stop funeral parlor. There were two more funerals that had to be done that day, and he was late.

"Listen, Mr. Bury Em Deep, if you play ball with me, I'll play ball with you. I can make sure that the entire Mothers Board and the Elder Royal Priesthood members use your funeral services when their time comes."

"How you gonna do that?" Mr. Bury Em Deep asked. The reverend now had his attention.

"They'll do what I tell them to do. As a matter of fact, I can tell them that the bishop here has also preplanned his funeral and will be using your economical and professional services—"

The bishop cut him off. "Why me? How come you ain't gonna use his services when you die?"

"Did I say that I wouldn't use his service?" The Reverend Knott Enuff Money forgot that the bishop who was not as quick as he should've been in matters of deceit was sitting next to him. "Of course, I will preplan my funeral, but I just ain't worked out all the details yet." He turned away from the bishop and back to Mr. Bury Em Deep. "Do we understand each other?" he asked.

"My mind is telling me to get that in writing from you. But, if you cross me, I'll make sure that you get the cheapest coffin made out of plywood with termite eggs embedded and pay the most money for it when you die," Mr. Bury Em Deep replied. "And you can be sure that I'll bury you bald 'cause you ain't fooling nobody with that cheap wig."

The degrading reference to his Jheri curl did it. "I've got hair!"

"No, you don't! What you got is what you bought. I ain't stupid or blind. That dried-up thing on your head is a number 2203 Ebony Maybe. That rug runs for about $39.99 from Mizz Lo Down's Weave It and Achieve It Hair Emporium." Mr. Bury Em Deep stopped to let his words sink in before continuing, "Now, what you don't have are the details to Mother Eternal Ann Everlastin's instructions for the disbursement of her money!"

Reality revisited the Reverend Knott Enuff Money like a bad credit report. He started talking fast, with words shooting out like his mouth was a nine millimeter gun. "Okay. You-got-me. I got a bad haircut from Shaqueeda's and I had to run out and buy a hair-piece." He stopped and took a deep breath before continuing to fire off the unconvincing lies. "Mizz Lo Down didn't have what I needed, so instead, I bought this hairpiece." He was so good at lying, with the exception of taking a pause to breathe, he didn't even flinch.

Oh, he's good, the bishop thought as a smile crept across his pale face.

"Whatever," Mr. Bury Em Deep replied. He didn't have time for any of the reverend's games, but he did need the business. "My understanding is that Mother Eternal Ann Everlastin' left a lot of her wealth behind distributed in checks, some endorsed and some not; some delivered and some to be delivered to several people. Those who received the endorsed checks are free to cash them and do what they want. For those who got checks that were not endorsed, well, they will have to deal with her nephew, Buddy, because they'll need his signature to make those checks valid." Suddenly Mr. Bury Em Deep started to giggle. "You do remember that you tossed Buddy out of your church some time back? Unless, you've gotten a check or you think you'll be getting one, whether you deserve one or not, I guess you've got some serious fence-mending of the butt-kissing variety to do."

The reverend pondered the new revelation and nodded at the bishop, signaling that the bishop should remain quiet.

In the meantime, inside the limo, both Ma Cile and Sister Betty finally woke up. "I'm glad we took a little nap," Ma Cile said and yawned as she straightened her hat, which had fallen to the side.

Sister Betty pushed away from Ma Cile, using her elbow to do it. She sat up straight and yawned until she thought her mouth would tear. She hadn't realized just how tired she was and then the reason for her tiredness and sadness reappeared. She shook off the sadness with a whispered praise to God and replied, "I'm glad we took a nap, too, Ma Cile."

As the limousine turned the corner of Redemption Avenue the large cross on the church's steeple suddenly came into view. "I see we're back at the church." Sister Betty craned her neck to see how many cars were still in the church's parking lot. "I'm glad there's still a lot of people who stayed at the church. I imagine they've already started eating and celebrating Mother's going on home."

The reverend and the bishop rushed out of the car, past Mr. Bury Em Deep, without saying good-bye. They didn't bother to help Ma Cile who was having a hard time maneuvering her wide hips to get out the car. "I must've swollen up while I slept," she murmured. "I don't remember having such a hard time getting in here." She forgot that when she got into the car, she did it head first. This time she was trying to back out.

Sister Betty remained for another moment to thank Mr. Bury Em Deep for all the care he showed in putting away Mother Eternal Ann Everlastin'. "I'm sure she would've loved every moment of this day, especially since she was the star." She tried to add a little levity to the moment.

"Well, she certainly got what she paid for. And, I wish most folks were like her—"

"You mean make their plans ahead of time?" Sister Betty thought she'd finish his sentence.

"No. I wish most folks would pay ahead of time." Irritation suddenly replaced his caring manner. "I get tired of folks either not having enough insurance or they have to wait until either the first or the fifteenth of the month, and don't get me started on how they have to wait to see if the church is gonna kick in a little cash." He would've kept up his complaints but the short honk of the horn from the driver reminded him that they needed to leave. "I hope to see you soon, Sister Betty. It's been a pleasure."

I hope it won't be too soon, she thought, but instead replied, "Have a blessed day." Sister Betty turned around and caught up with Ma Cile who seemed to be in an extra hurry. "Wait up, Ma Cile. Why are you rushing?"

Ma Cile mumbled something but all Sister Betty could hear was "pig foot fajita."

She moved a little faster to make sure that Ma Cile did not get inside the church's dining room and cause a scene.

11

Money Cometh in a Hurry

While Mother Eternal Ann Everlastin' was being laid to rest back at the cemetery, there were quite a few who had attended the funeral service and just as many who had not, but just didn't feel like cooking at home. They all came together and went downstairs to eat. Many of the people were packed, five deep, inside the church's spacious dining room. Elevator music played softly in the background for the first hour. Once that time had passed, several got up and started dancing the Electric Slide while saying it was the Holy Cha-Cha slide to those who were truly saved. It was the part of the home-going celebration that they loved the best.

Church folks just love to dance for whatever reason.

In between the noisy slurping of delicious foods, where they served everything from the succulent fried chicken with rice and gravy to the okra-laden jambalaya surrounded by buttermilk biscuits so light they could've almost floated, everyone continued with their reflections and tales of what Mother Eternal Ann Everlastin' had meant—or in some cases didn't mean—to them.

There was one table that sat in a far corner of the dining room away from the holy merrymakers. That was where Sister Betty and Ma Cile chose to sit and grab another much-needed breath. On the way to the table, Ma Cile had jumped the line at the buffet and no one tried to stop her or said anything as she filled her plate with food. While Ma Cile feasted on a huge platter of pig feet fajitas, Sister Betty thought back about the funeral and hoped Mother Eternal Everlastin', wherever she was, was truly satisfied. Sister Betty also scolded herself for not insisting on getting up to say something at the service.

Sister Betty thought about how strange it was that she was about the same age as Mother Eternal Everlastin', and although a lot poorer, apparently she was in better health. She chuckled a little to herself as she thought about the true meaning of being rich or poor. She was on a fixed income and yet she felt all the more richer for having Christ in her life.

It was moments of reflections like those that truly kept her grounded. On the other hand, it hadn't been that long ago when Mother Eternal Ann Everlastin' had Sister Betty hold on to one of her bank books. It was during a time when she felt that perhaps she was spending either too much money or giving away too much. When she showed Sister Betty how much money was in that one particular bank book, Sister Betty had never seen so many zeros in front of a decimal point. In her bank book they were mostly behind it. Little did Buddy know it, but whenever they got around to reading Mother Eternal Ann Everlastin's will, he would be a very wealthy young man. She hoped he would not drink away such a gift.

Sister Betty continued to be remorseful because she had not spoken up. She wanted to speak to Ma Cile about it, but between the loud chewing of pig feet fajitas dripping with jalapeño peppers and Uncle Charlie's Combustible Hot Sauce she was devouring and quite possibly the secret dip of the snuff, conversation was out of the question. Sister Betty continued to ponder about life's lessons when a soft voice interrupted her thoughts.

"May I sit here with you, Sister Betty? And, how are you, Ma Cile?"

Sister Betty recognized the voice even before she looked up. It was their district councilman, Mr. Hippo Crit, who was also an attorney. He was, as usual, meticulously dressed in a black suit that fitted his wide shoulders better than any coat hanger. He was very tall, cinnamon-colored, and looked like he could've doubled for Denzel Washington better than Denzel could.

"Yes, you may sit here," Sister Betty replied as she pointed to an empty seat, which held her and Ma Cile's pocketbooks. "I don't remember seeing you at the funeral," she added.

Ma Cile only nodded a greeting. Only the reappearance of Mother Eternal Ann Everlastin' herself would keep her from her food.

"I was there, but there was so much going on. I must say that new usher—Sister Mentol Kase, I believe that was her name—she packed quite a wallop. I figured I'd better hang around the service; Buddy might've wanted to sue. Anyway, Sister Betty, we need to talk about a personal matter. Can you come to my office around nine o'clock Monday morning?"

"For what reason?" Sister Betty asked suspiciously. She liked Councilman Hippo Crit, and he'd helped them out in a few crises, but she did not always trust him.

He slid his chair over closer to Sister Betty's and out of Ma Cile's hearing. "You have to promise me that you won't say a word to anyone. It's about Mother Eternal Everlastin's will."

"About what?" Sister Betty was stunned. She didn't think a long friendship and holding on to a bankbook for a while would cause Mother Eternal Everlasting to leave her anything. Everything she did was done out of the goodness of her heart and because that's what God would want her to do. To be of service to others was its own reward, she always thought and believed.

The councilman saw the puzzled look on Sister Betty's face. He looked over at Ma Cile to see if she had gotten the hint to leave. She had not. "It's okay, Sister Betty. There's nothing wrong." Since it looked to him that apparently, Ma Cile was drowning her sorrows in a platter of food and wasn't paying attention, he continued, "I can't tell you everything now but I can tell you this. Mother Eternal Ann Everlastin' even in her death is still depending upon you. She will need you to leave Pelzer for just a little while."

The councilman stopped and looked around again. "It appears that the folks from Mother Eternal Ann Everlastin's church have already left. I need to catch up with their pastor." He laughed quietly and added, "I guess if I go down to central booking, I can probably find him there with the first lady. It should be very interesting to see what happens when they come face-to-face since I noticed that the Reverend Bling Moe Bling didn't go downtown with her when the police took her away."

Before Sister Betty could wrap her mind around what he'd said and she could ask another question, Councilman Hippo Crit had excused himself and was up and out the door.

Ma Cile had finally finished eating. She was burping and speaking at the same time. With every word, out came the smell of pig and hot sauce. "Did he say leave Pelzer? Ain't that what he said?" She ate with her mouth, not with her ears. She'd overheard bits and pieces of the private conversation. "Ooh, Sister Betty, you gonna take me with you, ain't ya? Imagine that, Mother Eternal Ann Everlastin' still needs us to do something, even after she gone, she still needs us." Ma Cile was beyond excited and rewriting Mother Eternal Ann Everlastin's instructions to include herself. It was all Sister Betty could do besides find another pig feet fajita to stick in her mouth to quiet her.

"Ma Cile. Hush. Didn't you hear Councilman Hippo Crit? We can't say anything to nobody until Monday morning. You got to promise me you aren't going to tell nobody. Another thing he said, I might be leaving Pelzer for a little while not we might be going."

Ma Cile completely ignored Sister Betty's clarification of what was said. "I can't take Li'l Bit and June Bug with us. I'll see if Shaqueeda can keep them with her." Ma Cile suddenly lost her appetite. She was so excited that she completely ignored the fact that the will was to be read to Sister Betty and not her.

The thought of taking Ma Cile on a trip was scary enough; taking Li'l Bit and June Bug was too close to lunacy. She was grateful that Ma Cile at least had the foresight to realize that. If she'd only realized that the invitation wasn't for her then everything would've been fine.

Sister Betty just kept quiet and listened to Ma Cile go on and on. It was going to be a long weekend.

On the other side of the dining room there sat another lonely figure. He had his head down, cradled in his hands with his shoulders heaving. "She sure was a lovely person. I'm going to miss her," Reverend Knott Enuff Money said, weeping and lifting his head toward the ceiling and speaking loudly to no one in particular. He suddenly dropped his head, which caused a few loose strands of his Jheri curl tresses to land in a glass of lemonade. Of course, unbeknown to him, the acid from the lemonade immediately frizzed up the ends of his hair, but he had other things on his mind. With greed riding him like a witch on a broom, sweeping sympathy out of the way, he quietly added under his breath, "I've got to get that check signed."

He tried once more to summon a little compassion, and only a little came. "That old lady certainly knew the true and biblical meaning of giving. I'm gonna miss her!" He stifled a pretend sob as he looked around the church's dining hall.

The bishop had gone around to greet a few people who had stayed behind from the funeral. He did it to get some feedback on his delivery of the eulogy. He refused to believe that he actually heard people saying that they wished he'd shut up.

There was no one near the Reverend Knott Enuff Money to hear his insincere lament, so he decided to save the phony tears for another time. He was determined to get that unsigned check signed and to have a new Jacuzzi put into his church for baptisms.

"Mother Eternal Everlastin' would have to die before she endorsed that check!" This time he cried, with sincerity, "Oh why? Why did you leave me, Mother?" The ushers, including Brother Willy and others on his pastors aid committee, would have normally ran over to comfort him, but they were eating. So, again, he lamented alone, but not for long.

Reverend Knott Enuff Money needed a plan. Perhaps, the Reverend and Most Righteous All Aboutme could help. After all, that man knew quality, and he certainly knew money and all of its sources; he also knew low people in high places. He would probably live to regret it, but he was going to need the assistance of Brother Tis Mythang to help him win Buddy over.

The Reverend Knott Enuff Money's new mantra was now "Money, cometh in a hurry."

12

Wee, Cheatem and How

When Monday morning rolled around, Sister Betty was still exhausted. She couldn't seem to get her strength back. Even after much prayer and especially asking God to forgive her for questioning His ways, she was still somewhat numb from Mother Eternal Ann Everlastin' death.

Sister Betty showered and then ate a light breakfast of deep-fried, peanut-battered catfish with a dab of cheesy grits and diet peach-flavored tea. Sister Betty went over in her mind the disturbing conversation she'd had with the Councilman Hippo Crit. She stopped pondering long enough to wash her breakfast dishes before she called Ma Cile to make sure that she was ready for what lay ahead that day.

Sister Betty went to her favorite spot beside her living room couch and knelt for a few moments. She moaned a little and she meditated a little. When she finally found her voice, she again asked God for strength and above all, for an understanding of what was going on. Crying out to God lately had been hard since Mother Eternal Ann Everlastin's rather odd way of dying, and she was concerned that He was going to leave her in the dark again about His will. Apparently, God was not ready to share His plan. So, without her usual vision from God, she rose. She called Ma Cile who had nagged her into letting her go to the law office with her, and then she waited for a taxi to arrive.

She heard a car honking, so she grabbed her shawl, her family-sized Bible and went outside. Instead of a taxi, she was surprised to find that it was Tiny, Mother Eternal Ann Everlastin's chauffeur.

"Good morning, Sister Betty." He opened the back door, took the Bible from her hand and then helped her climb inside. "I know this must be a big surprise for you to see me still doing my duties for Mother Eternal Ann Everlastin'."

"Well, I must say, I'm definitely surprised." Sister Betty was more surprised than she let on because Tiny was not wearing his chauffeur uniform. He basically wore the same type of outfit that he wore when he delivered Buddy to the funeral. "I don't want to seem ungrateful, but why are you still driving the limo?"

"Well, you know Mother Eternal Ann Everlastin' always believed in getting her money's worth."

"Yes, she sure did." Sister Betty had to laugh at that remark because up until the time she died, Mother Eternal Ann Everlastin' still had the first divorce settlement check from her first deceased husband, Deacon Myzer. She had kept it to let folks know that she'd been paid enough money not to take any guff from anyone—and she never did. "But, Mr. Tiny what does that have to do with you continuing to drive this limo and picking me up?"

Tiny closed the door to the limo after Sister Betty was seated comfortably in the back then climbed behind the wheel. He started the engine then turned to face Sister Betty. He had just a hint of anger covering his words as he answered, "Mother Eternal Ann Everlastin' had a verbal agreement that she would always pay me a month in advance. She thought she was doing me a favor to make sure that I was always around, and I certainly needed the money. Well, she had just paid me for next month when she died. And, you better believe that Mother had it all worked out that, no matter what, I would work out any advance salary paid to me."

"Now, I know she was thorough, but was she that thorough?" Sister Betty asked. She finally had a reason to laugh as she tried to take it all in. Her friend didn't miss a trick. She had everything covered from her funeral to still running things after she died. "My goodness, I'm gonna miss that woman something terrible." Sister Betty chuckled.

"I guess in my own way, I'm gonna miss her too," Tiny said quietly, "but at least she and I didn't discuss what I would wear if it came down to me finishing out my duties under unusual circumstances. I've never felt so relaxed and at ease; although, I still feel a little sad that some of the last things she and I said to each other last Sunday were not very pleasant."

Sister Betty laughed and said, "Oh, I'm sure Mother Eternal Ann Everlastin' ain't still mad about that where she is now."

Tiny looked in the rearview mirror and caught Sister Betty's attention. He laughed as they both said at the same time, "She's still mad!"

The conversation during the rest of the way to Ma Cile's house was lighthearted. Neither Sister Betty nor Tiny could figure out what exactly her role would be in whatever plans Mother had left to be carried out.

Ma Cile busied herself with tidying her parlor and making sure that all her windows and doors were shut before going outside to wait on the porch for Sister Betty. She was excited about the possibility of leaving Pelzer on a little trip for a short while but was sad that it had to be at the expense of Mother Eternal Ann Everlastin'.

She'd sent her grandchildren, Li'l Bit and June Bug over to Shaqueeda's to play with Shaqueeda's five children until she returned. The way Ma Cile had it figured out, Shaqueeda's was the best place for them to be since there were so many other children there and plus, she knew that Shaqueeda would slap them upside their heads with hair rollers if they got out of line. Ma Cile laughed at that thought. *How hard could a pair of soft rollers be?* She didn't have time to think on it much longer because a limo was pulling up in front of her house.

It took Ma Cile a few seconds of tapping her forehead as she tried to line up her good brown eye with the false blue one to see that it was Tiny in the driver's seat. He was driving Mother Eternal Ann Everlastin's limo with Sister Betty in the back.

After letting her rocker rock back and forth several times, she was able to extricate her wide hips from its grip. She came down the stairs, stepping like a sidewinder snake, from side to side until she reached the bottom. "Sister Betty! What are you doing in this big ole car with Mr. Tiny? How come this looks like one of Mother Eternal Ann Everlastin's big cars?" She stooped down and poked her head through the open back window and gave Tiny a nasty look. "Oh, I see. You just gonna up and wait until my friend die and then you just gonna take over her fancy car. You ought to be skinned alive—" She paused and looked over to the other side to see a look of surprise on Sister Betty's face. Of course, Ma Cile mistook the look of surprise as one of fear. "What you do to Sister Betty? Did you make her git in this fancy car?"

Ma Cile was about to heave her hefty girth around to the driver's side where Tiny sat looking very much like the coward that only Ma Cile could make a man feel.

Sister Betty recovered first. "Ma Cile, please calm down. Mr. Tiny is here to drive us because that's what Mother Eternal Ann Everlastin' wanted him to do for us. You do remember how you said the last time we was all together that Mother may not have wanted to be uppity but that you wanted to be uppity?"

Ma Cile stopped and thought about it. She did remember thinking that uppity may have had something to do with a car. She smiled, then apologized to Tiny for scaring him. She didn't bother to wait for him to gather his wits and open the door for her. She opened it and poured herself into the backseat of the limo and sat down next to Sister Betty.

"I guess we gonna find out just what po' Mother Eternal Ann Everlastin' had in mind for her last say-so." Ma Cile sat up straight and tapped Sister Betty on the wrist. "Are you gonna be okay, Sister Betty?" Ma Cile asked.

"Don't be too concerned about me, Ma Cile. I'll be alright. But you look kind of piqued. You sure you want to go with me? We can turn around and take you back, if you'd like."

Ma Cile did have a look of sudden concern. It wasn't because of what lay ahead at the councilman's office; it was because she suddenly realized that she'd forgotten her snuff canister. She hadn't done that on purpose in about twenty years. However, her need to know what was going to happen outweighed her momentary need for a dip of snuff. "I'm okay. Let's go on and see what Mother wanted us to do."

Sister Betty didn't bother to admonish Ma Cile that Ma Cile wasn't requested to attend the meeting. It would've been futile. When Ma Cile made up her mind about something, it would be easier to get social security benefits on the first try than to get her to change it.

Tiny, in the meantime, checked his watch. The meeting was set for nine o'clock. He had about five minutes to get Sister Betty there and another two weeks before he could officially be off Mother Eternal Ann Everlastin's payroll. He couldn't wait!

Of course, he should've known better. If he didn't know, he'd soon find out that two weeks to him didn't necessarily have anything to do with what Mother Eternal Ann Everlastin' had planned.

Sister Betty and Ma Cile cuddled together like two birds of a feather as they tried to figure out what was in store for them, while Tiny continued the drive downtown, counting the days until he'd officially be off the payroll.

In the meantime, a couple of other birds had beaten them downtown, and they were of the human buzzard variety.

Downtown, on the west side of Pelzer, South Carolina, didn't look like most of the business districts found in many of the big Carolina cities. Instead of large affluent buildings that housed the successful businesses of Pelzer's east side, the west side looked like a litter-strewn field of double-wide one-story buildings. It was actually just a spruced-up trailer park. Each one of the trailers displayed a business name plaque and had a security guard wearing a baseball cap and carrying a baseball bat, performing minimum protection of limb and property.

Several of Pelzer's rent-a-cops patrolled the area. They walked around, misusing their limited authority by picking on anyone who wandered onto the property without some type of gift for them—either a cup of coffee or a doughnut and quite often both. They were trying to vent their anger and shortcomings for failing the regular police test. Therefore, most of the trailer owners usually kept their motor's running and the gear shift in neutral in case the security got too out of hand. Of course, they also kept the front of the trailers always facing the highway.

The first row of trailers was where attorney Mr. Cheatem kept his fly-by-night somewhat legal law business. He advertised his over-priced office space as the law firm of Wee, Cheatem and How. The one-window office came furnished with one desk, one filing cabinet with a broken lock, soiled black-and-white linoleum instead of car-peting, an electrical system that always shorted out and a dingy gray wall telephone with a five-inch telephone cord. It was also a few doors down from the office of Councilman Hippo Crit.

Making sure that they were not seen, Reverend Knott Enuff Money and Bishop Was Nevercalled had rushed downtown as soon as word had spread around the church's dining hall that Mother Eternal Ann Everlastin's attorney wanted Sister Betty to come to his office.

Ma Cile had spread the word as soon as Sister Betty had told her not to say anything.

Reverend Knott Enuff Money didn't need to be a brain surgeon to figure out that it had something to do with Mother Eternal Ann Everlastin's will.

He needed to make sure that it was definitely Mr. Cheatem who was handling Mother's last will and testament.The previous night, he'd called Mother Pray Onn under the pretense of being concerned about her and somehow, he figured to get the information he needed about who was handling Mother Eternal Ann Everlastin's affairs.

He had started off by telling her about the screwup made by Brother Flipper when he hadn't delivered her message. Of course, he'd added his own version of how upset he'd been that no one informed him of her hospitalization and that other heads would roll. "I just know you're gonna be alright. You just take your time about rushing to get out of there," he'd said. "I'm just glad to know that your daughter, Sister Carrie Onn, spent the night there with you attending to your every need. I was wondering why she wasn't at the service so she could've reported to you."

From the angry words that Mother Pray Onn had shouted at him through the phone, he found out that Sister Carrie Onn hadn't been with her mother at all. He had no doubt that when she did finally show up, Mother Pray Onn was gonna hurt her. Of course, he didn't bother to mention that he'd heard that Deacon Laid Handz's room was on another floor, and it was probably where Sister Carrie Onn had been.

Actually, Sister Carrie Onn was an afterthought. He hadn't even missed her at the funeral. And, Mother Pray Onn had been so mad that he didn't bother to mention anything about Mr. Cheatem.

After they arrived downtown and spread around gifts of much-appreciated, stale doughnuts with runny jelly centers and cold, sugar-free coffee, the Reverend Knott Enuff Money and the bishop found Mr. Cheatem's office. They banged the door knocker several times, then they waited.

A few seconds later, over the sound of rustling papers, a raspy voice spoke from the other side of the door. "Who's there? I don't know nothing, and if you can't prove I did something, then get away from the door. I have a gun and I'll learn how to use it!"

Looking around again to make sure that none of the rent-a-cops were coming, the Reverend Knott Enuff replied, "Open the door! It's your former pastor, Reverend Knott Enuff Money."

Suddenly, the shutter that covered the peephole in the door opened. It moved from over the peephole just enough for a single ray of sunlight to enter.

On the other side of the door, Mr. Cheatem peeked out. His eyes were deep black and as round and as tiny as the peephole in the door. After recognizing his former church brethren, he opened the door, dressed in a brown Colombo knockoff outfit and sandals that were obviously too small. His toes flowed from the sandals like crab pincers. He squinted his little beady eyes and looked around the hallway to make sure they were alone. Not taking any chances that someone could possibly jump out of the shadows, Mr. Cheatem then snatched them inside.

The Reverend Knott Enuff Money and the Bishop Was Nevercalled were very lucky. They could've gotten hurt when Mr. Cheatem grabbed them with his deformed hands. His ashy, reddish-colored hands looked like a pair of crab claws, with long curved nails that were in need of a serious manicure.

It was the first time that the Bishop Was Nevercalled had been inside of Mr. Cheatem's law office. One of the first things he noticed was the stack of brown-and-gray tweed suitcases that were crammed and piled high near a closed window encased in security bars. The suitcases had wheels on the bottom and could be pulled easily, just in case a quick getaway was necessary.

Even though it was broad daylight, there were also several large lit candles strategically placed around the room. They were in different colors, and each candle holder had a string attached to it. He later found out that Mr. Cheatem kept them lit like that so that the strings could be pulled and cause the candles to fall over and the place could burn down in the case of a sudden raid.

"What can I do for you gentlemen this afternoon?" Mr. Cheatem asked as he hurried to remove piles of papers that were caked with dust, from a chair. "Have a seat. I'm sorry that I only have one that I can offer."

Both the reverend and the bishop tripped over each other as they raced to get to the one chair. They ran around where Mr. Cheatem stood, as if they were playing a game of musical chairs. "It's mine!" the reverend said as he pushed the bishop out of the way, which caused the bishop to fall against the stack of suitcases.

The suitcases plummeted like a pile of old children's Legos and, of course, because they were on wheels, they rolled over near the candles. Both the bishop and Mr. Cheatem threw themselves in between the rolling suitcases and the lit candles. "Stop those suitcases before they knock the candles over!" Mr. Cheatem yelled. "Y'all gonna burn my business down."

"Who's gonna pay for the rip in my pants leg?" the bishop asked as he unhooked his tattered pants leg from the wheel spoke. "I'm waiting for an answer."

While the bishop waited for his answer, Mr. Cheatem got up off the floor and went over to the reverend who sat watching with disgust.

Standing over the reverend, Mr. Cheatem whispered, "I hope it's not about that little check that bounced the same week that I left the church. It's been slow for the past several years that I've been gone, but I promise to make it good as soon as I can. Business has been a little slow. I've been looking for something that can enhance my cash flow without alerting Uncle Sam, but it just ain't happened yet."

Reverend Knott Enuff Money smiled back at Mr. Cheatem, which only made Mr. Cheatem more nervous. Making sure that he was not overheard by the bishop, he put one arm around Mr. Cheatem's shoulder and gently guided him over to where the lone filing cabinet sat. He leaned over and whispered, "We're supposed to be here on a little business." He stopped and pushed a strand of his Jheri curl wig out of the way and then winked. "Just follow my lead."

Mr. Cheatem gave Reverend Knott Enuff Money a puzzled look then suddenly, his eyes bulged with an all-knowing smile. He knew the reverend was up to something, and whatever that something was, it was for certain that Bishop Was Nevercalled was not in on it. And, if the bishop was not in on it, then whatever that plan was, it had to be about money. That also meant it would be split two ways. "No problem." Mr. Cheatem smirked and winked back as he envisioned his share of whatever the reverend was about to perpetrate.

The Reverend Knott Enuff Money didn't say another word. Instead, he just let his hands drop from Mr. Cheatem's shoulders. He then went over and stood by the bishop who was still holding his torn pants leg in place with one hand.

While the reverend slunk over to set up the bishop—no doubt a checkmate—Mr. Cheatem hustled over to the back of the room and pretended to rumble through the dust and the papers. He kept looking back over his shoulder as he waited for the reverend's signal. His head bobbed and weaved as if controlled by a spring each time he tossed a bundle.

He didn't have to wait long. The reverend was about to go into an Academy Award–winning performance. Denzel Washington could've taken lessons.

The Reverend Knott Enuff winked at Mr. Cheatem as he reached into his front pocket to get a safety pin so that the bishop could pin his torn pants leg and free his hands. He even went so far as to help the bishop across the room to sit down in the single chair, which he'd moved into a corner.

Having placed the bishop in a "victims" position, the reverend walked back over to where Mr. Cheatem stood. He was still rummaging through the bogus papers. "Mr. Cheatem," the reverend said as he turned around to make sure that the bishop was trying to pretend that he wasn't trying to listen, "can we please see the first set of insurance policies or legal papers that you have from the divorce settlement of Mother Eternal Ann Everlastin'. We want to make sure that everything is in order for her nephew, Buddy, when he comes here this morning." He leaned in a little closer to Mr. Cheatem and mumbled, "What I really need to see is the will."

The Reverend Knott Enuff Money looked back over at the bishop. He could've blinded the bishop with a smile so wide and bright as he signaled that he had everything under control.

To the Bishop Was Nevercalled, the Reverend Knott Enuff Money's overconfident smile suddenly looked like the one he'd seen on the face of a sneaky and laughing hyena on the Discovery television channel. It was from one of those scenes where the hyena was on a hunt in a dense jungle. The hyena hadn't seen the victim yet, but from the smell, he knew it was wounded.

The bishop wasn't wounded—not yet. But he was sitting there with a dumbfounded look upon his face in a lone chair over in a corner with a torn pants leg near lit candles in the office of a lawyer of questionable reputation. What did he have to worry about?

The bishop's concern lessened somewhat and then immediately heightened again. He almost stuck himself with the safety pin that had reopened as the reverend bent over, seemingly to help Mr. Cheatem look through the mysterious papers. He could tell that they were conspiring among themselves.

Bishop Was Nevercalled's neck seemed to stretch about another inch or two as he strained to hear what was being said. He didn't have to wait much longer as the reverend started reading through several documents handed to him.

"I can't understand all of this legalese nonsense, and there are coffee stains covering the name." His eyes darted back and forth like an old manual typewriter as he scanned over the papers. He threw the papers down, which caused a few of the sheets to land precariously close to the lit candles. "None of these papers tells me what I need to know. There's no mention of Buddy's name in any of them."

"Are you sure?" Mr. Cheatem asked. He wasn't sure if what the reverend was saying was a part of the plan or not. He snatched the papers up from the floor, starting with the ones which were closest to the lit candles. "Here." As he extended the papers to the reverend, he winked. "Look at them again. That's everything I have." He added a little bass to his voice when he said the word *everything* to see how the reverend would respond.

The reverend did just that. He reread the papers, and that's when he got hotter than those lit candles. "Hold on a moment!" His voice went up about two octaves. He'd completely forgotten that he didn't want the bishop to know exactly what he was up to. "This Last Will and Testament is dated five years ago. Don't you have a more up-dated will?"

"Huh?"

"Where are all the codicils, the wherefores and the whatnots, plus all the details where Mother had mapped out her own funeral directions and wishes?"

"Say what?"

"The instructions for her money." The tiny beads of sweat now banded with the greasy Jheri curl juice that flowed free, and it caused more stains on the papers. "I need to know about her money. I also need to know who has the current power of attorney, if it's not you, until a permanent one is named!" He was becoming so mad that if he'd cocked his bulging eyes, he would've shot someone with them.

"Did Mother die?" Mr. Cheatem looked truly shocked as he ran his clawlike hands through his hair, pulling out a few loose strands in the process. "Her daughter was her next of kin, and I haven't heard anything from her." He sprinted across the room and picked up the unplugged telephone. "I've been meaning to get this thing turned back on, but I do still have my pager. When did she die?" He was beginning to turn from red to purple because there were several papers that he'd meant to file to make the will legal. Somehow, while he was trying to stay two steps ahead of the law, he just hadn't gotten around to it.

Now it was the reverend's turn. "Huh?"

"I really meant to do it, last year when I drew it up for her."

"Say what?"

"Her daughter had insisted that her mother redo her Last Will and Testament to include an update on who could and would not be invited to her funeral. She usually did the update at her home every two weeks—"

Everything Mr. Cheatem was saying suddenly turned into background noise as the reverend tried to figure out what he was talking about, and when did Mother Eternal Ann Everlastin' have a daughter? Who was the daughter?

And then, the most intelligent question to be asked since they'd arrived came from the most unlikely source, the bishop. He was still sitting in the chair, holding on to an open safety pin and his torn pants leg. He'd grown tired of hearing bits and pieces of the conversation. He hadn't heard everything that was said, but he did hear the words *Last Will and Testament*.

"Excuse me reverend. I-I don't mean to butt in. I have a question." He had started to stutter again, so he figured he needed to hurry and say what was on his mind while he had their attention.

The bishop turned his attention to Mr. Cheatem. "You were the last attorney Mother Eternal Ann Everlastin' hired, weren't you?"

"Mother Eternal Ann Everlastin'?" Once again, he raked his clawlike hands through his hair, snaring a few more strands as he slammed the file cabinet drawer. He almost caught the reverend's fingers. "I ain't never wrote no last will and testament for Mother Eternal Ann Everlastin'."

Now it was the bishop's turn. "Huh?"

"I only represented her during the hearings and investigations when her first two husbands died."

"Say what?"

"I only paid off a few folks to keep them from aggravating her with their nosy questions, and that was the end of our brief relationship."

"So who were you talking about?" the reverend snapped. "Whose papers are those?"

"Mother Pray Onn. I was talking about Mother Pray Onn and her daughter, Sister Carrie Onn." He stopped speaking long enough to throw his head back and look up at the ceiling. He then dropped his head, gripped the sides of the filing cabinet and tried to muster a couple of tears as he continued. "My goodness. I just spoke to her last night. She was in the hospital suffering from an infected pinky toe, and she wanted to discuss the possibility of suing your church for her injury. We were going to get together when she was released. I was gonna get an ambulance to bring her home. It was gonna be

for appearance's sake. I didn't know it was more serious than that."
Finally, one tear appeared because he was gripping the side of the filing cabinet so hard the blood started to drain from his hand, and it
hurt. "I'm gonna miss that old lady. When did she pass?"

"Sue my church," the reverend exclaimed. "That old woman
bangs a toe and she wants to sue. Let her just try it." He was about
to go off but the thought of his true purpose brought him back to
task.

Once again, the bishop asked a more important question. "Well if
you didn't write Mother Eternal Ann Everlastin's Last Will and
Testament, who did?"

"It was probably Councilman Hippo Crit," Mr. Cheatem answered, proud that he could finally contribute something.

"Ouch!" The bishop had finally stuck himself with the open
safety pin. "The councilman?" he asked as he sucked his thumb to
ease the pain. "I wondered why he was at the funeral. I didn't know
he knew Mother Eternal Ann Everlastin' that well. I thought he was
there for photo opportunities."

The reverend spoke up. "You know, he does have an office somewhere around here."

"He sure does. It's right down the hall," Mr. Cheatem offered.

"Why would he have an office down here in this dum—" the reverend blurted and then caught himself before he continued. "I meant
why would he be so far downtown in this establishment?"

"That office doesn't really belong to him. He only rents it because
he has another office across town in the Mo' Cheddar district. He
has the one down here so that he can help out the poor people of this
area. He also comes around when there's a high-profile ghetto case
or something. And, then sometimes, he just uses the office to store
stuff or when he doesn't want folks all up in his business."

For the first time since the reverend walked through the door, he
was finally starting to grow a little suspicious. "How do you know
so much about Councilman Hippo Crit's business?"

"I make it my business to know other folks' business and that's
how I handle my business."

The bishop was growing weary of the whole thing and asked,
"Well, tell us. Do you know if Mother Eternal Ann Everlastin's
nephew, Buddy, is the next of kin or the executor of her will?"

Mr. Cheatem looked like someone had asked him if he had passed
the bar exam. "How would I know. That ain't none of my business."

The Reverend Knott Enuff Money and the Bishop Was Nevercalled were so upset by the futility of their little exploration that they didn't bother to even say good-bye to Mr. Cheatem. They did, however, try to kick over one of the lit candles as they left the shabby office. All they managed to do was to scorch a wall that was already scorched.

They hadn't succeeded at anything but waking up that morning, and that was due to God's mercy and not their worthiness or an alarm clock.

13

Show Me the Money

The race to find out just what was in Mother Eternal Ann Everlastin's Last Will and Testament seemed to be on a lot of folks' minds that Monday morning. And although the Reverend Knott Enuff Money and the Bishop Was Nevercalled were not successful in their efforts to get information from the attorney, Mr. Cheatem, it appeared that the right people would.

Tiny drove into the parking garage under Councilman Hippo Crit's office in the downtown Mo' Cheddar district and parked the limo alongside several others. It was still early, not quite nine o'clock in the morning, but the rich never worked nine to five.

Sister Betty and Ma Cile had held hands and already prayed in the car. They felt that whatever it was that their friend had in mind, God would see them through.

"Are you going to wait for us?" Sister Betty asked as Tiny helped her and Ma Cile from the car. She waited patiently for him to answer because she knew he'd used most of his strength and breath trying to pull Ma Cile out.

"Yes, ma'am. I'll be here . . ." He stopped, then placed his hand over his heart. Then Tiny caught his breath along with a painful cramp. Ma Cile wasn't someone he should've tried to help lift without a good year's worth of workouts. "Councilman Hippo Crit says he needs me to be there for the reading too." He finally collapsed against the trunk of the limo and gasped, "The elevator is right over there. I'll be there in a moment."

Ma Cile couldn't understand what was Tiny's problem. "He

probably should've eaten sumpthin'," she said with a hint of concern.

"No, I don't think lack of food was his problem," Sister Betty replied as she looked at the girth of her dear friend and smiled, "but food definitely played a part."

It took another five minutes but Tiny finally pulled himself together, and he escorted the women up to Councilman's Hippo Crit's posh office.

Ma Cile was beside herself when she saw the deep carpet that made her feel like she was walking through soft grass. The smell of potpourri poured from a large pewter vase on the receptionist's desk. Ma Cile was okay until she spied a strange painting on the wall. She wasn't quite sure what to make of it and didn't know that it was a painting called *The Dream* by the famous Pablo Picasso. Tapping the side of her head usually caused her good eye to line up with the blue false one, but nothing seemed to change. She was about to tap herself into unconsciousness and would've if the councilman had not walked out from his office to meet them.

Looking like he had just stepped off the cover of *What a Girl Wants* fantasy magazine, the councilman greeted them. He had a full head of black hair that shone like each strand had been polished, and his mustache looked the same. His razor-sharp sideburns seemed to dance with his cheek muscles as he spoke. "Good morning, ladies. Mr. Tiny. Welcome to my office."

No one responded because they were all looking at Ma Cile who was still looking in awe at the Picasso.

"I hope you didn't pay too much for that," Ma Cile said as she pointed to the wall. "I thought you was a whole lot smarter than to pay good money for something that don't even look human. Why would somebody wanna paint someone with a head behind a head?" She stopped suddenly and realized that it could've been her eyes playing tricks on her as they so often did. So, she whispered into Sister Betty's ear, "That is one head with another head's shadow behind it, ain't it?"

"Looks that way to me," Sister Betty answered as she, too, struggled to figure out why someone would paint a human body in contortions.

Sister Betty's confirmation added fuel to Ma Cile's agitation. "Ya see. You've been took. I sho hope you handled Mother Eternal Ann Everlastin's business a lot better than you done your own."

He figured that the two old women had probably never been in a building past the third floor, especially not in an office as affluent as his. He didn't bother to try and explain the difference between a regular painting and an impressionist. Instead, he responded, "I'll try and do better."

Councilman Hippo Crit laughed and gently turned Ma Cile away from the painting. He'd only met her a few times in the past, and with each experience, her down-home naiveté somehow endeared her to him.

The four of them entered into the spacious office. The receptionist brought in cups of hot coffee for each of them and left, closing the office door behind her.

"Let's get down to this business. First of all, I need to tell you that I got a call from the county medical examiner. Apparently, Mother Eternal Ann Everlastin' did not die from the reported overdose of a York peppermint pattie."

"She didn't," Sister Betty exclaimed, "but that's what she was eating when she collapsed. I was right there and saw her."

"Yes, she did collapse while she was eating the peppermint pattie, but her death was caused by a massive heart attack. Apparently, Mother hadn't been taking care of herself as she should've."

"You mean she wasn't taken away in such an embarrassing fashion?"

"No, Sister Betty, she wasn't. I've taken the liberty of informing all the newspapers so that they can correct their first report of her death. And, of course, the York peppermint pattie company is sad about her death, but they are ecstatic that one of their products was not the cause."

Sister Betty just smiled a little bit as she again scolded herself for questioning God. She'd have a longer talk with Him when she got home.

"Now, we must take care of this unhappy but necessary business." He took a brown folder from his desk drawer and took out a long piece of paper with a blue cover on its back. "This is the Last Will and Testament of Mother Eternal Ann Everlastin'."

Sister Betty interrupted him. "I don't claim to know everything but shouldn't Buddy be here? He is Mother's next of kin."

"Buddy is here. He's in one of the other offices, trying to sleep off one of his alcohol binges." The councilman did not try to hide his distaste for Buddy. "Whether he was in here or not, it wouldn't matter. He still wouldn't understand the magnitude of what was going on in his state."

"Ain't he still in South Carolina if he's asleep in the other room? South Carolina is a state, even I know that," Ma Cile said.

Once again, Councilman Hippo Crit couldn't help but smile at Ma Cile. There was just something about her that seemed to get to him, and she could say no wrong. "Of course. You're right, Ma Cile. What I actually meant was that he was in no condition to participate in the seriousness of what we are about to discuss."

"Can we just get on with this?" Tiny interjected. "My time on Mother's employment clock is ticking, and my freedom is nigh. I'm also sure that Sister Betty would like to finish up here and get back home to whatever she needs to do."

Sister Betty didn't say anything, she just nodded in agreement. She felt very uncomfortable sitting there about to discuss the affairs of her recently departed friend.

Councilman Hippo Crit smiled and took a pair of glasses off his desk to read the document in his hands. "Okay. Mr. Tiny, I'll forgo all the legal mumbo-jumbo and start with you." He adjusted his glasses and turned over a few pages until he found what he was looking for. "Apparently, Mr. Tiny, you are not going anywhere for quite some time."

"Oh, you need to get a new pair of glasses. I've got less than two weeks of work that I still owe to Mother Eternal Ann Everlastin'." When the look on the councilman's face didn't change, the one on Tiny's did. He looked like he was about to cry. "We shook on it and everything." Then he started to get mad. "Two weeks is all I'm giving 'cause I ain't gonna be no dentist servant."

At first, the councilman was confused but when he considered the source of the confusion, he corrected him, "That's indentured servant."

"I ain't gonna be that either," Tiny said, fuming.

"Why don't we all just calm down and let the councilman tell us what's in the will," Sister Betty snapped.

Ma Cile didn't say anything but she, too, nodded in agreement.

Sister Betty was beginning to feel that old familiar ache in her left arthritic knee. She just sank back farther into her seat, clasped her hands in prayer and waited for the storm to come.

She didn't have to wait for long.

"Mr. Tiny, Mother Eternal Ann Everlastin' has requested that you continue in your capacity as her limo driver. Instead of driving her around, she has left a large and sizeable amount of money for you to take charge of Buddy. She has requested that you stay on and that you drive him back and forth to any AA meetings or rehab centers until he overcomes his alcohol addiction." He stopped reading and looked questioningly at Tiny. "Well?"

"AA meeting, my foot. I wouldn't drive him to a BeBe or CeCe Winans meeting. I said two weeks was all I was gonna stay for, and that's all I'm gonna stay for—"

"—Two million dollars if you stay at least three months with him."

Buddy didn't wait for the councilman to finish. "What's his schedule? I need to make sure that he gets to his meetings on time."

That was easy, the councilman thought. "I'll see that you get all the particulars." He then turned and looked at Sister Betty.

Suddenly Sister Betty's left arthritic knee started jumping on its own, like it knew the storm had arrived and was trying to hide. She would've sunk back farther into the chair, but if she had, she would've landed on the floor backward.

"Sister Betty, I told you the other day, after the funeral, that you would need to leave Pelzer for a while. I hope that you will be able to do just that and carry out Mother's last request." He stopped and flipped through more pages before he continued. "You're going to Maryland."

"Maryland? Why do we have to go to Maryland?" Sister Betty and Ma Cile asked in unison.

"You're going to church." Suddenly Councilman Hippo Crit was beginning to sense a change in the mood of the women, and it didn't look healthy. His health in particular.

"We can go to church right here in Pelzer," Sister Betty said as she inched her way toward the edge of her seat. "There's something else in them papers that you ain't saying, isn't there?"

"What I meant to say was that you will be going to a huge church convention in Maryland. There'll be music and a lot of things going on."

"You mean to tell me that Mother knew that she was gonna die in time for a big church convention?"

"Of course not. How could she know something like that?" The councilman lay the papers down on his desk. He then got up and came over to stand by Sister Betty's chair. "Sister Betty, what Mother actually wanted you to do was to visit three churches in the Maryland area whenever she passed on. It just so happens that those same churches will be a part of a large and well-attended conference that will be held next week. I just felt that you could kill two birds with one stone."

"Kill what?"

"I'm sorry. Poor choice of words, Sister Betty. Here's what I meant." He leaned down and rested his hand on her shoulder to assure her. "You can go to this conference instead of visiting each of the churches separately. You can do what you need to do, all at one time, and in one place."

"What am I supposed to do?"

"That's what I want to know. What is me and Sister Betty supposed to do over in Mary's Land?" Ma Cile chimed in.

He didn't bother to correct Ma Cile. He addressed Sister Betty instead. "You'll have to take a notice of a very substantial donation for a particular service to the churches. If we can all just calm down, I'll explain everything."

"Hold on," Tiny barked. "Ain't none of this so-called substantial donation coming out of my two million dollars, is it?"

"No, it's not."

"Well, go ahead and say what you got to say." Suddenly the second hand on his watch seemed to turn into a dollar sign. "I need to hurry and get Buddy to a meeting."

"I'm happy to see that you are so concerned for Buddy's welfare." Tiny was beginning to get on the councilman's nerves, but he had Mother's affairs to put to rest and he needed to get back to it.

"Sister Betty, here is a list of your instructions. On it there are three churches, like I mentioned before. They are Bethel AME Church. You would need to personally speak to its pastor, the Reverend Frank Reid. The other church is the Full Gospel AMEZ Church. That church is pastored by the Reverend John Cherry, Sr. You can speak to either him or the first lady, the Reverend Diana Cherry. The last church is the New Psalmist Baptist Church. That pastor is the Reverend Walter Thomas. Just like the others, you should speak to him, alone. All of them will be at the conference, and all of them will be receiving more than a million dollars each for their churches. I'll be calling them, personally, to let them know that you're coming."

"Why can't she just have a check sent to them? Why must we go there in person?" Sister Betty's right arthritic knee was shaking. With both her knees shaking so hard, she could've churned butter between them. "Is there something you are still not telling us?"

"I'm afraid there is."

"What is it?" Ma Cile asked. "We don't like traveling to places and we don't know what we gonna run into."

"Let me just tell you this. Carrying out Mother Eternal Ann Everlastin's Last Will and Testament will be like carrying out a *Mission Impossible* task or involuntarily appearing in an old *Outer Limits* episode."

"Why is that?" Sister Betty asked. She was familiar with the *Mission Impossible* television show but not with the *Outer Limits* one. Neither was something with which she'd want to be involved. Now her knees were beginning to jump so high they threatened to hit her navel.

"Buddy's going with you."

"What?" Sister Betty thought she'd heard him wrong.

"Huh," Ma Cile added. She had been too busy trying to figure out what to pack, so she hadn't heard much else. However, she did hear Buddy's name mentioned.

"What do you mean Buddy's going with them? I thought Buddy was supposed to be in my care. Are you trying to cheat me out of my millions?" Tiny was about to put his baseball cap on backward and go to work on the councilman's handsome face.

"You'll be going too."

The councilman didn't like the tone the meeting was taking on. Sister Betty's knees were jumping up and down like she was a puppet on a string. Ma Cile's mind came and went, depending on what was being discussed. Tiny looked like he wanted to kick some butt and could do a good job of it if provoked. He decided he needed to hurry up and tell them the entire plan before things got too ugly.

It was too late. Ugly had already awoken, and it was staggering through the office door.

Ugly just stood there staring into space. Ugly was shirtless with a pair of pants that were held up by one suspender, and it was looming in the doorway to the councilman's office. It leaned against the door frame for support.

"Come on in, Buddy." The councilman was not happy that Buddy had interrupted the meeting before he finished with what he had to say. He was also not happy that his overpaid receptionist had obviously left his door unattended. "Have a seat somewhere."

Tiny, realizing that if he started taking care of Buddy right away, he could be well on his way to getting his two million dollars, raced over to catch Buddy just as the man was about to leave the security of the door frame and kiss the floor. "Here let me help you, Mr. Buddy."

Buddy looked at Tiny through his hangover. He couldn't quite remember where he'd seen the man before, but he knew he had. "Who you? And, where's Jack?"

"I don't know Jack," Tiny said. He was a little confused because, besides the councilman and himself, there was no other man in the office.

"You don't know Jack." Buddy looked at him like Tiny was a piece of lint.

"Jack is Jack Daniel's liquor," Councilman Hippo Crit told Tiny. "As you can see, you will have to compete with Jack Daniel's for Buddy's attention."

"For two million dollars, I'd fight Tyson, Holyfield, Osama and Mother Pray Onn." He stopped and lifted his baseball cap to scratch his head, and added, "Well, perhaps not Mother Pray Onn. She's much too dangerous, but I'd certainly fight them others for two million dollars."

Suddenly game recognized game and the councilman knew why he didn't trust Tiny—Tiny was too much like himself.

The councilman pointed to another chair and said to Tiny, "Just sit Buddy down in the other chair and sit next to him so that he doesn't hurt himself on those fresh flowers."

"Councilman Hippo Crit, you were about to finish telling us what you didn't say at the beginning. What else is there that we need to know?" Sister Betty's knees hadn't stopped shaking yet, so she knew the councilman was still holding something back.

"I'm just gonna wrap everything up as best I can." He went and sat down at his desk and picked up the papers again. "Sister Betty, you can take Ma Cile with you, when you, Buddy and Mr. Tiny go to Maryland. Of course, you will be compensated, however, the instructions are that I cannot divulge the amount or the fashion in which the compensation will be paid."

Again, he stopped, and with a look that changed so quick, it would've taken a quick-motion camera to catch it, he added, "You will also have to dispose of a lot of Mother's property; however, the catch is that you only have three months to donate or sell the property that has not been bequeathed to Buddy or any other named inheritor, or it will be turned over to the state or to me to distribute as I see fit."

"You still talking about the state of South Carolina?" Ma Cile asked.

"Yes, I am." He took off his glasses and placed the papers back inside the folder. "Sister Betty, are we clear on everything?"

Her knees hadn't calmed down yet. She was certain that if he was truly finished then there was something that was going to happen. She was just as certain that she wasn't going to like it.

The councilman snapped his fingers as he reminded himself of a possible glitch. "Oh, there is just one other thing."

Sister Betty's knees suddenly felt like a match had been set off under them. Blast off!

"Reverend Knott Enuff Money has an unendorsed check that Mother Eternal Ann Everlastin' gave him before she died." He looked over at her, and with genuine concern in his voice, he added, "Please. You be careful, Sister Betty. I happen to know that his check is for fifty thousand dollars. Now, once he comes to see me, I can make that check good for him because Mother intended for his church to have the money; however, if he finds out that you are going to Maryland to give away more than three million dollars, then things might get a little ugly—"

"Why should he care?" Ma Cile asked. "He's got his money already afta you signs his check. Ain't that right?"

"He's the Reverend Knott Enuff Money," Sister Betty replied while the others smirked.

The meeting went on for another ten minutes. They discussed travel plans as well as what was to be bequeathed to Reverend Bling Moe Bling and the No Hope Now—Mercy Neva Church. They all agreed that the trip would start within the next several days and that the councilman would give Tiny a national list of places that held AA meetings. The councilman also promised that he would try to keep the Reverend Knott Enuff Money distracted. It was crucial that they get to Maryland and back without any problems.

To make Sister Betty feel more comfortable with her mission, the councilman told her a little more about what he'd been up to before they'd arrived at his office.

Somehow, he'd managed to set up events that would keep the Reverend Bling Moe Bling and his wife busy and out of their way. He'd also gotten the charges dropped against her over the weekend so she was in a much better mood to accept the huge check that Mother Eternal Ann Everlastin' had bequeathed their church.

He also found out that as it happened, Mother Pray Onn's infected toe had been more serious than she'd suspected, and she would be spending more time in the hospital.

As for Deacon Laid Handz, he'd been so happy to get the bedpan scraped off his behind that he hadn't even minded that Sister Carrie Onn was standing right there. She had donned a pair of surgical gloves, and posing as a nurse, she had helped with the procedure. Apparently, she had been very happy with the results of what she saw because she started shouting and proposing marriage right there in the hospital room.

For whatever reason, the councilman never mentioned the only two people left who could possibly interfere. They were Sister Ima Hellraiser and Brother Tis Mythang. Sister Betty didn't bother to bring up their names because she felt that Maryland was quite a ways from Pelzer, South Carolina. What business could they possibly have in Maryland?

All of these thoughts were circling in her head and yet, she didn't feel as comfortable as she should've been, and her knees had not calmed down.

The councilman walked side by side with Sister Betty and Ma Cile to the door as Tiny struggled to get Buddy out of the chair and through the office door. They had a quick benediction and the councilman walked them to the elevator. He pushed the close button for them and added as the door closed, "Please keep in touch, and let me know about your progress. And, don't worry. Everything will be just fine. Trust me."

Before the door to the elevator could completely close, the door to the second elevator opened. Out stepped two men who immediately shook the councilman's hand. One was tall and lean with a shiny, pale, bald head. The other man, shorter, stepped out, slipping and sliding in the falling grease from his Jheri curl.

What Sister Betty didn't know, but she was about to learn, was that when a politician said, "Trust me," it didn't necessarily mean that you could. In political terms, it had a special meaning. It meant, "watch your back because when I stab you with the blade handle, it hurts worse than the blade."

14

The Road Trip

Tiny had managed to get Buddy to one AA meeting during the week before they were set to leave for Maryland. Mother Eternal Ann Everlastin' had requested that Tiny stay with Buddy, without his family, in her house until everything was accomplished.

At first, Tiny's wife threatened to divorce him because she didn't believe what he told her; however, when he mentioned the two-million-dollar payoff and showed her the promissory note, she decided that three months was not that long of a separation. It took her less than five minutes to decide whether she would be upset if there were another woman involved or whether she wanted to go shopping in the Caribbean if she waited three months. She lied and told her husband that the warm weather appealed to her.

While Sister Betty packed all she could think to bring on the trip, she prayed. There were still things that didn't set right with her, but she couldn't put her finger on the exact one.

She'd read over the instructions from Mother Eternal Ann Everlastin' and after a few conversations with the Councilman Hippo Crit, she managed to understand a little more. She also understood that she was to call the councilman before she turned over the checks. He would tell her exactly when, how and if the pastors had done what was needed to get their monies.

With everything in place, Sister Betty hid the checks in a secure place and arranged for Ma Cile to meet at her house.

Ma Cile was still saddened over the death of her friend Mother Eternal Ann Everlastin', yet happy to be getting away from Pelzer.

She hadn't left Pelzer since she'd buried her husband and first met Sister Betty on the way back. This time, they'd be traveling again and in an uppity car due to the generosity of Mother Eternal Ann Everlastin'. With everything that she had to take care of, including settling her grandchildren with Shaqueeda, she managed, this time, to pack her snuff.

It was about noon before Tiny showed up at Sister Betty's house with Buddy in tow. He'd even put on his old chauffeur's uniform so that they would look prestigious. He'd also gotten the limo washed and waxed, and it was stocked for the long trip to Maryland.

For the first time in a long while, Buddy was momentarily sober. He sat up front with Tiny who had insisted that Buddy not be out of his sight. Buddy was clean-shaven, dressed in a pair of blue jeans and a tidy shirt that managed to cover his almost emaciated body. He sat still and didn't speak much. Somehow, during the AA meeting that week, he'd sobered up enough to understand that his only living relative had passed. That information made him sad, but when he found out that he could stand to inherit millions of dollars and property, that information made him want another drink and a talk with his friend Jack.

It was a struggle, but Tiny had managed to keep Buddy off the sauce by spiking his tea with a bottle of NyQuil cough syrup. His reasoning was that Jack Daniel's had about seventy percent alcohol and the cough syrup had about five. The cough syrup was the lesser of the two evils, and it kept Buddy quiet and out of his way.

"Are you ready to leave?" Tiny asked as he doffed his cap in a show of respect.

"Yes, I am," Sister Betty replied and then asked, "Who is that in the limo?"

Tiny laughed a little. "That's Buddy." He winked at Sister Betty and added, "The man cleaned up pretty good, didn't he?"

"He looks good. I'm sure his aunt would've been proud to see him like that." She waited until after Tiny took her bags to the car and blessed her house with prayer to protect it while she was absent.

While they drove to pick up Ma Cile, Tiny and Sister Betty once again went over their mission to make sure they were in sync.

Ma Cile was standing on her floral-laden front porch when the uppity limo pulled up. She was still a little sad inside, but her face just glowed from the thought of taking a trip.

It took Tiny two trips to Ma Cile's front porch to retrieve her suitcases. She had twice as many as Sister Betty. Whatever was in one of the suitcases smelled a lot like pork or something of the pork variety. He didn't have time to figure out what it was, so he just placed the suitcases in the trunk of the limo and returned to help Ma Cile.

Ma Cile waddled her way down the porch steps. She hugged an oversize pocketbook with her one hand and accepted Tiny's offer of help with her other. "I cain't wait 'til I git inside that uppity car."

The fact that Ma Cile was carrying that oversized pocketbook and hugging it like it contained her passport to Heaven was not lost on Sister Betty. She could only hope that it held an emergency change of underwear or anything but a tin of snuff.

But she knew better.

The two women greeted each other with their usual hugs and cheek kisses. Ma Cile's eyes accidentally lined up all on their own and she recognized Buddy sitting in the front seat. She was so happy to see him cleaned up. Ma Cile was just overjoyed at everything she saw inside the uppity car. And everything was just fine until Tiny decided to give the women a little privacy.

He pushed the button to have the privacy window roll up to separate the front of the limo from where Sister Betty and Ma Cile sat.

All the demons in hell shook with fear when Ma Cile started screaming. She probably scared about a thousand years off ole Satan's rule.

"Sister Betty! Sister Betty! This here uppity car is possessed. Git me outta here!" Ma Cile started screaming, crying, praying and then she took her oversized pocketbook and started banging on the window. "Satan, you let loose dis here car. Right now! I command you!"

Her screaming might've woke up the minions in hell but Buddy, with the aid of that shot of Nyquil, managed to sleep right through it while Sister Betty and Tiny tried to calm Ma Cile down.

Ma Cile had raised so much fuss that without considering the consequences, Sister Betty told her, "Ma Cile, take a dip of snuff."

Ma Cile grabbed the tin that held her pleasure. She yanked her bottom lip forward and poured so much snuff into it that if the car had spouted wings and flown, it would have been okay with her.

It was a good thing that they had only driven a few blocks away from Ma Cile's house because Tiny had to turn around and go back so she could replenish her snuff stash for the road trip.

Of course, Buddy slept through the entire thing.

15

When Is Enough Not Enough for Enuff?

For the past several days, it had taken every ounce of strength that the Reverend Knott Enuff Money had not to call or visit Sister Betty. He had kept to himself, not even bothering to talk with or return any of the bishop's phone calls. He did not even visit Mother Pray Onn in the hospital. Angry could not describe his foul mood.

He kept replaying in his mind the visit he had had with the Councilman, Mr. Hippo Crit. It had only taken him and the bishop about two hours from start to finish after they had arrived at Mr. Cheatem's office on the west side to get results. When they found out that Councilman Hippo Crit had the information they needed, they had driven like wild men over to his office on the east side.

When they first arrived, the councilman had tried to act real official and legal. He endorsed the check with Mother Eternal Ann Everlastin's power of attorney and told the reverend that he thought it was a great idea to replace the current baptismal pool with a Jacuzzi. He even gave the reverend the name of the place where he had bought his, and it would put about forty-five of the fifty thousand dollars back into his pocket if he gave his name as a referrer.

That was not enough for the reverend and the bishop. They needed to know everything, particularly how much power Buddy would have when it came to spending the inheritance.

Again, the councilman went into a litany of how wrong it would be to divulge that privileged information. However, after a wink and a promise in writing that they would deliver a sizable political donation to his next campaign, they got him to come around to their way of thinking.

"I can't in good conscience read to you what's in Mother Eternal Ann Everlastin's Last Will and Testament," the councilman said. Therefore, instead, he turned the papers around so that the writing faced the reverend, then he excused himself to use the bathroom. He told them he expected to be in there for about five minutes and when he returned, they had to leave.

It only took the Reverend Knott Enuff Money a few minutes to weave through all the legalese before he found what he was after. "Oh, my Lord." He almost had a coronary when he saw the names of three of the most well-known preachers on the east coast.

The near mild stroke only came after he'd read what Sister Betty's mission was about. "What-what-what—" He could not speak and his head started spinning.

The bishop caught him just as he was about to hit the floor. He dragged the reverend out into the receptionist's area and got him a glass of water. The water was not for the reverend to drink; it was so that the bishop could throw it in his face to revive him.

Again, the receptionist was on her permanent break and did not see what happened.

The reverend gathered his wits about him, enough to throw the remaining water in the glass in the bishop's face. He got up and pushed him into the hallway and onto the elevator.

He was still so livid he could have set the juice dripping from his Jheri curl on fire.

The sudden ring from his cell phone caused him to stop thinking momentarily. He was not going to answer the telephone until he saw a familiar name on the caller ID box. "Hello." He said it rather abruptly to let the caller know that he was in no mood for foolishness.

"What's your little problem? Shouldn't you be praying when you feeling so nasty?"

"I'm about to pray for you, Sister Hellraiser. I don't need any drama right now, so don't be calling me with none."

"I'm not calling you with any drama. I just thought I'd remind you that I will be leaving town this afternoon to cover a conference."

"So? What do I care about you covering a conference?"

"You got to pay for it, that's why you should care."

"I'm not paying for any conference. If you want to attend one so you can start trouble and then report that somebody else was the cause, well then, you'll be the one to pay for it."

"I told you weeks ago that me and Deacon Laid Handz was going to cover the conference. I really need to be there because I understand that the reverends Cherry, Reid and Thomas from Baltimore, Maryland, are going to be there—"

Reverend Knott Enuff Money's mind started spinning like a madman's. "Deacon Laid Handz is still in the hospital, thanks to your efforts. He won't be able to make it."

"I know that. Next time, he'll operate them cameras like he's supposed to. Anyway, the only other person I could get to go with me to operate the cameras was the Bishop Was Nevercalled. He said he's been trying to reach you to let you know, but he couldn't."

"I've been sort of out of touch for the past several days," he lied a little white lie.

"Well, I just found out something else that might interest you." Sister Hellraiser loved waiting for the last breath to lower her verbal axe. "It appears that Brother Tis Mythang is going to miss tonight's senior choir anniversary service because he's been asked to play for the conference. He left this morning, but he didn't know that I knew he was going." Sister Hellraiser counted to two before she lowered the coup de gras. "By the way, did you know that the Reverend Thomas is Brother Tis Mythang's cousin?" She let the word *cousin* marinate as the smile spread across her face wider than the one on a smiley face.

"Right now, Sister Hellraiser, I really don't care where he goes." That is what he told her as he pretended as though he had not heard her last jab. It was no secret. Everyone knew how in awe he was about those particular three mega-church pastors. He had dubbed them the Trinity.

The reverend thought about how Brother Tis Mythang had been a member of the church since he was a teenager. Never once had he ever heard him mention that his cousin was the renown Reverend Walter Thomas of the New Psalmist Baptist Church in Baltimore.

The reverend started nervously strumming his fingers against the side of the desk as the silence on the phone line became deafening. Sister Hellraiser was waiting for him to respond. It was expected that he would ask her how she knew. He would not ask. He would have said much more, but he couldn't wait to get her off the phone so he could call Brother Tis Mythang's cellular phone. Things looked like they may work out, after all.

The reverend decided to toss Sister Hellraiser a bone as he continued to not care about her last comment. "You know, I'm still upset about Mother Eternal Ann Everlastin' passing on so suddenly. I think

I need to get away too. I tell you what: I'll pay for our hotel rooms and the conference fees, but y'all are paying for your own meals."

His fingers were strumming as though they were possessed as they tapped rhythmically. He was really getting excited. Perhaps it was divine intervention. He knew it was not, but that didn't stop him from hoping.

"I mean," he continued, "I am your pastor, and as such, I should be there to make sure that y'all don't misrepresent my church's good name and reputation."

Finally, he had responded. Sister Hellraiser wasn't sure that he had not hung up, so she was happy to get another chance to toss a barb into the conversation. "We can't misrepresent the Ain't Nobody Else Right But Us—All Others Goin' to Hell Church's reputation. Everybody knows we already got a shaky reputation, and that we don't play or pray. Folks can't even begin to be in the same league with us . . . and by the way, keep that information about Brother Tis Mythang to yourself. I don't want folks to think I gossip."

The reverend didn't wait for Sister Hellraiser to finish. He interrupted and told her to be ready by five o'clock, then he hung up the phone while she was still ranting about her moral character.

He immediately called Brother Tis Mythang. When the reverend couldn't reach him on his cellular phone, he telephoned the bishop. He halfheartedly apologized for not getting back to him, and then he brought him up-to-date with what was going to happen. He told him about everything except the latest news regarding Brother Tis Mythang.

"Well, I'm about finished packing. I should be ready to pick you up about five," the bishop said.

"Good. Make sure you get some rest."

"Don't worry about me. I can get some rest at some point in the car," the bishop replied.

"How you gonna rest in the car while you driving all the way to Baltimore?" the reverend asked.

"Why am I driving all the way to Baltimore?"

"It's either you or Sister Hellraiser who will be driving." He stopped to let the thought sink into the bishop's mind. "I'm the pastor. I don't drive folks around. I am driven. Do you get the picture?"

"I gotta hang up and catch a nap. I'll pick you up about five."

It was about five-thirty when the bishop finally arrived at the reverend's house. He had made the mistake of picking up Sister Hellraiser from her house first. She needed to stop at a local Wal-Mart store for film and, of course, she ended up doing what came natural to her. She raised hell because the film came two in a pack and she only wanted three cartridges. She didn't see why she had to get two packs and pay for four.

The cops arrived and to no one's surprise, most of them knew her on a first-name basis. They gave her a summons for disorderly conduct from a special summons book, which they carried next to their pistols in their back pockets. The book of summonses already had her name typed on them. She thanked them and promised to see them at their next policemen's ball.

The policemen commanded her not to show up and sent her and the bishop on their way.

The bishop wanted to cry. Even he was smart enough to know that there were probably a dozen or more policemen between Pelzer and Baltimore who knew her on a first-name basis too.

He reached into the glove compartment of his car and pulled out a large bottle of Too Blessed 2 B Stressed Oil. He placed it inside the caddy on the driver's side car door. He needed to keep it handy just in case he had to drench that she-devil.

It was already past five, so the reverend fussed a little when they finally arrived at his home. When he found out why they were late, he, too, grabbed a couple of bottles of industrial-strength blessed oil. He was sure that the one bottle the bishop hid would not be enough to keep Sister Hellraiser's demons in check.

After waiting for another thirty minutes because Brother Tis Mythang had not returned any of the reverend's calls, they packed everything into the trunk of the car. However, the reverend was not a quitter. He made one last try at locating Brother Tis Mythang. Once again, he got a voice mail message: "*Praise the Lord for this blessed day. You want me so you got me. If you don't know who I am then you probably called the wrong number, but you be blessed anyway. However, if you are a bill collector or one of them demon telemarketers, then you ain't nothing but the spawn of Satan. I rebuke you and I curse you back to the pit of hell. Everyone else, you can please leave a message.*" Beep.

The reverend did not bother to add another message to the five he had already left. Instead, he made a mental note to find out if the reason he kept getting the voice mail was because Brother Tis Mythang might have been out of signal range. He had better been.

Just before they pulled off, the reverend and the bishop prayed a quick benediction. They prayed aloud for God's traveling mercies then in silence, they prayed to find a muzzle with a lock on it for Sister Hellraiser's lethal mouth.

Finally, with his seat positioned just right, the reverend lay back and meditated for a few moments. Whatever plan he concocted to get in the good graces of the Trinity had to be beyond reproach. Just as he was getting close to what he thought was a brilliant plan, Sister Hellraiser started complaining.

"Why did you buy a car with the emergency brake lever shaped like a frankfurter?" She kept yanking on the crank, causing it to make noises that sounded like sharp fingernails raking across a blackboard. "It should be underneath the dashboard and next to the accelerator."

Even the gunning of the motor before the bishop took off could not drown out the sound of Sister Hellraiser's annoying and nagging.

Unlike Tiny, the reverend and the bishop had not discovered the true medicinal purpose of NyQuil. If they had, then they could have hook up an IV bottle full of the stuff and jammed the needle into Sister Hellraiser.

They were about to enter into the twilight zone and Sister Hellraiser was their pilot.

16

Baltimore Bound

Brother Tis Mythang had his car windows rolled down, and he was singing at the top of his lungs. He looked at his reflection in the rearview mirror and, of course, liked what he saw. He wore a pair of white denim jeans with a white lacy headscarf tied like a pirate. A pair of white sandals and socks offset by a beige and white shirt-vest made him look like a tall cloud with just a hint of a storm brewing. He laughed and whispered, "Hmmm. I just love me some me." He could not help but to blow himself a kiss in the mirror.

He stopped profiling in the mirror when he came close to uniting with the rear end of a Mack truck that didn't share that opinion of him.

Brother Tis Mythang pulled a pair of pearl-rimmed sunglasses from his shirt pocket. He stroked the dashboard as he sang words of encouragement to his sometimes-it-worked-and-sometimes-it-didn't 1995 Hundai. That blue, twice painted used car and his Roland 600 electric organ were the two things of which he was most proud. "Come on, baby, do the hustle," he said repeatedly as he softly pumped and encouraged the accelerator.

Brother Tis Mythang's mind wrestled with the method he'd used to leave Pelzer. It was a shame to sneak away on the down low. He had managed to leave Pelzer without any hindrances or drama from the Reverend Knott Enuff Money or the other church members by ignoring incessant phone calls, leaving around midnight and driving along the back roads to the outer city limits.

As soon as he arrived home and found the message from the Baltimore conference coordinator on his answering machine, requesting him to come and play for his cousin, the well-known television preacher Reverend Walter Thomas, he went underground. The call came right on time. He needed something to cheer him up after sitting through Mother Eternal Ann Everlastin's funeral, especially after seeing Buddy. He hadn't seen Buddy since he was about nineteen and Buddy was in his mid twenties.

The moment the thought of Buddy entered his mind, Brother Tis Mythang raced into his bedroom and started throwing his clothes and a few accessories into a suitcase. He tossed them in without bothering to fold or wrap anything, much the way he wished he could pack away the memories of Buddy. *Get a grip*, he thought. "Buddy should've fought the feelings just like I have done," he said aloud as he shuddered from a sudden chill that seemed to prick him in odd places on his shoulders. It was as if someone or something knew that there was more to his story.

Brother Tis Mythang shook his head from side to side to bring himself back to the moment. He was trying to shake away any further thoughts about unpleasant things. A smile forced its way across his face and was determined to stay.

On the seat next to Brother Tis Mythang lay his survival kit. It was actually an old brown leather camera bag. It had several compartments to hold his necessities, like his James Brown, Dottie Peoples and Kirk Franklin CDs. There was a typed sheet of all the local Christian clubs located around and within the Baltimore and Landover, Maryland, areas. A bag of plastic cups lay snuggled against a bottle of lemon-flavored water. The water was a must-have as a part of his weight-maintenance plan, and his cellular phone. The items lay beneath a layer of paper towels and a large bag of Lay's potato chips. With a Hundai, that was about all he could fit in it.

The cellular phone had rang constantly since he had left the city limits. When Brother Tis Mythang saw the reverend's telephone number on the caller ID, he ignored it. Whatever drama the reverend had going on, he did not want any part of it. On the other hand, if the reverend had somehow found out about his unsanctioned-by-the-church, out-of-town gig, there would be consequences and repercussions.

Instead of thinking further about what may or may not be going on, Brother Tis Mythang turned up the volume and sang louder. He shook his shoulders and bounced in his seat to the rhythm of Dottie Peoples's, "On Time God." He leaned out the window, threw his head back, and hollered into the traffic, "Yes, He is."

Brother Tis Mythang drove all the way to the outer city limits of Baltimore without any concern for the possibility of mishaps. He was as satisfied as a lone mouse in a cheese factory. He was so happy and sang and prayed so loud that he did not even pay attention to the stretch black limousine and its occupants that overtook and passed him.

Too bad for him. The Bible says that one should watch as well as pray. There is a reason for that.

Brother Tis Mythang had driven nonstop for about four hours, and he was tired and hungry. Finally, he saw a chance to stop and he did. He pulled his car off the highway into the back of the crowded parking lot of the Rest Stop rest stop.

Tired as he was, Brother Tis Mythang was still humming to himself as he got out of his car. He went inside and immediately raced to the bathroom. He entered through one of the double swinging doors to relieve himself. After washing his hands and checking himself out in the mirror, he left.

There were many food marts to choose from inside the food court, so, he decided to treat himself. He maneuvered through the crowd and got on a line at McDonald's.

It was not enough to be obnoxious by humming loudly. Brother Tis Mythang decided that he would sing his order to the waiting cashier. He tried to sing it like he thought Donnie McClurkin would have: "Let me have . . . two all-beef patties, special sauce, lettuce, cheese, pickles, onions on a sesame seed bun."

Brother Tis Mythang's voice was almost as smooth as Donnie McClurkin's, but somehow the order just did not sound right when he sang it to the melody of "We Fall Down." He ignored the open-mouth stares and several snarls from the other patrons. With his bag of food in his hands, he went back to the parking lot and got into his car. He immediately unwrapped his hamburger and separated the buns. For reasons of his own, he tossed the lettuce, cheese, pickles, and onions out the window. With a napkin, he wiped away most of the special sauce, which left two huge clumps of beef on a bun. He was just strange that way. Brother Tis Mythang then drove away while trying to sing with his mouth full, "I Did It My Way." He almost choked from eating that dry hamburger.

Of course, had Brother Tis Mythang known how close he'd been to having his serenity sapped up, he would have choked. Ignorance and his hasty retreat from the men's bathroom saved him. He had no idea who had been in the bathroom too.

After several hours of stop-and-go highway driving, Tiny pulled the limo into a crowded parking lot at the Rest Stop, one of the many rest stops along Highway 301. He had to do it. Ma Cile's overdose of snuff had them all suffering. When she was not talking fast like a runaway speeding locomotive, she was being her "natural" self. She didn't say "excuse me" or open a window.

They could've hooked Ma Cile's butt up to the gas tank. She had passed enough gas to take them nonstop from Pelzer to Baltimore.

Sister Betty and Ma Cile left the limo to refresh themselves while Tiny rested against the side of it to get a breath of fresh air. He kept one hand on the hood of the limo to steady himself and one eye on Buddy whom he had nicknamed My Two Million.

"I can't wait until we get to Baltimore," Sister Betty said as she hustled toward the women's bathroom.

"I'm just hungry," Ma Cile replied. She wasn't in much of a hurry to use the bathroom since she'd done her worst on the way there.

Ma Cile waited inside the food court for Sister Betty and the two women ordered enough food to feed them, Tiny and Buddy, if he ever woke up to eat.

When they returned to the limousine, Tiny accepted their offer of food and declined a trip to the bathroom. All he wanted to do was to get back on the road to Baltimore.

As they pulled out of the parking lot, Sister Betty's left arthritic knee suddenly jerked. It jerked so hard that it caused her to spill her food and drink onto Ma Cile's lap. Tiny briefly took his eyes off the road as he handed her a wad of paper towels over his shoulder. As he turned back around to continue driving, he had to swerve. He narrowly missed colliding with a blue Hundai that was racing onto the highway from the other side of the parking lot. He didn't get a real good look at the driver because he was shaken by the near collision. However, the quick look he'd gotten made him think that the driver seemed familiar.

By the time they made it to the highway to continue on their way, Sister Betty's knees shook like aftershocks. She became agitated because she knew something was not right but couldn't figure out what. She apologized. "I'm so sorry, Ma Cile. I didn't mean to get you all messed up."

"That's okay. You didn't wet my snuff."

Sister Betty started to admonish Ma Cile but the sight of a familiar blue Hundai that stood still in the bumber-to-bumber traffic ahead caught her attention. It must've caught her arthritic knee's attention, too, because it started aching and shaking again. She did not want to believe that the car ahead looked exactly like Brother Tis Mythang's. There was no reason in her mind why he shouldn't still be back in Pelzer, especially since he had to play for the senior choir's anniversary, which was happening that same night.

Now Sister Betty was certain that trouble was not waiting until their arrival in Baltimore; it was riding on the same highway with them.

Of course, Buddy slept through it all.

Barely a few minutes after Brother Tis Mythang had exited the bathroom, another man with a pale bald head and with about as many chins as a Chinese phone book appeared from within one of the two stalls. It was the Bishop Was Nevercalled.

The bishop took Brother Tis Mythang's place at the washbasin. Since the bathroom was not too crowded, he felt it was okay to raise his voice. "Reverend Knott Enuff Money," the Bishop Was Nevercalled ranted, "if murder wasn't one of the top ten sins, I think I'd killed Sister Hellraiser before we crossed the border from North Carolina to Virginia."

"I know what you mean," answered the reverend, "but I can't talk about her right now. Something I ate has gotten me a little messed up." The men in the bathroom looked shyly at one another as a few more grunts came from inside the stall, followed by a sigh of relief, then silence.

The bishop ignored the unpleasant smirks from the strangers. He was obviously steamed and if he had to rant by himself, then he would. "I can't believe that crazy woman got us stopped three times before we even crossed over into Virginia. It was bad enough when we got stopped at that gas station when she caused a ruckus on account of she didn't like the one-cent increase in the gas price." His voice started to rise. "Let's not forget her going crazy when she couldn't buy three of the rolls of film from the two two-packs." He was starting to stutter. "B-but, when she almost got us arrested after she started throwing rocks at that state trooper's car because he was an old boyfriend and she saw him chatting on his walkie-talkie,"—his voice shot up into the soprano range—"and she thought he was talking about her . . . that tore the drawers . . ."

The reverend came out the stall and joined the bishop at the washbasin. He looked drawn and embarrassed, but decided to add his two cents to the bishop's rant. "It's too bad we didn't just toss a lighted match at her after we tried to drown her with all those bottles of blessed oil."

The bishop had to laugh at the reverend's last remark. "I bet you that she's probably fireproof."

"Yeah, she probably is. I know the devil's gonna have his hands full trying to burn that demon up," the reverend added.

One of the other men standing nearby couldn't resist butting in. He had been ogling the bishop and thought it would be a good way to introduce himself. "I bet she's probably gonna leave this world wearing gasoline-laced panties bought at a discount from Victoria's Secret."

Both the bishop and the reverend stopped and looked at the man like he was something they'd forgotten to flush.

The stranger caught the hint and swished his hips, almost as if he were trying to balance a hoola hoop, slowly out of the bathroom. He looked back over his shoulder to make sure they saw what they were going to miss.

By the time the reverend and the bishop finished washing their hands, both their moods and their bodies seemed a little lighter from getting rid of two wastes: bodily and Sister Hellraiser. They decided to give themselves a little more time from her vicious behavior by going over to the food court and ordering something to eat.

The bishop rubbed his growling stomach. "I am starving," he said, moaning as he tried to decide what he wanted to eat.

"Let's try that McDonald's over there," the reverend said as he pointed to a place that was sandwiched between a Baskin-Robbins ice cream parlor and an Arby's. It didn't seem to have a long line.

They had not taken two steps before the crowd started stampeding toward them. Hunger immediately fled as they looked at each other knowingly and said in unison, "Sister Hellraiser."

Knowing that there was safety in numbers, both the bishop and the reverend joined the stampede. They were bobbing and weaving, trying to keep sight of each other as they raced to the parking lot. Each secretly hoped that they could make it to the car and leave without Sister Hellraiser.

However, it didn't matter how fast they ran because when they arrived at the car there she sat behind the steering wheel. Sister Hellraiser looked angry and smelled like a combination of olive oil and tartar sauce. She screamed at them, "What took you two so long? We need to get out of here."

Reverend Knott Enuff Money stopped wasting his time trying to run to the car. He walked the last five feet slowly, and when he arrived at the passenger-side door, he said, "If you wasn't always starting something we wouldn't have to escape every other minute."

"I ain't rushing," the bishop said. "I'm still hungry, and I need to eat. We can pull into someplace else."

The reverend leaned into the window and snapped, "Ima Hellraiser, what did you do this time?"

"I didn't do anything. That woman should've moved her big feet and her tray of food out of my way when she saw me coming."

"Wha-what?" The bishop's stuttering returned to join his hunger pang. "I'm out here starving because you stepped on somebody's toes?"

"No," Sister Hellraiser answered with a frown on her face.

"Then why are we starving?" The reverend didn't really care what her reasons were. He just didn't want the bishop to sound more intelligent than he.

"It's because I could've sworn I saw Brother Tis Mythang—"

Sister Hellraiser didn't get a chance to finish. The reverend pushed the bishop into the backseat, almost decapitating him when the bishop's head didn't quite make it out of the way of the car roof.

"Follow him. Whichever way you think he went, just follow him!" The reverend couldn't believe it. If it was Brother Tis Mythang then what was he doing in the same rest stop and most importantly, why hadn't he returned any of the several messages he'd left?

Sister Hellraiser didn't have to be told twice. She sped away because suddenly she saw the woman whose toes she'd smashed coming toward the car. It looked like she might've had her entire family reunion with her. On the other hand, Sister Hellraiser also didn't reveal to the reverend another bit of observation. She knew without a doubt that she'd also seen Mother Eternal Ann Everlastin's limousine about an hour ago when they were in traffic. Although the limo was over in the third lane, there was no way she could have ever mistaken someone else for Ma Cile. She would have said something, but at the time, she was still miffed about having to pay extra money for a pack of film that she didn't need. However, it appeared that she might just get a chance to use it.

17

To Be or Not to Be—Welcomed

Brother Tis Mythang looked at his watch. It was early afternoon and the sun was still extending its warmth. He began to feel as wonderful as the weather, so he decided that instead of checking into a local hotel he would go directly to his cousin Walter's house. He drove his Hundai carefully through several neighborhoods. It took him twice as long as it should've to reach where he was going because he was afraid to stop and ask some of the undeniably thug denizens for directions. He actually thought they might hijack his Hundai or as it happened on another occasion, rough him up because someone thought he wasn't manly enough.

Brother Tis Mythang pulled up to a circular driveway. Microscopic pieces of multicolored gravel paved the driveway, and it looked like they were laid by hand. The driveway, magnificently lined with tall firs and sculptured bushes and dotted with several bonsai trees along the way seemed to stretch for about a mile.

The Hundai sputtered a little as if it, too, were in awe of the sprawling layout of Reverend Thomas's home. Brother Tis Mythang gripped the wheel of the car as though it were the first time he'd driven onto the palatial grounds. He gripped it until his fingers grew numb—not from fear but from the same unnecessary embarrassment he'd felt on several other occasions.

On the way there, he debated, as usual, whether he should check into a hotel then rent a more luxurious car before visiting. He'd done that once before and his cousin, the Reverend Thomas had reprimanded him thoroughly. "Cousin Tis," the Reverend Thomas had scolded, "God has no respect of persons. If I don't live according to

His word, none of my possessions will be my stay-out-of-hell cards."
His cousin had said a lot more to make him understand the price of
Salvation and its rewards, but that statement remained with him.
Yet, he still felt a little embarrassed by his lack of earthly riches. He
still had more inner work to do.

Reverend Walter Thomas stood, dressed more like a gardener or
another employee in his coveralls between the pillars of his spacious
home. He was a very humble man in dress and deeds. Yet, there was
no question about his spirituality and that God had shown favor
upon him. He had a few pounds more than the last time Brother Tis
Mythang saw him, yet he was still the color of a rich chocolate bar
and wore brown-rimmed expensive glasses that added to his handsome features. Although he told everyone he was in his late forties,
he could've just as well passed for someone in his late thirties. If he
had a hint of any embarrassment coming from his arriving cousin because of his common gardening attire, it never showed.

"Just leave your car where it is," Reverend Thomas hollered,
"and don't you worry about your bags. I'll have someone bring them
in for you."

Brother Tis Mythang turned off the engine of his Hundai just in
time. The car was beginning to sound like it was running on its last
rites. "Walter, I'm sorry I'm late. As usual, I got completely turned
around." He fibbed about why he was lost because he didn't want to
admit to not asking for directions.

The two cousins embraced as they entered the house. Brother Tis
Mythang accepted his cousin's offer of hospitality as well as his gratitude for his timely arrival.

They chatted about nothing in particular as they went out into an
area by an Olympic-size pool surrounded by many purple cloth-covered
long tables with gold umbrellas in the center that stood tall with authority among the high-back chairs and chaises. No doubt, the yard
was set in preparation for a grand party. They strolled a little farther
along a cobbled narrow path until they came to another small grassy
area and entered the solarium that stood next to a smaller pool. To
add to the uniqueness of the home, that particular pool's water was
the color of a special combination of yellow and blue and a hint of
something mysterious that gave it a brilliant aquamarine look and
feel of holy peace.

After they'd spent another five minutes discussing Brother Tis
Mythang's long drive from Pelzer to Baltimore, they got down to
business.

"I have another favor to ask you," Reverend Thomas said as he pulled a letter from the pocket of his coverall. "I received a letter by overnight express mail from an attorney in Pelzer. Perhaps you might know him."

"What is his name?" Brother Tis Mythang asked. He wasn't particularly happy discussing a possible legal matter when what he really wanted was to take a dip in the magnificent pool then play on the grand piano inside the huge living room.

"It's from an attorney named Mr. Hippo Crit." Reverend Thomas stopped and watched his cousin's eyes light up like a sparkler on the Fourth of July. "I take it that you are familiar with the man."

"Of course I know him. I know just about everyone in Pelzer, especially the good-looking folks." Brother Tis Mythang decided it was in his best interest to make himself seem very important since the letter was of obvious importance to his cousin. "What about him?"

"I haven't discussed this with the board yet, but apparently, the recently deceased and much beloved by me, Mother Eternal Ann Everlastin' has left about a million dollars to New Psalmist Church—"

"And you apparently seem to have a problem with accepting a million dollars. Do you want me to take it off your hands?" Brother Tis Mythang laughed nervously but he was serious if his cousin was too.

"No, of course, I don't have a problem with the gift. It's the part about how we will get the money that has me concerned."

"What do you mean?"

"Apparently, there's a little catch to it. We have to accept and then try to turn around one of Pelzer's most renowned preachers. It seems that Mother Eternal Ann Everlastin' didn't think he would receive a heavenly welcome if he's called in his present state of grace."

Brother Tis Mythang's puzzled look left no doubt that his mind was beginning to spin. "Whom are you talking about?" He suddenly had a feeling that he knew whoever it was.

"It is someone named the Reverend Knott Enuff Money; however, it didn't say what church he led." Reverend Thomas stopped and looked straight ahead as though he were searching. "I seem to recall Mother Eternal Ann Everlastin' mentioning him many years ago, but I can't remember for what reason."

"Oh Lord." Brother Tis Mythang's happy mood was fading faster than a red shirt in boiling hot water. "He's my pastor."

"Your pastor." Reverend Thomas began to smile. "This ought to be easy."

"What should be easy?"

"The task I have to perform in order to receive the entire million-dollar gift."

"Really. Why do you think that?"

"I know it will be easy because I'll have you, my cousin—my favorite cousin—to help me."

Brother Tis Mythang started to feel a sugar shock coming upon him from all the sweetened pleas. "Let me tell you about my pastor. Perhaps when you know what you will be up against you'll wanna have a fund-raiser instead and forget the gift."

Brother Tis Mythang spent the next hour giving his cousin the history, as he knew it, of the Reverend Knott Enuff Money. What he revealed cut away at the Reverend Thomas's enthusiasm like a pair of snipping shears. By the time Brother Tis Mythang finished with his revelation, Reverend Thomas's hope of getting the bequest was as sure as curing the common cold.

There was at least six hours before the conference would begin. They decided to use that time to rest and then come together again to plan. That meant that Brother Tis Mythang would have to spend more time at his cousin's palatial residence.

At least one good thing would come of his visit.

Loud snorts and bad breath clouded the interior of the limo as Buddy finally roused from his NyQuil-induced sleep. Buddy's last belch sounded and smelled like a barrel of pickled pig snouts and garlic cloves. The odor made Tiny's eyes water and his throat itch as he tried to maneuver the limo quickly around a curved track toward the back to the Hilton Hotel's underground garage in downtown Baltimore.

"I should've kicked your butt out at the curb when I dropped off Sister Betty and Ma Cile in front of the hotel. Two million dollars ain't enough money to smell your rancid breath."

Tiny was lying. He would've hooked up a hose from Buddy's mouth to his own and inhaled every stinking molecule for much less; however, when he remembered that Buddy had not used a bathroom during the entire ride, he panicked. He wasted no time in snatching Buddy out of the car and dumping him in a heap alongside the parking rail.

Buddy stared straight ahead, and in time too quick to measure, he watered the plastered Hilton Hotel garage wall with his own specially mixed body fluid. The smell of Jack Daniel's and bleach circulated around the enclosed area where the limo sat. Buddy started coughing like he wasn't the cause, and he had the nerve to look suspiciously at Tiny.

The fact that Buddy looked like he was about to accuse someone other than himself made Tiny clench his fists in anger. But when he also noticed that Buddy was sober enough to undo his zipper before he watered the cold cement, that told Tiny that Buddy could also walk by himself through the back of the Hilton. Instead of steadying Buddy as they entered the back door, Tiny gave him a hard shove.

The shove was rough enough to sober up Buddy a little more. The stinging pinch from his still-opened zipper nipped at his manhood.

"Whoa. What's wrong with you? Where the heck am I?" Buddy was still struggling with the open zipper on a pair of jeans that had shrunk from his body heat, while he ranted and staggered up against a bank of elevators in pain. He gave Tiny a look of distrust then suddenly became quiet, almost alarmed, when an elevator arrived with an accompanying gong that sounded like a doorbell. "Who's there?" Buddy asked as he looked inside the empty elevator.

He was awake, but still needed to sober up a little more. It took him a few seconds to realize that there was no one inside the elevator. He either realized it or got tired of standing up without the aid of resting against the wall. Neither of those things mattered because the aftereffects of the Jack Daniel's and NyQuil cocktail came back to visit. He staggered a few steps then he fell facedown, almost into the elevator just as Ma Cile and Sister Betty approached.

"I see you got Buddy out of the car okay," Sister Betty said as she looked down at Buddy while she handed Tiny a small envelope containing his hotel room key card. "You need to hurry up and get him standing before the bellboy comes with our luggage."

Ma Cile said nothing but the vacant stare from her false blue eye showed her displeasure. She rolled a severe and mean squint which was meant for Buddy, with her good brown eye.

However, the stare from Ma Cile's false blue eye focused on Tiny. Her stare made him feel like he had done something wrong—sinfully wrong. He snatched Buddy by the nape of his neck and with the other arm under Buddy's shoulder hoisted him up against the elevator wall. He stood in front of him so that the approaching bellhop wouldn't think anything was suspicious and to keep Buddy from falling down again.

The bellhop, a lanky young man of about twenty with smooth brown skin and red hair that made him look like a long stale pimento olive appeared to be rushed and a bit disconcerted. He walked briskly with his nametag, which read Larentz, dangling from his jacket like it wanted to escape. He was pushing a luggage trolley loaded with all their bags and carryalls. He said nothing as he sized up the odd couples. He definitely thought something was suspicious about the four but a nice tip when he delivered the men's bags to their room and the women, theirs too, soon drove away his concerns.

Sister Betty and Ma Cile were too excited and a little apprehensive about their mission to take advantage of a much-needed rest. They hung up their clothes while they stared in disbelief at all the unusual comforts of their room.

Sister Betty fondled the four down pillows stacked at the head of her bed. The embroidered pillowcases lay atop a queen-size bed. The bed looked inviting as several layers of white-on-white expensive sheets, a tan blanket and even an extra comforter sent welcoming vibes. She ran her hand along the chrome-plated siding to the closet doors.

For the next ten minutes, Ma Cile marveled at the small microwave and a coffeemaker along with several other items that she'd never used before. She was a woman of habit and didn't take to change quickly. The fact that she was one of the last people in Pelzer to switch from using an old wringer washing machine to an electric one almost made the local newspaper. It was newsworthy because she didn't switch until the late eighties. She had to do it because the only factory in the United States that had a subsidiary that made the rollers for the old wringer washing machine finally folded. Ma Cile was their only customer.

Sister Betty and Ma Cile did everything they could to avoid what they really wanted to discuss. Finally, Sister Betty was the first one to give in. "Ma Cile, you know I'm still not comfortable with this mission." She moved across the blue carpet with her tiny feet barely kissing the nap. She sat down slowly on the small dark blue sofa with flowery cushions. The sofa, a coffee table and two reclining chairs were the only furniture in a small area that served as a living room.

Ma Cile put down the tray of bathroom toiletries that she'd been studying. The pretty bottles with their odd shapes and exotic scents held her attention. She'd never smelled anything so sweet that was for the body. She came out of the bathroom and joined Sister Betty in the living room. After several tries, like the three little bears in the nursery rhyme, she finally found a recliner that comfortably fit her girth. The cushion emitted a small sound as though air was escaping or it was in pain.

"What seems to be the thang that's botherin' you?" Ma Cile had her own questions but figured she'd see what was on Sister Betty's mind.

"It's the money. I still don't understand why Mother Eternal Ann Everlastin' would want me to take the money when she could've just as easily had Mr. Hippo Crit send them preachers a check." She shifted around in her seat and reached into her bag to retrieve the papers that had her instructions. "I also don't understand why I couldn't tell the Reverend Knott Enuff Money where I was going. The money Mother left wasn't for him. There was nothing he could've done about it. I don't like all this secrecy."

"You seemed to be okay with it when we was back in Pelzer. What made you change yo' mind?"

"My left knee's been aching." Sister Betty started to massage it so hard that it began to look like she would take the skin off. "It's been bothering me ever since we left Pelzer. Whenever I think about the reverend and the bishop not knowing what's going on, it gets worse."

"I wasn't gonna say nuthin' but I seen how yo' knee almost put yo' eye out in that fancy car. It was about that time that I started gettin' a little antsy myself." Ma Cile stopped as she sensed that Sister Betty was truly becoming agitated by the way her knee jerked up and down, almost as if it were possessed. "Sister Betty, you and me both know how to pray. Don't you think this would be a good time?" Ma Cile leaned forward and moved aside a few papers that lay on the coffee table next to her recliner. "If you want, you can come and sit in this here fancy rocker and I'll git up and see about getting us some tea." She then rose from the recliner and went to help Sister Betty from the sofa.

"Thank you." Sister Betty didn't try to resist Ma Cile. Instead, she let Ma Cile's strong hands gently pull her from the sofa and lead her to the recliner. "There's another thing . . ." Her voice trailed as though she had lost her place in time.

"Why don't you just rest and let me lead the prayer."

Ma Cile went to her large oversized tote bag to retrieve her Bible. "I'll just get my Bible." Normally, she'd have read from Sister Betty's large family-size Bible but for whatever reason it didn't lay out in the open. Sister Betty always kept it out in the open or in her hands. In fact, when Ma Cile thought about it, she hadn't seen Sister Betty bring it out to the limo.

Suddenly Ma Cile's hands started to shake. She didn't need a dip of snuff to tell her that Sister Betty was more upset than she'd let on. In practically all the years they'd been friends, she had never seen Sister Betty without her big family-sized Bible.

Now it was Ma Cile's turn to panic. She sat down on the same sofa where Sister Betty had sat. As she looked across at Sister Betty who now sat in the recliner with both knees now jerking, she started praying. Ma Cile prayed hard, and the harder she prayed the more both her hands shook. She went from pleading to God for His mercy to reciting the Lord's Prayer. As Ma Cile lifted her arms in supplication, the fatty flab from under her arms flapped, her false blue eye twitched, and as for her good brown eye, it just stared straight ahead as if it couldn't believe what was happening.

It had been a very long time since Ma Cile had led a prayer when she was in the presence of Sister Betty. It was always her best friend whom she thought had the supreme connection with Heaven. Nevertheless, when Ma Cile thought Sister Betty was in trouble and now could not get a prayer through, she didn't think twice about stretching her arms toward the beginning and the end of both their faiths—their God. She prayed until she was exhausted. When she looked up and saw that Sister Betty was suddenly smiling like her old self and that her knees had stopped jerking, Ma Cile gave God more praise.

"Thank you, Ma Cile." Sister Betty was truly happy that she'd let Ma Cile come along. She wasn't feeling up for a spiritual battle by herself and she was happy that God had given her a helpmate. "I didn't realize that I didn't have my Bible until I saw yours. God always has a ram in the bush."

The two women chatted a little less and prayed a lot more. They soon realized that their prayers had reached next door to the room Tiny and Buddy shared. Tiny called and was in a much better mood. He told them that he had finally gotten Buddy all settled down in one of the reclining chairs. He felt he could catch a little nap on the sofa before it was time to drive them to the conference.

Hearing from Tiny that everything seemed to be all right gave Sister Betty permission to relax a little. She tried to keep Ma Cile company for a bit longer but finally excused herself to go and lie down in the adjoining room. Even though she and Ma Cile had prayed for about an hour, she felt she needed to meditate. There was something more that God had for her to do, and she wasn't too sure that it had anything to do with what Mother Eternal Ann Everlastin' had in mind.

Ma Cile excused Sister Betty then marveled at how she hadn't touched her canister of snuff since they'd left the rest stop. For reasons unknown to her, this particular prayer had taken away the desire. She didn't know how long it would last but she was secretly happy for the rescue. She gave God another round of praise and decided that she, too, would go into the room and lie down.

Both the women instantly fell asleep, fully dressed and on top of the covers. Every so often one of them would mutter something or move around.

Perhaps it was God ministering to them.

As Sister Betty slept, she felt as though she were floating on water and the water appeared to change colors—sometimes blue and other times green. The depth went from deep to shallow. Off in the distance, she saw Buddy, and he was smiling at her. Buddy was also dressed in a brown suit, clean-shaven, and he was sober.

Sister Betty stirred slightly as she marveled at the colors she saw in her dream. Suddenly, the water parted and that's when she also saw the Reverend Knott Enuff Money. He was without his ever-present Jheri curl wig. The reverend was with three other men she did not know. A swirling mist arose from the center of the parted water as it turned different colors and came together again. The mist seemed to elevate the three men who were all black and surrounded by thousands of other people who stood side by side on invisible tiers and they too appeared to be of all colors.

One of the strange men stepped away from the Reverend Knott Enuff Money. He was tall, slender and the color of smooth chocolate. He looked to be about in his mid-forties. He was very handsome and wore what looked to be very expensive eyeglasses that sat precariously on the bridge of his nose.

An amber-colored light danced as if possessed around the second man. With the rays of light encircling him like a cocoon, he stepped out of it and away from the Reverend Knott Enuff Money, his arms raised in acceptance. He appeared to be a little shorter and heavier than the first man. He had silky black, wavy hair with a tiny touch of gray that peppered his hairline. Sister Betty thought him to be about fifty. Unlike the other two men, he wore a long purple robe with the initials F and R. He, too, seemed unusually good-looking, brown-skinned with only a few freckles. The robe billowed then opened without a trace of wind. He stood with a book in one hand while the other one held back one side of his robe, revealing his black pants, starched-white shirt and an expensive lavender silk tie with matching suspenders.

The last man was just a little shorter than the second man. He looked to be in his late fifties and had a beard that circled his lips. He was of regular build yet he looked like someone who was very much into a health regiment. His skin was as smooth as costly satin and the color of a pecan. His dome was in the process of balding and seemed designed to enhance his appearance. He appeared to be the most powerful of the three, and his presence defied description.

This time it was a strong hum, something like the sound of satisfied bees that seemed to invisibly envelope their lower bodies. The three men didn't seem to either notice or hear the humming as they stepped backward with their collective feet barely touching the water that was beginning to churn beneath them. They looked up into a sky, which was void of color and seemed endless. Their eyes were steadfast, revealing nothing, then they began laying their hands upon the reverend. He did not resist them. He could not resist them.

In her dream, Sister Betty saw the reverend suddenly rise from the center of the three strange men and as he rose, Buddy approached him.

Sister Betty turned over in her sleep and mumbled, "Thank you, Jesus" as she drifted further into her consult with God.

Ma Cile, in the meantime, slept without moving. She felt as though she could not do anything but surrender to what was happening to her. She, too, dreamed.

In Ma Cile's dream, she was standing alone and dressed completely in white. She stood in the middle of a beautiful green pasture with grass that came up almost to her thighs. She stood with her legs slightly apart and with both her hands raised and her palms open, a white dove lit upon each one.

As the dove hovered over her open palms then rose, a ball of bright warm white light descended from the heavens. The ball of warm light kissed each of her open palms gently as if it wished to bless them. As the ball of light lifted, a spring of water erupted from the center of each palm, then suddenly Ma Cile looked around, and she was not alone.

The pasture had completely filled with people of all colors, shapes and sizes, and in the center of the mass of people stood three strange men. The men were of various ages, shapes and hues and looked very distinguished, very spiritual as they stood next to the Reverend Knott Enuff Money and another young man who had his back turned. Then all three men vanished and reappeared. As strange as it was, Ma Cile felt that she should've known the men, but she didn't. She almost didn't recognize herself in the dream either. Both her eyes were the same color; they were brown. And, as she stood in the middle of the pasture, all the people except the three strange men and the young man who stood with his back turned, started to approach her. They wanted to touch the water that sprang from her palm. "Thank ya, Lord," she mumbled and smiled in her sleep.

There were only five hours left before the Baltimore church conference would begin and both women slept for about three of them. They would need all the rest they could get. They would have to share their strength with those who were much weaker.

While Sister Betty and the others slept in the luxury of tan-brocade-wallpaper suites at the expensive Baltimore Hilton Hotel, the Reverend Knott Enuff Money, the Bishop Was Nevercalled and Sister Ima Hellraiser had no place to lay their heads. The three of them ended up looking like pitiful peons. They each wore a pair of sunglasses to hide their identity while booking into the dwarf accommodations of the roach motel. People and bugs checked in at their own risk at the Motel 5, and no one left the light on for them.

It wasn't that they couldn't afford to stay at the Hilton but Sister Ima Hellraiser being who she was, for sport, just couldn't resist raising a little hell at the Hilton.

It all started earlier in the afternoon when they finally arrived in Baltimore. The reverend and the bishop were famished because they still hadn't eaten during the entire trip from Pelzer. Instead of immediately checking in the hotel, the two men rushed toward the hotel's restaurant and told Sister Hellraiser to check them into their rooms. They'd bet each other that she couldn't possibly mess that up.

Of course, they'd have done better to bet that a pig cloaked in feathers could fly farther than a robin in a windstorm.

Sister Hellraiser had sashayed up to the hotel's check-in desk, and with her best and most insincere smile, she asked for three of the hotel's most expensive suites. It wasn't her money so she felt like splurging—as long as it was on her terms.

Even after the long drive, she still looked fresh. There was no reason why she shouldn't have looked beautiful, after all her job was to aggravate and she always did her job well. She didn't have to touch up her makeup or her hair. The Hilton couldn't have asked for a better-looking guest.

Leave it to Sister Hellraiser to soon make being ugly a prerequisite for getting a room.

The breakdown in communication came about when the hotel clerk told Sister Hellraiser how much each suite would cost. "That'll be $350 per suite for each night of your stay." The hotel clerk whose badge read Anthony hadn't bothered to look up as he was busy putting the information into the computer so he could program the room keys for her. He assumed that she had heard him. His fingers flew quickly across the keyboard like little hummingbirds on crack. He stopped only long enough to push from across his blue eyes a few brunette tresses of his long shaggy hair. "Ma'am, if you'll just give me your credit card, I'll have you all set up and then call a bellboy for your bags." He pushed the reservation slip off to the side ready to swipe as he waited for the credit card.

Sister Hellraiser, true to her name and nature, reached across the counter and snatched the slip. Her eyes popped so hard it loosened one of her false eyelashes. "You must be kidding." She stopped speaking long enough to take the hanging eyelash between her fingers and squeeze it back onto her eyelid. "It's because I'm black. I know it's because I'm black. Haven't you heard of affirmative action? Don't you have a special rate for poor black working people?" she asked, not expecting him to answer. She thought she'd shock and embarrass him into giving her a cheaper rate even if he had to use his own employee discount to do it.

Anthony's face reddened, and he could feel his old southern tenacity return as he stood his ground while staring back at Sister Hellraiser with equal disdain. He looked around to make sure no one was looking then he reached across the counter with one hand and again pushed aside a few of his long brunette tresses. He hissed through his perfectly aligned white teeth, like a seasoned cobra who didn't bother with the other snakes, "No, ma'am. We do not have the poor black working folks discount. We had to discontinue it because too many white folks were asking for it."

Sister Hellraiser stood rooted to the hotel's carpet in her Gucci pumps in disbelief. No one had ever challenged her like that.

Anthony didn't wait for her to recover. He snatched back the slip almost ripping off one of Sister Hellraiser's press-on fingernails in the process and tore it in half. He then picked up the telephone and made a nuisance-removal distress call.

Twenty minutes later, the reverend and the bishop, with their hunger sated and their blood pressure soaring, after they were stupid enough to admit being with Sister Hellraiser, stood on the curb sur- rounded by their luggage while their car was brought to them. They were livid and wondered if Baltimore had a death penalty. They wanted to kill Sister Hellraiser.

It was all they could do to get out of the Hilton in one piece. The reverend had dragged Sister Hellraiser onto the sidewalk and to the car with her arms flailing around like a propeller on a crop duster. While she pitched hell, she nearly decapitated the bishop who stood in horror trying to remember the words to the twenty-third Psalm as he tried to get the car door open.

The reverend's face became twisted just like a corkscrew. He'd had enough. He snatched a greasy plastic cap from his pants pocket and covered his Jheri curl to keep it in place. He then balled up his fist, tossed his head from side to side, and started shuffling his feet like he was stomping roaches. He was about to lay the smack-down.

Suddenly, he stopped. He had a better idea because he didn't want to work up a sweat. "Lord, just give me the strength," he hollered as he ran around and opened up the trunk of the car to look for a crow- bar or anything to use as a weapon. He also didn't want to mess up his clear-polished nails. The first thing he saw, he grabbed. He slammed down the trunk of the car and dashed around to the pas- senger side. "I'm gonna get you! So help me, I'm gonna get you good!" He raised one of his hands and instead of spraying Sister Hellraiser with the last bottle of the blessed oil, he flipped the tip of the can of WD-40 lubricating oil that he held. "I warned you," he screamed, as he prepared to spray her and her trouble-causing demons.

The bishop's eyes widened with horror. "Don't do it, Reverend! She ain't worth you doing time for hurting her. You know you al- ready got a criminal record and a couple of pending IRS investiga- tions."

The mention of doing time and the pending IRS investigations by the bishop stopped the reverend in his tracks.

"You better thank God that the bishop stopped me from hurting you," the reverend snapped as he jumped backward, almost tripping over a stray tree branch. He was hot enough to warm hell up another degree or two.

Sister Hellraiser just stood there mute. She just couldn't seem to get her thoughts together to retaliate; however, that didn't mean that she wouldn't, but she wasn't thinking fast enough.

"I-I don't want anything to take your mind off why we are in Baltimore," the bishop stuttered. He spun around like someone had tied a rope around one of his legs and pulled as he snatched the can of WD-40 lubricating oil from the reverend's hands. He then ran a few feet and jumped at Sister Hellraiser, screaming, "I'll do it myself!"

It took the reverend, bishop and the she-demon another thirty minutes of screaming and accusing one another of sabotage and the sounds of police sirens as they sped down several Baltimore inner-city streets and back roads. After getting a lot of unintelligible and sometimes purposely wrong directions from neighborhood denizens who either wanted to be paid for their information or were too drunk to remember what they knew, the three soon found themselves parked in front of a small, dingy, pay-by-the-hour Motel 5. As they got out of the car, Sister Hellraiser swung at yet missed the bishop because she slipped from the lubricating oil that still clung to her shoes. No matter what her condition, she was still willing to throw down with a nasty attitude to match.

It took them another five minutes to pull one another off one another and walk the ten feet from the curb into the motel lobby. They walked inside the lobby fussing louder than most of the people who frequented the motel would have ever done. In fact, a few of the women who stood around wearing skirts that looked more like narrow strips of bright-colored cloth around their waists with teased hair of various hues, five-inch spike heels and who were obviously drugged out, frowned on them as being undesirable.

A diminutive clerk in a black-and-white striped short-sleeve shirt and a red cap with the brim turned sideways kept his head down and ignored the fracas. His midnight-black skin glistened as perspiration seeped down the side of his fat, round jowls. He looked like a lawn jockey statue as he stood barely tall enough to look over the counter as he chewed on the tip of an unlit cigar that looked like a few people had already chewed it. His name was Big Tom, and he worked the afternoon shift at the Motel 5, so he was used to strange people engaged in even stranger activities on the sleazy premises. He finally looked up and glanced across the top of the counter at the loud newcomers, then spat on the floor. He assumed that the three were into some kinky, role-playing, and without inquiring as to the length of their stay, he pushed a key across the desk as they approached. "Y'all can continue whatever it is that y'all doing in the privacy of your own room." He stopped talking and leaned over the counter with his flabby chin resting upon it and leered with his beady brown eyes at one of the working girls who was pushing her skirt up higher than the legal limit. "You only got about three hours to do it 'cause we only got one room left. There's a church convention in town so we're gonna be very busy tonight, and rooms are gonna be filled with those who want one last fling before they give up sinning." Big Tom leaned back from the counter and laughed again. "Some of them who will be here tonight, well they fall down on a regular basis and they have standing reservations."

The reverend, the bishop and Sister Hellraiser, exhausted more from their squabbling than the long drive, had no choice but to take the room. They took the key and opened the cheap wooden door then walked into a cheaper-looking almost barren room. Fortunately for them, there was at least a queen-size bed and an old wooden, armless chair that was fitted with a thick but stained yellow cushion.

Each one was too tired to fight the other over the meager accommodations. Instead, they dropped their luggage in a heap and argued about how they were going to divide the last paper cup of Ramen noodles that Sister Hellraiser had pulled out to taunt them. Of course, they couldn't do that without a fight. By the time they got finished pulling and snatching on the fragile paper cup they had slivers of noodles, mashed peas, slimy carrots and cold soup broth, over every part of their bodies but their mouths.

If they were exhausted before the noodle fight then they were near comatose from all their snatching and pulling. They called the fight a draw and dashed the few feet to the bed. None of them bothered to undress. They fell on the bed causing the springs to creak as if the bed was haunted. They didn't care that they landed side by side with the reverend's dry Jheri curl tresses stabbing Sister Hellraiser's neck. They were so tired that with their heads barely touching the one long pillow with a frayed pillowcase, the reverend and Sister Hellraiser turned over and collapsed almost in each other's arms.

The Bishop Was Nevercalled, being the tallest of the three, barely had enough strength to pull the old chair inch by inch to the side of the bed. He lay on the old lumpy mattress with his legs hanging off the side of the bed and his knees resting against the dirty chair cushion. The bishop was snoring before he realized that the stain that his knees rested upon was still fresh.

The three occupants of the sleazy greasy motel room were in a deep sleep, as if they were in comas. They all smelled as bad as week-old alley trash and they snored loud enough to cause the other motel undesirables to complain to the front desk. They would stay that way until it was time for the conference later on that evening.

The accommodations at the Motel 5 left a lot to be desired and it certainly wouldn't be confused with its other closely named competitor, Motel 6. This Motel 5 not only didn't welcome them with a light on, it didn't even leave a flashlight on in the window.

18

The Conference

Brother Tis Mythang awoke from his nap, bathed and got dressed. He marveled as he surveyed the guest room where his cousin had placed him to relax. The room, like the rest of the house, oozed with opulence. There was a king-size canopy bed with matching five hundred thread dark gray cotton sheets that sat in the center of a red-and-gray Indian rug. The rug had a border of deeply polished wood that embraced the sunlight that crept through the open bay windows. A three-tier swinging crystal chandelier hung over a light gray chair and ottoman in the far corner of the enormous room. A red-and-gray brick fireplace took up an entire wall with a lighted picture of Jesus praying in the Garden of Gethsemane hanging over the center of the mantel. In another corner, next to a heavy oak door that led into a bathroom that seemed as wide as Brother Tis Mythang's apartment bedroom was a small table with a water fountain. As water streamed down a replica of a mountain, soothing sounds of singing birds came forth in whispers. *Walter, you've done a fantastic job on decorating your house. I'm glad you never married and let a woman mess up your sense of style,* he thought. For a fleeting moment, he also wondered why his cousin never married. He'd never asked and his cousin never said.

Brother Tis Mythang had only stayed at his cousin's house a few times since his late teens, and he always favored that particular room. Whenever he spoke about his own apartment to people who didn't know better, he gave the description of that guest room.

Brother Tis Mythang went over to the open doors that led to an open balcony. It took his breath away to smell the intoxicating mixture of flowers and pine. He inhaled the essence of the garden below once more then leaned over the balcony to check on his car. The front of it could barely be seen from behind a tall hedge. He was glad that he'd opted to leave his Hundai parked in the hedges behind the toolshed. He had already made up his mind not to drive his little gas guzzler to the conference. Not only would the car look out of place among the many more expensive automobiles, but the engine really needed rest for the long drive back.

Brother Tis Mythang again, as he'd done when he walked up the stairs to the guest room looked in awe at the family pictures that hung in expensive gold-gilded frames along the eggshell white wall. He stopped about midway and smiled. There hung a picture of his grandmother who the family affectionately nicknamed Ma Precious. Ma Precious was the mother of his cousin Walter's father and the mother of his own mother, Laura.

Unlike Walter, Brother Tis Mythang never knew his father but he was reared with an abundance of love from both his mother and his Ma Precious when they lived in Charlotte, North Carolina. Both women used to pretend to fight over who had the right to chastise him, who could dress him with colorful outfits that sometimes would've looked better on a daughter rather than on a son and who loved him the best. Ma Precious always won out by giving his small-framed body an extra hug, letting his curly hair grow longer than necessary or giving him more pieces of his favorite candy—red watermelon slices—whenever his mother wasn't looking.

Despite all the love and attention his mother and grandmother lavished upon him, there were times when he felt that perhaps they secretly wished he'd been a girl. Whenever those occasions arose, he'd add a little more dip to his hip or sway to his hair and they'd heap even more gifts upon him thus confirming in his young mind that they loved him in spite of him being a male child. As Brother Tis Mythang grew older, he also learned that those very same actions would either draw unwanted men to him or men who would attack him.

His mother, Laura, was very small-boned, almost beige-colored. She was a short woman with long black hair that she wore, until she died, in a long ponytail pulled back from her oval face. She was never able to do much for him because she'd stayed sick. He remembered that she'd spent most of his teenage years in and out of hospitals. It wasn't until several years after she'd died at the young age of thirty-five that he discovered that she could've lived longer had she taken better care of herself.

The revelation came when he'd been looking for mason jars to fill with Ma Precious's homemade strawberry and rhubarb jams. He'd accidentally pushed one of the old shelves from its ledge and it went hurling toward the rear of the walk-in pantry. When he went to where it had landed, he found a large box that was tied in such a manner that made him think that it was never meant to be discovered. That was enough to make him want to look inside.

He never forget what he'd found. There were several bound dark red journals inside a shoebox. The aroma from several violet-scented sachet packs stuffed inside the box rushed his nostrils fast enough to make him feel a little heady. The packets hadn't lost their freshness. But it would take more than a whiff of a flowery aroma to protect him. It wasn't enough to cover the hurt he soon discovered written with a noticeably shaky hand in faded ink on the pages of the journals.

Brother Tis Mythang remembered sitting down on the cold pantry floor, his legs crossed and hands unsteady. He'd fluctuated between whether or not he should let well enough alone.

Apparently his mother had discovered a lump in one of her breasts but had decided that if she went to see a doctor she wouldn't be able to work steadily. She'd needed to work to keep a place to live and a meal on the table. Although Ma Precious never wanted any money from her, his mother had decided that whenever she wasn't laid up in a hospital that she would work. She had stubborn and unreasonable pride and wouldn't depend upon her mother any more than she had already. Between the hospital bills and other necessities, she never had enough. "Laura, you need to stop trying to be a superwoman. I got a pension and this house is paid off. You don't have to kill yourself trying to work a third shift at that Broyhill factory," he'd heard Ma Precious argue, her words landing on the barren ground of his mother's psyche. His mother's decision to give in to her own stubborn pride eventually cost her her life.

Brother Tis Mythang willed himself back to the present. It would do no good to revisit the past because every time he'd just get angry with his mother for leaving him. "She didn't have to die, Ma Precious," he said as he stroked her picture. "I guess I came by my stubbornness honestly."

He stepped back from the picture, and a smile appeared on his face as he looked at the beautiful woman in a long white dress with a high frilly collar and frilly sleeves. Her jaw was set with determination, and there was a confidence etched upon her face that seemed to make her twin dimples sit unusually deep within her cheeks.

Ma Precious was the opposite of Brother Tis Mythang's mother. In the picture, she sat regal, like a queen, with her arms around both he and Walter. The two boys were her only grandchildren. She was probably in her sixties when the picture was taken but she looked a lot younger. Like her daughter she, too, had a beautiful oval face and wore her long silver hair in a ponytail that hung thick and fanned across one breast and almost down to her waist. That long hair and their oval faces were their only resemblance.

Ma Precious was originally from New Orleans, the Bayou country, and she had the distinction of lineage from a long line of women known to be root workers. No one messed with her, and she laughed at their fear because she didn't believe in roots, only whenever it suited her purpose, although she'd never let on about it. She believed in God, and she believed in Him with all her heart.

Ma Precious had an exotic look like one of those old turn-of-the century mulattos who tried to pass into white society to avoid the pressures of being mixed. However, Ma Precious was proud of her black heritage; she was almost boastful about it. She was tall, yet shapely, built sturdy and continued to take care of herself despite the early death of her husband.

Brother Tis Mythang never remembered Ma Precious being sick a day in her life. When she passed suddenly from an embolism that had traveled from her leg to her heart and then burst, everyone was shocked. It took him a long time to get over her death. It seemed that one moment he angrily questioned God because his mother had suffered so long before she died then the next, he wrestled with God because his grandmother was taken away suddenly, without suffering or a warning. He was not prepared for either of their deaths.

Ma Precious had left a lot of money to both he and Walter. He ran through his inheritance like a bull in a china shop. He spent it on expensive trips, jewelry and gave gifts to several of his friends, including Buddy. He used up the money on everything except what he should have and wrecked his life in the process.

In the meantime, Walter had pastored a small church with only a few hundred faithful members who needed more space. He'd taken his inheritance and added it to the funds raised for the construction of the new building and today, he had more than he'd ever expected.

God had shown favor upon Walter because He had trusted him with a little and he'd shown good stewardship.

The thought of Mother Eternal's sudden death flashed through Brother Tis Mythang's mind. He willed it away. He hadn't been prepared for her death either. He wasn't too sure that he was prepared for his own.

Brother Tis Mythang looked down the winding stairway, and when he saw no one in the foyer below, he leaned forward and planted a light kiss on the picture of Ma Precious and continued downstairs.

By the time Brother Tis Mythang reached the bottom of the long, winding stairway, his composure had returned. He was happy once more. Licking a finger he slicked back a stray strand of his black curly hair and strutted slowly into the den. He would take a few steps then stop and look into one of the mirrors to check his reflection from different angles. The wide grin on his face beamed with approval. "Tyson Beckford had better watch out," he said.

"Tyson who?" Reverend Thomas asked. He sat over in the corner in a metallic gray oversized easy chair with his feet resting on the matching ottoman, out of view of the doorway. He wore a burgundy suit and a white shirt with a burgundy collar. His tie was burgundy and black and matched his socks. The Stacy Adams shoes were deep burgundy.

The Reverend Thomas had been lounging in his den for about ten minutes, enjoying a moment of solitude. Earlier, he'd telephoned the Reverends Cherry and Reid to discuss the night's conference. After their intense discussion and because of several new revelations, he needed time to meditate. He was about to have a glass of cold lemonade and a bit of prayer before the interruption of Brother Tis Mythang's sudden entrance. His self-appreciating comments broke Reverend Thomas's concentration.

Brother Tis Mythang stopped short when he suddenly saw his cousin but not before he let out a short, high-pitched scream. "Walter, you scared me. I didn't know anyone was in here." He recovered then walked over to where his cousin sat. "Tyson Beckford is a supermodel." The sour look on his face didn't mask his disapproval. "You need to come out from that pulpit more often and check out the rest of the world." He followed his last comment with a nervous laugh as he realized that he was a guest as well as a relative. "Do you like what I'm wearing?"

Brother Tis Mythang was dressed in a silver Hugo Boss suit with a peach-and-black-striped tie and matching socks. His shoes were polished so bright that one would need sunglasses before looking at them. He checked the buttons on his black shirt to make sure they, were buttoned completely and not out of line. He also knew that his smile and fashion were all he had left. They represented his rent money, which he decided to worry about later.

"Walter, you look like a million dollars." Brother Tis Mythang sang the word *million* to remind his cousin of his impending reward if all went well that night.

"You're not fooling me," the Reverend Thomas said, laughing. "Cousin, I'm way ahead of you. I've been sitting here praying and reading the Word while waiting for God to show me what to do."

"I hope you lit a few dozen candles as well as danced the Macarena and the Hokey Pokey too. Trying to change Reverend Knott Enuff Money will sap up all the spirituality you've got stored."

"I won't be doing this alone."

Brother Tis Mythang lay a sympathetic hand on his cousin's shoulder and mimicked in a heavy voice, "'You've got God on your side.' That's what you were going to say, wasn't it?"

"Actually, I was going to say that I've already spoken with the Reverends John Cherry and Frank Reid. They're to receive financial bequests as well; however, it seems that there will be others from your church arriving here tonight. I wasn't able to get much more information than that. I don't know if they're male or female. I don't know if they're young or old. I actually don't know how many. The one thing I do know is that the three of us, Cherry, Reid and me have got to watch as well as pray." He stopped talking when he realized Brother Tis Mythang was no longer listening.

Brother Tis Mythang jumped back and did a little shuffle and shout. He'd stopped listening to his cousin as soon as he'd heard the names of the Reverends Reid and Cherry. "You mean to tell me that I'm going to be playing in front of those two dynamic speakers and their congregations? They have about ten thousand people between their churches." He shouted some more and then stopped. "Walter, why didn't you tell me this before? I've got to make sure that I have some of the songs I hear on their broadcasts in my repertoire."

"Cousin Tis, calm down. Yes, they're both coming to the conference tonight; however, as I've tried to explain to you before you went into your shout, they, too, are a part of the effort to bring Reverend Knott Enuff Money to a level where God can truly use him." The Reverend Thomas stopped and snapped his fingers as he remembered something more. "You know I suddenly realized something. All three of us—Reid, Cherry and me—tried to call your pastor on the day they had Mother Eternal Ann Everlastin's funeral. The Reverend Knott Enuff Money never returned our calls. That's very impolite."

"Impolite is what he is." Brother Tis Mythang didn't really want to discuss his pastor. He wanted to know about the parts the Reverends Cherry and Reid played. "Why are the other two pastors involved?" He suddenly felt important and on a different level since his cousin obviously didn't mind sharing a confidence with him.

"Apparently, Mother Eternal Ann Everlastin' has a bequeath for each of them, and it will be given, if and when we can bring God's deliverance down upon your pastor," the Reverend Thomas replied.

Brother Tis Mythang let out a nervous laugh. He thought about mimicking the words from one of his favorite television series, *Mission Impossible: Reverend Walter Thomas, if you should decide to take this mission . . .* Instead, he said, "Here's something that might help." He reached into one of his pants pocket and pulled out a ten-dollar bill from his wallet. He extended his hand with the bill folded in half. "The Reverend Knott Enuff Money only listens to the crisp sound of money. You will need this ten and a lot more because there ain't no way without God stepping down from His throne in Heaven into the conference in the flesh that you're gonna turn that man around." He pressed the bill into his cousin's hand and laughed again. "You'd better take it. You can forget about that million dollars. This will be the only money you'll see coming in from Pelzer."

The Reverend Thomas pushed his cousin's hand aside. The look of concern seemed almost painful as he asked, "Well, if you truly feel that way then why do you continue to attend a church where you have no faith in its leadership? Why do you want to put your salvation at such a risk?"

The Reverend Walter Thomas continued with his questions, omitting any further references to which others might be coming from the Ain't Nobody Else Right But Us—All Others Goin' to Hell Church that night. His words took on the tone of a mini-sermon, and as he spoke, quoting Bible verses, Brother Tis Mythang's concern with his outward appearance faded while he finally realized that his soul stood naked in sin and in danger of hellfire.

Brother Tis Mythang became uncharacteristically quiet as they left the house and got into the Reverend Thomas's luxury Town Car. While they drove the several miles to the conference venue, the Reverend Thomas's admonition repeated itself in Brother Tis Mythang's mind. He tried to replace his cousin's questions and warnings with the different songs and melodies he'd play later on that night. Nothing worked. For the first time since he'd joined the Ain't Nobody Else Right But Us—All Others Goin' to Hell Church, he questioned his membership and its questionable rewards.

19

Return to God's Love

It was almost eight o'clock and the evening sun was beginning its descent. It seemed to shower the sky with shades of purple, red and yellow as it bid the day good-bye. Spit-polished limousines and other luxury cars were parked in a roped-off section for the VIPs at the conference's host church, the New Psalmist Baptist Church. Their occupants stepped out of the expensive vehicles in dazzling arrays of colors and styles. The men and women, with entourages surrounding them, were considered the most beautiful and the more spiritually-minded as they walked with heads proud as if they alone were communicating with and being led by God.

Some of the distinguished men and women were pastors, some bishops and practically all of them well-known television personalities. There were even several world-famous gospel singers sprinkled throughout the parade of celebrities. One such person was the queen of gospel, the evangelist and pastor Shirley Caesar. A small yet powerful woman, from Raleigh, North Carolina, her lifetime of singing God's praises using an obviously anointed voice had garnered her worldwide attention. Unlike many who would later on bring the flock to their feet, that night, she lived the life she sang.

Shirley Caesar was accompanied by the Reverends John and Diana Cherry. The Reverend John Cherry was considered a very devout preacher whose drive to reform the church seemed plagued with resistance and several lawsuits, each of which had failed. His wife, Diana, a few years younger than her husband and also a dynamic speaker was a beautiful woman, physically and spiritually. She dressed impeccably and her bright silver hair framed her face as though the color and style were created specifically for her. They sandwiched Shirley Caesar between them as though to protect the shy gospel sensation from the many television cameras blanketing the sidewalk, which were apparently making her nervous. No matter how many times Shirley Caesar appeared in front of millions of people, she was still shy, and her only purpose for singing was to praise God.

Bishop Frank Reid took his position in front of New Psalmist Baptist with outstretched arms to welcome the conference attendees. His friendly, no-respecter-of-persons manner was apparent as he greeted the well-known and the unknown. His salt-and-pepper hair seemed darker and lighter at the same time as the bright camera lights poured over him as he stood dressed in white-on-white attire. His wife, Marla, stood eye to eye with her husband in height and was considered a full-figured woman. She looked almost angelic. She, too, was dressed in an all white pearl-beaded floor-length gown and matching high-collar short sleeve jacket. Her superb, unblemished dark complexion made her famous bright overly-white teeth even brighter. They were about to be interviewed by famous gospel television host Dr. Bobbitto Jonas.

Dr. Bobbitto Jonas had served the gospel community for more than twenty-five years. He'd received honors from all over the world for his unselfish drive to bring the best of gospel to the masses. He, too, was a singer and producer, and he knew the ins and outs of the gospel community from the musicians to the singers, from the record companies to the record producers, and his wealth of knowledge and contacts were extended to all, regardless of race or religion. Dr. Jonas was also famous for his custom-made stage attire and the conference was another opportunity to show the men how he felt dressing for television and any major appearance ought to be done.

Dr. Jonas took one last look at his six-foot slender reflection in the camera lens and liked what he saw. The makeup he wore made it seem that there was not one freckle on his fifty-year-old face and his mustache appeared as though it were sculpted, hair by hair. It didn't matter to him that others said behind his back that he dressed a little too daintily. In his eyes, he looked exquisite standing before his television cameras dressed in a powder-blue Ciccone ensemble complete with satin shirt. His shoes were the same color as his suit and were obviously handmade. He looked away from admiring his reflection just in time to see that the Reverend Frank Reid and his wife stood at the entrance to the three-story brick church, which was the size of a small stadium and seated about seven thousand people. The Reids were ready to greet their conference guests, so he signaled for the cameras to start.

Dr. Jonas flashed his best television smile and went to work on the various celebrities who had flocked to the conference. Those who regularly appeared on his weekly gospel music television program, *The Bobbitto Jonas Gospel Music Show* poured all kinds of tributes his way, and at the same time managed to get in a free plug about their own television ministry, record album and latest concert appearances. Some of them even managed to remember to thank God for allowing them to be in such a holy place and for their anointed ministries, whatever they happened to be.

Everything was going smoothly until the gospel songbird herself, Miss Dottie Peoples, walked up before the cameras to greet Dr. Jonas before she continued into the church. She walked slowly so that the cameras could catch every inch of her magnificence. She was in her forties but had the seasoning and class of someone much older. Her signature coif of polished black beehive hair was pulled back from her chocolate-brown face to reveal makeup that was flawless, as was everything about her, from her long diamond-studded earrings to her silver Valentino gown, which cloaked her body like it never wanted to leave it. She was as well known for her beautiful custom-made gowns as she was for her well-recognized robust voice. Dottie Peoples could warble in notes that were either four notes below or above middle C, and not one note was flat. She was so cool on stage that those who came to see her perspired more than she as they clapped their hands, stomped their feet and tried to sing along.

Dottie Peoples was just about to say hello into the microphone to Dr. Jonas when it happened. Hell broke loose from its foundation and, of course, there was only one person who could've caused such a fuss. It was none other than one of her biggest fans.

"Dottie! Dottie Peoples. Oh my Lord. It's *my* Dottie."

Brother Tis Mythang had sprinted from his cousin Walter Thomas's side, waving his hands so fast it looked like he was trying to fan a fire. As soon as he'd spotted her, he lost all three of the big Cs—his class, composure and couth. Everyone back in Pelzer knew that if they really wanted to get Brother Tis Mythang to send someone to the nearest emergency room or the morgue, all that was needed was one bad word against Dottie Peoples. She, Kirk Franklin and the great James Brown ruled in the musical kingdom of Brother Tis Mythang.

Unfortunately for Brother Tis Mythang, he wasn't in Pelzer, and before he could get within ten feet of his musical love, several security men threw him and his Hugo Boss suit onto the ground.

Of course, the entire thing was caught on television. With the way things were going for Brother Tis Mythang that particular scene was bound to end up on the show's repeat schedule.

Both Dr. Jonas and Dottie Peoples stood mute, looking like they'd seen the ghost of the late Reverend James Cleveland return to claim back his legendary gospel throne. They didn't know what to say or do.

Fortunately for Brother Tis Mythang, the Reverend Thomas raced over and ordered the security to free Brother Tis Mythang and help him to get on his feet.

"Cousin Tis, what is wrong with you?" the Reverend Thomas snarled. He was both upset and embarrassed. "Why would you attack Dottie Peoples?"

Brother Tis Mythang stood with his head of disheveled curls hung in shame. He never meant to embarrass himself or his cousin, but he'd been a fan of Dottie Peoples for a long time and this was the first time he'd had a chance to see or meet her in person. Well-known celebrities didn't exactly flock to the little town of Pelzer. His eyes began to water, and it wasn't certain whether it was from his brazen act or his ripped, spent-all-his-rent-money Hugo Boss suit. Everyone but Brother Tis Mythang could see that it was only a torn pocket.

"I just wanted to meet her and say hello." With every word of explanation came another tear. The grown man was standing there crying with the cameras still rolling and picking up his every word. "What will Miss Peoples think of me now?" he whined. Brother Tis Mythang could see his dream of playing "On Time God" while Dottie Peoples sang, strutted and shouted across the stage disappear. What effect his outburst had on the Reverend Thomas never crossed his mind. "I'm never gonna play the organ for her now." He stopped and looked at his cousin with eyes that looked like he'd just seen a horror movie. "Oh no! They probably won't let me play for anybody tonight." His face became a mask of contrition and tears. It was enough to move the most hardened heart.

The Reverend Thomas could only pray. He didn't know what else to do. He'd never witnessed such a display, and although he knew his cousin Tis was a bit eccentric, he had never expected a display like what he'd witnessed.

The Reverend Thomas's quick prayer must have worked. From

out of nowhere Dottie Peoples appeared. She'd hidden behind one of the cameramen when the fray had begun. From her hiding place she'd heard through the camera monitors what Brother Tis Mythang had said. When she saw and heard that the Reverend Walter Thomas was not only trying to calm down the young man but was obviously a relative, she knew everything would be okay.

Dottie Peoples reached out and touched the shoulder of Brother Tis Mythang. "Young man," she said as she gently tried to turn him around to face her.

Brother Tis Mythang could've been in the midst of a roaring and stampeding elephant herd but he'd still recognize Dottie Peoples's voice. His body reacted faster than his mind because before he knew it he'd spun around twice, and there she stood. In all her regal beauty was his Dottie Peoples standing close enough for him to reach out and touch her, which was all he'd wanted to do anyway.

"Are you alright?" A look of real concern had taken the place of the fear she'd shown only moments before. "I'm sorry I overreacted," she added. "It was my fault for not looking to see that you were with the Reverend Thomas."

The class she possessed had let her take the blame for something that was not of her own doing in order for the young man to recover a bit of dignity.

The Reverend Thomas looked at Dottie Peoples. He'd seen her quick wink and returned her smile. He was well aware of what she was doing and his smile showed his silent appreciation. He also understood that the cameras were still on them and that she'd taken control of the broadcast direction so that the conference could get back on track and off the commotion.

With no more drama for the moment, the cameras turned back to Dr. Jonas and he continued with his overexaggerated greetings and compliments.

Dottie Peoples was a true anointed professional in every sense and her display of charity for the conference's sake took nothing away from her genuine concern for the young man who obviously was an ardent fan.

Brother Tis Mythang's thoughts of his torn suit and anything that might've embarrassed him on nationwide television disappeared as soon as Dottie Peoples spoke directly to him. As much as he could chatter with the best of them, he still couldn't or wouldn't say a word back. He just stared into the beautiful dark, round doe eyes of Dottie Peoples and gave God praise in silence.

Of course, because he didn't speak aloud didn't mean that all was well. After all, there was a hell-raiser in every crowd to squash any notion of forgiveness and peace, and that night was no exception.

The Reverend Walter Thomas was just about to walk both Dottie Peoples and Brother Tis Mythang through the throng of onlookers, consisting mostly of those who couldn't afford to attend the conference who still wanted to ogle the celebrities, when he sensed a change in the crowd. He looked around but didn't see anything unusual and thought perhaps he was just being too sensitive. He certainly had a reason to be after everything that had gone down.

The distant noise started off like the annoying hum of a broken buzz saw. Normally, Brother Tis Mythang would've noticed or at least heard that something was amiss but he was too busy wallowing in the attention from Dottie Peoples.

And just like claps of thunder that could be heard but not seen, powerful words that cut through the air like lethal daggers into the heart of peace and quiet arrived.

"Brother Tis Mythang, what are you doing here? You ain't got no business here with all these classy folks."

The nasty blast of agitation had a familiarity that tossed Brother Tis Mythang's serenity harder than a bucking horse with his tail ablaze. He thought he was dreaming. Baltimore was at least seven or eight hours away from Pelzer, and no one from there should be at that particular conference, yet, he'd know that vicious voice anywhere. "Oh Lord, please don't let it be that hell-raiser." He just dropped his head in surrender like someone had karate chopped him in the back of his neck because he knew better. After the embarrassment he'd just suffered on nationwide television, to have a hell hound chasing him on his special night seemed only fitting.

Both Dottie Peoples and the Reverend Thomas also heard the annoying questions from within the crowd of onlookers but they couldn't determine which of the women in the crowd had spoken; however, one glance at the defeated look on Brother Tis Mythang's face told them that he definitely knew. It also told them that perhaps if they wanted to get inside without any further drama they needed to leave Brother Tis Mythang to face his own demons.

"Why don't we just let you stay out here for a moment to compose yourself," the Reverend Thomas whispered to his cousin. "We'll meet you inside." He didn't expect any resistance, and he wasn't disappointed when he received none. He felt bad when he saw

Brother Tis Mythang just standing and staring into space, but not bad enough to stay out there with him.

Dottie Peoples thought she was helping when she pointed to the woman who was trying to get Brother Tis Mythang's attention. "There's the woman who called out to you." No sooner had the words left her mouth than Dottie Peoples regretted getting involved. One look at the approaching woman told her that she meant business and didn't much care about the television cameras or the spirituality of the event.

Dottie Peoples didn't wait for the Reverend Thomas to escort her inside. She ran ahead of him in her five-inch Prada high heels and inside the church like she heard someone calling her to the stage.

The strange woman walked through the crowd, which had parted to let her through without her asking. She had a scowl on her face and her snarling lips looked more lethal than a machine gun. Her body moved with a swagger of certainty as she approached him with the intensity of a spotted she-tiger on the prowl. She never took her eyes off her prey—Brother Tis Mythang. Wearing an obviously red-dyed wig and a long mauve-colored form-fitting dress that was a bit wrinkled, the honey-colored shrew wasn't to be denied her victim.

"I know you heard me," she said with her lips curled. She was not going to be denied her fifteen milliseconds of fame before the television cameras, especially since she'd kept mum about seeing his car on the highway as they were driving from Pelzer. With each word, she poked Brother Tis Mythang in his chest with one of her long, pearl-pink polished fingernails like she was beating a conga drum.

He never felt it return but his voice had done just that. It was probably loosened by the pokes from her sharp fingernails. "Sister Hellraiser, what in the world are you doing here?"

Before Sister Hellraiser could respond, she was interrupted by another voice.

"Never you mind why she's here. Why haven't you returned any of my phone calls? We knew you were trying to sneak off somewhere when we saw you back on I-95." The Reverend Knott Enuff Money was on a roll. He didn't know whether to continue his tirade or get back on track with his own personal mission.

The assault from the Reverend Knott Enuff Money was a big surprise. Brother Tis Mythang had focused on surviving the verbal assault from the always lethal Sister Hellraiser. He never noticed that she was not alone. He didn't need a tarot card or a vision to tell him that if his pastor was there with Sister Ima Hellraiser, then the bishop was somewhere bringing up the rear.

"This is just lovely. I-I-I'm so excited," the Bishop Was Nevercalled stuttered as he waved back to the crowd, which had formed around them to see what was going to happen next to Brother Tis Mythang, the poster boy for bad luck. The bishop waved as if he were doing the crowd a favor just like the celebrity he always wanted to be. He seemed to want to confirm Brother Tis Mythang's thoughts of impending disaster.

Sister Hellraiser was about to block the Reverend Knott Enuff Money from confronting Brother Tis Mythang any further. It wasn't because she cared about Brother Tis Mythang; it was because the Reverend Knott Enuff Money had stepped in front of the one camera that had stayed behind to take outtakes. It was on her. "Move out of my way," she snapped. "This is my moment, and I'm about to get a close-up."

She didn't have to ask the Reverend Knott Enuff Money twice. From the corner of his eye, he saw them—the Trinity, the Reverends Cherry, Reid and Thomas. They were standing in the archway of the church talking with Dr. Bobbitto Jonas. "I don't need Brother Tis Mythang. I'll deal with him later, that is if I ever decide to let him back inside my church or sit at my organ." He had his eyes deadlocked on the three mega-church pastors and hadn't bothered to notice that Brother Tis Mythang had used the distraction to his advantage.

Brother Tis Mythang fled to the side of the church with a foxlike quickness.

The Reverend Knott Enuff Money was about to lose the microscopic bit of dignity he had left from his short stay at the Motel 5 as he rattled his brain for a few introductory Bible verses to impress the Trinity.

While the bishop signed autographs for those who thought he was somebody because he acted like he was and Sister Ima Hellraiser posed for the television camera by showing a little more leg than she should've every time the cameraman acted like he was moving away or losing interest, the Reverend Knott Enuff Money straightened his cobalt-blue Ralph Lauren tie. The tie was the only piece from his ensemble that didn't need an iron.

Just like Sister Hellraiser and the bishop, his clothes were a bit wrinkled, but there wasn't any way to iron clothes at the Motel 5 because there wasn't an iron to be found on the premises. It wasn't necessary for most of their patrons who had sense enough to take their clothes off before carousing.

With his imaginary caution flung to the wind, his alleged dignity left back in Pelzer and his late mother's words—"We have got to build a fancy church. God said His people should have the very best. How we gonna show folks how prosperous God is if we ain't showing prosperity?"—echoing in his head, he set off to worm his way into the inner sanctum of the mega preachers.

The Reverend Knott Enuff Money's feet picked up the pace as he zigzagged through mobs of people and several thorny rosebushes toward the archway of the church where the three pastors stood. "Mother," he whispered as his face took on a look of determination while he quickly looked skyward then focused again on his mission, "I'm about to do it. I'm gonna learn all about prosperity at the feet of the Trinity. If they knew how to get old, tight-fisted Mother Eternal Ann Everlastin' to leave them millions of dollars while all she donated to me was fifty thousand then I need to sit at their prosperity table and lap up some of those crumbs of knowledge." He needed to assure himself, so he continued with words of self-encouragement. "Why should I settle for my congregation purchasing a baptismal pool with a Jacuzzi? I have fifteen hundred members who believe that I deserve an Olympic-size baptismal pool and so much more. If I can get in on some of that fortune, then I could possibly lower the tithes from fifteen percent to ten percent." He stubbed his foot on a rock at that last thought.

During the time the bishop was building his imaginary fan base and Sister Ima Hellraiser was almost to the point of mooning the cameraman to get herself on film, there were other situations popping up.

There was still Sister Betty and the others. The four figures were trying to make their way into the church from the parking lot but they had to keep stopping. It seemed that Sister Betty's arthritic knees were jumping again. In order to keep her from doing harm to herself and her waist-length bosom because her knees were jerking so hard and so high, Tiny had to carry her like he was setting a chair out. Unfortunately for him, the knee jerks didn't lessen until they got within about fifty feet of the church. Both he and Sister Betty were fortunate that one of her knee jerks, which kept popping him in his face like hail hadn't completely knocked him out. "I'm sorry, Mr. Tiny," Sister Betty kept repeating each time she sucker-punched him with one of her bony knees.

There was nothing Ma Cile could do to help Tiny with Sister Betty's bad knees. She knew that it meant that somewhere around them there was trouble either happening or about to happen, but she had her hands full just trying to steady Buddy.

He had recovered from his drunken stupor but not without consequences. He had the shakes so bad, he looked like he was dancing the Bankhead Bounce as his head, shoulders and torso twisted like a contortionist to music, which only he heard.

Ma Cile was losing her patience. "Buddy, if ya step on my bunion one mo' time, I'm gonna slap ya so hard 'til you'd wished you'd never heard of yo' friend Jack Daniel's." She still wasn't sure why someone would call liquor by a man's name instead of White Lightning, but she didn't have time to figure it out.

Even with a bad hangover, Buddy knew the truth when he heard it. Buddy had no doubt at all that Ma Cile would've slapped the liquor taste out of his mouth and praised God, all at the same time. His body suddenly stopped shaking; however, he still needed Ma Cile's assistance in walking a straight line to the church, so he held onto her massive arm, and like a good little boy, he kept up with her as well as kept his big mouth shut.

It wasn't five minutes later before Sister Betty and the others saw the reason for her knee jerks. The man running like the devil was chasing him, with long Jheri curled hair flapping in the wind, could've only been one person. "Oh no," Sister Betty murmured. "What are we gonna do now?" The others stood there like statues. The reverend was the last person they expected to see that night especially since, as far as they knew, they'd left him in Pelzer.

They didn't know that the Reverend Knott Enuff Money was racing off to bulldoze and bluff his way into the good graces of the Reverends Cherry, Reid and Thomas. He was so determined to meet the mega-church pastors before they went inside the church and joined others of their impressive distinction that he never saw Sister Betty and the others pass by. He didn't even take the time to give his frizzy Jheri curl a splash of activator.

He was on a mission and, as usual, he hadn't considered the consequences of his impending actions. However, he was sure his mama was somewhere turning over in her grave with pride. He was about to walk in some high cotton with the big boys.

By the time Sister Betty and the others regained any semblance of composure, the reverend had raced out of sight. "I don't know how we are gonna do what we came to do now with the Reverend Knott

Enuff Money running around here." Sister Betty stopped and clasped her hands together in prayer. She looked upward toward where all her hope and strength lay and began to pray. "Lord, I don't know how or why the reverend is here in Baltimore, but I suspect that you do. I've been in the dark ever since I started on this mission, and I still don't see any light at the end of this long tunnel. It seems that every time I think I got a handle on thangs, something else happens. Heavenly Father, I need your help—"

Before Sister Betty could finish her plea, Ma Cile butted in and finished the prayer for her, "Yessir, Lawd. Could you please do what Sister Betty asks in a hurry. I'm hungry and this here man, Buddy, is about to make me sin." Ma Cile turned and looked at Sister Betty who was looking back at her like Ma Cile had lost her mind. So Ma Cile, not quite understanding what was the problem, quickly added, "Amen."

"Why did you do that?" Sister Betty asked Ma Cile. "Why did you interrupt my praying?"

"I did it to help you out," Ma Cile replied with a wide grin on her chubby face. She was so proud of herself that she didn't even try to thump her forehead to make her bad eye line up with the good one.

"How was that supposed to help me?" Sister Betty asked suspiciously but nicely. She didn't want to offend Ma Cile.

"You know the Bible says when two and mo' are standing together, Heaven listens mo' closely." Ma Cile grinned as she gave her own interpretation of the Holy Word. It was so loose it would take a lot of prayer to bind it to the real meaning.

Sister Betty needed a reason to laugh and she did at the sweetness of her best friend's intentions, although she was sure that somewhere in the back of Ma Cile's mind was also the need to get everything over so she could get a dip of snuff.

While Ma Cile and Sister Betty were praying, Tiny had grabbed Buddy and leaned him against a fence. Like the others, he'd seen the Reverend Knott Enuff Money rushing toward the church; however, unlike the reverend, he'd also seen the three pastors leave the church's doorway and walk around toward the side of the church chatting with Dr. Bobbitto Jonas.

Tiny looked over at Sister Betty and Ma Cile. He saw that they appeared to be fine so he used that opportunity to run after the preachers. He said a silent prayer and hoped that Buddy wouldn't do anything stupid while he was gone.

* * *

It was while the Reverend Knott Enuff Money had bent over to momentarily massage his aching foot, after he stubbed which against a rock that the Trinity left the doorway. He spun around looking like a wild man as he searched through the throngs of conference attendees who had not gone inside yet. "Where are they?" he railed under his breath. "They were just here." He wanted to cry. "How could they have just disappeared?" He suddenly stopped and pounded his fists together. *How could I be so stupid? Of course, they're inside. They must've gone inside,* he thought. With that revelation in mind, he straightened his clothes and marched into the church, smiling like he'd just found out the secret to success.

A few minutes later what he found out was that he'd forgotten that Sister Hellraiser still had the conference confirmations for the three of them in her possession. Five minutes later, he found himself again on the outside looking in.

While the Reverend Knott Enuff Money stood outside holding a pity party for one, Tiny had managed to locate the mega-church pastors. He put on his best smile and offered a handshake to each of them as he introduced himself. With the preliminaries out of the way, Tiny went straight to the meat of the matter. "Pastors, I guess by now, y'all know that Sister Betty has come all the way to Baltimore to see the three of you." He waited for a reply. There was none so he continued talking as the pastors appeared to be sizing him up.

"She brought the checks."

"Oh, that Sister Betty," they said in unison.

"Where is Sister Betty?" the Reverend Cherry asked. "We need to clarify a few things with her."

"Yes, we do," the Reverend Thomas added, then said, "We do, however, offer our condolences to you for the loss of your employer, and one of our most loyal tithers, Mother Eternal Ann Everlastin'."

"We'd love to discuss it with you but it's Sister Betty that we need to speak to about this most delicate matter," the Reverend Reid chimed in.

"I'll go and get her," Tiny replied. He spun around so fast he appeared to be nothing but an illusion.

By the time Tiny returned to retrieve Sister Betty and Ma Cile, they had moved over to where he'd left Buddy. Ma Cile had Sister Betty and each had Buddy by one arm, and they were praying for him. He got to them just in time to hear Sister Betty say amen.

"I found them," Tiny said. "We need to hurry. They won't have much time before they have to speak before the audience. If we work things right, I can have us back on the road to Pelzer by midnight."

Tiny was suddenly in a big hurry to unload his passengers and get on the road to collecting his two million dollars. Also, it was starting to get a little too spiritual for him. He wasn't really that much of a praying man, and too many church folks always made him nervous. In his mind, he felt that too much religion would undermine his good times. Tiny took over the job of lugging Buddy, and he led the women to where he'd left the pastors.

The pastors were still standing practically in the same spot where Tiny left them. He introduced Sister Betty and Ma Cile and purposely omitted Buddy; however, when he saw the pastors were giving him a strange look, he mumbled, "This is Mother Eternal Ann Everlastin's nephew, Buddy."

At the mention of Buddy's name, the Reverend Reid smiled. "It's a pleasure to finally meet you, Buddy. Your aunt has mentioned you over the past several years, and she always asked me to pray for you, which I did, gladly."

Ma Cile looked over at Buddy who was still struggling to keep one eye open. She then turned to the Reverend Reid, and asked, "When did you pray for him? Was it once a year at a one of ya converacations or sumpthin'." Ma Cile didn't wait for an answer. She took the Reverend Reid's hand and added, "You gonna have to do better'n that to kill that boy's demon. I can help ya out 'cause I know the demon's name."

The Reverend Reid was caught off guard by Ma Cile's sudden familiarity and questioning of his praying skills, and even more so that she could name demons. He could only reply by asking, "The demon's got a name?"

"He sho do," Ma Cile said. Her false blue eye seemed to take over and on its own it rolled around in her head until it looked accusingly over at Buddy. She then hissed, "His demon's name is Jack, and it's even got a last name, too. It's Daniel."

It was the serious look on Ma Cile's tired face and the twitch coming from her false blue eye that caused everyone to laugh—everyone but Ma Cile. She didn't have a clue as to what was so funny, after all, she was only trying to help.

"Why don't we all just step inside my study," the Reverend Thomas said. "I don't think we want to continue this serious discussion out here in the vestibule."

As the Reverend Thomas opened the door to his study and showed everyone to a seat, Sister Betty was struck by the study's simplicity. There was nothing in the study that looked like it belonged to a very wealthy and prosperous preacher. There were plain brown wooden chairs with thin eggshell-white cushions. The desk seemed ordinary in that it wasn't the long cherry-wood one that she'd seen in other pastors' studies, including the Reverend Knott Enuff Money's. There was a bookcase and at a glance she could see various Bibles and concordances. There were many reference books, and against the back wall was a small table that held a computer, a printer and a fax machine. The walls were painted off-white and they seemed to have a stucco-type façade. Two hanging lights lit up the room, and there was a telephone console at the end of the desk. There was not a picture of Jesus hanging on the cross. Instead, there was a small three-foot wooden cross that hung with a piece of purple material draped over each side where Christ's arms would've been. Everything was plain and simple. That's what it was that seemed strange to her—it was definitely the simplicity.

At the suggestion of the Reverend Cherry, everyone held hands and had a short prayer before starting the meeting.

"We all pretty much know why you've come to Baltimore, Sister Betty. Although I'm sorry that it had to be under these difficult and sad circumstances. Mother Eternal Ann Everlastin' was a longtime supporter of our various ministries, so we definitely feel your loss—"

"Not only because she was such a staunch supporter of our humanitarian efforts but because she was a beautiful person, inside and out, and she really cared about God's people as well as people in general," the Reverend Reid added. It was important to him that no one think it was entirely about Mother Eternal Ann Everlastin's money.

"I know that we are short on time this evening and that you have a service that will begin shortly, so I'll get to the point." Sister Betty lay one of her small wrinkled brown hands across the desk and slid the introduction letter from Councilman Hippo Crit across it to the Reverend Thomas. "I don't know how you gonna do it, but it's gotta be done before I can approve of y'all getting the million-dollar donations."

"Sister Betty," the Reverend Thomas replied, "we understand the requirements, but there's nothing we can do about it until we come to Pelzer."

"Why do y'all need to come to Pelzer after we done drove all this way?" Ma Cile asked.

The Reverend Cherry who'd been quiet and prayerful while the discussion was going forth took a chance and answered Ma Cile. After hearing several commentaries from her, he wasn't too sure about how much she really knew or if she was just being eccentric. "Ma Cile, you know we must encourage and help your pastor to seek the true path to leading God's people. He has to learn that it is about a personal relationship with almighty God and not with the almighty dollar. We need to do that in person. We can pray for him on our knees here in Baltimore, but we'd like to show respect and learn about the man, personally. We are taking this quest very serious."

"I know all that," Ma Cile shot back. She quickly put her hand over her mouth, indicating that she was apologizing for the tone in her voice. "I just need to know why y'all thought y'all needed to come to Pelzer to see the Reverend Knott Enuff Money."

Tiny couldn't take the back-and-forth conversation, so he put it all to rest. "Pastors," he said with reverence because he was still a little edgy being surround by all the church paraphernalia, "the Reverend Knott Enuff Money is already here, in Baltimore."

"Really?" the Reverend Reid said with a surprised look. "Where is he staying? Is it far from here? Perhaps, we can all go and visit him tomorrow, if he's still in town."

Sister Betty looked almost embarrassed as she revealed, "He's here. My pastor is here at the conference."

"He's here already?" the Reverend Reid asked. "How will we know him? Perhaps one of you can point him out."

"He'll be wearing a Jheri curl," Sister Betty said.

"Nobody wears a Jheri curl anymore," the Reverend Thomas responded and laughed.

"He's not just anybody," Sister Betty replied. "He's our Reverend Knott Enuff Money. If he's still wearing a Jheri curl after all these years since the fad was over, you can imagine how hard you will have to work for the money that Mother Eternal Ann Everlastin' has left to all of you. He thinks he needs his Jheri curl more than he needs water."

Before anything more could be revealed to show how difficult the task would be, another log was thrown on the fire.

"Yeah, and he ain't by himself either," Ma Cile added. "He's here with the bishop."

"The bishop?" the Reverend Reid asked. "Which bishop?"

"Bishop Was Nevercalled," Ma Cile said. She turned and looked at Sister Betty with a look that showed her shock. According to the bishop, he was supposed to be very well known, so she was surprised that these pastors didn't know him.

Before Ma Cile could say anything more, the Reverend Cherry intervened and said, "Well we are not here tonight to discuss whether someone has been called. We need to get on with what we're supposed to do about your pastor."

Ma Cile still couldn't understand why there was so much confusion. She thought she'd clear things up by adding a little more information to the brew. "You know the Reverend Knott Enuff Money also brought a hell-raiser with 'em."

"Who's a hell-raiser?" the Reverend Cherry asked. He really didn't want to ask Ma Cile any more questions, but he wasn't able to stop himself once his mouth opened.

"Ima Hellraiser," Ma Cile answered sheepishly. She thought everyone would know Sister Ima Hellraiser; she was almost as famous as her mother, Sister A. Real Hellraiser.

"Aw, Ma Cile. You being too hard on yourself. We know you don't mean to start no trouble. Things are just a little confusing right now," Reverend Cherry said softly.

"Huh?" was all Ma Cile could reply.

"Have mercy," was all Sister Betty could add before she hung her head, almost in defeat.

Tiny just shot a look of exasperation at the surprised looks on the pastors' faces and suddenly things became so confused until it was he who began another prayer session.

After a while things calmed down in Reverend Thomas's study, and as the air cleared and the situation became clearer, they devised a plan to deal with the Reverend Knott Enuff Money. "I'll send someone to find him. It shouldn't be that hard to find a preacher with a Jheri curl."

"Is he for real?" Tiny mumbled under his breath. "It's gonna be a long night."

In the meantime, the Reverend Reid placed a phone call to the home of Councilman Hippo Crit. He explained the latest development to the councilman, and was taken aback that the councilman was not at all surprised to learn that the Reverend Knott Enuff Money was already in Baltimore.

That's when Sister Betty's knees started jerking so hard that everybody in the study huddled together like they were inside the *Exorcist* movie. The only thing that didn't happen was Sister Betty's head spinning around. Of course, Buddy was the only one in the room not worried. He was sitting in the chair beneath the cross. Even in his stupor, he knew how to draw nigh unto the cross when danger came to call.

It was indeed time for another miracle and Tiny supplied it. He insisted that they pray again. He'd prayed more in one hour in Baltimore than he'd done the entire time he lived in Pelzer. He figured God owed him since he hadn't bothered Him in the past.

When they finished praying, Sister Betty, Ma Cile, Buddy and Tiny were given VIP passes and told that someone would come soon to escort them to wait in the celebrity guest room, offstage. From that room they could watch the conference in comfort on the special video hookup to a wide-screen television monitor.

When all was said and done, the Reverends Cherry, Reid and Thomas assured Sister Betty as they left to go to the auditorium for the conference that with the Holy Ghost power they possessed between them, they should be able to bring the Reverend Knott Enuff Money into his true calling, if indeed God had ever really called him.

Hopefully, they had enough power to get past the spiritual challenges about to come from Sister Ima Hellraiser and the Bishop Was Nevercalled. They'd have a better chance of growing hair on a watermelon. Whichever way it went, Sister Betty and the others would be able to witness the feat from the safety of the celebrity guest room and they would be forever grateful for the refuge.

Outside, under the light of the moon, Brother Tis Mythang walked around the church grounds. He was awed by the magnificence of the four giant circular lights nestled deep inside the black five-foot metal floodlights. There was one placed at each corner of the New Psalmist Baptist Church. The brilliant streaks of yellow and orange beams panned back and forth, crisscrossing across the night sky as though they were trying to light a path for the spirit to come down to Earth. The brilliant lights announced to the city of Baltimore that there was something incredible about to happen inside the New Psalmist Baptist Church, and if they were outside watching the lights then they weren't important or spiritual enough to be a part of the big celebration.

Brother Tis Mythang took his time looking around as he entered and saw that the front hallway leading to the church's huge auditorium was packed. It was a long winding hallway decorated with crimson stucco walls and high gray ceilings that seem to climb toward Heaven. Along one side of the wall hung the pictures of many great leaders who had at one time either led a revival or were pastors of the same stature as the host. Gold plated picture frames were suspended by wire, looking like hanging icicles. The pictures were of well-known personalities such as the Bishop T. D. Jakes of the Potter's House in Dallas, Texas; Bishop Paul S. Morton of the Greater St. Stephen Missionary Baptist Church of New Orleans, Louisiana; and the Reverend Floyd H. Flake of the Greater Allen Cathedral of Jamaica, New York, and seemed to tower above the others who included the great evangelists such as Jackie McCullough, a raspy-voiced tall woman from Brooklyn, New York, who seemed to mesmerize congregations with her anointed speech pattern that seemed to reveal God's plan in simplicity. There was also another one of his favorite speakers, the wonder woman, Juanita Bynum. She came up from the streets of poverty to the level of prophetess. She was anointed with a plan for the single woman that elevated women and freed them from destructive patterns. He was breathless as he took in their portraits, among the great men and women, that were also scattered along the walls.

Brother Tis Mythang walked a little farther into another large room that was set up as a rehearsal room complete with instruments and a sound system. He was overjoyed that there were choirs from all around the country. A few of the choirs, like the Mississippi Mass Choir and Hezekiah Walker's Tabernacle of Praise from Brooklyn were vocalizing. By each choir outriffing or singing in a voice that was lower in register than the other, they were mentally challenging one another. The conference attendees who stood milling around in the outer hallway waiting for the main auditorium doors to open, loved hearing the choirs battle. They felt privileged to get a small taste of what was to come.

The vocalists came in all genres. There were gospel rappers, quartets, soloists and a few who accompanied themselves on the piano and organ. Each of them, no matter who'd ever won a Grammy or Stellar award, felt blessed to be there that night. That also included Brother Tis Mythang, and the wide grin on his face showed it. He'd never played outside of Pelzer, or won an award from his peers but he acted like the others just needed to know who he thought he was.

"I'm gonna be playing for y'all tonight," he happily announced. "I don't need no sheet music 'cause I can play anything."

"You play by ear?" asked one of the Brooklyn male choir members. He went by the nickname of Wonder Boy. His voice reminded most people of James Cleveland whom people affectionately called Superman.

"Yes. I most certainly do." Brother Tis Mythang's bony chest poked out like he thought he was a musician's musician.

"Well, you'd better play it right or you gonna get tossed out on your ear." Wonder Boy looked Brother Tis Mythang straight in the eye while he spoke. "We ain't got time to rehearse with you because it's almost time to have prayer before we go inside."

"Is that why you're acting so funky" Brother Tis Mythang snapped, "and in church no less, because you ain't prayed yet?"

"Yes," Wonder Boy replied with a straight face. He meant every word he'd said, and he wanted Brother Tis Mythang to know it.

Brother Tis Mythang was determined to meet the challenge head-on. "Well, I guess I need to inform my cousin, the Reverend Walter Thomas, who pastors this big church that you don't seem to have any faith in the musician he personally picked and that you out here commenting on situations you ain't prayed about yet."

Wonder Boy wasn't aware of the kinship, but he knew when to fight and when to retreat. "I'm a bit stressed, so please accept my apology." He filed away the insult for payback at another time and walked away.

Of course, Brother Tis Mythang had never been to Brooklyn, New York, so he thought he'd won the battle. The battle perhaps, but certainly not the war.

In the center aisle of the auditorium one of the cameramen was waging his own battle. He was trying to fight off the unwanted advances from Sister Hellraiser. She had decided from the time they were outside the church that she and the cameraman were going to become a team. She envisioned luring him back to Pelzer so that he could do the job that Deacon Laid Handz never seemed to get correct. It didn't matter to her that her scandalous behavior was becoming chatter fodder for anyone sitting within two rows of the camera. Things only got worse when she hiked her dress and tried to climb the crane where the frightened cameraman fled to operate a boom camera from the safety of a bucket seat that was suspended at the end of a long pole. If the boom camera had risen to the top of the auditorium, it would not have kept Sister Hellraiser from chasing that cameraman. She didn't even know his name and he was determined to keep it that way. After ten minutes of the camera swaying and the control booth screaming at the poor reception they were getting, the cameraman surrendered, and he let Sister Hellraiser sit beside him in the boom bucket. He made her promise that she would just sit and be quiet.

Sister Hellraiser promised the cameraman that she would; however, her promise was worth about as much as Monopoly money in a collection plate. There was no doubt that before that night was over, he'd wished he had gone into something safer, like fighting a lion, butt naked, without a whip or a pistol.

While Sister Betty and the others waited, one of the conference ushers, a short woman with warm brown eyes who looked to be in her early twenties, approached them. She wore a matching white uniform that fitted snuggly around her tiny waist and a little cap that sat upon a pulled-back ponytail, of dark brown curls. Her uniform was bright white and not some other shade of white as some ushers would wear. Her badge simply read CONFERENCE USHER and under those words, in tiny letters, was the name Livvie.

Livvie opened the door to the celebrity guest room and in a voice befitting her small stature said, "Please come in and make yourselves comfortable. There are cheese, fruit and sandwich trays over in the corner and plenty to drink in the refrigerator." She pulled a few paper plates and utensils from a cabinet, then she went over to turn on the television monitor and adjusted the volume.

Before Livvie could move her finger off the adjustment knob Tiny rushed over and turned it up.

"I'm sorry," Livvie told Tiny, "I thought I had it loud enough."

As she spoke again, Tiny turned up the volume once more. That time he did it with one hand on the volume control and the other covering his ear.

"Evidently, you have everything under control," Livvie said and left.

No sooner had the door closed behind her than Tiny lowered the volume.

"Thank you for doing that," Sister Betty said. "I wanted to scream every time she spoke."

"Me too," Ma Cile chimed in. "Her voice reminded me of something I saw on television with my grandbabies. I just can't think of what it was, but they had that same whiny voice."

"She sounded like one of them munchkins. If she'd spoken another word and hurt my eardrums, we'd be in here praying a different kind of prayer," Tiny said. He meant what he said.

It took a moment for Livvie's whiny, squeaky voice to leave their systems. To recover from the effects of her voice, Tiny and the others went over to the table and started to gorge themselves on the fruit, cheese and sandwich platters. Sister Betty took out her false teeth and went to work on a slice of watermelon, swallowing seeds and most of the rind. They ate the food like it was placed in the guest room especially for them and that none of the other celebrity guests at the conference had to eat.

Ma Cile's hunger revisited her like a pot of bad pinto beans. She was beginning to feel a gas buildup from not eating, so she started with the cheese platter. She knew that cheese had an unpleasant effect on her system but she wanted it, so she ate it. Both she and the others would suffer the consequences of her actions later.

When they finished eating Tiny excused himself to drag Buddy into an adjoining room to help him change and become a little more presentable. For the first time that day, he only had to drag Buddy a little because apparently the NyQuil was finally wearing off, and for that, he was thankful.

Sister Betty again looked around the celebrity guest room and marveled at its simplicity. Everything about the Reverend Thomas seemed so unassuming. *Perhaps this is why Mother Eternal Ann Everlastin' is leaving him so much money. None of this looks like it belongs to a man who has so many members and is so famous. The Reverend Knott Enuff Money would have chandeliers hanging in the bathroom if he pastored a church this fine,* she thought as she pocketed her false teeth and nibbled on a sandwich.

It was while Sister Betty and Ma Cile waited in the celebrity guest room that Tiny returned with a cleaned-up version of Buddy.

"Didn't he clean up good?" Tiny asked as he entered the room with Buddy who was trying to smile and looking a little silly. He turned Buddy around to show him off then he sat him down on a sofa near the television monitor. He started to say something else about Buddy but then he suddenly had his third revelation regarding the need for prayer.

Tiny was the first to spot the outrageous behavior of the deadly and beautiful Sister Hellraiser. "Sister Betty," he snapped, "would you please come over here and look at this?" Pointing at the television monitor without throwing something at it took all the control he could muster. "That crazy woman is sitting up in a bucket with one of the cameramen. She's going to mess up the conference."

"Who?" Sister Betty asked as she slipped her false teeth back into her mouth before going over to where Tiny stood before the monitor.

"Who else!" he hissed, then cringed.

Sister Betty didn't have to ask twice. She immediately knew who he was talking about but she was used to Sister Hellraiser's antics, and as far as she and Ma Cile were concerned, it was par for the course. "What do you want me to do?" she asked Tiny.

"Let's pray," Tiny replied, "and let's do it now."

"I think we'd better pray."

Sister Betty's eyes widened as she looked at Ma Cile.

Ma Cile's eyes suddenly lined up on their own as she looked directly into Tiny's.

Unless Tiny was a ventriloquist, he hadn't said a word. Each of them, one at a time, like a row of dominoes looked over at the figure who was speaking while lounging on the sofa; it was Buddy. In his new sobered condition, he wanted prayer.

That's when Tiny found religion. He could not believe that he'd found God in the celebrity guest room at the New Psalmist Baptist Church in Baltimore. He hadn't seen Buddy that sober since . . . never.

Ma Cile was the first to recover and go over to sit down next to Buddy. She had been on the verge of excusing herself to take a much-needed—in her mind—dip of snuff to follow that cheese taste in her mouth when she'd heard a voice suggesting they pray. "Buddy," she said, "do ya really want to pray?" She truly wanted to believe him, but she still hadn't got past the fact that he liked to drink alcohol. It wasn't that she wanted to be judgmental, after all, she dipped snuff, which in her mind wasn't anywhere near as bad as drinking spirits, but she just didn't want to be made a fool. If she was going to delay taking a snuff dip, he had better be for real.

"If y'all don't wanna pray with me, I'll understand," Buddy said, his words husky and throat scratchy from years of alcohol abuse. He was starting to get a little clarity in his continuously fuzzy world. Even when he stayed drunk, there was always a little area of his mind that never forgot God. He just thought that God had forgotten him and had banished him to a modern-day Sodom and Gomorrah way of life.

The tears that sprung from Tiny's eyes were genuine. He was truly happy to see Buddy clean and sober. And, for the first time since they'd left the Councilman Hippo Crit's office, it wasn't about the two million dollars—not entirely.

They gathered and helped Buddy to stand because, although he was sober, he was still a little wobbly. Then the four of them gathered in a circle and they had prayer. Afterward, Tiny and Sister Betty took time to bring Buddy up-to-date. Ma Cile would've stayed for the discussion but her cheese concoction and the need for a dip of snuff was about to explode within her, so she excused herself to find a bathroom.

Buddy barely remembered his aunt's funeral, and he couldn't remember why he was among strange people who seemed to care a lot about him, so he was happy for any information they gave.

Buddy hadn't been happy for all of about ten minutes before something on the television monitor caught his attention. Seated onstage at one of the organs was Brother Tis Mythang. Drunk or sober, he'd always know that face. "What's he doing here?" Buddy demanded.

"Who?" Sister Betty asked.

"Him," Buddy said loudly. The bass and the power in his voice had completely returned with the shock of what he saw before him. "What is Brother Tis Mythang doing here?" He was becoming very angry, and his voice rose as he spoke. "Is he here with y'all?" He turned and started for the door, almost knocking Sister Betty down as he did. "Y'all trying to set me up again."

"What are you talking about?" Tiny asked as he grabbed Buddy by the arm and spun him around. "Who's trying to set you up? Why would we want to do that?"

For reasons that he wasn't sure about, Buddy looked at the shock on Tiny's face, and he believed him.

Over the noise from the auditorium that began to filter into the celebrity guest room, Buddy began to tell them how and why the Reverend Knott Enuff Money had him thrown out of the church and the part, he believed, that Brother Tis Mythang had played.

20

When They All Get Together

The auditorium inside the New Psalmist Baptist Church was completely filled with the energetic attendees and the pulsating music that announced that the conference's Welcome Night ceremony had begun. As customary, they would start with a few songs, listen to several testimonies and sing about three selections.

One of the visiting deacons from nearby Landover, named Deacon Muss Bee had been appointed to lead the devotion service. Deacon Muss Bee was a member of the Sho 'Nuff Saved by the Promises Temple. He was a fifty-two-year-old, slender, dark-haired white man with protruding, capped front teeth, yet with his mouth closed and the tiny mole that sat just to the left of his top lip, he looked like he could've been the long-lost twin to actor Roberto De Niro. He was married to Deaconess Clara Could-Bee, who was a thirty-year-old, full-figured black woman who loved to wear teased blond wigs, which only made it more probable that he could've been Roberto De Niro's lost twin brother since they both had a thing for dark feminine flesh.

The two of them loved each other and were inseparable, which was a good thing, because they were going to need each other.

Deacon Muss Bee knew that the devotional service was only to last about fifteen minutes, so he started inviting the testimonies and songs. "The night is growing long, and we all have something to thank God about, so let's get started." He waited and no one jumped to the call.

Deacon Muss Bee decided he'd set it off by singing the first song. He decided to sing the song that every church deacon sang, at one time or another—"Jesus On the Main Line." He looked like a snaggle-toothed crocodile with his crooked teeth and his giant overbite threatening to puncture his bottom lip with each note. By the time he got to the second verse, his throat began to feel a little scratchy. Before he could motion for one of the ushers to bring him a glass of water, he went into a coughing fit and one of the caps that covered his front teeth flew out of his mouth, leaving nothing but the sharp, thin peg for show.

Before the audience could realize that he'd lost his cap and he became embarrass, his wife, Deaconess Clara Could-Bee, jumped to her husband's rescue. She pretended to get the spirit, and she started shouting and waving her hands. She danced and pranced her way right over to her husband's side, and with the hands of a seasoned thief, she pulled something from her pocket and appeared to anoint his mouth. Actually, what she'd done was snap a square piece of white Chiclet gum onto the peg, which once held his cap. Fortunately, that part of the conference service was not filmed because the unsightly and uneven mess of teeth in Deacon Muss Bee's mouth would've had folks trying to adjust their television's horizontal bar.

The Bees were truly a team. Deacon Muss Bee only missed the second verse of the song and no one knew the reason why. Of course, when the audience saw a strange woman anoint the deacon's mouth and he was able to resume singing, they got the spirit too. Everyone in the first two rows got up and started throwing their hands in the air and waving them like they just didn't care.

Deacon Muss Bee would've kept the devotion service going but the sweet peppermint juice from the Chiclet gum started to run onto his tongue, causing him to become hungry. Also his other cap was beginning to slide off its peg, and he didn't know if his wife had another piece of gum.

While Deacon Muss Bee brought the devotion service to a close, Dr. Bobbitto Jonas had changed into another power suit. This time it was a chocolate three-piece Versace with matching shoes. He took to the stage as though he owned it. As he scanned the faces of those whose careers he'd helped launch, he smiled and began to sing. He didn't have a great voice but he knew good singing when he heard it. After a few bars of "Come On In the Room," accompanied by his long-time organist and best friend, Darryl Lee, he had the audience stand as he paid homage to the conference hosts Reverends Reid, Cherry and Thomas.

"Saints and friends," he said, then stopped to look over to the double row of seats where other noted pastors were seated, "I give homage to the remarkable men and women of God who have come to this great church, New Psalmist Baptist, and brought their congregations with them." He stopped again and waited for various sections of the audience to finish clapping.

Each section clapped louder than the next as Dr. Bobbitto Jonas introduced the visiting pastors and announced their home churches. He smiled and directed the audience with a wave of his hands to calm down so he could continue.

"I want to bring to the stage, these next men of God. Let me introduce them to some and present them to others." The organ music started playing as if on cue to further excite the audience before Dr. Jonas continued again. "You would have to be living under a cold rock in outer space not to have heard of these anointed and precious servants of the Most High King. Show some love for the Reverends Reid, Cherry and Thomas as they make their way to the stage. Y'all had better hold on 'cause it's about to storm up in this place." He did a little two-step prance around the stage then continued. "Shout if you wanna. Sing if you wanna. Clap if you wanna. You can even bring some of that paper money up here to the steps of the stage." He stopped at that point because he caught the disapproving looks shot his way from the Reverends Reid, Cherry and Thomas who were standing off stage. But he was a professional and knew how to correct a mistake. He just started prancing around again and said, "Come on, children of the Most High. Y'all know I was just kidding about that last part, but I guarantee you that you'll be completely worn out after they bring word from the Lord.

"Pastors Reid, Cherry and Thomas, come on out here and receive all this love that's waiting for you." They walked slowly from behind a purple velvet curtain and onto the stage. Dr. Bobbitto Jonas took a few steps forward and greeted each preacher with a hard handshake, as if to affirm that he was as much a man as they, and after he added a hug, he left the stage. Of course, the entertainer in him wouldn't let him leave the stage without again turning to the audience, waving and throwing a kiss.

Bright overhead camera lights cloaked the trio, leaving a shadow trailing behind them. The shadow gave them an aura of holiness, as if God Himself approved and was escorting them. The visual effect was not lost on the more than two thousand people who welcomed them with choruses of hallelujahs.

Because the Reverend Thomas's church was the host church for that evening's conference event, it was he that took the microphone to give the welcome address and to introduce the conference co-hosts.

"Praise the Lord, my brothers and sisters in Christ. The Reverend Cherry of the Full Gospel AMEZ Church, Reverend Reid of Bethel AME, and myself are so proud and honored that you are here at the New Psalmist Baptist Church tonight. We are all here to celebrate the fifth anniversary of our Back to God's Love conference." He stopped, then he waited until the approval applause ebbed. "Tonight, we have many special guests who have decided that it was not robbery to give of their services and their time to come to Baltimore and help us praise God, as well raise the necessary funds for our various charities."

That time, many people stood and waved their hands, Bibles or handkerchiefs to show their unity with the reverend's remarks.

"I'm now going to hand the microphone over to the honorable Reverend Reid. He will come to you in his own way. After the Reverend Reid, the final remarks before the musical portion of the program begins will be given by the Reverend Cherry." He stopped long enough to allow the Reverend Cherry to walk to the other end of the stage and take his seat in a high-back red-velvet cushioned chair. Waiting also gave the audience a chance to let their excitement build.

The Reverend Thomas implored while raising his hands, "Let us all stand on our feet and receive the Reverend Reid with a hearty amen."

The people, most notably the congregation members of Bethel AME, the Reverend Reid's church, went wild as the handsome preacher slowly took the microphone from Reverend Thomas. He scanned the audience and smiled while the camera came in close to show his wife, First Lady Marla Reid, sitting in the front row. She threw him a kiss to show her support then the Reverend Reid continued.

Reverend Reid watched Reverend Thomas exit the stage to confer with Bobbitto Jonas and said, "I want to thank you, my good friend and conference cohost, Reverend Thomas." He stopped and clasped the stand as he eased the microphone into its holder. He then nodded toward Reverend Thomas who stood off a few feet away out of the camera's range and gave a wide grin to express his approval of the service thus far.

Reverend Reid laughed a little then told the people, "Come on, y'all. We are gonna be here all night if y'all keep on acting like you love God that much!"

Reverend Reid sure knew how to work it. About two-thirds of the people in the audience went wild.

Back in the celebrity guest room, all four of the people inside did the same when they recognized the Bishop Was Nevercalled seated onstage in the front row of visiting dignitaries.

The Bishop Was Nevercalled had changed his outfit as well as turned his collar around. He was grinning like everyone in the audience was cheering for only for him and not for God. In his mind, he had finally arrived.

It hadn't taken much for the bishop to ingratiate himself into the group of pastors as they'd waited to be seated on the stage. All he'd done was change into an all black regulation preacher's outfit and turn around a short white collar. He'd said "praise God" real loud one time, grabbed a Bible from a nearby table and got in line with the others. No one on line noticed that he carried the Bible upside down.

On stage, the conference ceremony continued as the Reverend Reid gave a short speech concerning the mission of the Back to God's Love conference.

Sister Ima Hellraiser had calmed down a little after her climb to the top foray into the bucket seat of the boom camera. Although she wasn't afraid of much, she had been so determined to hook up with the cameraman that she'd forgotten that she was definitely afraid of heights. Sister Hellraiser looked down across the many rows of conference attendees and drew a quick breath. She, then, did something that she seldom did, except in extreme circumstances—she prayed.

Sister Hellraiser prayed in silence because when it was all said and done, she still had her mama, Sister A. Real Hellraiser's DNA, and that was enough to make her believe that no one should see her sweat—not even the Lord.

Back inside the celebrity guest room, Sister Betty and the others started another prayer session after they recovered from the shock of seeing the Bishop Was Nevercalled out of his element. He was trying to look pious as he sat onstage among other truly anointed pastors and dignitaries.

And, outside sitting on a bench was the Reverend Knott Enuff

Money. He was sitting there with his head bowed and cupped in his hands. He had one leg resting on the bench seat and the other just dangling back and forth. In the light of the moon, he looked like a disheveled lost soul as he muttered his complaints to a couple of invisible people—the late Mother Eternal Ann Everlastin' and his dead mama.

21

Will the Dead Please Stay Dead

The blaring rhythm of the music poured from inside the church with enthusiasm. The syncopated notes from the organs, pianos, drums and an entire horn section cavorted with the echoes of stomping, frenzied dance that flew through the air. The sounds had hitched a ride on a passing night breeze and landed right at the feet of the Reverend Knott Enuff Money. The praises pouring from within the church could not break through the bitter argument he was having with the spirits of his mother, Sister Am Money, and Mother Eternal Ann Everlastin'.

"It's y'all's fault," the Reverend Knott Enuff Money whined. "Mama, you was always pushing me to have a big church, a big congregation and a big bank account. What did it get me, Mama? Tell me. What did it get me?" He stopped as though he were listening to his mother's reply. Hanging his head while he clasped and unclasped his hands, he continued, "Let me tell you what it got me, Mama. It got me a multimillion-dollar member whom I lost to a former circus performer who claimed that he got a call from God on his cellular phone to preach." The reverend was starting to lose it as the sounds of laughter seemed to rise violently from his insides.

"Imagine that! You wanted me to get in good with the big boys, the mega-church preachers." He raised his head and looked over toward the church. "Well, here I am. I'm here with the big boys." He laughed again. "Oh, I'm sorry. Did I say I was here with the big boys? Let me clear up that little mistake." He got up from the bench and pointed toward the church. "You see, I'm not exactly here with the big boys 'cause the big boys are on the inside. You can see that I'm still on the outside—like always."

As tears welled and started to pour from his eyes, the reverend made sure that he pushed a loose strand of his Jheri curl out of the way. Even in his darkest hour, his hair never lost its importance or got wet unless it was from activator.

The Reverend Knott Enuff Money plopped down again onto the bench. He turned around as if there were someone sitting on the other side and began to whine again.

"And you!" he said angrily. "You. The one and only everyone-got-to-kiss-my-feet Mother Eternal Ann Everlastin'. Look where you've brought me." He stopped again as if he were listening to a response. "I'm in Baltimore. I'm thousands of miles away from Pelzer and in Baltimore. You could've left me a million dollars for my church—for your *former* church. You could've done that, but, oh no. You just had to give me a trifling fifty-thousand-dollar check—a check that you didn't have the decency to even endorse before you up and died. I had to jump through hoops just to get it signed." Again, he stopped and with a flicker of his hand, he pointed to the New Psalmist Baptist Church building. "Look over there. You see that church building?" The reverend squinted through the tears and wept. "You could've seen to it that my church looked every bit as refined as that one."

The reverend rose from the bench, and with as much anger as he could muster, he said, "Do me a favor. Since I know that both of you are probably in hell laughing at me, roll over and with your pitchfork, I want you to poke my mama. You make certain that's she's still awake. I wanna make sure that both of you are hearing me real good. Y'all have ruined me."

The Reverend Knott Enuff Money fell again onto the bench. "God could've probably done something with me if Mama hadn't ruined it."

The reverend was so busy lamenting his life that he never saw someone looking at him from behind a nearby bush. It was the usher, Livvie. She'd been there for a few moments listening to the wailing from whom she was certain was a madman; however, she'd looked hard and there was no one other than the man with a Jheri curl crying on the bench. She was certain that he had to be the Reverend Knott Enuff Money. She tried to give him a moment to pull himself together, but he was taking too long. She didn't want to miss any more of the conference.

Livvie stepped out from the shadow of the bush and approached the bench. "Excuse me," she said quietly. "Are you the Reverend Knott Enuff Money?" she asked with as much reverence as she could muster.

The interruption of another voice frightened him. The reverend jumped off the bench in a single bound. As he tried to see clearly through his bloodshot eyes and blurred vision, he saw a figure in white. He didn't know what to make of it so he naturally thought he'd seen a ghost. "I'm sorry, Mama. Please forgive me, Mother Eternal Ann Everlastin'." He wasn't sure which of the two women the figure clad in white could be, so he apologized to them both.

"I'm sorry if I startled you," Livvie said. "They're waiting for you. Let me take you there."

The Reverend Knott Enuff Money wasn't going without a fight. He still thought that the woman in white was really a ghost from hell. "No, I ain't goin' to hell!" he bellowed.

"Really," Livvie remarked. "I've not come to judge you. I'm here to escort you to Reverends Cherry, Reid and Thomas."

"Oh Lord," the reverend yelled again. "If those men of God didn't make it, I ain't got no chance at all." Like a man drowning in his sin, he suddenly saw his entire life flash before him. There wasn't much that pleased him.

It took some doing, but Livvie finally got the Reverend Knott Enuff Money calmed down. She took a tissue from her pocket and handed it to him so that he could dry his puffy eyes.

Livvie didn't want to appear nosy but she just had to ask as they walked toward the church entrance, "Reverend Knott Enuff Money, why were you sitting out here all alone and crying on that bench?"

The Reverend Knott Enuff Money was taken by surprise at the sincerity in her voice. She appeared to really be concerned, so he did what he always did when he found himself in an embarrassing situation—he lied. "Oh, that. That wasn't nothing. I was just rehearsing some lines for a play that I'm doing when I get back to Pelzer." That little lie quickly erased the revelation of a sin-filled life that had appeared a second ago when he thought he was hellbound. He figured that he'd save face since there wasn't anything else that was much saved about him.

"Really," Livvie said. "I'm quite a bit of an actress myself." She was telling the truth. She was acting like she believed him.

They walked the rest of the way in silence. Neither of them wanted to say anything more for which they'd have to repent.

After they entered the church, Livvie escorted the reverend to a small blue room with mirrored walls. It was a room that was used for changing and was adjacent to the pastor's study. She told him that she was certain that the Reverend Thomas would not mind if he borrowed one of several robes that hung neatly in plastic suit bags in the closet. Then she left, and was glad to do so.

The Reverend Knott Enuff Money looked at the various robes. There appeared to be about ten of various colors and for various occasions hanging as though they expected him. He had no doubt that they were probably gifts from the congregation since he'd never personally bought a robe.

The Reverend Knott Enuff Money went inside the small bathroom. He washed and pulled himself together. When he came out, he went back to the closet and claimed a red robe with gold trimmings. It had a dove insignia above the breast, and according to what the reverend saw in the mirror, it fitted him perfectly. He couldn't stop smiling as he envisioned himself as the copastor of the New Psalmist Baptist Church. He'd be satisfied with that title. The three megachurch pastors were expecting him, and there was nothing, he thought, from that point on that could spoil his night. One look over at the television monitor, which had the sound turned off, changed all that.

The reverend couldn't believe his eyes. There was the bishop sitting on the same stage, elbow to elbow, with some of the biggest names in the religious community.

Then he screamed—and it wasn't the word *hallelujah*. He could feel the heat rising from his body. If he'd been near freezing water, he could've jumped in and turned it into a hot spring. He would've steeped like an old teabag.

The Reverend Knott Enuff Money paced inside the dressing room. He came up with one payback after another for the bishop. "How could he do this to me?"

As he was about to go into another tirade, another figure on the television monitor caught his attention. It was the Reverend Frank Reid. "Reverend Reid!" the reverend exclaimed. He quickly forgot about revenge on the bishop and turned up the volume. "Maybe he's gonna mention my name. After all, that usher said that the three of them wanted to see me."

It was amazing how right there in the Reverend Knott Enuff Money's worst hour he could still jump into a pool filled with truth and sink right to the bottom with an anchor made of delusions.

The muffled sound from the television monitor rose and became clearer as it delivered the words of the Reverend Frank Reid; however, all the Reverend Knott Enuff Money heard was the last few sentences of a fiery summation. He had completely missed the mini-sermon.

The Reverend Knott Enuff Money had been so busy having a blast at his own delusional pity party where he served himself too many helpings of wishful thinking that he missed a message that could've possibly turned his life around.

He would've heard the Reverend Frank Reid's very well-thought-out review. He'd spoken about the need for the Back to God's Love conference and its benefits to mankind. Speaking slowly, he'd laid out which acts had brought about the current condition of the world. He'd stopped, donned a pair of glasses that lay perilously close to falling off his nose and read several passages from the Bible. Spurred on by the shouts of "amen" and "preach," he'd interpreted how the church should fit into God's plan of reconciliation.

Pointing and opening his arms, as if to embrace the large audience of true believers, the Reverend Reid told of a great man—the Son of God—and his ultimate sacrifice. With his voice rising and falling in a cadence that scattered condemnation and that seemed to be a special gift of many great preachers, he demanded that all mankind be of service to one another. After his summation, he had each member of the audience turn to those on either side and repeat the words, *I love you, and there's nothing you can do about it.* With that last command, the audience stood and more choruses of hallelujahs spilled from their lips, and many started a praise dance.

At the very least, the final words coming from the dynamic Reverend Frank Reid prevented the Reverend Knott Enuff Money from focusing on his anger and petty jealousy toward the bishop. He had missed a lot, but unknown to him, there were still more lessons ahead.

The Reverend Frank Reid's mini-sermon had lasted about fifteen minutes, and the Reverend Knott Enuff Money had heard less than five minutes of it.

But it was enough time for the Reverend Knott Enuff Money to listen and learn what he'd already imagined in his small mind—that the mega-church preachers knew how to manipulate their members.

The Reverend Knott Enuff Money couldn't take his eyes away from the television monitor. It seemed as though the auditorium was about to explode with its support and praise for the Reverend Reid.

Sprinkled throughout the huge auditorium were many women of all shapes, sizes, skin tones and ages. The vast majority of them were wearing big designer hats and even bigger hair. They were clad in expensive tailored, colorful dresses. Many clutched their Bibles in one hand while throwing up their other, pointing it approvingly toward the Reverend Reid.

He marveled also at the men of all shapes and sizes. Some were dressed in custom-made suits with the collars turned around.

The Reverend Reid looked at his watch. He was right on time but before he left the podium, he told the audience that there would be a twenty-minute intermission. During that time, he told them to make sure they purchased the various conference-related tapes, CDs and books as well as T-shirts and hats that were being sold in the lobby. "Most of the proceeds from these sales will be used for the furtherance of the Back to God's Love reformation," he explained.

Once again, the Reverends Cherry, Reid and Thomas came together onstage and dismissed the crowd for intermission.

While the crowd, spent from all of their praise aerobics, poured out from the auditorium into the lobby to take advantage of either the conference merchandise on sale or to take care of other personal needs, Brother Tis Mythang decided to see more of his cousin's church.

He wandered into a nearby large white room with maroon-colored stripes. It had several chairs and horizontal coat racks and was obviously meant for choir gatherings. A wide grin flooded his face as he looked at the many pictures that hung in the spacious room. He saw the picture of a stocky young man with pecan-colored skin, wiry hair and a wide gap between his teeth. "John P. Kee!" he squealed. He started to leave the room so that he could explore further but something caught his attention. "Oh my goodness," he said as he looked closer and laughed at a picture of a diminutive young man dressed completely in white and surrounded by about twenty other young people. "Would ya look at my boy, Kirk Franklin."

Brother Tis Mythang spun around after looking at the picture of Kirk Franklin and started doing a little dance that resembled the old Twist, as he sang one of Kirk Franklin's hits. "Stomp . . ." He continued humming the melody as he left the room to go down the hall.

By the time Brother Tis Mythang arrived at the next large room, he'd just started humming another Kirk Franklin song. "Someone asked a question . . ." He stopped because he thought he heard voices coming from inside.

Brother Tis Mythang looked at the sign on the door. It read CELEBRITY GUEST ROOM. He placed his ear against the door to see if he could hear better. As he listened, he thought he recognized one of the voices. *I don't know nobody that would be in there,* he thought.

Brother Tis Mythang, being who he was, couldn't help himself. He opened the door to the celebrity guest room, and it didn't take but a second before he wished he hadn't. The first thing he saw when he opened the door was the face of Ma Cile, and she had her eye right on him—her false blue eye.

If Brother Tis Mythang thought he was shocked, it wasn't anything compared to how Ma Cile felt.

"Lawd, looka here. If it ain't Brother Tis Mythang," she shrieked. Her sudden yelp caused the others to turn and look.

"I don't believe this—" Tiny snapped.

"Ouch!" Sister Betty hollered. Her knee had jerked and slammed into her other one.

"Well, if it ain't an old dirty chicken showing up right here in—" Buddy would've continued to rant, but suddenly he couldn't remember exactly where they were in Maryland, and besides that, his throat had unexpectedly gone dry, and he was feeling the need for his friend Jack Daniel's.

Brother Tis Mythang couldn't say another word. He collapsed into a nearby chair, and with vacant eyes, he just stared at the four figures who faced him.

Tiny was the first one to recover, and he walked over to where Brother Tis Mythang sat half in and half off his chair. "Are you okay?"

Brother Tis Mythang looked up at Tiny. Recognition crept across his face and triggered a response. "Didn't I leave all of y'all at a funeral?"

No one saw him move, but Buddy sprang from across the room and was about to light up Brother Tis Mythang. "Funeral! Let me show you who's gonna get buried." Buddy's voice had returned, and it didn't need a sip of Jack Daniel's to bring it. He was ready to toss aside all of the praying he'd done since he'd arrived at the church and fight.

Tiny, Ma Cile and Sister Betty sprang up to stop Buddy from seasoning Brother Tis Mythang with what looked like an onslaught of near-missed, peppered punches. Within minutes, everyone in the room was shouting or trying to stop others from doing it.

Two of the church ushers who were passing by stopped at the door. "It sounds like they're having their own praise party inside," one of them said to the other.

"Well, let's just let them do whatever they feel like. People have got to get their shout on wherever and however they can," the other usher added as they walked away.

There was at least fifteen minutes to go before the conference would resume. The Reverends Cherry, Reid and Thomas rushed into the pastor's study. They each grabbed their briefcases, which had been locked and placed inside one of the sliding door closets. Out of the room they raced and went inside the small room adjacent to the study.

When the three pastors entered the room with briefcases dangling at their sides, they were met by the sight of a strange man. They found the Reverend Knott Enuff Money sitting in a chair with his eyes still glued to the television monitor. The men didn't bother to interrupt him; instead they, too, concentrated on what he was watching.

Two of the four cameras had panned across the auditorium and zoomed in on several groups of attendees and dignitaries who were standing around, apparently making small talk. Many of them were very animated. Using exaggerated hand and head movements, hats and hands were shaking across the auditorium while they waited for the conference to resume. The room remained quiet until once more, there was a close-up of the bishop. The camera only showed a second of the back of his head as he exited the auditorium, but the reverend knew that bald dome anywhere. What he didn't know was where the bishop was going.

The Reverend Knott Enuff Money was on the verge of being pulled back into his fit of emotional jealousy when he felt the need to turn around. If he lived to be a hundred and two, he would never forget the sight. Standing before him were his Trinity.

The Reverend Knott Enuff Money was in the same room and standing face-to-face with the Reverends Thomas, Cherry and Reid. He couldn't move. He couldn't speak. He could only stare. His brain was working rapidly to regain composure, but his sly silver-tongued mouth, for the first time, just wouldn't cooperate.

The Reverend Knott Enuff Money had spent almost a lifetime plotting instead of praying to get where he now sat. His mother had spent much time and energy convincing him that he was equal to any mega-church preacher on the planet.

Now, he could only stand, feeling condemned before these great men of God, much like Ananias, the man who lied to the disciples.

Acts 5:1-Ananias, through the act of the Holy Spirit had died for lying; the Reverend Knott Enuff Money was instead standing before great men and dying from embarrassment.

The feeling of panic was making its rounds, and it found the Bishop Was Nevercalled, a ready and willing victim. He'd just overheard one of the other preachers discussing which of them would stand behind the Reverend John Cherry when it was his time to bring the final message of the evening. He hadn't planned on participating in the conference; he was just happy to be onstage among the other greats. When his hand involuntarily flew up to volunteer to stand behind the Reverend Cherry, he only felt a little intimidated. The deed was done, and his desire to participate was accepted. He found out that he'd be reading from the Bible whatever scripture the Reverend Cherry requested. He could've passed out but chose to vault from the auditorium instead.

As the Bishop Was Nevercalled fled down lobby halls and around a corner, his heart pounded, his veins threatened to pop in his skull and his mind was mentally packing to leave. "What's-what's . . ." he stopped and leaned against a wall. Tearing away the collar from around his neck, he lowered his head to look at where he wished he could go—under the floor; anywhere but where he stood. There was no way he could get up before thousands of people and read the scriptures for the Reverend John Cherry.

It wasn't because he was shy. It wasn't even because he stuttered, although his speech impediment definitely played a part in his fear. The Bishop Was Nevercalled didn't want to stand up on the stage to read because he couldn't. He couldn't read, not even when he wore reading glasses for his astigmatism. He hated those glasses because of the way they made his eyes look. Seeing him in those glasses made folks think that they were staring at a specimen under a microscope. His eyes always looked out of focus and much too big for his face.

He'd never been able to fully grasp any junior high or even high school level of reading. He'd left school in Murfreesboro, Tennessee, at the age of thirteen. It was back in the early 1950s.

Both his parents, Bea and Haint Nevercalled, born of poor German heritage, seemed destined to continue their legacy of poverty. Although young and hardworking, they were yet unlearned and barely eked out a living as migrant farmers. Back then, most of the migratory families were Negro and because there were so few poor white families, his family stood out wherever they lived. Everyone around them had a name, including the Negro families—the Howards, the Ackers, and even a Chinese family by the name of Lee. But whenever anyone talked about his family, they wouldn't say, "Have y'all seen or heard of a family who goes by the name of the Nevercalleds?" Instead, they were just referred to as the po white trash that farmed down over on Mr. So and So's land.

The first nine years of his life had been spent with his parents. They were indigents, migrating from one poor dirt farming town to the next. Everywhere they lived, each wooden and drafty one-bedroom claptrap on cinder blocks seemed the same.

Although his parents couldn't' read, they loved to quote scriptures. Whether they were quoting them correctly, they never knew. They also had a habit of making up scripture for things they felt needed it. They'd spend the warm spring and hot summer months sowing and planting on borrowed land while quoting scriptures. When the breezy fall season came around with an Indian summer as its captive, they'd reap and can vegetables on borrowed land while quoting scriptures. During the winter, if the weather wasn't too bad, they'd walk into a nearby town. For long hours, behind stained makeshift tables made of splintered clapboard, his parents would stand shaking, their rail-thin bodies almost vibrating from the cold. They would sell whatever extra harvest of corn and beans they could spare. It was all they had to bargain. It was also all the field owners gave them as payment for their grueling labor. They did what they had to so that they, too, could have the bare necessities while they lived on borrowed land and quoted scriptures.

Of all the necessities they needed, schooling was never one of them; besides, they never stayed long enough in one place for him to attend any school full time. Seldom was he able to take a test, let alone pass it. Whenever he was promoted to the next grade, it was basically because he was too big or too old to be in the current class. Of course, any grade advancement he received, his parents attributed to their quoting scriptures and faith.

By the time the bishop had left his unbearably unstable home, which fell far below the poverty line radar, there were only a few *things he knew for sure. He knew that from that time on he'd never live his life on another piece of land that wasn't his own and that as long as he could remember every book and verse from the Never-called family Bible edition, he'd make it.*

The Bishop Was Nevercalled traveled throughout the south for the next ten years or so. He did seasonal odd jobs without murmuring. He was a good worker and an even better son. Whatever monies he earned, he always made sure to send a little to his parents. It usually took a while for his parents to receive the monies because by the time the bishop sent the letters, they'd often moved on to another farm. By the time the bishop turned thirty, both of his parents had died. They had exhausted themselves, not because they wanted to but because they'd had to. They'd worked themselves to death. That would never happen to the bishop, not if he could do anything to prevent it.

He had only been in Belton, South Carolina, for a short while before he met the Reverend Knott Enuff Money. The reverend was in his early twenties and the bishop was about thirty-two-years old. They were introduced by the reverend's mother, Sister Am Money.

The bishop needed to be where he could hear scriptures quoted since he couldn't read, and every Sunday, he'd walk past the church with the loud preaching and beautiful music. Before he knew it, he found himself attending services at the Bound and Determined Glory Maintenance Center in that little town of Belton, South Carolina. The church had been founded and pastored by the Right Reverend Will Money, and it became his second home.

Sister Am Money had invited him to lunch one day to formally meet her son, Knott. It was after a noonday prayer service. He didn't know her that well, but she was different from most pastor's wives he'd met at various churches in his travels. She always looked ambitious, and he liked that. Unlike some of the other church members who seemed to tolerate him, his skin color and his scripture quoting stuttering voice, she genuinely seemed to like him.

From the time he stepped foot through her door and instantly became friends with Knott, he loved the Money family. It never mattered to him that Sister Am Money was a black woman. He loved her, and he learned to look upon her as a surrogate mother.

He liked the way Sister Am Money seemed to constantly urge her son to try and surpass any imaginary success her husband had garnered. She always wanted better for her son, and she also wanted much of the same success for the bishop. He remembered her leaning over the oven one evening. She'd baked a lemon meringue pie. He was sitting at her kitchen table waiting for Knott to come downstairs so that they could all ride to service together. As she fussed over each and every toasted white meringue peak, she turned and asked him to come and stand beside her.

"Was," she said, "you see this meringue? It's white with just a little bit of brown on the top." Sister Am Money laughed as she pointed to him, poking him in his bony chest. "That's you." She started to laugh even harder at her own inside joke. "You're white, a little undone, but if you play your cards right, you'll always have Knott on your side; he's the brown on the top."

He was a bit surprised and a lot confused. All he could say was "Yes, ma'am."

"You best pay attention to what I'm trying to tell you." She had her long hair tied back and wound in a bun, which she'd covered with a clean and ironed pink scarf. It was her "I ain't playing" scarf.

"The topping on this pie ain't fit for eating while it's just plain white and uncooked. It's not until the peaks on the top turn brown that you know it's time to take it out of the oven." She took a worn handkerchief from the breast pocket of her apron, and she wiped the sweat from her brown furrowed brow. Grabbing a chair, she sat down then continued with a serious yet controlled look upon her face. "You and Knott, y'all need to always stay together. He ain't going nowhere near success without you, and you ain't gonna get no closer to it without him. Even if y'all marry—and I hope you do—you need to make sure your wives get along and not cause no friction between the two of you." She'd instantly made the bishop and her son codependents.

The bishop and Reverend Knott Enuff Money remained friends, but they did not remain married to their spouses.

The past few minutes of remembering bad experiences heaped on to what was about to be another terrible incident was too much for the Bishop Was Nevercalled. His heart felt as though it were trying to punch a hole in his chest to escape.

He reached into his pocket and pulled out a handkerchief to wipe the pouring sweat from his face. *I-I-I need to find the reverend,* the bishop thought. His emotional state was becoming so bad that he even stuttered in his thoughts.

From a distance, the bishop could hear the music playing inside the auditorium. It sounded like they were playing songs from the various invited musical guests' albums. He knew that time was passing quickly and that they would be looking for him to return to the stage to read the scriptures as Reverend Cherry would direct. His mind was so far gone into a panic, that even if he knew which scriptures he would be asked to read, he couldn't recall them.

As he wandered aimlessly down the hallway, he found himself in front of a door. In the shape he was in, he didn't bother to try and figure out the words written on the door, he just opened it and walked in.

Sitting in a wooden-back chair with a firm cushioned seat, surrounded by Reverends Cherry, Reid and Thomas, sat Reverend Knott Enuff Money with his Jheri curl so frizzy, one could almost hear it crunch. The surprised look on Reverend Knott Enuff Money's face told the bishop that the reverend had been looking for him too.

Bishop Was Nevercalled was two for two. He couldn't read words, and he couldn't read faces.

For a brief moment, the bishop was so happy to see Reverend Knott Enuff Money that he'd all but forgotten that he was trying to escape from the mega-church preachers who were in the room too.

Unfortunately for the bishop, the Reverend Knott Enuff Money was also glad to see him, it was just not for the same reasons. "Bishop, where have you been? Come on in," Reverend Knott Enuff Money said with his mouth set so tight, it looked like a straight line. He said the words slowly yet each was said with a touch of sugar-laced vinegar to both comfort and distract the bishop from the daggers he tossed with his blazing brown eyes. It was much the same way he spoke whenever he was trying to get the last mite from one of his unwilling members.

Before the bishop could respond, the other three preachers walked over to him and each extended their hands in greeting. "Welcome, Bishop."

It was Reverend Thomas who calmly guided the bishop farther into the room so that the door could be closed. "We're happy that you took time out of your busy schedule to join us."

The look of panic hadn't been lost on the men, but they needed to return to the business at hand with Reverend Knott Enuff Money.

Realization hit the bishop like a baseball player hitting home plate. He didn't need to be spirit-filled to know he'd interrupted something very serious, and he wasn't quite sure if he needed to be in on it. As he quickly turned and met the eyes of Reverend Cherry—

the very man whom he'd been trying to avoid—he frowned in defeat. The air in the room seemed to leave slowly, as if the very righteousness from the mega-church preachers were soaking it up.

"Why don't you have a seat right here. Sit next to your pastor," Reverend Reid said as he pulled out another chair from among several that were surrounding a small round table. "We've been having a chat with Reverend Money, and we see no reason why you shouldn't be included."

"We don't have much time because the conference will be restarting shortly," Reverend Thomas added. "In the meantime, there are some other people we need to bring in." He went over to a wall phone and pressed a few buttons. "Sister Livvie, please go into the celebrity guest room and bring our guests to my prayer room." He paused as if he were listening to a response from the other party. "Yes, that's correct. I'm in the small prayer room that is adjacent to my study." Again, he paused then said, "Thank you."

Even if Reverend Knott Enuff Money was upset, how could he stay that way when he'd just overheard the Reverend Thomas ask Livvie to bring celebrities to meet him? The only thing that he momentarily regretted was that he would have to share the moment with the bishop. He'd have preferred to tell the bishop about his experience, so that he could relate it the way he wished it had happened and not necessarily the way it did.

It didn't take but a few minutes before there was a knock on the prayer room door. Livvie stuck her head in first to announce that she was there with the Reverend Thomas's guests.

Thinking that it would bad manners to sit when celebrities entered the door, both Reverend Knott Enuff Money and Bishop Was Nevercalled stood. They both had replaced their looks of confusion with ones of appreciation and respect.

They kept on cheesing, showing nothing but pink gums. They looked like two human mounds of Silly Putty with their grins wide and their lips almost puckered, ready to suck up to whoever the celebrities might be, when all of a sudden their faces dropped. Like cartoon characters, their faces plunged, as if there were two ton weights attached when in walked Sister Betty, Ma Cile and Tiny.

It was Reverend Knott Enuff Money who was the first to recover. He wasn't sure what Sister Betty had told the mega-church pastors, so he had to think fast to save his questionable reputation.

If he'd have thought that hard back in Pelzer and put that much effort into getting his members saved, he would've been a much better pastor.

"I don't know what these people have said about me," he said. "They're a little upset with me now because they probably don't think I should've come to Baltimore." He stopped speaking.

Even Reverend Knott Enuff Money knew that he was beginning to sound like a blabbering idiot, and he didn't want to entirely lose favor with the mega-church pastors, so he decided to turn the tables. He instead started to act like a sympathetic fool. By the time he was finished, they'd all have to take out their pocket versions of *Crazy to English* dictionary just to keep up.

"We'll just have to pray for them," Reverend Knott Enuff Money added as he sat down again, " 'cause you know that Sister Betty thinks that God called her."

"God does call women too," Reverend Thomas replied.

"He most certainly does. I can assure you that God called my wife," Reverend Cherry chimed in.

"On the telephone?" Reverend Knott Enuff Money asked.

Of course, since that little bit of information was omitted when they'd spoken with Sister Betty earlier, it caused the three pastors to abruptly turn and look at her like she had a stick of broccoli stuck between her teeth.

Sister Betty, herself, was caught off guard. Her left knee hadn't jerked once to alert her to possible trouble since they'd entered the room. Instead of acting like she'd been found to be insane, she decided to tell her story again for the umpteenth time.

Sister Betty took her time and summed up how back in 1984, she'd received a phone call from God. She told them that God had said that He was coming by her house that day, but never said when. Sister Betty told how she'd mistreated and dismissed a hungry child, a homeless man and a prostitute who'd come to her house for assistance. She went on to let them know that God had showed her that one of the true values of her Christian walk lay in her service and love for her fellow man.

"God does work in mysterious ways," Reverend Thomas said as he searched his mind for a biblical reference to God making telephone calls.

"Yes, He does. After all, He's prepared to make the rocks cry out if we don't," Reverend Reid commented.

"Well then, I guess if God can make a rock cry and call forth Lazarus from the dead, He can certainly make a telephone call too,"

Reverend Cherry said. By the time he'd added his two cents, he'd already written a sermon in his head about another way God could call someone.

When the three mega-church pastors seemed to understand and accept what Sister Betty told them about her telephone call from God, Reverend Knott Enuff Money tried another tactic. "Ma Cile dips snuff, the heavy-duty kind, and it makes her eyes roll around in her head. She scares everybody she comes into contact with," he mumbled as he suddenly felt the need to cower in his chair. From the stunned, angry and bulging look shot from Ma Cile's eye (the good brown one), he wished he'd kept his motor mouth shut.

Ma Cile had her fat fists balled up and her false blue eye cocked like she could've shot and beaten him to pieces. "What ya sayin' 'bout my business?" She forgot about Reverends Cherry, Reid and Thomas being in the room. She was in a hurry to waddle her way over to where the frightened and still trembling Reverend Knott Enuff Money sat. He'd turned a shade darker and looked almost the same color as his chair.

Ma Cile kept balling and unballing her stubby tight fists, and her lips twisted, her false blue eyeball still rolled and she was ready to anoint. The only thing that stopped her was the strong pull by the tiny hand of Sister Betty and the sight of Tiny standing ready to pounce.

Tiny was actually ready to leave. He didn't want to use most of his impending two million dollars on hospital bills, which is what would've happened if he messed with Ma Cile.

It was a good thing that Sister Betty got her sudden gift of power from on high or from somewhere because that hallucinogenic snuff high was telling Ma Cile to go ahead and slam dunk her pastor.

Ma Cile was so furious, she had gotten one of her hands raised way back over her head, like she was gonna pound him like cornmeal. Starting from the book of Genesis, she was gonna slap that Reverend Knott Enuff Money at least sixty-six times, all the way through to Revelation.

Ma Cile wasn't entirely innocent of all charges from Reverend Knott Enuff Money. She was feeling extra guilty, not only because what he'd said was true, but that she'd taken a dip of snuff when she'd left the room to make a phone call to Shaqueeda to check up on Li'l Bit and June Bug. She hadn't enough restraint not to take that dip when she knew better.

While the Reverend Knott Enuff Money sat like a statue, Ma Cile backed off, then apologized to everyone in the room, the three pastors in particular.

"I'm sorry," Ma Cile said. "It's just that my pastor knows how upset I gets when folks talk about my bad eye." She wasn't totally consumed by the snuff euphoria. She purposely left out the reference to her snuff habit and went on to relate about how, as a young girl, one of her eyes was damaged by a kick from a stubborn mule.

Reverend Cherry nudged the elbow of the Reverend Thomas and whispered, "I'm glad she cleared that up. I've been exorcising, ready to toss a pail of blessed water upon her and trying to stay clear of that demon-possessed eye ever since Ma Cile stepped through the door."

Reverends Thomas and Reid stood side by side as they nodded their understanding to Ma Cile. Reverend Reid then pretended to cough as he and Reverend Thomas then mumbled under their breaths "that eye scared me too" to each other.

In the meantime, the bishop made his first smart move of the day. He just stood there slumped in his black suit, collarless, with his mouth zipped and staring off into space. He looked like a skinny Pillsbury Doughboy. His forehead became paler and furrowed with intensity as he mentally clicked his heels three times while silently praying that he could be somewhere else.

It was Reverend Cherry who suddenly remembered that there was someone missing from the group. "Where's your other friend?" Reverend Cherry asked as he looked around the room.

Reverends Reid and Thomas quickly turned, too, and looked toward the door as if they thought that someone would be standing there. "Wasn't he left in the celebrity guest room with all of you?" one of the pastors asked.

Now it was time for Sister Betty's intuitive and psychic kneecaps to start doing the jerk. Her knee shook as if her kneecap was trying to dance the twist by itself. She didn't have to wait for trouble to come; it was already there.

"Oh, you must mean Buddy," Tiny answered. "We left him in the other room, and he was about as sober as any one of you," he proudly added. He especially wanted the Reverend Thomas to know that he was on top of keeping Buddy sober as well as safe.

Right away, Sister Betty's knee kicked its dance up a notch and started to act like it wanted to spin or pop a wheelie.

Ma Cile suddenly felt as if she needed a double scoop instead of a dip of her snuff.

The three pastors needed to know what in the world was going on, so they slipped off to the far side of the room. Ma Cile's flickering eyeball and Sister Betty's dancing knee were about to make them almost question their faith. They began to hold hands and pray for answers.

The Bishop Was Nevercalled finally found his voice, but could only ask, "Did they say that Buddy was here? Here in Baltimore?" He shot a questioning glance toward his coconspirator, Reverend Knott Enuff Money.

Tiny took that opportunity to unknowingly add more fuel to the fire. "Yep. He's in the other room down the hall. As a matter of fact, he's with your choir director, Brother Tis Mythang."

"He's alone with Brother Tis Mythang?" Reverend Knott Enuff Money barked. "Both of them are together?"

It appeared that every stray and effeminate-acting chicken in the frilly church coop seemed to be coming home to roost, and they were flying in wearing boas and seeking vengeance.

Reverend Knott Enuff Money knew he'd had a reason to panic as the room seemed to shrink around him. He'd been so close to being embraced by the three mega-church pastors he'd affectionately nick-named the Trinity. However, instead of being embraced, he knew he was about to be embarrassed.

All eyes in the room were suddenly upon him and his partner in crime, the Bishop Was Nevercalled—all eyes including Ma Cile's false blue eye, which was jumping around in its socket like a Mexican jumping bean.

It was Reverend Thomas who first realized when he and the Reverends Cherry and Reid had finished praying that more time had passed than they'd thought. "We can continue this discussion later," he said. Turning to Reverend Knott Enuff Money, he added, "Reverend Money, we would be so honored if you'd join us onstage along with the bishop."

"That would be a wonderful pairing," Reverend Reid added. He didn't have a clue as to what the Reverend Thomas was leading up to, but he felt that that he needed to go along with the plan.

"I've got another idea," Reverend Cherry added with enthusiasm. "Why don't I have the Reverend Knott Enuff Money read the scriptures along with the bishop? They can take turns reading alternate verses as I bring the Word of God and the conference to a close."

All eyes in the room looked over toward Reverend Knott Enuff Money. He had recovered from the impending assault from Ma Cile when he heard the Reverend Thomas's gracious invitation to join the mega-church pastors onstage. Even his dried and frizzy Jheri curl seemed to suddenly look moist.

"Well, praise God!" Reverend Knott Enuff Money replied. "I'd be honored to stand on the same stage with the three of you." In his mind, he'd already begun practicing how to inflect his voice with more bass as he would read the scriptures and, perhaps, he'd toss in a whoop or two.

Reverend Cherry then turned to the bishop. "Bishop Was Never-called," he said humbly, "I know that you were told that it would be only you reading to support me. I hope you don't mind that we've asked your pastor to stand and read along with you."

There was a strange look that began to creep along the bishop's face. The Reverend Cherry had noticed its beginning when the Reverend Thomas had first suggested that the bishop share the reading with his pastor. The Reverend Cherry had only just met the bishop and hoped that he didn't overstep the bishop's authority when he'd agreed with the Reverend Thomas's suggestion, yet, he didn't want to misread him either, so the Reverend Cherry continued speaking, thinking that he'd found a way to celebrate the bishop's status. "By the way, Bishop Nevercalled, how many churches do you preside over?"

That's when the Bishop Was Nevercalled passed out.

Reverend Knott Enuff Money was always quick on his feet. He wasn't always correct; he was just always quick. He spoke up fast. "My goodness! The Lord has slay the bishop in the spirit." His eyes squinted involuntarily as he looked over at the mega-church pastors to see if they could tell he was lying. He couldn't tell if they did or not. So he, without looking at Sister Betty, Ma Cile or Tiny because he definitely knew that they weren't fooled, started humming, "Help him, Jesus" while mumbling under his breath, "wake up" over the bishop, as if he was laying on hands.

Both Sister Betty and Ma Cile looked at each other and shook their heads in mutual annoyance at their pastor. He never seemed to know when to quit. They retreated to a corner to get out of the way of the lightning that they were sure was gonna strike that room.

Tiny, just from that brief show he'd witness by the Reverend Knott Enuff Money, decided that when they returned to Pelzer, he was definitely going to visit the Ain't Nobody Else Right But Us—All Others Goin' to Hell Church. *If they're running a con like this every Sunday, then I know I can go to that church and not feel condemned.*

I can get my church points the easy way with this man. God certainly won't blame me 'cause I'll be following the Reverend Money, he thought.

He was thinking wrong because he'd never picked up a Bible and learned to follow Jesus and not the money, reverend or otherwise.

Reverend Cherry couldn't afford to waste any more time because the sounds of the musicians tuning up told him that the conference was about to restart. "We must all get ourselves together." He glanced over at the bishop still lying on the floor and the Reverend Knott Enuff Money hovering over him, and asked, "Reverend Money, do you think you'll be finished praying in time to join us on-stage?"

"Oh, I'll be there," Reverend Knott Enuff Money responded as he let go of the bishop's head, which caused it to hit the floor with a heavy thud. He then used the arm of the chair to support himself as he stood. He was surprised at how stiff his knees felt after only bending for a short time. He wasn't used to bending unless it was to pick up coins in the street or something; he definitely didn't bend to pray.

"What about the bishop?" Reverend Thomas asked.

"What about him?" Reverend Knott Enuff Money replied. His mind wasn't on the bishop. Even while cradling the bishop and pretending to pray over him, the reverend's mind had already scanned the room to determine which decorating idea he could use in his own study, the new one that he was gonna have his members build.

"Will the bishop be joining you on stage?" Reverend Thomas asked with a bit of agitation added to his words.

"Why yes, of course, he will." The reverend needed to find a way to have all the stage time to himself. Without the bishop, the cameras would be on him. "We'll join you. I'm gonna help the bishop get himself together." He then asked Tiny to escort Sister Betty and Ma Cile back to the auditorium. He could handle the bishop by himself.

As Reverend Thomas walked past the Reverend Knott Enuff Money, he suddenly took a step back and looked. "That robe looks good on you." He had a conspiratorial smile that seemed to almost light up the room, but only he and the reverend knew why. "I have to look in my closet when the conference is over. I believe I have one just like it."

Reverend Knott Enuff Money caught the hint from Reverend Thomas; it translated to "Don't think about keeping my robe. It'd better be hanging in my closet when the conference is over."

"Perhaps, we'll compare robes after the conference," Reverend Knott Enuff Money replied. "I'll make sure to bring this robe to your main study so we can compare."

Reverend Thomas smiled as he and the others closed the door behind them. Even with the door open only a few seconds, the stampeding of feet could be heard outside as the people piled past on their way to return to the auditorium.

Reverend Knott Enuff Money waited another few seconds before he snapped, "Come on, Bishop. Everyone's gone. Get up."

"I thought I was gonna pass out," the bishop said as he attempted to get up.

"You did pass out," the reverend snapped. "What's wrong with you? How many opportunities come along like this? If you didn't want to get on that stage, why didn't you just say so?"

"I want to be onstage. I just don't want to read onstage," the bishop replied sadly.

"I forgot all about that," the reverend replied with concern. He truly felt compassion for the bishop, and that would be the excuse he would give to him for what he was about to do.

Reverend Knott Enuff Money threw up his hands at the bishop.

The bishop threw up his hands, too, but not quick enough.

Reverend Knott Enuff Money snatched the horn-rimmed glasses from the bishop's face and threw the glasses to the floor.

"Wha-t . . ." the bishop stammered, "Whaaat are you doing?"

"I'm helping you out," the reverend answered as he put the finishing crush on the bishop's glasses with the sole of his shoe. He turned the heel of his shoe back and forth as if he were putting out a cigarette.

"I-I can't see." The bishop's stuttering was getting worse. "I-I-can't see well without them."

"You can't *read well* without them either." The reverend smiled, with his eyes giving conspiratorial winks so fast they looked like broken signal lights.

The bishop looked down at the pile of glass that was once his bifocals and burst out laughing. "You know what, you-you're a genius."

"I-I know," the reverend replied as he mocked the bishop's stutter. "Now, let's get out of here before they start without us."

Of course, each of the men stopped to check each other's robes. Impressions were important. Neither of them seemed to remember that they'd already made impressions—bad ones that had nothing to do with how they looked and more about how they acted.

Narrowing his eyes like tiny slits, the bishop moved his bald head from side to side as if he were getting into a wrestling stance. Because of his severe astigmatism, it was the only way he could focus. He also had to be within a foot of an object to see it clearly. "You-you look pretty good." He peered a little closer. "Tha-a-t robe is saying somethin'. I ain't seen that one b-b-before—"

A grin spread across the reverend's face that would've made a Cheshire cat jealous. He turned and looked into one of the nearby mirrors and smiled again. He then dabbed a little blessed oil, which he poured from a bottle that sat on the Reverend Thomas's desk onto his dry and frizzy Jheri curl, and he smiled some more, which meant for the bishop to continue with his praises.

The bishop couldn't see the manipulating look upon the reverend's face too clearly, but out of habit, he continued, "I-I do believe that you're gonna be able to-to hang with the big boys on that stage. You look like you-you was born to preach, the way that robe is fitting."

The bishop sputtered and stuttered sugar-coated words at him so fast until it was amazing that the reverend didn't turn into a diabetic.

"I do look good. I look like new money . . . the new Reverend Knott Enuff Money."

The two of them laughed at the reverend's corny joke; the reverend even harder because it was apparent to him that the bishop hadn't caught on that it was a borrowed robe from Reverend Thomas.

"How do I-I look?" the bishop asked in a manner that was begging for the reverend to return the compliments he'd bestowed.

"You're alright," the reverend said. "You look like you could be hanging someplace too." He didn't bother to tell the bishop that the bishop needed to fix the collar that was hanging around his neck like a loose noose. It wasn't enough for the reverend that the bishop would be unable to read behind Reverend Cherry; he didn't want the bishop to look as good either.

"Thank you," the bishop replied.

Reverend Knott Enuff Money replaced the bottle of blessed oil on the desk and opened the study door. The two men left the study with the reverend leading the bishop, just like he always did.

At the same time all the drama was going on inside the study, back inside the celebrity guest room, Brother Tis Mythang and Buddy were squaring off—Buddy dressed up as well as he could under his drunken circumstances and Brother Tis Mythang still wearing his designer suit. They paced, sizing up each other. Their eyes were locked by a key of suspicion and dislike, and their bodies ready to spring forth into battle at the slightest provocation. Although their silent and intense looks of intimidation went on only for a few minutes, it seemed much longer.

Buddy would have spoken up first, but the shock of being sober had him dumbstruck. Riding all the way up to Baltimore, hyped up on NyQuil cough syrup and the remnants from a bottle of Jack Daniel's liquor had him rethinking each word he wanted to say, which gave Brother Tis Mythang enough time to do his usual thing. He set it off.

Brother Tis Mythang hadn't quite expected that type of silent reaction. He was ready to roll up his sleeves and rearrange several of Buddy's still existing brain cells. "Oh, so now you're trying to act like you're too out of the loop to know that she's left you a ton of money." He stopped before going into another volley of words designed to whittle Buddy down to the size of a miniature toothpick. The expression on Buddy's face told him that the man really didn't have a clue.

"You've got some nerve. You think just because Mother Eternal Ann Everlastin' died that you can just waltz back into folks' lives? You still ain't nuthin' but a loser, and whether you're rich or not, you'll always be a loser." Brother Tis Mythang held up a thumb and forefinger to form the letter L for emphasis.

"It was always about the money." Brother Tis Mythang's voice was beginning to rise, and he didn't care who heard what he had to say. "When you decided to pull that stupid move at the church—I know you remember that!" He leaped toward Buddy and came almost nose-to-nose. At that point, he felt he had nothing more to lose. "You could've stayed and fought Reverend Knott Enuff Money. You could've also stayed in the doggone closet!" The color of his skin was beginning to change, and his skin tingled from the anger that was rapidly coming to a boil.

"All you had to do was to continue to pray. We had a deal. No one asked and we wouldn't tell. The same emotional ribbon of fear and embarrassment is what tied us together." Brother Tis Mythang could feel the anger moving over to give room to the tears that were beginning to seep from his eyes, eyes that didn't want to see what was standing before him and a mind that was fighting not to return to a place in time that he'd left long ago.

"I'm sorry." Buddy wanted to say more but his brain hadn't caught up yet, and Brother Tis Mythang cut him off.

"Sorry. You're sorry." Brother Tis Mythang was at his limit for patience. It was time to launch Buddy's sorry excuses to where they belonged. "Tell it to God when He judges your sorry butt."

Brother Tis Mythang walked away. He went over to the other side of the room because he was starting to feel a little faint. No doubt it was from the hidden anger that suddenly burst forth into the open, and threatened to burst some of his blood vessels. He could feel his blood pressure starting to rapidly elevate, but he wasn't going to stop berating Buddy until he'd had his say.

"Every time you and I had those feelings that we knew God didn't allow, we prayed. That was the deal, Buddy. We would pray until we got delivered. It didn't matter that we were young and starting to prefer our own kind—" He let his eyes rest on the far wall where there hung a model of the cross. It was draped with a strip of purple cloth around the top and wound around the places where Christ's hands were nailed. Then he continued as he hung his head in shame— "What we felt was an abomination, and we understood that."

Again, Buddy's response was the same. "I'm sorry."

Brother Tis Mythang felt his body spring forth. He didn't feel the floor beneath him as he ran toward Buddy. The veins in his hands throbbed as he reached out for him. "Don't say that word again. Don't you ever tell me about how sorry you are. I already told you how sorry you are."

Brother Tis Mythang found himself towering over a frightened Buddy. He had his fists raised and was about to forget that he was inside the church or that he'd just looked to the cross. "Why couldn't you have just kept your big mouth shut? You never had to get up and announce that you were gay. We already knew that some folks thought that we both were. But you knew better. You knew that I—" He stopped and started pounding his chest. "You knew that I would never act on whatever it was that I was beginning to feel. You knew that I was praying for deliverance, and when you stood up and told the entire congregation that you were gay, you took me down with you. You slapped a gay bull's-eye on me."

Brother Tis Mythang stopped pointing toward himself and threw up his fists again toward Buddy. "I was sitting right there beside you when you decided to mess up both our lives. Everyone knew that we were close. I stuck with you because I knew what you were going through. A friend was all I ever was or tried to be to you."

There was no stopping his tears as Brother Tis Mythang sobbed. "Everyone whispered behind our backs about how strange we always acted. You were right there the night Sister A. Real Hellraiser stood up and called us Sister Buddy and Sister Tis Mythang, and then she pretended that she'd misread the names on the paper while the entire congregation laughed at us. They laughed not because what she'd said was funny. They laughed because she'd said what they were all thinking."

Brother Tis Mythang stopped sobbing as he felt a tingling sensation rushing through his body. The feeling spread to the tips of his extremities—his fingers and toes felt the sensation of sharp needles but he couldn't stop. He could've been on the verge of a stroke, but he couldn't stop. "I sat right there in that pew waiting to go up to that organ and play." A nervous laugh cloaked in a hiss escaped from his snarling lips. "Do you know what I was going to play on that organ?" He'd asked a rhetorical question and didn't care if Buddy answered or not.

"No." Finally, Buddy had found another word he could use to respond; however, he still was unable to stop adding, "I'm sorry." He folded his arms over his head just in case Brother Tis Mythang wanted to hit him. While Brother Tis Mythang continued with his barrage of accusations and the searing tension rapidly began to replace the air in the room, Buddy began to silently pray.

"I was going to play 'Just a Closer Walk with Thee.' " Again, he let out a nervous chuckle. "Imagine that. I was about to play a song that was supposed to bring us closer to God, and you stand up and say something so vicious and untrue that it sent us about as far away from Heaven as possible, and it got you kicked out of the church, and me . . ." He raised his eyes and leveled them at Buddy who still had his head hung as though he'd fallen asleep.

Brother Tis Mythang snatched Buddy's face up by the jaw and snapped, "As for me, your stupid sense of timing sentenced me to an eternity of being judged and placed under a spiritual microscope by churchgoing, spiritually deprived people who will probably fill up hell so that there won't be room for me." He let Buddy's jaw drop, almost hoping that he'd broken it. "I've been ridiculed and teased by some church folk because people think that I walk and act not as a man should. The funny thing is that I've never tried to change my walk nor my mannerisms to be accepted by anyone but God. When I promised Him that I would never act on my 'unnatural' feelings, I meant it. I told God that I would stand on His word until my change came. I may be judged for a lot of things, but it won't be for an abomination." He found himself suddenly hitting the back of a chair that sat next to him. "Can you say that! Can you?"

"Yes, I can."

Brother Tis Mythang was about to go into another round of pent-up testimony. He felt like a ton of bricks lifted off his chest with each scream, but he thought he'd heard Buddy wrong. "What did you just say?"

Buddy lifted his head while saying, "Amen," then he met Brother Tis Mythang's stare. "I've never acted upon my feelings either—"

"Did you just say amen?" Brother Tis Mythang couldn't get past hearing that word uttered from Buddy's lips, not even as Buddy continued to speak, and he looked like he was speaking with a sober mind.

"I never intended to act upon my feelings either. When we said that we would pray until a change came, I meant it, just like you did." Buddy stopped, and without any fear, he slowly got up and made his way over to where Brother Tis Mythang stood, still leaning against the wall. "I knew better, but I only said what I did that night because I wanted to prove how hypocritical the Reverend Knott Enuff Money was acting when it came to certain folks in the church." Buddy was surprised at himself, at how easily the words were beginning to come to his mind and exit his mouth.

Buddy let an unconvincing smile rest upon his face as he took the seat next to where Brother Tis Mythang continued to stand. "I should've told you what I was planning to do. I didn't think it would be such a big deal considering some of the other testimonies that we'd heard in the church that night." He stopped to cough. The words were coming faster and clearer, but his throat still felt raspy. "We heard folks testifying about habits that went from fornicating to stealing. How did I know that the reverend was gonna go to the lengths he went?"

Brother Tis Mythang was beginning to calm down, even though he really didn't want to do that. He was not only suddenly intrigued with Buddy's unexpected sobriety, but no matter the circumstance or situation, he still liked hearing secrets. He was still angry, but he was also still curious. "Buddy, what in the world are you talking about? You stood and told the people that you were gay—not as in happy to be there, but full-fledge gay. You had folks thinking that we both were gay. You got kicked out of a church. Is that the result you were going for when you came up with that plan, the one you failed to share with me?"

"No, not exactly." Buddy suddenly looked defeated, even though it was only moments ago that he'd been praying. "A couple of weeks before, I'd overheard the reverend and the bishop talking outside the sanctuary. They hadn't seen me because I was standing between the blessing dispenser and the ATM. I don't remember what they said, word for word. It seems a little fuzzy to me now . . ."

"You're kidding." Brother Tis Mythang couldn't help throwing in a barb or two. "You've been drunk for a few years. Don't be surprised if you don't start to taste lint on your tongue too."

Buddy ignored Brother Tis Mythang, even if what he said was true.

"The two of them were running their mouths on and on about how there were certain folks in the church that even if they'd committed a dozen murders, so long as they continued to pay a lot of money in support of the church and the pastor's lifestyle, the two of them wouldn't care."

"Well, what did that have to do with you? Or us, for that matter? It wasn't like we were putting in fifteen percent every week, and even if we were, fifteen percent of nothing would've still been nothing."

Buddy nodded in agreement then went on. "It was when the bishop threw in his two cents and said that the unlimited pardons would extend to only the family members of the very rich and giving members of the congregation." Buddy's eyes began to widen as he saw the look of understanding rapidly spread across Brother Tis Mythang's face.

"Let me get this straight. You mean to tell me that from what you overheard, since your aunt, Mother Eternal Ann Everlastin', was giving up the big bucks, no matter how crazy you acted you'd always have a home? There wasn't no one at the Ain't Nobody Else Right But Us—All Others Goin' to Hell Church that could've put you out?"

"Exactly!" Buddy's face lit up when he saw that Brother Tis Mythang truly understood and perhaps, he was ready to forgive him.

Brother Tis Mythang sprang from the wall and landed in the middle of the room. He spun around and snapped, "But they threw you out anyway! Apparently, Mother Eternal Ann Everlastin's money couldn't hold an eternal seat for you." He looked over at Buddy and shook his head. "You know I was just beginning to think that perhaps you'd sobered up enough to think straight. Do you know how stupid you just sounded?"

"I wasn't thrown out of the church because I said I was gay," Buddy insisted.

"It had to be because you said you were gay. Your aunt had more money than Fort Knox, and they didn't throw you out until you stood up and made your closet exit announcement."

"They didn't throw me out until the Reverend Knott Enuff Money found out that I'd placed a stop payment on one of my aunt's huge donations," Buddy shot back.

"You did what?" Brother Tis Mythang thought he'd heard wrong. "You put a stop payment on a check that wasn't even yours, and for that, I had to suffer all these years?"

His rage climbed another degree as he hissed, "I stayed all this time out of sheer stubbornness. I refuse to let those hypocrites run me away. Staying there became a habit."

Brother Tis Mythang had returned to his old self. Suddenly the tragedy was all about him.

"The check had been drawn from a joint checking account that I shared with my aunt. It gave me an opportunity to only put a temporary hold on the check to see if the reverend truly meant what I'd overheard. You and I were accepted as long as my aunt's checks continued to pour into the church. When I put a halt to that—temporarily or not—the reverend tossed me out."

Buddy had explained that it was never his intention to act on his feelings, and that he'd even tried counseling after he was driven from the church. When he eventually told Mother Eternal Ann Everlastin' about the real reason he'd intercepted her donation to the church, she became very angry and wouldn't believe him. She eventually stopped speaking to him, and she stopped paying for his counseling. Slowly, and over a period of months, he slid deeper into a dark depression and even deeper into alcoholism. It was a fifth of Jack Daniel's that took the place of all of his friends, his church and his aunt. Jack Daniel's seemed to be the only thing that would accept him for who he was.

Brother Tis Mythang couldn't let Buddy do all the testifying. He revealed that he, too, always knew that there had to be something more to Buddy's sudden disclosure, but he was so satisfied to blame Buddy for all the stares and accusations from many of the church members, even though, deep inside, he knew those actions he would've no doubt received, whether Buddy had never uttered a word. In his mind, Buddy's betrayal gave him a comfort zone, a way out so that he didn't have to face his own demons. He could just continue to wallow in his emotional juices as he sometimes overextended a hand or a wrist or put a little too much girlyness in his mannerisms. More often than not, he did outrageous things to get attention, and it didn't matter if it was unworthy attention, as long as it was attention.

Brother Tis Mythang abruptly changed the conversation. "You know you could've spoken to me at your aunt's funeral. You acted like you didn't know me and that hurt." He stopped and smiled before adding, "I just thought I'd put that out there since we're airing dirty laundry and other feelings."

"I heard that I was at her funeral. I don't remember much. Although, I do remember a little bit about someone hitting me."

Brother Tis Mythang couldn't hold it in. He started laughing so hard that his stomach began to knot up. "Hit you. Sister Mentol Kase knocked you farther into unconsciousness."

"Why would she do that?" Buddy asked.

"Because you were part Indian." Brother Tis Mythang's face muscles were beginning to hurt from the laughter.

"What are you talking about? Why would she have something against that? Was she prejudiced?"

"I don't know if she was prejudiced, but she certainly didn't like no one who was part Slap-a-ho."

The expression on Buddy's face became twisted as he started to laugh too. "You mean to tell me that I told that same old tired joke of mine to someone at the funeral?" He started wringing his hands as he continued to chuckle. "You remember when I used to tell folks that nonsense just to make them mad and call them names without actually calling them a name?"

"I sure do," Brother Tis Mythang uttered. His stomach was still tied in knots but he continued to laugh. "When you said that, I was at the organ. I started playing that whistling melody from that Clint Eastwood movie. You should've seen the look on that woman's face as she turned your lights out!"

"And, all this time I thought it was from the effects of that Jack Daniel's."

"Perhaps it was Jack and Sister Mentol Kase who knocked you out." Brother Tis Mythang held his stomach as he made his way over to a chair to sit. "You know even when them feathers poured out the sides of Mother Eternal Ann Everlastin's casket and were touching you where you were stretched out, you still didn't move."

"Feathers. Please tell me that she wasn't buried in those flamingo feathers that she liked."

"Feathers and the feet."

"Did she wear the ones she had dyed blue?"

"You'd better believe she did." Brother Tis Mythang's eyes suddenly went serious. "You know, I still can't believe that she died on her birthday from the sensation of a peppermint pattie." The seriousness didn't last for long. "I tell you that nobody couldn't have left this planet the way Mother Eternal Ann Everlastin' did, but her. When I tell people how she passed, they still can't believe it."

"That's not what killed her."

"Of course, that's what killed her. I heard all about it from Brother Juan Derr, and you know I just had to tell everyone about it."

"Well, you'll be telling a lie if you continue."

"What are you saying?"

"Back in the hotel, Mr. Tiny tried to explain things to me. I didn't understand everything, but I do know that she actually died from a massive heart attack while she ate the peppermint pattie."

"Boy, I gotta hand it to your aunt. Even in death, she still rules."

Buddy and Brother Tis Mythang continued talking, and by the end of their conversation, they'd made up and forgiven each other. It was Buddy who reached out to hold Brother Tis Mythang's hands while they prayed.

Buddy straightened the tie that had become undone on Brother Tis Mythang, then he gave him a friendly pat on the back. "Well, do you think you can show this loser where everyone went?"

"Did I call you a loser?" Brother Tis Mythang said. He frowned with a look of mock indignation.

Buddy returned the look of pretended indignation with one of his own. "I believe you mentioned that I was a rich loser."

"You mean, it's all about the Benjamins?"

"I certainly ain't talking about the tribe of Benjamin." Buddy laughed.

Brother Tis Mythang checked his watch. "There's only about another five minutes left before everyone will have to return to the auditorium. I guess we can go now and find the folks who brought you up here.

"Although, I have to admit, I'm surprised that you rode all the way up from Pelzer to Baltimore in the same car with them and didn't find a way to shoot them for what they did to you. I don't think I could've survived a ride with the Reverend Knott Enuff Money, especially with the bishop and a Hellraiser riding herd."

"What are you talking about?" Buddy asked. "I didn't come here with the reverend and the bishop." He spread his hands wide as if to show how surprised he really was. "I didn't even know that they were here. And, you know I wouldn't go near none of those Hellraisers."

"You mean to tell me that you drove up here by yourself, drunk?"

"No, of course not. I didn't drive here drunk by myself. I came here drunk with Sister Betty . . ."

"Oh, Claude." Brother Tis Mythang grabbed his head between his hands and mumbled. He'd meant to say, *Oh Lord*, but he was so shocked, it came out, *Oh Claude*. "Wait a minute. Sister Betty can't drive."

"She didn't drive," Buddy replied. "Mr. Tiny drove the limo and Ma Cile came with us."

"Ma Cile!" Brother Tis Mythang unclasped his head and started laughing so hard, he was getting out of breath for about the fifth time. He added, wheezing, "You mean to tell me that Ma Cile is up here in Baltimore?" He tried to catch a gulp of air. "Just tell me that she didn't bring her snuff with her."

"I supposed she did. I seem to remember her and Sister Betty discussing it." Buddy suddenly stopped as though his brain was just catching up to the conversation. "Are you saying that the reverend and the bishop are really here too?"

"That's right, and they brought that lovely she-demon, Sister Ima Hellraiser with them. Although, I haven't heard of any catastrophes in the past hour or so. I guess Sister Hellraiser must be someplace where someone has either knocked her evil self out or tied her up." He chuckled to himself at the thought of someone knocking out Sister Hellraiser before he continued, this time, with a serious tone to his voice. "On another note. I'm on the verge of making some serious connections here in Baltimore. This is my cousin's church, and he's doing some major hookups for me. I don't need those crazy folks from Pelzer messing things up for me." As an afterthought, he added, "Or you."

"Oh my goodness," Buddy exclaimed. "We'd better do something."

"We need to pray," Brother Tis Mythang said. "And we need to do it quick. I hear some of the musicians starting to tune up, and I'm supposed to be onstage. I ain't about to be late for my debut performance, so let's do this."

"I need a drink!" Buddy replied.

"We need to pray hard," Brother Tis Mythang said as they rushed toward the door, choosing to ignore Buddy's last statement. "Hopefully, you can find your way back to Sister Betty and the others."

"You know, you're right. Let's not leave just yet. We need to stop right now and just pray until the heavens open up," Buddy said as he closed one eye and peeped with the other. He stayed that way as he watched Brother Tis Mythang hang his head and begin to say a quick prayer. When the prayer was about over and ready to come to the amen part, he quickly closed his other eye and thought, *When we finish I may need a drink.* Condemnation pricked his heart so he silently asked God's forgiveness for thinking about a drink.

Both men rushed out the door. It didn't take Brother Tis Mythang but a quick glance to recognize Ma Cile from the back and Sister Betty walking beside her. He always thought the two of them together looked like a black Laurel and Hardy. He pushed Buddy ahead of him. "Hurry up. Go catch up with Sister Betty and Ma Cile. I'll see you after the conference, and we can chat some more."

Buddy gave Brother Tis Mythang a high five and watched him dash down the hallway in the opposite direction from Ma Cile and Sister Betty. *He can pray all he wants, he still prances when he runs,* he thought. Not wanting to waste more time wandering around a place he'd never been before by himself, he then rushed off to catch up with Sister Betty and Ma Cile. He didn't have to run too far because Tiny came from out of nowhere and fell in step with him.

"You look like he didn't hurt you too bad," Tiny said to his investment as he looked him up and down. "I can't bring you back to Pelzer all banged up." He didn't mean to say it, but he found himself adding, "We do care about you, Buddy." Tiny caught the approving nods from Ma Cile and Sister Betty. It made him feel more comfortable as he smiled and lay an arm across Buddy's shoulder while adding, "We all care about you."

Buddy wasn't quite sure how to react. In the past, he'd always let Jack Daniel's handle his conversations—with the exception of the one he'd had earlier with Brother Tis Mythang. All the sudden caring was beginning to get to him, and he wasn't sure if it was because he'd prayed or if it was because he was suddenly a wealthy man. He decided it was the result of prayer, so he gave a heavy sigh and whispered, "Thank you." He placed a hand on Tiny's shoulder in affirmation. "I truly thank you."

Neither of the manly men wanted to show any more emotion

than was necessary, so they raced to catch up with Sister Betty and Ma Cile who had walked on ahead to give them privacy.

As they walked down the long hall, they could almost feel the electricity in the air from voices sending praises skyward. Their eagerness to join the Back to God's Love conference was spurred by another blast from the horn section accompanied by the wailing of an electric guitar and applause. Without saying a word, Ma Cile, Sister Betty, Tiny and Buddy walked a little faster to join the festivities inside the auditorium. None of them were disappointed as a mixture of anointing and good old-fashion hallelujahs permeated the air from one side of the auditorium to the other. The crowd was ecstatic, sending joyous praises back and forth as though their words were a spiritual ball in a game of holy volleyball.

The Spirit of God had to be pleased.

22

It's Time to Change

While Sister Betty and the others were taking their seats, Dr. Bobbitto Jonas strutted onto the stage again. And, as was his habit, he'd changed into yet another flamboyant outfit; this time he'd opted for a wine-colored Giorgio Armani two-piece suit with a matching cream-colored tie. Of course, his shoes shone bright enough to almost cause blindness to those in the first three rows.

There wasn't a dumb or courageous fly in the entire auditorium that dared light on him. Even the Miss Evil One herself, Sister Ima Hellraiser was mesmerized by the sight of the handsome man who pranced across the stage with more of a flair than most men. Any other time, she might've tried to do or to start something to upset the tranquility of the moment, but she was still cowering like a frightened child afraid of heights inside the camera bucket that hung high in the auditorium.

Hopefully, with God's grace and mercy, she'd stay right there because at the rate her troublemaking skills were soaring, that was about as close to Heaven as she'd ever get.

Dr. Bobbitto Jonas finally arrived at the microphone. As long as the moving camera lights highlighted his every step and he had the audience wrapped around his every gesture, he was gonna take his time. He relished the attention and made sure that the audience knew he appreciated the support by blowing kisses and waving. Everyone, from the front row to the nosebleed section, was shown a little love.

"Come on, y'all. We've got to get this part of the service started."

Dr. Jonas laughed as he pretended to wait with both hands on his hips as the audience finally came to attention.

For some crazy reason known only to Dr. Jonas, he decided to sing a hymn a cappella. Clothes, he wore them well. Words, he spoke them very well. Singing, his pitch was about as correct as a footless man trying to kick a football. He couldn't sing and everyone knew it but him; however, since he was the one and only Dr. Bobbitto Jonas, his notes as flat as tortillas were tolerated.

He started off singing a verse of his signature song, the one that he mangled the most, "This Little Light of Mine." By the time he got to the words, "I'm gonna let it shine," the microphone started squealing as if it couldn't take those crushed notes being breathed upon it any longer.

The entire first two rows started yelling, "Thank ya, Lord." With that little bit of praise to God and misunderstood encouragement, Dr. Jonas thought he'd start up the song again, but the microphone wasn't having it. That microphone started humming and barking until every word he sang sounded like that Chihuahua from the Taco Bell commercials.

A lot of prayers must've gone up with an urgency because he suddenly stopped singing. He laughed nervously as he strutted across the stage and blamed the devil for sabotaging his solo.

If that were true, then it would've been the first time that Satan ever got a "thank you" from the church crowd.

When it seemed like the audience was growing impatient because the hallelujahs had quieted down, with the exception of someone yelling out, "Let's get on with it," Dr. Bobbitto Jonas took another microphone from a stagehand who suddenly appeared from nowhere. He started introducing the various vocalists and choirs, those waiting in the wings and some who were visitors in the audience. All were invited onstage for a short gospel jam session. It seemed like a good idea since he needed to fill the time until the Reverend Cherry was ready to speak and bring the conference to a close.

In the meanwhile, Brother Tis Mythang had also come onstage and had taken a seat at another organ just a few feet from where Dr. Jonas's musical director, Darryl Lee, sat. The two of them had met earlier backstage and had an instant respect for each other's musicianship, softness and penchant for originality and on-the-spot improvisation.

Of course, Brother Tis Mythang never bothered to mention the fact that he'd never used most of the accessories and sounds that were a part of the instrument he was about to play. He felt he didn't need to reveal that little detail because, after all, he was Brother Tis Mythang, cousin of the Reverend Walter Thomas, the pastor of that church.

The audience went wild when Evangelist Shirley Caesar and Yolanda Adams appeared together onstage then were later joined by Pastor Donnie McClurkin. The trio appeared so spiritually grounded in the gift of voice and the message, that they sang until many audience members became overwhelmed, either by the spirit or the rhythm and had to be taken from the auditorium—and that wasn't even fifteen minutes into the program. There was at least another ten minutes to fill.

The other Christian and not-so-Christian celebrities followed onstage and also whipped the crowd into a frenzy with their short praises and testimonies, which ultimately left the audience panting for more.

Everything was going right on schedule with no one the wiser that time was being killed until Dr. Bobbitto Jonas brought out Dottie Peoples to wrap up that part of the program. She had changed into a black-and-white, rhinestone-encrusted gown that probably cost more than a year's tithes for the every Sunday churchgoer. The shimmer from the dazzling stones caused those sitting in the first three rows to become giddy with jealousy. She had the famous Mississippi Mass Choir as backup.

The choir leader for the Mississippi Mass Choir was unable to attend because of illness, and in his stead stood the body of elasticity itself, Ricky Dillard. Ricky was a cocoa-complected, thin, handsome young man of about thirty who when he wasn't leading his own choir called the Gospel Choir Excellence held his hands limp at the wrist. He was someone who could and who did literally contort his body when he conducted a choir. He looked like he was leading the choir in Tae-Bo, and he looked very sexy doing so.

The auditorium was totally silent with respect for Dottie Peoples and Ricky Dillard as they waited for the magic to begin. No one even breathed hard enough to make a noise. With the exception of the low hum from several of the air conditioners, anticipation was felt in the air.

And, then it happened. It happened quicker than it took one of the old church mothers to get into the spirit and start shouting whenever someone dropped a dollar nearby.

Somebody didn't pray hard enough because Brother Tis Mythang, who hadn't been informed that Dottie Peoples was going to do a solo with a choir backing her lost his mind. He had always wanted to play "On Time God," and no matter what Miss Peoples thought she was going to sing, that's what he was going to play.

Ricky Dillard had just bent over backward with the back of his head touching the heels of his shoes and sprung forward like someone had kicked him; that was the cue for the choir to start singing "Testify."

The choir had all turned to the left so that when they started singing, Miss Peoples could prance and shuffle in her rhinestone heels toward them and begin to sing her verse.

That's what was supposed to happen.

Ricky Dillard hadn't so much as sprung forward about a foot and the choir was into singing the fifth note, when Brother Tis Mythang started pounding on the organ, his version of "On Time God."

Brother Tis Mythang was so into doing his thing, that he never realized that the only sounds being made were the ones from him and his organ. By the time he got finished with the mustard and tried to ketch-up, it was too late.

While Brother Tis Mythang, still high on his self-imposed ego trip, mangled and rewrote the musical portion of the program, the entire stage of dignified celebrities, including the Dr. Bobbitto Jonas, had started to empty into the musician's pit, where all the other musicians with an ounce of sense scattered for safety. All with the exception of Brother Tis Mythang.

Brother Tis Mythang had the nerve to stand like he was about to pound that organ into splinters. He was basking in his own glory juices. He was winking like he had something in his eye and had his head going from side to side, almost rotating. While his feet raced from pedal to pedal, he offered the awestruck audience a smile that looked like he'd just discovered new cheese. The organ's notes were just about to launch into the second verse of his song when his smile was cut short by a hard thump across his teeth from a rhinestone earring. The rhinestone earring weapon was quickly followed by the delivery of a rhinestone high-heel shoe.

That jewelry assault, which was quickly turning Brother Tis Mythang's top lip into a blubbery mass, was then followed by a chokehold by Ricky Dillard. He stood behind Brother Tis Mythang, and grabbed him with both his hands cupping Brother Tis Mythang's chin. Ricky Dillard pulled him backward like he was bending a slingshot but refused to release. No matter how much Brother Tis Mythang tried to wiggle, Ricky Dillard was bending him to his will.

A few of the other Mississippi Mass Choir members, which by then included the Wonder Boy from the Brooklyn choir, grabbed him by his legs. They pulled at Brother Tis Mythang's legs like they were trying to make a wish, as Ricky Dillard held on to his chin grip. If Brother Tis Mythang ever completely changed and desired to have children, he'd surely have to adopt. They tore Brother Tis Mythang asunder. It would be a long time before he played with or on any organ.

About twenty irritated ushers, both men and women who were all sizes and nationalities and included five midgets who were ex-cons, finally recovered enough to rush to the musicians' pit and rescue Brother Tis Mythang. They did it hesitantly and even managed to toss in a few punches and kicks of their own as they pretended to help him get up.

The audience and the other celebrities who were off stage were shocked, although many of them were secretly glad to see Brother Tis Mythang get his comeuppance since he'd made it a mission to let them know that he was part of the Reverend Thomas's family.

Even Sister Betty, Ma Cile and Tiny as well as Buddy who'd kept alternating between wanting to pray and needing a drink couldn't believe their eyes, yet, they weren't all that surprised at Brother Tis Mythang's antics.

"Jesus, have mercy on us!" Sister Betty whispered as she desperately fought to keep her poor arthritic knees and legs from hopping around. At the rate her legs were going from all the bad karma, she was bound to have to soak in a vat of Ben-Gay before everything was over.

"And, save a little mercy for him," Ma Cile urged on in prayer. Just seeing what had gone down suddenly made her crave a snuff dip, but she didn't want to move and miss any more drama.

This is just another reason why I have just got to join the Ain't Nobody Else Right But Us—All Other's Goin' to Hell Church, thought Tiny as he laughed to himself.

The drama had been so overwhelming that even Sister Hellraiser had gotten up the courage and moved an inch in order to see everything that was appearing on the camera screen from inside her camera-bucket hanging prison. When she finally took a chance and moved over that inch, it was all the lone cameraman needed to bolt and escape down the side of the camera lift.

Sister Hellraiser was all alone in the bucket, and it was no one's fault but her own. At least her fear of heights would keep her out of the way. The only other fear she had was that no one would climb up to help her out. She was even too scared to scream for help. It seemed that Hellraiser wasn't so tough after all.

Reverends Cherry, Reid and Thomas were shocked, embarrassed and dismayed to say the least, but they were persuaded by the ushers, along with Reverend Knott Enuff Money and the Bishop Was Nevercalled not to enter into the fray. So instead, they prayed. This time when the prayers went up, they went down on their knees. There was the gnashing of teeth, the pounding on the chests and the outstretch of arms as they were all on one accord in their need for God to intervene. In a hurry!

The only exception to the fervent prayers was that the mega-church pastors were praying for literal peace, and Reverend Knott Enuff Money was praying for piece too—he wanted a piece of Brother Tis Mythang's behind.

Down in the musicians' pit, pieces of music charts and broken drumsticks lay among the turned-over chairs and music stands. It was a mess. After the ushers removed Brother Tis Mythang and the remnants of his expensive suit, everyone finally calmed down. The musicians returned from out of hiding and put things back together as best they could under the circumstances. They would have all left but they hadn't been paid, so they stayed and decided that whatever musical arrangements were played, whether right or wrong, they would just say that they were jamming or improvising.

She was totally embarrassed, but Dottie Peoples went back on-stage, accompanied by Dr. Bobbitto Jonas who because he'd had sense enough to stay out of the fray, still looked good and in one piece. In her disheveled yet elegant appearance, with her upswept beehive hairdo now hanging to her shoulders, Dottie Peoples apologized to everyone but Brother Tis Mythang.

The audience gave her a rousing round of applause to show their support for what she'd done as well as to accept her apology, and the conference festivities continued.

With only Darryl Lee at the organ along with the other musicians, Dottie Peoples and the remnant of the Mississippi Mass Choir that hadn't gotten their clothes torn from the fight sang the song that would've initially ended her time onstage. She sang "On Time God."

All Brother Tis Mythang had to do was wait and he'd have gotten his chance to shine. Instead, he lay in one of the outer rooms, one tooth missing, lips puffed and twisted like he'd had a shot of collagen, with a black eye that was very shiny from the heavy amount of Vaseline lathered upon it to keep the swelling down.

Dr. Bobbitto Jonas invoked the crowd to give Dottie Peoples and the choir another round of applause. He then apologized again and with another wide grin, he told the audience, "Now comes the part of the program that we've all been waiting for. You heard Reverend Thomas welcome you. You've also heard Reverend Reid tell you what and why we are here for the Back to God's Love conference. It's time, and I'm honored, my brothers and sisters and all of you out there in television land, to bring it on home."

He turned his head toward Darryl Lee who cued the musicians to start playing softly. "Stand to your feet and give God some praise." He stopped while the audience stood, clapping as they did. "Oh, that's fine if you're clapping for me." The audience started clapping harder as if God were counting the times and the effort.

Dr. Jonas smiled again and said, "Now I know, without a shadow of a doubt, that God is pleased."

As if it were prearranged, Darryl Lee raised one hand from off the organ keys and cued the musicians to play a little louder. The horn section tooted. The drummer drummed and tossed one drumstick up in the air a few inches, then caught it just to show he could. The rest of the musicians hung in there and slid notes wherever they could. The frenzy was building and the church was about to go up.

Dr. Jonas pranced and performed hand acrobatics, tossing the cordless microphone from one hand to the other as he continued his announcement. "Here he is, the man who's behind the reformation of the church and God's people everywhere ... the anointed and gifted, none other than the ... Reverend ... John ... Cherry."

He worked that crowd like an ole massa.

23

My Brother's Keeper

Reverend John Cherry smiled as he strolled onto the stage. It wasn't a smile made of courage or even one made of an overrated ego. He smiled because finally there was a forum and purpose to share the vision and ministry that God had bestowed upon him.

For more than a year, he'd preached the reformation of the church from not only his pulpit, but from any that he'd occupied. Preaching a message that both condemned the church in its present state while outlining an anointed plan to bring it back to God had been challenging.

Reverend Cherry had led his huge congregation in a widely publicized battle against its head church. He'd publicly disassociated his church and sizeable assests from his former head church which he described as a bureaucratic puppeteer. He'd taken a lot of hits, some publicly, a few politically, and for the most part, religiously. But Reverend Cherry would not budge from his determination to do whatever God lay upon him to run the hypocrisy out of the church—from the pulpit to the front door.

As Reverend Cherry took a pair of reading glasses from his robe pocket, he scanned the audience. He marveled at the many faces of the men and women who had sacrificed to come out that night. With the exception of the previous embarrassing moment when Brother Tis Mythang had inappropriately caused so many of them to react so unbecomingly, they seemed to be of one accord in their desire to return to God's love.

He adjusted his reading glasses upon the bridge of his nose then his face lit up again. Sure enough, sitting as elegant and as poised as a woman of God could be was his wife, Diana.

With a small silver-colored scarf with white crocheted trim that lay across her lap and covered her legs modestly to mid-calf, Diana Cherry sat, gazing at her husband. She was his never-wavering source of support, and she relished the role because she truly believed in her husband.

There was a lot going on backstage during the time that Reverend Cherry had spent getting his thoughts together and enjoying the respect and honor lavished upon him by the audience. Four maroon cushioned high-back chairs had been placed behind one of the curtains.

It took some doing but one of the sound engineers managed to attach a wireless lapel microphone to the neckline of Reverend Knott Enuff Money's borrowed robe. The lapel microphone had to be changed several times because the perspiration and the activator juice that ran from the reverend's Jheri curl kept soaking the microphone head. Every time someone from the sound booth did a microphone check there was a crackling sound from the reverend's microphone. Finally, someone with a little creativity placed a small piece of sponge on the head of the microphone, and placed a rubber band around it to hold it in place.

By the time they raised the backdrop curtain to reveal Reverends Thomas, Reid, Money and Bishop Was Nevercalled sitting in their respective chairs, no signs of backstage drama were seen.

Once again, the audience responded to the sight of the pastors and the bishop with enthusiasm, and the men they responded with wide grins to show their appreciation.

Reverend Knott Enuff Money put on his best pious-looking face and with a Bible spread open in his hands, he sat up straight in the high-back chair between Reverends Thomas and Reid. He looked up at the auditorium ceiling and truly gave thanks. He also thought about his mother and how awesome it would've been to have her see him sitting between two mega-church pastors as though he had been born to be there at that place and time.

While Reverend Cherry continued, this time with a little more bass in his voice, as he gave the people a brief summary of his topic and his outline points, Reverend Knott Enuff Money moved his head quickly from side to side. Backstage, he had already informed Reverends Thomas and Reid about the bishop's "supposed" accident, which had left the bishop's glasses smashed beyond repair. He even tried to look ashamed and unenthusiastic that it would be he instead of the bishop who would read the scriptures for Reverend Cherry.

Both of the pastors seemed to be okay with his awkward lie. If they didn't believe his flimsy explanation that the bishop had tripped and fell facedown, which caused him to shatter his glasses without leaving so much as a mark on his white face, they weren't showing it.

Reverend Knott Enuff Money's main concern for that moment was the bishop. All during the time the reverend had lied to the pastors, the bishop acted like he wanted to stop him. The only thing that prevented it was that the bishop was more afraid of being discovered as illiterate than he was of getting some on-air camera time. But, that was backstage. Now that the program had started and the cameras were panning back and forth, the bishop looked like he was ready to spring from his seat. The reverend sat there hoping that the bishop wouldn't get too caught up in what was happening with the spotlight on someone other than himself.

However, just like the reverend was busy sneaking peeks at the other pastors on the stage, they, too, were watching him; and they weren't the only ones.

Sister Betty, Ma Cile, Buddy and Tiny were watching him. They'd all agreed that if they asked for visitors to stand and give their names as well as their church's name that they wouldn't. They would've sprouted wings if they could have to fly away and distance themselves from the reverend and the bishop.

Sister Ima Hellraiser had no choice but to watch Reverend Knott Enuff Money too. She was still trapped in that camera bucket with about two feet of space between her and the camera monitor. And, when the cameraman escaped, she was left literally hanging. All she could do was watch and hope that somehow Reverend Knott Enuff Money and the bishop would do what they always did, which was to make fools of themselves. When she'd seen Brother Tis Mythang carried from the auditorium in disgrace and disarray, she thought the rest of the evening might be boring until someone came to rescue her; however, from just one look at the hyenalike grin on the reverend's face and the envy-green tint covering the bishop's complexion, she knew there was more to come.

As Reverend Cherry prepared to go into his speech, the shuffling of his papers was heard all over the auditorium through the speakers. He took his time and looked over several and when he was satisfied that all was in order, he began.

"Again, on behalf of myself and my esteemed colleagues,"—he stopped then pointed to the chairs behind him, nodding to each of the men and turned back to face the audience—"I thank you for your time and will try not to wear out your patience.

"However, I do want to take a moment and give a special acknowledgement and thank you." Reverend Cherry walked from behind the podium, clasped his hands and walked close to the edge of the stage. "I would be remiss if I continued without first of all asking for a moment of silence for a woman of God who exemplified what God meant when the question was asked 'Am I my brother's keeper?' "

He began to pace across the stage, and with a look of sadness that sprang upon his face like a sudden summer rain, he continued, "Mother Eternal Ann Everlastin' is dead. Now let us give her a moment of silence."

Not everyone thought they needed to participate in the moment of silence.

"Ain't that the old rich woman who always came here from down south wearing blue chicken feathers?" one of the audience members who was wearing a hat with a crown so high it looked like the Leaning Tower of Babel was overheard asking. "She had exquisite taste in hats."

"I believe that they were aqua-colored peacock feathers," whispered a very thin woman sitting next to her. The tall black-and-white striped hat she wore made her look like Dr. Seuss's *Cat in the Hat*. She moved closer to the other woman as she looked around to make sure no one overheard. "I wonder who got her hat stash?"

As some folks will do, whether they should or not, the two women continued their whispered commentaries. They couldn't shut their mouths for one moment—not for respect or to be obedient—as they continued their comparison dialogues about the late Mother Eternal Ann Everlastin's one-of-a kind church hats.

"Mother Eternal Ann Everlastin' passed away several days ago," Reverend Cherry related as he crossed the stage to return to the podium. "She was a very wealthy woman and she thought much of the Reverends Thomas, Reid and myself. She thought enough to leave each of our churches, one million dollars."

For the first time since Reverend Cherry had asked the audience to give Mother Eternal Ann Everlastin' a moment of silence, the two blabbering women did just that. The mention of the million-dollar gift shut them up completely. The only thing that moved in their seats were their hands, quickly covering their hearts from the shock.

The two women weren't the only ones sitting in shock. Masks of angry greed suddenly replaced the ones of piousness upon the faces of Reverend Knott Enuff Money and Bishop Was Nevercalled. They looked like they had gas as their bodies began to swell with resentment.

"As we understand it," the Reverend Cherry continued, crossing his arms, "it was Mother Eternal Ann Everlastin's birthday and she was about to host a church Mothers board anniversary at her home church, No Hope Now—Mercy Neva. She was her usual happy self. Then suddenly while standing at a podium, such as this one, God sent for her to come on home."

"It-it wasn't quite tha-at simple," the bishop stuttered as he tried to whisper into the Reverend Knott Enuff Money's ear. "She was feel-feeling high off-off a York pepper-peppermint pattie. Tha-at pattie killed her."

Of course, as often as the bishop tried, he still couldn't be counted on to shut his mouth. No amount of whispering, unless he did it so low only dogs could hear him, would've worked. He was whispering directly into the Reverend Knott Enuff Money's lapel microphone.

Everyone in the New Psalmist Church, inside and out of the auditorium, overheard the bishop.

At the sound of the bishop's unintentional revelation, Reverend Cherry's short neck turned around so quick, his whole body felt the whiplash. It was as though he'd asked the entire auditorium to give Mother Eternal Ann Everlastin' another moment of silence. Again only a low hum from the air conditioners was heard. And, for the first time in his thirty years of preaching, Reverend Cherry couldn't say a word.

Well, he wasn't by himself. Reverends Thomas and Reid sat in their seats looking shell-shocked. Suddenly, as if on cue, both men let their heads drop as though they'd started praying. The truth was that they were trying to hold back laughter. They didn't want to laugh. They definitely didn't want to be seen laughing so, therefore, they dropped their heads to muffle their laughs. Like many preachers who liked to tell a little joke or relate some funny situation that they'd witnessed, each one knew that as soon as they could, they'd work that little comment into one of their sermons.

Reverend Knott Enuff Money was the only one with the presence of mind to try and move around in his seat. It was only because he looked around for a hole in the stage floor to hide and, of course, he didn't find one.

The poor bishop again sat wiggling in his seat, his complexion beet red from embarrassment as he wished, again that he could've clicked his heels and fled to Oz.

Sister Ima Hellraiser almost caused the camera bucket to turn over. She was laughing so hard, she made that bucket swing from side to side. It was a short-lived laugh because in addition to being deathly afraid of heights, she was also afraid of roller coasters. All that giggling and moving about she did made the bucket seem like one. She quickly shut her mouth and again went back to cowering inside the camera bucket. She also stopped because she'd laughed so hard that she was beginning to feel the early urges of a necessary visit to the bathroom, and there wasn't one inside that bucket—not yet.

That last embarrassing act sealed it for Sister Betty and the others. There was no way they were going to admit to being members of the Ain't Nobody Else Right But Us—All Others Goin' to Hell Church.

All of them would take their secret church affiliation back to Pelzer with them, with the exception of Buddy. He'd gladly agree to reveal everything he knew. He was getting more sober by the minute.

Reverend Cherry decided to take the high road. He continued to speak as though nothing had happened. "Reverends Thomas, Reid and myself, we've decided to donate the million dollar gifts from Mother Eternal Ann Everlastin' to the Back to God's Love Foundation." They'd also decided to claim, by faith, the repentance of the Reverend Knott Enuff Money.

On the heels of that announcement the audience stood to give the mega-church pastors an ovation. Both Reverends Thomas and Reid got out of their seats and came forward to stand for a brief moment beside Reverend Cherry to accept the applause from the audience as well as to show their solidarity.

That's when both the reverend and the bishop started choking. One of the ushers had to run onstage to bring them each a glass of water.

I don't believe this! They can't do that. I needed to get some of that money for my church, Reverend Knott Enuff Money thought as the water and the color drained fast from his face. He was so shocked that his mocha-colored complexion turned almost as white as the bishop's complexion used to be.

The bishop sat back in his seat looking stiff as a board. He was sitting there with his eyes bulging, forehead furrowed and his mouth and jaws set so tight that air could neither get in or out. He wanted to say something. He even wanted to think something, but he was afraid that perhaps his thoughts would transmit through the wireless lapel microphone on the reverend's robe.

While the bishop and the reverend sat in their seats, both verged on the brink of a stroke, the other preachers made their way back to their seats. Their faces shone with pride that they were able to do something good with the monetary gift.

The only thing that took away their momentary joy was the look on the Reverend Knott Enuff Money's face. If looks could've killed, the sharp knives thrown by the reverend's eyes would've had them all filleted and dead. Without saying a word, both Reverends Reid and Thomas looked at each other with sad looks of disappointment. Each man knew that it would take a miracle to turn around Reverend Knott Enuff Money. It was apparent that the reverend did not agree with what they'd done.

However, none of the drama that was in the process of unfolding was witnessed by the Reverend Cherry. He was still basking in the audience's appreciation and so, he continued to speak.

"Let me tell you why we feel it is important to have a reformation of the church and why it's equally important that a message of getting back to God's love is so important." He adjusted his glasses, looked down at his wife Diana who gave him a nod of approval and spoke again.

"The church is supposed to be a place of refuge, particularly when you have just escaped the clutches of the devil. And, before I go any further, I want to ask one of our esteemed guests, tonight, Reverend Knott Enuff Money, if he will do me the honor of turning to 2 Peter 2:14."

Some of the color that had just drained from the Reverend Knott Enuff Money's face returned when he heard Reverend Cherry introduce him to the people with the word, esteemed. In his mind, he thought that perhaps it was the inappropriate behavior of the bishop that they disliked, and that these mega-church pastors truly thought of him as one of them.

How the Reverend Knott Enuff Money always managed to slip on and off the island of Denial was a work of art. He was beginning to believe his own hype.

Before they'd come onstage, Reverend Cherry had already told Reverend Knott Enuff Money which book of the Bible he'd chosen. Even the Bible that the reverend carried already had a bookmark that was clipped to the page in the appropriate place. So Reverend Knott Enuff Money stood, proud, and was just about to read from 2 Peter 2:14 when Reverend Cherry flipped the script on him.

"Hold on a moment, Reverend Money. The spirit is telling me to start off from another place." Reverend Cherry closed his eyes for a moment, and with one hand cupping the elbow of his other arm, he leaned back and then said, "Turn to the book of Genesis."

Well, what should have been an easy thing to do suddenly became a chore as the Reverend Knott Enuff Money started thumbing through the index, looking for the book of Genesis. In all the years he'd pastored, he would always preach from a book of prewritten sermons. He never had to study or read from a Bible. All he had to do was just read from a script, throw in a few whoops, toss a hand-kerchief in the air while covering one ear as he railed back and forth, and he had the congregation going. There were even a few times when folks actually got up and started to shout.

Reverend Knott Enuff Money got nervous and dropped the Bible. Bishop Was Nevercalled swiftly picked it up and handed it back to the reverend with the page to the book of Genesis already open.

Bishop Was Nevercalled may not have been able to read but even he knew that Genesis was the first book of the Bible, so as he handed the Bible to the reverend, he gave him a look that read, *You owe me, and you owe me, big time.*

Again, Reverend Cherry took the high road and decided that per-haps the reverend was just nervous. "Turn with me, if you please to Genesis 4:9. Y'all know the story, so I won't go into it in detail. It's the verse where God asked Cain as to the whereabouts of his brother, Abel. Cain replied, 'Am I my brother's keeper?' " He took off his glasses and looked over the crowd of people and then asked the question, "Are you your brother's keeper?"

While Reverend Cherry was in the midst of getting the audience worked up and ready to receive his message, Reverend Knott Enuff Money secretly thanked God that he'd managed to dodge that bullet. He quickly flipped to the page where the bookmark still held fast to 2 Peter 2:14.

"I want you to think about that question as I continue to go into the message and the word tonight," Reverend Cherry said. He turned around and nodded toward Reverend Knott Enuff Money, all the while wondering why his colleagues, Reverends Thomas and Reid, still had their heads bowed. *Perhaps they are praying for me and this service,* he thought.

"As I said before, the church should be a place of refuge when you've been kicked, stomped and almost dealt a death blow by day-to-day life."

He hadn't meant to do it but Reverend Cherry found himself quickly looking back at Reverend Knott Enuff Money before continuing. "There are many false teachers out there and they will draw men and women in through the lust of the flesh." Sticking one hand out from his side, he said, "Reverend Money, please read now from the second book of Peter."

Now it was time for Reverend Knott Enuff Money to shine. It was the moment for which his mother, without any fight from him, had groomed him. He was onstage with the big boys. His Trinity. His mega-church preachers. He took a step forward so that it would appear that he was so holy that he needed to come out from among the others who sat watching him closely.

Pushing back strands of Jheri curls, which again had lost their moistness and crackled into the wireless lapel microphone, the Reverend Knott Enuff Money prepared himself to read. In preparation, he held the Bible in one hand, took his other hand and covered one ear, and as was his habit, he threw his head back and cried out, "Oh Lord . . . oh Lord."

For whatever reason he'd forgotten just that quick that he was only doing the reading and not the preaching. It took a strong yank on the hem of his robe from the bishop to bring him back to the planet. He played it off by crying out again, "Oh Lord. Reverend Cherry, what I'm about to read is so deep—"

Reverend Cherry and no one else on the stage were fooled. "I know," Reverend Cherry said sternly. "Just read the word, Reverend Money. Just read the word and stop at verse twenty-one." He put emphasis on the word *stop* so that the reverend knew he meant business.

And, Reverend Knott Enuff Money began to read thusly. "Ahem," he said into his lapel microphone. He wanted to make sure that in addition to having all eyes upon him that his every word was heard. "*Having eyes full of adultery, and that cannot cease from sin; beguiling unstable souls: a heart they have exercised with covetous practices; cursed children . . .*"

"Stop right there!" Reverend Cherry looked as though he was about to jump from the stage into the audience as he pointed his finger at them. "Having eyes full of adultery, and that cannot cease from sin!" he roared. "I told y'all that we are supposed to be 'our brother's keeper,' but how can we be that and have adulterous eyes? How can folks come to the church seeking refuge and instead they are met by supposedly men and women leaders who look at them with adulterous eyes." He stopped to let his words sink in. "Read on," he said as he pointed back toward Reverend Knott Enuff Money.

"*Which have forsaken the right way, and are gone astray, following the way of Balaam the son of Bosor, who loved the wages of unrighteousness; But was rebuked for his iniquity: the dumb ass speaking—*" The reverend's hands were becoming wet with perspiration. He didn't like reading for Reverend Cherry as much as he thought he would.

"Who was that he said was speaking?" Ma Cile asked as she tried to adjust her false blue eye, which suddenly looked like it was going to sleep.

"He said that he was a dumb . . ." Buddy suddenly remembered that he was still in church and corrected himself. "He said he was rebuked for speaking," Buddy hissed.

"That's what I thought I heard," Ma Cile said. She looked over at Sister Betty to say something to her but found Sister Betty with her head cradled in her hands and praying. Ma Cile didn't want to disturb her so she looked past Sister Betty to where Tiny sat. She wanted to say something to him, but he was praying too. So Ma Cile just sat back in her seat and turned her attention back to Reverend Knott Enuff Money.

Reverend Knott Enuff Money continued. As long as Reverend Cherry didn't tell him to stop, he would read. "*. . . the dumb ass speaking with man's voice forbad the madness of the prophet. These are wells without water, clouds that are carried with a tempest; to whom the mist of darkness is reserved for ever.*" He was starting to feel a little uncomfortable. He was starting to feel convicted, but he didn't know why because he really didn't understand everything that he was reading.

"Stop right there, Reverend," Reverend Cherry said with a loud voice. "These are leaders who love to tell you anything that they think you want to hear. They're unlearned in the ways of truth, according to God's Word. I said 'unlearned' not uneducated. They know that when a soul is wounded that it is in an unstable mental condition, but they will tell you anything because they don't have your best interest at heart. They are whispering words that are sweet to the ear just so that they, themselves, can receive a financial benefit." He stopped speaking and came from behind the pulpit to face the audience. "And the men and women of God are not alone in courting you with honey-coated words and promises of fulfilled dreams. The government is no better. Both of them will put their own spin on things just to get you to dig into your pockets and support their perceived lifestyles and programs." He walked slowly back to the pulpit, giving the audience a chance to ponder what he'd just said.

"If I tell you that if you send me fifty dollars that God will give you the desires of your heart, then that means that you don't believe the Word of God. For the Bible says, *Seek ye first, the kingdom of God, and His righteousness, and all these other things will be added unto you.*"

Reverend Knott Enuff Money felt his mouth suddenly going dry. He wasn't sure if he'd be able to read any further. He tried licking his lips as he listened intently to what the Reverend Cherry said, as he remembered some of his own, not-quite-so-spiritual fund-raisers.

He can't be pointing no fingers at me, the reverend thought as he shifted from one foot to the other. *I never asked anybody to send me money directly. All I did was tell them to send me a hundred dollar bill and write the words* send me a blessing, *on the bill.* He struggled to find a place in his heart where there was no condemnation. So far, he couldn't.

"Listen to me," Reverend Cherry urged. "The government once put people in jail for writing numbers. They were called policy writers. But then one day, the government discovered that they could add to their already swelling finances if they legalized the numbers game."

Now it was the bishop's turn to squirm. "Please don't say the word *lottery,*" he mumbled to himself.

"The lottery," Reverend Cherry explained, "ain't nothing but legalized number running. I mean you have to be mentally unstable to look at a sign that says, 'one-in-a-million chance of winning,' and you plop down your hard-earned money."

Suddenly, the bishop's head dropped as if someone had sneaked up behind him and delivered a karate chop to his neck.

As far as the audience was concerned, he looked like he was praying right along with the Reverends Reid and Thomas. They seemed to constantly lower their heads as if they were getting busy signals from Heaven and weren't hanging up until they got through.

"Reverend Knott Enuff Money, read on. I'll tell you when to stop.

Tell us what thus saith the Lord," Reverend Cherry said as he took a small white towel from the pulpit and began to wipe the perspiration from his forehead. "Come on, Reverend. Tell it!"

Reverend Knott Enuff Money seemed lost as he stood, convicted and marinating in his own guilty juices. Somehow, he found his voice and continued to read from the Bible. It seemed as though each word he spoke was pointing at him.

"For when they speak great swelling words of vanity, they allure through the lusts of the flesh, through much wantonness, those that were clean escaped from them who live in error. While they promise them liberty, they themselves are the servants of corruption: for of whom a man is overcome, of the same is he brought in bondage. For if after they have escaped the pollutions of the world through the knowledge of the Lord and Savior Jesus Christ, they are again entangled therein, and overcome, the latter end is worse with them than the beginning. For it had been better for them not to have known the way of righteousness than, after they have known it, to turn from the holy commandment delivered unto them."

As he finished speaking the last words, from the verse, he added, as humbly as he could, "Amen."

"Thank you, Reverend Money," Reverend Cherry said as he nodded his head toward the Reverend Knott Enuff Money, indicating that he was pleased with what he'd done. Reverend Knott Enuff Money had a strange look upon his face as he slowly took his seat, and Reverend Cherry couldn't determine why.

As far as Reverend Knott Enuff Money was concerned, Reverend Cherry didn't tell him to sit down a moment too soon.

His entire body felt unusually warm, and there were fleeting accusatory images, almost like a slide show that began to run through Reverend Knott Enuff Money's mind. They were the faces of some of the poorest members of his congregation. A hazy collage of young and old who had given parts if not all of their meager savings and earnings. They stood in lines and poured money into many baskets and even threw their envelopes upon the steps that led to his altar, just because of the insincere promises he'd made—honey-coated promises that poured from him with each cupping of his ear or a loud bass-infused word meant to sweetly kiss the ears of those who listened. He'd watched smiling greedily with the bishop by his side as well as other preachers as each of the congregation members opened their wallets, hoping to buy a slice of promised eternal life.

When Reverend Cherry was certain that Reverend Knott Enuff

Money had managed to sit down without incident, he turned back to the audience to finish his message. "I know the hour is growing late, and I certainly thank Reverend Money for lending his voice in support of us tonight."

Reverend Cherry started off the applause first, then the audience followed in kind. But, it was all that Reverend Knott Enuff Money could do to raise his hand in appreciation. The condemnation had sapped his strength. He was trapped between feeling that he probably should change and not truly wanting to do it.

It would take a little more of a miracle to bring him on in. Somehow, Reverends Reid and Thomas felt that a little more help from on high was desperately needed, so they continued to pray.

Reverend Knott Enuff Money was experiencing both mental and physical changes on the stage, none of which was lost on Sister Betty. She, too, felt that another powerful prayer session was in order to bring her pastor to his senses.

As far as Tiny was concerned, he just clasped his hands and started praying for God to just show up and shove the reverend real hard. He didn't realize that with all the praying that he did for Buddy and Reverend Knott Enuff Money that he, too, was storing up a little grace for himself.

It was time to bring his message home. The Reverend Cherry took another look at his wife, Diana, who still sat looking adoringly at her husband, as First Lady Marla Reid did the same at hers.

"Second Peter 2:14–21 summed up quite specifically why we need this reformation for the church. I'm talking about those men and women of God who try and lead their flocks while their hearts want what their eyes see. And, as long as they feel and act that way, they can't do anything about sin but to sin."

"Their words and deeds seek to entice unstable souls. They do it without conscience because they've done it for so long. They have become cursed."

"They've left the true way to the cross, choosing instead to sin because they covet the rewards of sin on this side of the grave. And, just like Baalom, the son of Bosnor, he was a prophet who often sold his prophecies to the highest bidder and was condemned for it. Chastised. Number 31.8 and the Bible says that a dumb beast spoke with a man's voice. Some of you know that Baalom was a prophet who cared nothing about the proper use of his position or his gift. He only wanted to market it."

A few moans and choruses of hallelujahs and amen rose and spread like echoes. Some people even gave one another high fives either because they truly agreed with the message or wanted to take the attention away from themselves.

Reverend Cherry seemed oblivious to the audience's response as he twisted and turned his body while gripping the sides of the pulpit with both hands. His face became contorted, his eyes narrowing and rolling, almost at the same time. There was no mistaking his irritation as he spat out the words. "They are destitute of spirit. Their words are learned and pretentious. They speak big words that are primarily designed to overwhelm you with their show of superiority. They say that they want to show you how to be free when they, themselves, are slaves and servants to corruption. It would be better if they'd never learned or have known the righteousness of God; for if after they have escaped the pollutions of the world through the full personal knowledge of Jesus Christ, they again became entangled in sin even though they overcame, their last condition is worse for them than the first."

The audience members as well as those on and off the stage sprang to their feet. The applause for Reverend Cherry ricocheted around the auditorium until the sound became almost deafening.

"Come on, church," he implored. "Come on. Let's go home. For the Word of God promises that if my people, which are called by my name, would humble themselves and seek my face, turn from their wicked ways and pray, then will I hear from Heaven, forgive their sin and heal their land.

"People all over the world are going to extreme measures to get folks to turn to their god. They are willing to kill and deprive their brothers and sisters of the most basic rights of freedom of choice. Almost three thousand people lost their lives on that horrific date of September 11, 2001. Why? It was because some determined zealots wanted to insure that their voices were heard using the most abdominal acts and they did it, according to them, in the name of their god. Love for one another, I truly believe, could've prevented that tragedy."

Again, the applause of agreement blanketed the auditorium.

"Well, if we are going to truly return to God's love then we need to start right now and continue to do so." He walked again to the edge of the stage and pointed toward the audience. "There's something I want for all of you to do again." Stopping once more, he scanned the audience to make sure he had everyone's attention. "I want each of you to turn to the person on your right and repeat these words: *I love you, and there's nothing you can do about it.*"

The auditorium erupted as people repeated after the reverend and some even hugged the person sitting to their right. This time the majority of the people meant it.

"Oh, that's very good," Reverend Cherry said, laughing, "but we're not finished yet."

The auditorium calmed down to await what he had in mind.

"Now, I need you to turn to the person to your left and say, 'I love you too. There's nothing you can about it either.' "

It suddenly became like a Fourth of July celebration as the auditorium crackled and exploded as echoes of "I love you" rippled throughout. It was an amazing sight.

It was also an amazing and foreign feeling to poor Sister Hellraiser. Being trapped in the camera bucket kept her from participating in the love fest. She'd been forced to listen to the message. A foreign feeling of wanting to belong invaded her being, and she not only felt afraid but abandoned. She whispered the words, *I love me.* She whispered and she secretly hoped that with all the wrong she'd done that God did too.

Reverend Cherry turned and beckoned Reverends Thomas, Reid and Money along with Bishop Was Nevercalled to come forward and stand with him. Reverends Reid and Thomas were the first ones to rise. Smiles erased their concerns. They extended their hands, which indicated that the reverend and the bishop should accompany them. So with Reverend Knott Enuff Money and the bishop sandwiched between them, they lifted their hands, each of them, and sincerely gave God the praise.

The five men gathered around the pulpit, still praising God while embracing the warmth, respect and love from the audience. There seemed to be no end to the applause or the pockets of people shouting while being circled by several ushers.

This time, it was Reverend Thomas who stepped forward and took the microphone. "It's time, my brothers and sisters. It's time to return to God's love. It's time to stand up and hold fast to your faith. Playtime and playing church is over." He became overwhelmed and passed the microphone to Reverend Reid while he began to engage in his own dance to give God the glory.

Reverend Reid seized the opportunity to keep the praises going. "Do you love Him?" he shouted into the microphone, the question reverberating around the auditorium. "I said, do you love Him?"

"Yes, we love Him. Give God the glory," came the responses.

"Then, you need to return to God's love!" Reverend Reid saw that both his fellow cohosts for the conference were now shouting. They were going from one end of the stage to the other, their arms extended toward the auditorium ceiling. They looked as if they were trying to get as spiritually close to Heaven as they could in their outpouring of praise.

Reverend Reid suddenly found himself looking at Reverend Knott Enuff Money. And even though Reverend Knott Enuff Money just stood there encased in a layer of shell shock, Reverend Reid thrust the microphone into the reverend's hands.

It was the loud and irritating sound of feedback, caused by the proximity of the pulpit's handheld microphone to the one on Reverend Knott Enuff Money's lapel that shocked him into the present moment. Fortunately, the sound engineer took care of the problem by cutting off the sound to the lapel microphone.

For whatever reason the audience started to calm down as they waited to hear what the out-of-town pastor had to add. Even Reverends Cherry and Thomas had stopped shouting. Sister Betty, Ma Cile, Buddy and Tiny had all shot forward in their seats, even though they'd just sat down. Sister Hellraiser, still trapped in her camera-bucket prison, listened intently. There was something different about their pastor, but none of them knew what it was.

"I'm sorry," Reverend Knott Enuff Money whispered into the microphone. His face glistened from the mixture of tears and perspiration. His Jheri curl lay matted on his forehead and didn't move as he shook his head slowly side to side. "I'm so sorry."

As if to show that the spirit of God was truly moving in the place, evidenced by the way things seemed to happen in threes, Reverend Knott Enuff Money, through his stinging tears, found himself looking directly at the faces of Sister Betty and the others. He gripped the microphone with power. The microphone felt slippery and was about to fall from his perspiring hands. His voice faltered and again, his throat threatened to close, but not before he looked directly into the face of Buddy.

With their eyes locked, Buddy heard the words, *I'm so sorry,* whispered from the mouth of Reverend Knott Enuff Money again. And, this time, those words of apology were truly meant for him, and they came from the man of God whom he'd blamed for many years for his downfall.

Now it was Buddy's time to cry. Ma Cile clasped his hand to show she was there if he needed her. Tiny clasped his other hand to say the same. But Buddy shook off both their hands and extended his hands toward the stage. He mouthed the words, *It's okay. I forgive you,* and with his shoulders heaving with heavy sobs, he sat down. He rested his head on his chest and continued to cry as both Ma Cile and Tiny embraced him.

Sister Betty found herself standing on her feet. Several ushers raced to catch her as she started to shout and throw her tiny hands around in the air. "Thank ya, Lord," she hollered while managing to slap the elaborately decorated hats off three of the women in the next row.

The three women, all at least a hundred pounds heavier than Sister Betty, spun around in shock. They took one look at their expensive church hats lying tangled on the auditorium floor. They looked at one another with eyes that read, "thank you, Jesus" one moment and "maim that demon" the next. They lifted their fists and were cocked and ready to fire and get their shout on too. Both at the same time.

But the ushers arrived in time to save Sister Betty from any unwanted laying on of hands.

So Sister Betty shouted on, Buddy cried on and Ma Cile and Tiny just sat there looking confused. They didn't know what to do. It was Tiny who finally cleared up their confusion as he whispered into Ma Cile's ear, "I guess this praying stuff really does work."

Ma Cile just turned and with her false blue eye looking as if it were standing at attention while her good brown eye looked like it was saluting, she replied, "Prayin' always works." *Particularly, since I ain't wanted a dip of snuff or a pig foot fajita in about an hour,* she thought.

In the meantime, things were beginning to calm down, both on the stage and in the audience. Reverends Reid, Thomas and Cherry had each said a final word of thanks to the audience, and they'd given the benediction, but not before bringing back Dr. Bobbitto Jonas and all the other celebrities who had attended and entertained on behalf of the Back to God's Love conference.

Once they exited the stage, Reverend Knott Enuff Money and the Bishop Was Nevercalled found themselves encircled by the megachurch pastors. The Reverend Thomas was the first to take their hands, and they all started praying again, and this time both the bishop and the Reverend Knott Enuff Money meant every word they said.

Neither the bishop nor Reverend Knott Enuff Money said a word during the prayer. They didn't have to. There was a certain glow about their faces and their eyes lacked the smugness that they usually showed. The words from Reverend Cherry along with the manner in which all the mega-church pastors had treated them caused them to rethink their relationship with God. Only time would tell how deep the seeds of conviction were planted—time and their actions. After all, it took the reverend's mother a while to plant those seeds of greed and narcissism, and it would take some time for those roots to die, but die they would.

Just as they had ended the prayer and were about to leave to converse with other visiting pastors, evangelists, deacons, deaconesses, entertainers and other people of notoriety, they were approached by Dr. Bobbitto Jonas.

Even Dr. Jonas looked different. His smile was bright and his handshake firm as he told the Reverend Cherry just how much he'd enjoyed his closing message. "All of you just took us to another and higher level. I haven't seen this much offer of salvation and reunification with the Lord served up in one place in a long time." He then offered to shake the hands of both the bishop and the Reverend Knott Enuff Money.

"Sir," he said to the bishop, "I'm quite sure that had the hour not been so late, you'd have had words that probably would've taken us over the top. I do hope that you plan to come back and share your ministry with the rest of us. As a matter of fact, I would like to invite you to the taping of my next program."

"Thank you," the bishop responded, and he didn't stutter when he spoke. "I would love that very much."

Without prodding, Reverend Knott Enuff Money added, "The bishop would be a welcome asset to your program. And, of course, you haven't heard anything until you've heard God truly use him. I know God has something special for him and for your audience." He'd said exactly how he felt, and he truly meant it. It was the most he'd said since the piercing of his mind, heart and soul by the arrows of truth delivered by Reverend Cherry.

"I'll be prayed up and prepared," the bishop said. He'd already determined that if he had to attend night school six days a week he was going to learn to read the Word of God for himself. He had also made up his mind to return not only to God's love but to being an obedient son of the royal priesthood.

"Well then. It's a date," Dr. Jonas agreed and produced a broad grin. He was about to turn and say something to the Reverend Knott Enuff Money but stopped when he noticed that the reverend's attention had been diverted. "We'll chat later, Reverend Money." He wasn't sure if he'd been heard or not because the reverend was rushing toward two other people standing near the exit sign.

"This is *my* pastor," Brother Tis Mythang began to brag. "He was the one you saw up on the stage getting saved tonight."

Normally, Reverend Knott Enuff Money would've been upset and angry at such an affront to his position with God, but he wasn't. What Brother Tis Mythang said was true. He truly felt like he'd met God for real and for the very first time, so instead of admonishing, he offered his hand in greeting.

"Reverend Money, I'd like for you to meet one of the people that I love the most in the world." Suddenly, the expression on the reverend's face changed. It was as if he'd been able to see clearly for the first time. "Isn't this . . ."

"Yes, it is!" Brother Tis Mythang giggled.

"But I thought . . ." the reverend said as confusion took the place of the recent smile he'd had.

"Well, think no more. I'd like to introduce to you Miss Dottie Peoples." Brother Tis Mythang spoke as though either he wasn't aware, or didn't care that he was standing there grinning like a chipped garage-sale Cheshire cat. He seemed happy to be in the presence of Dottie Peoples even with a torn suit, a slightly busted bottom lip and with one shoe missing.

Her lipstick looked a little smudged. There was now an ashy color to her beautiful chocolate brown skin. She was still missing one of her rhinestone earrings and there was a small tear in the seam of her dress as well as the deflation of her signature beehive hairdo. It had to be her. This was the same woman who had led the charge to literally disarm and bust Brother Tis Mythang to pieces. The reverend was totally confused.

"I'm pleased to meet you," the reverend said with caution. For all he knew, perhaps both of them got hit on the head during their scuffle, and that was why they were acting so strange. When he'd seen Brother Tis Mythang beckoning to him while he was standing with Dr. Jonas and the others, he'd had no idea what he was walking into.

"We've made up," Brother Tis Mythang said as he squeezed Dottie Peoples's hand. "I apologized to her again."

"Again?" the reverend asked.

"Yes. I sort of made a pest of myself earlier this evening," Brother Tis Mythang said shyly. "In fact, I've been apologizing to a lot of folks tonight. I'm really feeling this back to God's love idea."

"I've apologized to my new friend too," Dottie Peoples added, smiling and squeezing Brother Tis Mythang's hand. "After all, the battles are never ours, and I certainly can't react, inappropriately every time someone does something I don't like."

"Come with me, Dottie." Brother Tis Mythang stopped, and again, humbleness coated his words. "I hope you don't mind me calling you Dottie. You are my shero."

"No problem. I would be honored."

"Good. I want to introduce you to some of the other members of my church." Brother Tis Mythang offered his arm to Dottie Peoples. "I'll see you later, Pastor," he said, as he almost dragged Dottie Peoples off to the other side of the room.

They were quite a sight. Dottie Peoples, still looking lovely without her rhinestones, with smudged makeup, a torn dress and with droopy hair. And, of course, Brother Tis Mythang felt like a prince, complete with his busted lip, torn suit and slight limp because he was only wearing one shoe.

Just as the Reverend Knott Enuff Money turned to rejoin the others, Livvie touched him on the arm. "Reverend Money," she said softly, "please come with me. Reverends Cherry, Thomas and Reid along with the bishop are waiting for you in the pastor's main study."

Reverend Knott Enuff Money didn't say anything. He was about talked out, so he just followed her as she led him through the hallway, past people who held out their hands to shake his; not because he'd done anything special, but because he'd been onstage and read the Word of God. That accounted for a lot as far as most were concerned. For the first time since his mother had convinced him to go into the ministry and seek a mega church as a legacy, the reverend was truly humbled. Much of the curl had gone out of his Jheri curl, and he didn't care. He only knew that he felt undeserving of such respect. He was, indeed, uncomfortable, and it showed.

To the people who were offering him encouragement, he didn't seem uncomfortable. He looked humbled, and they linked that to the fact that he'd apologized for some unknown reason. To them, he was not only humble, but brave. Most of them, unrepentant, would enter their graves without ever apologizing for anything they either did or were perceived as doing wrong.

As Livvie and Reverend Knott Enuff Money strolled toward the pastor's main study, Livvie smiled to herself. *This is hardly the man I found mumbling to himself outside on the bench. God, you are truly a miracle worker and I thank you,* she thought.

A smile suddenly broke out upon the reverend's face again. It was as if he'd read the usher's thoughts. This time, it was he who started humming "On Time God," and he meant that too.

24

Forgiveness: a Kingdom Principle

Livvie opened the door for the Reverend Knott Enuff Money to enter into the pastor's main study then closed the door behind her

Reverend Knott Enuff Money couldn't quite believe his eyes. Inside the simple but tastefully decorated room seated together and waiting for him was the bishop, the three mega-church pastors, Sister Betty, Ma Cile, Tiny, Brother Tis Mythang and Buddy who looked strange in a sober state.

It was Buddy who stepped from the midst of the others and embraced Reverend Knott Enuff Money. It had been years, yet each man in his own silent manner set aside that part of history to start anew.

"You know you're gonna have to join the choir again when we return to Pelzer," the Reverend Knott Enuff said. He gave out a healthy but nervous laugh and added, "Y'all know this man can tear up a hymn."

"Which him?" Brother Tis Mythang asked as he pointed to several of the men in the room.

"You still gonna act crazy with that busted lip of yourn?" Ma Cile barked. She'd had enough for one night, and she wasn't about to let Brother Tis Mythang's flippant tongue spoil things. "You need to quit teasin' folks," she snapped. "Some of us got another dose of religion tonight," she scoffed. Her false blue eye tried to cross her good brown one as if to let him know that she meant business.

At the rate she was going, she'd need another dose of a good sermon to get back on track, if it didn't take but a couple of teasing words from Brother Tis Mythang to derail her good feeling.

"I'm sorry, Ma Cile," Brother Tis Mythang said. "I guess it's gonna take a while for me to know when to shut my big mouth."

"Better not take long," she snapped.

"I'm surprised you could still open it since your swollen lip was trying to meet your nose," Buddy added with sly wink. It was his first day of sobriety and he didn't need anyone pushing him into backsliding. He knew the road back would not be easy but he was determined. If he was gonna be a rich man, he was gonna be a sober one.

The entire room burst into laughter. The tension all but dissipated as the Reverend Thomas offered another apology for the actions of his cousin Brother Tis Mythang while offering Reverend Knott Enuff Money a chair.

"We're just waiting for one other person, but until that time, why don't we just get to know one another better," Reverend Thomas said. "We don't have to go into the reasons why most of us are here this evening. We know that already."

Reverend Cherry stood and placed three envelopes on the desk where Reverend Thomas sat then returned to his seat.

Reverend Thomas leaned back in his swivel chair and said, "Each of us,"—he pointed to Reverends Cherry and Reid—"were promised a million dollars if we somehow embraced you, Reverend Money . . ." He stopped and folded his hands together. With as much tact as he could muster, he added, ". . . and, persuaded you·to, perhaps, change your way of thinking as well as how you pastored your church."

"Say what?" Reverend Knott Enuff Money replied. "You mean to tell me that none of you really meant what you said out there?" He became agitated, and angry words poured from his mouth. "Y'all ain't no better than me. Here I thought y'all were truly into serving God, and it was all about the money. All that stuff wasn't nothing but talk." His eyes began to mist. "But that's alright. I like what I'm feeling on the inside. I like me! I'm gonna praise—" He was interrupted and surprised by a strong knock at the door.

He wasn't the only one. Everyone in the room sat there with their jaws dropped almost down to their necks.

The door opened and again, it was the usher Livvie. As she stepped aside, in walked the Councilman Hippo Crit. "How's everyone doing?" he asked. "I'm sorry it took me so long to get to this meeting, but it was hard to get through the mobs of people trying to leave the church, and I needed to stop in the men's room."

Either he didn't or couldn't read the shocked looks on everyone's faces—everyone with the exception of Sister Betty.

"I thought you'd never get in here," she gushed. "Things were about to get pretty messy."

"Really? I'm sorry. I was so taken with the messages coming from the pastors . . ." He stopped and walked around the room to shake each pastor's hand. "Where are my manners? I'm the Councilman Hippo Crit. Which of you is Reverend Thomas?"

"I'm he," Reverend Thomas said as he rose again. "We spoke yesterday on the telephone."

All eyes were on the councilman. Under any circumstances, his expensive attire, good looks and educated words would command attention, but this was different. He took confusion to another level in their minds.

And then, as if an atom bomb had dropped in the room, everybody looked over at Sister Betty. She would've met their eyes, but she was trying to adjust her false teeth so that she could speak clearly. It wasn't a pretty sight. She looked like she had a mouth full of pink Bubblicious gum.

"Sister Betty, you wanna explain what's going on here?" Reverend Knott Enuff Money urged. He was almost ready to tear into everybody in the room because he felt betrayed. The sudden appearance of the councilman had thrown him and apparently the others, too, especially the bishop, Tiny and Buddy. The three of them looked as if they were in a trance as they sat with their eyes bucked and fixed.

The bishop looked apprehensive but he wasn't quite sure why he should've been. The events of that entire evening had him messed up.

Tiny looked confused but he was actually cracking up on the inside—mentally cracking up. He wasn't quite sure if the appearance of the councilman meant that the deal was off and he wouldn't be getting his two million dollars. He'd brought a switchblade with him and he wasn't afraid to use it. After putting up with Mother Eternal Ann Everlastin's eccentric ways and these crazy folks, he'd earned every dime.

Poor Buddy looked confused because he thought the councilman looked familiar but he couldn't figure out why—he'd been too drunk when they'd met.

Sister Betty quickly clicked her gums several times to make sure that the false teeth had a snug fit. Satisfied that the teeth wouldn't fall out, she began to speak slowly as she rose from her seat. "I know that y'all are probably wondering what is going on, and I don't blame none of you if you get a little upset with me, but I had to follow instructions."

"What instructions, Sister Betty?" Ma Cile asked. She was starting to feel sad because her best friend hadn't told her everything.

Sister Betty knew Ma Cile very well and tried to assure her as best she could. "Ma Cile, I couldn't tell you or anyone. I wanted to tell you but I couldn't."

"Perhaps, it would be better if I explained," the councilman interrupted. "You just fill in the gaps just in case I forget something." He only added the last part because he didn't want Sister Betty to feel slighted as she was one of his best political supporters.

"All of this started several months ago," the councilman said as he removed his suit jacket to make himself comfortable. His tan shirt contrasted with his cinnamon complexion, and the outline of his sculptured arms escaped no one's attention. All eyes were on him, and they all had their own reasons as to why.

"Mother Eternal Ann Everlastin' had visited my office to revise her will. It was her habit to do so every six months for the past ten years that I'd been her attorney. There was always some new charity or venture and a usual project or two to which she wanted to bequeath a large sum of money. When she showed up at my office last spring she told me that she'd had a vision, and that it would sound crazy to me, but she needed my help."

The councilman turned toward Reverend Knott Enuff Money and the bishop and began again. "Reverend Money," he smiled and said, "Mother Eternal Ann Everlastin' always knew that you had good in you; however, she could never trust you. Not that she couldn't totally trust you with her money but she couldn't trust you to honor your calling. It was never her intention to question your calling. That was something between you and God; however, she did question your handling of God's business. And, that was the business of saving souls."

Reverend Money said nothing. He couldn't. Everything stated so far was true.

"And you, Bishop. Mother admired you in her own strange way. I'm not going to put your business out in the street, but Mother knew all about your background and where you came from and how you arrived at the Ain't Nobody Else Right But Us—All Others Goin' to Hell Church."

The bishop looked up at the ceiling, refusing to allow anyone to see the embarrassment he felt. He kept silent while the tears that moistened the collar of his robe told it all.

"What Mother Eternal Ann Everlastin' couldn't and wouldn't admire for a long time was the fact that you did nothing to overcome the one thing that could've set you apart and made you your own man.

"Anyway, from what I've witnessed here, tonight, that's all in the past. As for Sister Betty's part. The day that I had everyone meet in my office, I had already spoken to her earlier. It was her love for her friend that made her an unwilling participant in Mother's outlandish plot."

"Can we get to that plot before we all need one?" Tiny quipped. He still wasn't sure if he liked the way the conversation was going.

"That's right," Brother Tis Mythang added. "In one sentence or two, can you please name that plot?"

A few nervous laughs spread among them.

"Okay," the councilman said, throwing his hands up in surrender. He'd almost forgotten that he wasn't in a courtroom or in a political arena. "In summation: Mother Eternal Ann Everlastin' wanted to use the reverend's favorite thing to lure him into facing his calling. She knew that he loved and admired Reverends Cherry, Reid and Thomas." He paused. The councilman turned toward the pastors and remarked, "By the way, did you know that he named the three of you his Trinity?"

All three of the pastors looked at one another too stunned to even bat an eye. They didn't know whether to accept Reverend Knott Enuff Money's title of Trinity as admiration or blasphemy, so they just simply smiled and nodded with apprehension in the direction of Reverend Knott Enuff Money.

"She used that admiration," the councilman said, "along with the reverend's love of money to lure him to this conference. She'd expected to be here to see her vision through, but we all know that we can't know from one day to the next where we'll be. Mother Eternal Ann Everlastin' felt that if any of the godliness from these pastors would rub off on the reverend, and he saw just how well they were blessed while yet doing God's work, he'd change his ways.

"All the pastors had to do," the councilman continued, "was to persuade the reverend to honestly consider changing his ways. Mother knew that it wasn't a foolproof plan but she believed in her vision."

"That explains the reverend, but what about Mr. Tiny, the bishop and myself. How did we fit into my aunt's plan?" Buddy asked. He was getting more nervous by the moment and suddenly felt like he wanted the company of his old friend Jack Daniel's but he fought the urge.

"Actually, Buddy," the councilman said, "your aunt had made provisions for you to be well cared for in a facility that treats people with alcohol addictions; however, Sister Betty came up with a way that we could carry out Mother Eternal Ann Everlastin's final wish for you and help Mr. Tiny too. It was Sister Betty who since it was left to her to find a place for you to receive treatment thought about hiring Mr. Tiny."

All eyes rested upon Sister Betty who sat still clicking her false teeth out of nervousness. She was so wound up that she kept curling her lips, which made her look like an angry snarling cat.

There was no response from Sister Betty so everyone turned back to face the councilman.

"Hold up!" Tiny snapped. "You mean to tell me that Mother Eternal Ann Everlastin's estate was gonna pay me two million dollars just to get her nephew to some AA meetings because Sister Betty decided so."

"Exactly," the councilman replied.

Finally the bishop found his voice and stood and spoke, his face still pink from all the near disasters that had occurred that night. "If-if Mother wanted the reverend to change and was willing to-to leave huge donations if he could be persuaded to do that, how do I fit in? Who was gonna get paid for me?"

"Oh, nobody was gonna get paid for you, Bishop. Mother felt that if she left enough for you to further the education you always chased,"—the councilman was trying to use codes so that only the bishop would know what he meant—"with your educational needs met, you could make your own money and head up your own church and affiliations."

The bishop didn't move from his spot. He raised an eyebrow and when what the councilman said still wasn't comprehensible, he remarked, "I'll make an appointment to see you when we return to Pelzer."

"I sort of thought you might," the councilman responded. "I've already made an appointment for you to come in on this coming Wednesday morning at nine o'clock."

"Let's get back to me," Tiny interrupted. "Buddy looks sober, and I'm sure he'll be going to all his AA meetings for the next two months." He started rubbing his hands together and snapped his fingers. "Do you think I could get an advance on that two million?"

Finally, Sister Betty spoke up. "I've already made arrangements with your wife. She got the money transfer earlier this afternoon."

"She got my money?" Tiny almost passed out. "How did you know that Buddy was gonna be sober tonight?"

"Mother wasn't the only one who God speaks to." Sister Betty rose slowly from her seat and stood next to the bishop who still hadn't moved an inch. "God showed me in a dream this very afternoon what He was gonna do, and I took Him at His word."

Sister Betty smiled at Tiny in an effort to calm him. "I only had the councilman wire her enough to keep her from being mad at you for not coming straight back to Pelzer."

"I'm not going straight back to Pelzer?" Now he was really confused and a lot concerned. "Where am I going?" Tiny asked, not really knowing if he wanted to know.

"Well, you are going to first drive Buddy to the Lettie Peugeot Clinic in Boston, Massachusetts. It will take about a week to get him adjusted and we've already made arrangements for you to stay with Evangelist Margaret Acker. She's the pastor of St. John's Church."

"Why would I want to do that?" Tiny asked. "I don't even know the woman."

"She's got a check waiting for you," the councilman answered.

"Ahem." Brother Tis Mythang gulped, clearing his throat as loud as possible. "What about me? Did Mother leave me anything?"

"No, she didn't," Sister Betty replied. Before she could say anything further, Reverend Knott Enuff Money spoke up.

"Don't worry about it, Brother Tis Mythang. She left me fifty thousand. I'll make sure that you get something. You've been playing that organ at the church for many years, and we've never even so much as taken up an offering for you. I'd like to do something for you."

"Is this some type of *Twilight Zone* joke?" Brother Tis Mythang asked suspiciously. "Where's the camera? Y'all just waiting for me to make a fool of myself on television, right?"

"Ya did that already." Ma Cile laughed.

Brother Tis Mythang never said another word as he sank into his chair. He took a chance and looked back at Reverend Knott Enuff Money whose look of repentance was still there. He believed that his pastor meant what he said, so he smiled to let everyone know that he was okay with things.

The hour was nearing eleven-thirty and everyone was becoming restless; however, by the time the councilman and Sister Betty finished revealing Mother's entire plan and what monies and gifts were being bequeathed, everyone left satisfied.

Buddy and the Reverend Knott Enuff Money promised each other that they would have dinner one evening when Buddy returned to Pelzer. "You mean out in public?" Buddy asked.

"Yes, and because you're rich, you can pay for it," the reverend said, laughing. He was amazed that he didn't feel any jealousy toward the mega-church pastors or anyone who'd received financial gifts from Mother Eternal Ann Everlastin's estate, and he felt good about it.

Just as Reverend Thomas was about to turn off the lights in the pastor's study, both Sister Betty and the councilman stayed behind. "Can we speak to you for just one more moment, Reverend Thomas?" Sister Betty asked.

"Of course. What can I do for you?" He hoped there was no irritation in his voice but he was almost completely exhausted from the night's events.

Sister Betty took him by the hand and said a quick prayer as her tiny hands reached up to clasp his shoulders. When she finished, she laughed and said, "You know in all that was going on in here tonight we forgot to give these release papers to you and the Reverends Reid and Cherry."

"I'm confused," Reverend Thomas said. "There's still more spiritual work to be done with Reverend Money. When it's done, we will be happy to take the monies and donate them as we promised we would."

Councilman Hippo Crit flipped the off switch for the Reverend Thomas and gently urged him and Sister Betty out into the hallway, firmly closing the door behind them. "You've met the requirements already," the councilman said.

"We have?" Reverend Thomas asked hesitantly. "When?"

"When you persuaded the reverend to consider changing his ways. That's all that was required. Mother didn't expect you or the other pastors to change the reverend. Only God can do that. She only wanted you to provide a forum and deliver a message that would make him want to be more like you and understand that a personal relationship with Jesus was necessary. You've done that and more. From this point on, it's up to the reverend and God."

"Thank you," Reverend Thomas said. "Thank you so much."

"Just make sure that you return it to God's love," the councilman teased, "and with interest."

No sooner had the councilman, Sister Betty and Reverend Thomas reached the exit to leave through the auditorium than they heard loud voices.

Reverend Thomas was the first to run into the auditorium. He thought he was hallucinating. He saw several of his male ushers. The men were trying to coax a female down from the camera bucket, but she was too petrified to help herself.

"Come on down, miss. We'll help you," one of the ushers yelled.

"We won't let you fall," another usher confirmed.

One by one the ushers said and did everything they could to coax Sister Hellraiser down from the scaffold, which held the camera bucket.

It was only when the councilman walked over and stood by one of the rows of seats directly under the scaffold that Sister Hellraiser seemed to even consider coming down.

"Sister Hellraiser, what are you doing up there?" the councilman asked as he again took off his jacket, revealing his sculptured upper body.

Even though by that time Sister Hellraiser was almost hysterical, from her self-made prison and a desperate need of a bathroom visit, she thought she recognized the voice calling up to her. She inched herself up the side of the bucket and peered down. She couldn't believe her eyes. *I've been up here too long,* she thought as she plopped down again inside the bucket.

"Come on, Sister Hellraiser. This is Councilman Hippo Crit. I've flown all the way here from Pelzer for the conference, and I don't know about you, but I'm starving. I sure could use the company of a beautiful woman," the councilman implored. He winked toward Reverend Thomas as though they were two men who knew how to handle a woman.

Reverend Thomas agreed with the silent message and returned the wink.

Sister Hellraiser came out the bucket so fast no one knew she was climbing down the scaffold until several but certainly not all of the ushers turned their heads aside so as not to see under her dress as she descended. Those who didn't turn their heads stood there smiling with their arms stretched out, pretending to wait to help her.

Sister Hellraiser, being who she was, took the liberty of leaping from the last several rungs of the scaffold into the arms of two of the ushers. Even when she was too scared to get out of the bucket to come down to use a bathroom, she could still make a dramatic entrance when it suited her.

She smoothed down the wrinkles in her dress with both hands, making sure that she showed a little more leg than necessary, which was how she got into the mess in the first place. "I'm so surprised to see you here in Baltimore," she said to Councilman Hippo Crit. Without waiting to be asked, she almost stepped on Sister Betty's foot as she twirled and clung to the councilman's massive arm. "I was waiting for the cameraman to return so I could show him the proper use of that modern equipment," she lied.

"Really?" the councilman replied. He would've said more but he was too busy formulating a plan to rid himself of Sister Hellraiser. As far as he was concerned, he was just trying to be a gentleman when he lied to her and shouldn't be held to the promise of dinner.

He would become the first black president before Sister Hellraiser let him out of that promise.

And she would become the first lady before Sister Betty warned her that her dress was caught up in the waistband of her dress.

Those males ushers went home that night feeling more blessed than they had been in a long time.

25

Life Can Come From Death

Early the next morning the sun shone exceptionally bright. It was as though the moon had gleefully shared the blessed events of the previous night as it faded. So with the weather quite warm for a fall day, they all met outside the spacious home of the Reverend Thomas to get ready for the return to Pelzer. All except Tiny and Buddy who would continue driving north up to Boston.

The bishop and Reverend Knott Enuff Money had stayed up most of the night in a prayer watch with Reverends Cherry and Reid. Even though neither felt tired when they should've been, they decided after they'd arrived at Reverend Thomas's that it would be better not to try and drive back to Pelzer. Since Reverend Thomas lived alone and had plenty of room, he invited the reverend and the bishop to spend another day with him and offered them the use of his guest rooms.

Brother Tis Mythang had spent that night at his cousin Reverend Thomas's house. He'd tried to get an early start, but his Hundai wouldn't go. *It probably died from culture shock*, Brother Tis Mythang thought. It had made its last trip and would be buried unceremoniously in a junkyard somewhere in Baltimore.

"I don't know what I'm gonna do now," he said sadly. "I don't have transportation."

"Don't worry about it," Reverend Knott Enuff Money said. "When we return to Pelzer, we'll see about getting you another car." Suddenly generosity seemed to become an addictive drug, and he liked it.

"But what about now?" Brother Tis Mythang asked. "I'll still need to get back, and I really need to be back in time for the young people's service tonight."

"I almost forgot about that. I had asked Reverend Bling Moe Bling if he would conduct the service in my place."

"The reverend who?" the Reverend Thomas asked.

"We'll tell you about him, la-later," the bishop replied. His stutter wasn't completely gone but it was a lot better.

Ma Cile and Sister Betty finally arrived from their hotel by taxi. After hugging and greeting everyone, they sat wearily down on one of the futons to rest. "We're gonna leave in about an hour and a half to return to Pelzer," Sister Betty announced.

Before she had a chance to say anything more, Brother Tis Mythang did what he always did—he butted in.

"How are you two going?" Brother Tis Mythang asked out of curiosity. "Ma Cile, are you gonna drive a rented car or something?" He was feeling pretty good after hearing the reverend promise to buy him another car when they returned to Pelzer.

"Boy, I ain't fixin' to hear none of yo' foolishness," Ma Cile barked. "I ain't got myself together yet and ya just needs to leave me alone."

Brother Tis Mythang translated Ma Cile's warning to mean that she'd not had her snuff yet.

For once, he was right. She hadn't eaten either, and those two things were fuel for a dangerous explosion.

"We're gonna fly," Sister Betty said, trying to change the subject. "Neither one of us has ever been on a plane, so we're gonna fly back with the Councilman Hippo Crit and Sister Hellraiser in his private jet," Sister Betty said proudly. "I'm so excited." She turned toward Ma Cile who sat looking like she could eat anything that came near. "Aren't you excited too?"

"I ain't excited. I'm hungry!" Ma Cile countered. "I gets excited when I eats!"

Sister Betty decided to leave Ma Cile alone until she could finish eating a plate of silver dollar-sized blueberry pancakes drowning in a pool of low-fat syrup. It was the best that the Reverend Thomas could do since he felt he needed to fix something for her to eat in a hurry. He'd jumped up, almost running everyone over as he dashed into the kitchen the moment Ma Cile's false blue eye seemed to stare at him accusingly.

While Ma Cile ate, Brother Tis Mythang convinced Sister Betty to phone the councilman and see if he could fly back with them. It would give him a chance to get back to Pelzer in time to rest up before the service.

Sister Betty did what she'd promised. She phoned the councilman and got the okay for Brother Tis Mythang to fly back with the rest of them, so Brother Tis Mythang rushed inside and gathered his things.

The cab ride to Baltimore International Airport was uneventful, and for that Sister Betty was grateful. They found out where the councilman had his plane but before they could go through the airport to get to it, they had to go through security.

Although the airport was bustling with people coming and going, both Sister Betty and Brother Tis Mythang whipped through security with no problem. Somehow Ma Cile had gotten separated in the crowd, and there were a few people who were in line between her and the others. While Sister Betty waited for Ma Cile to go through security, she decided to use the bathroom.

She would only be in the bathroom for a few minutes and didn't think that Ma Cile would have any problems in that short time.

She should've known better. Sister Betty knew that whatever the commotion was about that she heard outside the bathroom, it could've only involved one person—and, of course, she was right.

Ma Cile stood, legs spread a little with her small carry-on bag between them on the ground. She had both her chubby hands raised, palms up.

It was apparent to Sister Betty that somehow Ma Cile had sneaked a dip or two of her snuff because Ma Cile's eyes were bright with fear as her eyeballs tagged each other. She looked like she was about to urinate on herself every time a security person, one on each side of her, waved their lighted batons. Each security officer scanned every inch of her body, particularly the palms of her hands. There was a crowd, all ages and nationalities, surrounding Ma Cile and the security personnel. Every time a baton scanned over Ma Cile's open palm, it buzzed. But there didn't appear to be anything in Ma Cile's hands, although Brother Tis Mythang would later say that it was probably snuff residue.

They waved and buzzed over Ma Cile for a few minutes more then decided to let her go on her way, especially after she started passing nervous gas. The foul-smelling gas and Ma Cile's peculiar eyes of two different colors gave her a pass to go anywhere in the airport she wanted from that point on.

Normally, Ma Cile would've fussed and threatened to maim or kill but she didn't. She was frightened because she thought the embarrassing incident was the dream she'd had back in the Baltimore hotel. Ma Cile's wide hips swept folks aside as she sprinted through the airport, trying to escape to the safety of the councilman's airplane.

Sister Betty and Brother Tis Mythang thought they would suffer a stroke trying to keep up with her.

It took some doing but they made it to where the councilman was waiting. "Any problems?" Councilman Hippo Crit asked as he pointed to the airplane to indicate that they should board. He started to say more but one look from Sister Betty said, *Don't ask.*

Sister Betty and Brother Tis Mythang gave out a lot of *oohs* and *ahs* as they climbed aboard the plane. "This plane reminds me of the ones that used to land on *Fantasy Island.* All I need to do is get on here and find a midget named Tattoo, and I'm just gonna pass out." It was the first time that day that Brother Tis Mythang was truly glad that his Hundai had decided to croak.

While Sister Betty and Brother Tis Mythang were excitedly going on about the plane, Ma Cile had her own concerns. She touched the shoulder of the Councilman Hippo Crit to get his attention. "Befo' I gets on this here plane I gotta ask ya sumpthin'." Ma Cile let her false blue eye wind down from its rotating motion before she continued, "And ya better tell me the truth."

Councilman Hippo Crit looked from Ma Cile over to Sister Betty, silently and desperately trying to get Sister Betty's help. However, both Sister Betty and Brother Tis Mythang were still ranting on about the plane and ignored him. "Yes, Ma Cile," he said, his voice shaking. "What do you want to know?"

"I wants to know who's driving the plane. I also wants to know how fast we gonna be goin and how long befo' we gets back home to Pelzer."

Hoping against all odds that Ma Cile couldn't remember her questions in the order she gave them, the councilman took a chance with his well-being and answered, "We'll be in Pelzer in about an hour and a half. Just add the extra hour that it will take us to drive there from the Greenville-Spartanburg airport, and it's going to be around two and a half." He looked almost ashen as Ma Cile eyed him up and down like she was welding a scalpel, whittling him down as she did.

"Good. I should be home in time to whup them heathens' butts and have supper ready befo' the sun sets." Just like the councilman had suspected, she'd forgotten her other questions. Ma Cile waddled her wide hips away from him and caught up with Sister Betty.

Councilman Hippo Crit had once again outmaneuvered another one of his constituents but he'd rather have played tennis against one of the Williams sisters than to have dealt with Ma Cile—Ma Cile didn't play.

The plane was named the Blue Flamingo. It was a small Gulf Stream II SP. It held about twelve passengers, each of whom would have their own flat screen monitors to watch any program they chose. There were plenty to choose from because the plane stocked about two hundred DVD and VHS movies as well as CDs, surround stereo sound and wireless headsets.

The Blue Flamingo also had about six feet of headroom, which meant the councilman only had to bend his neck a little while standing. It was painted blue and white on the outside and sported a huge blue flamingo feather, which ran from the nose of the plane to the tail. The interior was all white with the exception of the coral full-size luxury lavatory with a gold-plated vanity. And, on every seat lay a blue flamingo feather and a large round chocolate York peppermint pattie.

The small plane was a very expensive gift to the councilman from Mother Eternal Ann Everlastin' who felt extremely grateful since he'd successfully represented her when the deaths of her three husbands were extensively investigated. The use of the blue flamingo feathers and the peppermint patties as a welcome to the passengers were also her suggestions, which were usually dispensed as commands.

When Sister Betty, the councilman and Ma Cile got to about the middle of the plane, they were surprised to find Sister Hellraiser already on board. She was seated, still looking shocked and still dressed in the same clothes from the night before. She sat erect as if someone had poured starch down her back. Her usual flawless complexion looked jaundiced. There were two tightly fastened seat belts around her waist and across her chest. She looked like the star of a B-rated horror movie trapped in a straitjacket or a child's car seat.

Ma Cile looked over at Sister Hellraiser but didn't say a word. She was still trying to calm down from the unsolicited airport fondling she'd just received, and she realized that she'd packed her snuff canister in her suitcase, so she was in no mood for Sister

Hellraiser's current drama. She also remembered that Shaqueeda had been leaving messages for her, which only meant that her heathen grandchildren had caused trouble. She would cause trouble, too, just as soon as she could get her hands on the two of them.

Brother Tis Mythang would always be himself and, therefore, couldn't help asking the councilman, "How did you get Sister Hellraiser to fly? I thought she was petrified of heights. Ain't heights the source of her dilemma?"

"I'd like to know the answer to that myself," Sister Betty chimed in. She had just finished a silent prayer for God's traveling mercies upon them as well as thanking Him again for all that had been done. "Although, it does fit in with the miracles I've seen so far."

The councilman didn't say a word at first. He flexed his perfect biceps as though he were trying to indicate that he'd had to roughly subdue Sister Hellraiser. When he saw the surprised look on everyone's face, he laughed and nodded toward the petrified Sister Hellraiser. He went to his seat and fastened his seat belt, never saying a word, choosing instead to wink at Brother Tis Mythang.

"Oh no! Not him too," Ma Cile blurted when she caught the wink. She always considered the councilman to be a man's man but certainly not Brother Tis Mythang's man. Her jaw dropped and literally landed atop the first of her two fat chins.

"Hush, Cile," Sister Betty shot back. Ma Cile looked shocked and hurt at the harsh reply. Sister Betty knew assumptions could lead to all kinds of problems, and when Ma Cile assumed something, she was usually wrong, and the results would be devastating.

"I'm sorry, Ma Cile. I guess I'm just very tired," Sister Betty sweetly said to reassure her best friend that all was well. The hurt look on Ma Cile's face disappeared and was replaced by the hungry look that had occupied it before.

Brother Tis Mythang ignored the low-buzzing chatter coming from where Sister Betty and Ma Cile sat. No matter what people might've said or thought about Brother Tis Mythang, like the councilman, he, too, knew women. He started laughing so hard, he almost rocked the small jet from side to side as he returned the councilman's wink and sat down in his seat with a loud thud. He adjusted his seat belt but kept rolling from side to side, laughing every time he looked over at Sister Hellraiser.

Sister Betty couldn't figure out what was so funny and her curiosity was getting the better of her. She finally got Brother Tis Mythang to calm down enough to speak. "What's so funny?" she asked. "Do you know how the councilman got Sister Hellraiser on the plane?"

"Yep," he answered. His jaws were starting to ache from the laughter.

"Will ya stop yo' stupid giggling and tell somebody!" Ma Cile hissed. Her chubby hands were pawing the sides of her seat out of nervousness and hunger. She was just itching to get at somebody and his body would do just fine.

"Okay." Brother Tis Mythang laughed. He leaned over in his seat and got close to both Sister Betty and Ma Cile. In between gulps of laughter, he blurted, "He told her that he was looking for a wife."

Brother Tis Mythang's revelation lightened the tension on the plane. In fact, they were laughing so hard until they never noticed that the plane was airborn.

That's when Ma Cile remembered her first question to the councilman, but she became too angry to repeat it again.

It took some doing on Sister Betty's part but she kept Ma Cile strapped in her seat. When she told Ma Cile that because of her weight the small plane might fall from the sky if she moved around, Ma Cile made it her business to sit still.

Ma Cile also would make it her business to give the councilman the business when they landed for not answering all her questions.

While the others took the opportunity to catch a nap after the serving of a small snack by a very unattractive and nondescript young black woman who was both their stewardess and copilot, Sister Betty and Ma Cile took time to chat a little more. Sister Betty didn't want to sleep. Being so high up in the clouds made her feel like she was so much closer to Heaven, and she didn't want to miss anything. She acted like she expected to see either God or one of his angels peering through the small windows.

Ma Cile didn't sleep because she still didn't know who was driving the plane.

The two women chatted on about whether Reverend Knott Enuff Money and Bishop Was Nevercalled would really go through with their desires of a new relationship with God. There was some laughter regarding Tiny's trip to Boston with Buddy and how the two of them would fare. They also talked about the message of returning back to God's love and its importance. The one thing they both agreed upon was that Mother Eternal Ann Everlastin' was a kind-hearted control freak who had managed to get her way, even after death. While the women talked away, the councilman came over and sat down with them.

"Sister Betty," the councilman said, all the while watching for any signs of displeasure from Ma Cile. There didn't seem to be any so he continued, "I still have a little unfinished business concerning Mother Eternal Ann Everlastin'.'"

A questioning look accompanied by raised eyebrows appeared on both Sister Betty's and Ma Cile's faces. "What unfinished business would that be?" Sister Betty asked.

Ma Cile didn't say anything but when she leaned forward in her seat with a menacing sneer, she didn't have to.

The councilman thought it would be a good time to bring his business to an end. So, from his briefcase, he retrieved two envelopes and gave one to Sister Betty and the other to Ma Cile.

"What are these?" Sister Betty asked as she turned the envelope over several times. "I don't understand."

Ma Cile did the same and, of course, she understood even less.

"It's the final wishes from Mother Eternal Ann Everlastin'," he said with a smile. "There's just one more thing she has for you to do."

Finally Ma Cile spoke up. "Ya mean to tell me that Mother always had sumpthin' for me to do too? I thought I was just here to be with Sister Betty." Although, she didn't know what was in the envelope, just the idea that Mother Eternal Ann Everlastin' had thought about her, after all, made her happy.

Sister Betty wasn't taking it quite as well as Ma Cile. "Councilman Hippo Crit," she said as nicely as she could, "I can't do nothing more for her." She raised her hands in surrender. "I'm bone-tired, and I just want to go home and rest. I loved Mother but I'm really too old to be doing any more of the . . ." She stopped. She wanted to say the word *crazy* but chose another descriptive word, ". . . any more of her *unusual* requests." Sister Betty cupped her chin with one of her tiny hands and slowly turned her head away from the councilman and Ma Cile. She squinted from the glaring sun as she looked out the window, scanning the beautiful blue sky and down through the fluffy clouds. She almost wanted to cry. "I'm sorry, Mother," she whispered.

Ma Cile chose to question the councilman further. The idea that Mother Eternal Ann Everlastin' would trust her enough to leave her something to do was about to blow her mind. "Cain't I open my envelope? I wants to see what she had fo' me to do," Ma Cile said cheerfully as she tried to lift the flap with one of her chubby fingers.

Looking around to make sure that Brother Tis Mythang and Sister Hellraiser were still sleeping and couldn't hear what he had to say, the councilman tapped Sister Betty on the arm to get her attention. When she turned to face him, he said, "Sister Betty, please hear me out. Both you and Ma Cile have something very simple to do for your good friend. All Mother Eternal Ann Everlastin' has requested is that the two of you move."

"Move!" Ma Cile and Sister Betty hollered in unison.

"Shush. Please keep your voices lowered." Fortunately, the low hum from the jet's engines had drowned out the women. "In the envelopes are the deeds to your new homes."

"What . . ." Sister Betty replied. The rest of the words were stuck in her mouth.

"Huh?" Ma Cile said nervously. "What new home is you talkin' 'bout?"

The councilman looked at his watch and realized that he only had a short time to explain everything, so he needed to get started.

"Mother Eternal Ann Everlastin' always remembered how the three of you met. She also remembered that it was you Ma Cile who made sure that Sister Betty had someplace to stay when she arrived in Pelzer, a stranger and alone. She never forgot the kindness that you showed Sister Betty on the bus after you'd just buried your husband, Charlie. You could've wallowed in your own misery, but instead you chose to help a stranger."

"She also remembered how when you first met her while working for the woman, Ms. Maximum. It was you that made sure she had clothes to wear and food to eat. You always had enough for someone else even when you barely had enough for you and your own children."

"You've worked hard enough. Ma Cile, it's time for you to rest. The house is big and already furnished. There's a bedroom for you and each of your grandchildren. Mother knew you very well, and it pleased her to be able to do this for you."

"I don't know what to say." Ma Cile cried instead. At first it was just a low sob and then it grew louder.

"Also, Ma Cile," the councilman added, "it's already paid off."

That's when Ma Cile buried her head into the folds of her dress and cried harder.

Sister Betty listened to all that was said and still couldn't respond.

It wasn't because she wasn't happy for Ma Cile; it was because of all the praying and dreaming she'd done, God hadn't revealed the latest turn of events. Not that He had to but as far as she was concerned, it would've been nice if He had.

The councilman could see that Sister Betty was still shocked, and she looked anxious and thrown. "Sister Betty," the councilman said as he reached over and took one of her tiny hands in his, "Mother always had a certain fondness for you. She especially loved how when everyone thought you'd lost your mind when you said that God had called you that you never wavered in your belief. Your strength was also a source of strength to her."

"I loved her," Sister Betty finally said. "I loved her like a sister."

"She knew that. She also left you a home. Now, understand that she knew how much you love your small home and that there was nothing wrong with it, but she also felt that you deserved a better home, so your home is close to Ma Cile's. The both of you will be living on the same block, and there's only one house between you. The two of you will be able to still remain as close as ever. Your house is also furnished and paid for."

The councilman took advantage of the shocked silence that stilled the voices of Sister Betty and Ma Cile. He went on to tell them about the monthly stipend that Mother Eternal Ann Everlastin' had set aside for them and that it would be available for as long as they lived.

What he didn't tell them was how Mother Eternal Ann Everlastin' had it set up so that it wouldn't interfere with their monthly Social Security payments. He felt they didn't need to know that, and what they didn't know they couldn't testify about.

In no time at all both women got over their shock and talked excitedly about the prospects of moving into their new homes. "I hope it's not too far from the church," Sister Betty said.

"We can always call a cab if we need to go places," Ma Cile countered.

"We can hire Mr. Tiny," they said at the same time.

"But he's got two million dollars coming. He ain't gonna want to work," Ma Cile said after she thought about it.

"Not if Mrs. Tiny gets her hands on that money." Sister Betty chuckled. "He'll be looking for work again."

Conversation dwindled between the two women, and it gave each of them a chance to really comprehend how the latest revelation would change their lives. Ma Cile lay back in her seat, and with hands crossing her massive chest, she thanked God and Mother Eternal Ann Everlastin' for giving her something that her poor husband, Charlie, had died trying to do. She hadn't even told Sister Betty that she was almost three months behind on her mortgage payments and had received a notice of a possible foreclosure if she didn't pay up. That situation alone was one of the reasons why she was so anxious to go to Baltimore and get out of Pelzer. She needed a break. She didn't know what was going to happen to Li'l Bit and June Bug because she was much too old to work, yet the grandchildren were growing so fast and needed much more than she was able to afford on a fixed income. Her daughters in her opinion, could not properly raise the kids up north where morality wasn't important.

"God, you sho' is good to me," Ma Cile mumbled under her breath. "I also thank ya for not letting me and Sister Betty be scared while we up here so close to yo' throne." She mumbled praises as she drifted off to sleep.

Sister Betty, on the other hand, chose to continue surveying the wide skyline. She marveled again at God's handiwork. She was captured by the beautiful layers of red, orange, brown and blue that dappled the sky as far as she could see. It seemed that God was laying out a panorama of what He had in mind when He made His people in so many different colors. When all the colors came together, there was power and magnificence. She decided that when she did move into her new home that she would plant a garden and it would be round, with flowers of the same colors as those she saw in the sky.

"Thank you, Jesus," Sister Betty whispered as she continued to look at the heavenly landscape. She kept her eyes glued to the sky even as the plane descended.

The plane finally landed and Ma Cile also got a chance to see who drove the plane. She was too thrilled. In just one weekend, she'd managed to travel around in luxury, something she thought she'd never do in her lifetime.

Sister Betty got off the plane with a little help from the councilman and Brother Tis Mythang. As usual her knees had stiffened up, but she was too blessed, in her opinion, to let it bother her.

Somehow, they managed to unstrap Sister Hellraiser. She'd fought them like they owed her money, but then, she remembered that Councilman Hippo Crit had said he was looking to marry. She decided to act ladylike but it was all for nothing. As she departed the plane again no one bothered to tell her that the back hem of her dress was still tucked into the dress's waistline.

Everyone was feeling too good to set her off, so they watched as she raced down the tarmac after the councilman who thought he had enough of a head start to avoid her.

In the meantime, while their luggage was being unloaded, both Ma Cile and Sister Betty decided to open their envelopes and read for themselves what Mother Eternal Ann Everlastin' had given them.

It was Sister Betty who started laughing first. She was laughing so hard, she had to stop and take out her false teeth before she swallowed them. Her tiny arms were just flailing around like she was trying to ward off a hoard of angry bees.

Ma Cile took a little longer to read the paper in her hands. She read the words once, tapped her forehead to straighten out her eyes which seemed to be dancing with glee, and read it again. Then Ma Cile started laughing too.

"Oh Lawd," Ma Cile said and laughed, "Sister Betty, do ya believe this?"

"Yes, I do," Sister Betty said, all out of breath from laughing hard. "Ain't this just like Mother Eternal Ann Everlastin'?"

Brother Tis Mythang raced back to see what was wrong with the women. They were laughing too hard to explain, so they showed him the letter instead, pointing to a particular paragraph. Brother Tis Mythang quickly read the paragraph and started jumping up and down. "Ooh, I can't wait," he said, laughing. "When's moving day?"

"We don't know yet," Sister Betty replied.

"Mother Eternal Ann Everlastin' sho was sumpthin' else," Ma Cile said as she tried to catch her breath. "She's got us livin' in fancy homes and in a fancy neighborhood. She sho had thangs planned out."

"She sure did." Brother Tis Mythang laughed as he reread the piece of paper in Ma Cile's hand.

"It seems that God used Mother Eternal Ann Everlastin' to do His work," Sister Betty said, finally catching her breath, "that's why she bought us expensive homes on both sides of Reverend Knott Enuff Money's house. He ain't got no choice but to stay on the right path."

"You right," Ma Cile added, "and I'm gonna keep my eye on him too."

"Which one?" Brother Tis Mythang said as his imagination ran wild with pictures of the reverend being confronted by Ma Cile's roving eyeballs every time he left his house.

"He'll never know," Ma Cile replied. She was in a good mood and didn't mind Brother Tis Mythang's teasing.

"What are you two ladies going to do with your old homes now that you'll be moving on up?" Brother Tis Mythang asked.

Sister Betty and Ma Cile stopped walking. They had not given that part any thought.

"Well, I guess that's something we will have to figure out," Sister Betty said.

"You can have mine if you got about fifteen hundred dollars," Ma Cile said, "but you'll need to have it in about two weeks."

"Are you teasing me?" Brother Tis Mythang asked slowly. All the laughter had gone out of his voice and surprise had taken over. "I have a little more than that right now."

"Well then," Ma Cile smiled and said, "when I moves out, you can move in. I'll see if the councilman will put some law words on a piece of paper to make it fo' real."

Sister Betty was moved beyond words. Her best friend constantly amazed her. Then, she remembered the words of the councilman concerning the reasons for Ma Cile receiving her gift—it was because she was always giving. It was then that Sister Betty decided that she, too, would see who needed a home. Of course, she would seek God about it. After all, it was in that very same house that He'd called her on the phone in 1984 and changed her life, and it was there that He, so many times, revealed to her through prayer and fasting what she was supposed to do. Whoever received her house as a gift would have to be approved by God.

Epilogue

Within a month's time, both Ma Cile and Sister Betty had moved into their new homes. The women prayed and fasted for about a week to make sure that their homes were blessed. They wanted to always be available for whatever God wanted them to do. And, they were sure that there were other spiritual adventures to come. Sister Betty eventually gave her home to a small family from a nearby homeless shelter. It would be years later before she discovered that the father in that family would go on to become a very famous motivational speaker. It was because of Sister Betty's generosity that he not only gave his life to God, but was able to form a network that raised funds to build homes and give better lives to other families in need.

Brother Tis Mythang moved from his tiny eclectically decorated apartment into Ma Cile's furnished house. She'd shared with him the reason why she needed the fifteen hundred dollars, and he didn't mind paying it since it was to keep the house out of foreclosure, and he kept his big mouth shut about it. He seemed almost a new person after his trip to Baltimore. There was a newness about him both physically and spiritually. He still teased and ran his mouth about silly things when he shouldn't, but he was a much happier person and God was certainly working on him. He also renewed his friendship with Buddy who was still away in Boston receiving treatments for his alcoholism.

Tiny eventually took a job driving Ma Cile and Sister Betty around town. He had to because just as Sister Betty predicted, by the time he'd returned to Pelzer with Buddy, his wife had prespent most of the money. He still managed to keep a small portion of it secreted away, but if he wanted to keep that money, he needed to pretend it wasn't there, so he drove the women around town and kept Ms. Tiny out of his business.

Buddy overcame his addiction and learned to fight it day by day. He and the reverend set up a luncheon date. They managed to iron out a lot of their difficulties and again, Buddy accepted the reverend's apology. They were both wrong with what they'd done in the past. Buddy, although now wealthy, decided to do more charitable work for others less fortunate and even more work on himself; that meant he'd have to stop buying into what others thought about him and discover who he really was. He'd finally discovered that God didn't make junk and he could eventually become a worker for Him.

The Bishop took advantage of Mother Eternal Ann Everlastin's generous gift of funding his education. Three times a week, he took night classes at a school in nearby Belton, South Carolina. It would take some time, but he had plenty of that, and even more determination. In no time at all, he fully expected to learn to read well enough to lead, instead of follow.

At first with the Reverend Knott Enuff Money's house sandwiched in between Sister Betty's and Ma Cile's new homes, the reverend wasn't sure if he agreed with the way God was moving around the chess pieces of his life. He soon found out that God never did things the way man would have; if He did then He wouldn't be God. He also soon learned the benefits of having the women as neighbors. It was a couple of weeks after he'd returned from Baltimore. Mother Pray Onn and Deacon Laid Handz showed up at his door uninvited. Needless to say, when Sister Betty and Ma Cile intervened, the deacon and Mother Pray Onn's visit was cut short . . . very short.

The reverend put to rest most of his demons, including those which his mother had heaped upon him and truly gave his life to God. In the beginning, the membership at the Ain't Nobody Right But Us—All Others Goin' to Hell Church began to dwindle. The reverend wasn't preaching sweet, sticky, words that clogged up the sinner's ears so that the truth would not get in. There were many people that weren't happy about it. He also was no longer consumed with the outward appearance of wealth, either for himself or his church and that drove some folks away. But he kept up his fellowship with Reverends Cherry, Reid and Thomas, and with their guidance and the leading from the Lord, Reverend Knott Enuff Money did just fine. He also mended fences with Reverend Bling Moe Bling and invited him to attend a meeting in Baltimore with the mega-church church pastors. Reverend Knott Enuff Money had decided that if those men could work on him then they could probably do the same for the Reverend Bling Moe Bling.

Finally, the councilman had to take Sister Hellraiser to dinner and the theater. That was her price for the way he had misled her. No one knows how the date turned out because neither had been seen for weeks. Only a Hellraiser could arrange that, and, of course, that would be another story.

Rest in peace Mother Eternal Ann Everlastin'.

PSALM 12: 1-8

1   Help, Lord; for the godly man ceaseth; for the faithful fail from among the children of men.

2   They speak vanity every one with his neighbor: with flattering lips and with a double heart do they speak.

3   The Lord shall cut off all flattering lips, and the tongue that speaketh proud things.

4   Who have said, with our tongue will we prevail; our lips are our own: who is lord over us?

5   For the oppression of the poor, for the sighing of the needy, now will I arise, saith the Lord; I will set him in safety from him that puffeth at him.

6   The words of the Lord are pure words; as silver tried in a furnace of earth, purified seven times.

7   Thous shalt keep them, O Lord, thou shalt preserve them from this generation for ever.

8   The wicked walk on every side, when the vilest men are exalted.

BLACK STEEL

Struggles, they attacked me
Though I had no permanent shape
They found me and when they did
I was thrust into a fire
And without my permission
I was shaped and hammered in that fire
Only to be quickly submerged into cooling water

Often, certain blessings came upon me
And when I gave no thanks
Without a second thought, I was
Thrust again into the fire
Hammered and reshaped
Again, quickly submerged into cooling waters

At an age when knowledge should have ruled me
Instead, I searched for more comfortable things
There were consequences; so again into a fire
Chastised with life's repercussions and reshaped
Once more quickly submerged in cool waters

After repeated lessons, good and bad
After being consumed over and over in the fire
I became hard, impossible to break,
My spirit soared with invincibility
"Now I see," said my reason for being
***Black Steel** only comes about*
After the thrusting into many fires
And the cooling off in many waters
I have arrived; I am ready for Spiritual warfare
I am a supernatural weapon
*I am God's **Black Steel***
*Only to bend and to be used . . . by **His Will***

Pat G'Orge-Walker © 1999

MOTHER ETERNAL ANN EVERLASTIN'S DEAD

PAT G'ORGE-WALKER

ABOUT THIS GUIDE

The questions and discussion topics that follow
are intended to enhance your group's reading
of this book.

Suggested Questions for Book Club Discussions

1. What, if any, spiritual message did you get from the story?

2. Do you believe in having comedy in the church?

3. Do you believe that you can never stray too far for God to forgive?

4. Are there unlearned leaders, such as Bishop Was Nevercalled?

5. Are there any other characters in the story you feel should be reclaimed? Who? Why?

6. Is the author exposing spiritual challenges in a comedic manner or just making fun of people in the church?

7. Can you actually think of people who have some of these flawed personalities?

8. From reading the story, were you able to determine which characters belonged to which race? How could you tell? By actions? By dialogue?

9. Do you believe that judgment begins with the church?

10. Do you have to be a "Believer" to enjoy these stories?

11. Do you believe that parents or caregivers can negatively shape someone to the extent of the reverend and the bishop's experiences? If not, why?

12. Do you believe this particular genre, gospel comedy, can work as well on film and television as it has on stage?

Suggested Questions for the Author

1. What is Christian comedy fiction and why is it worthwhile?

2. Why do you write Christian comedy fiction?

3. How did you become published by a publisher not known for Christian fiction?

4. What impact have you seen Christian comedy fiction make on the lives of others?

5. What has been your greatest reward in writing Christian comedy fiction?

6. How do you respond to those Christians who say reading fiction of any kind is a waste of time, and that people should be reading the Bible?

7. How are blacks represented in Christian comedy fiction stories?

8. How are blacks represented as writers in the Christian fiction genre?

9. Why has it taken so long for blacks to break into the Christian fiction genre? Racism?

10. How is your particular comedy accepted in other cultures?

11. As a preacher's kid, do you feel more responsibility for what you write concerning the church?

12. Are your characters based upon people you know or have met?

13. What is the market like for Christian fiction, comedy or otherwise? Black Christian fiction?

14. What if anything is the difference between your self-publishing success and your major publishing experience?

15. What advice would you give to new authors wanting to break into the genre?

16. Show me the money! Aren't you jumping on the Christian fiction bandwagon because there are big bucks to be had?